Santa Montefiore was born in England in 1970. She has written seven novels which have been translated into over twenty-five languages and sell all over the world. She lives in London with her husband, the historian Simon Sebag Montefiore, and their two children. To find out more about her novels, visit Santa's website at www.santamontefiore.co.uk

Praise for Santa Montefiore:

'Santa Montefiore has proved herself a talented novelist'
She

'The kind of book you can't wait to get back to' *Tatler*

'Sheer heaven' *Bangor Chronicle*

'Appealing' *Mail on Sunday*

'Thoroughly readable . . . with good old-fashioned romance' *Evening Standard*

'Absorbing' *Vogue*

'A story told across continents, with grand themes and strong emotions' *Yorkshire Evening Post*

'Ambitious . . . contains all the basic ingredients of a satisfying saga' *Sunday Telegraph*

Also by Santa Montefiore

Meet Me Under the Ombu Tree

The Butterfly Box

The Forget-Me-Not Sonata

Last Voyage of the Valentina

The Gypsy Madonna

Sea of Lost Love

SANTA MONTEFIORE

The Swallow
and the Hummingbird

HODDER

Copyright © 2004 by Santa Montefiore

First published in Great Britain in 2004 by Hodder & Stoughton
A division of Hodder Headline

This paperback edition published in 2007

The right of Santa Montefiore to be identified as the Author
of the Work has been asserted by her in accordance with the
Copyright, Designs and Patents Act 1988.

A Hodder paperback

1

A CIP catalogue record for this title is available from the British Library

ISBN 978 0 340 832608

Typeset in Plantin Light by Palimpsest Book Production Limited,
Grangemouth, Stirlingshire

Printed and bound in Great Britain by
Mackays of Chatham plc, Chatham, Kent

Hodder Headline's policy is to use papers that are natural, renewable and
recyclable products and made from wood grown in sustainable forests.
The logging and manufacturing processes are expected to conform to
the environmental regulations of the country of origin.

Hodder & Stoughton Ltd
A division of Hodder Headline
338 Euston Road
London NW1 3BH

To my son, Sasha Woolf

Acknowledgements

I would like to extend my deepest gratitude to the following people who helped make this book possible: Captain Denis Robinson, who shared with me his experiences of the Battle of Britain and answered endless questions with patience and humour; Eileen Brittle and Joan Laprell, whose recollections of the war were both fascinating and often hilarious; Hugh Kavanagh, an avid bird-watcher, who provided a vital service when reference books failed to deliver; Ian Bond, who initiated me into the wonderful world of walnut trees and even inspired me to join the Walnut Club!; Lia Rueda, who invited me to her beautiful farm in the north of Argentina and enlightened me on the agriculture there; Annabel Elliot and my uncle, Jeremy Palmer-Tomkinson, who remembered, somewhat hazily, life in the 1960s; and my father, who has taught me throughout my life about farming, flora and fauna.

My mother deserves high praise for editing the first manuscript with such dedication and for all the colourful stories she has woven over the years of her life in South America, which I have remembered in detail and ruthlessly poached. I am enormously grateful to my aunt, Naomi Dawson, for coming to my rescue in the weeks following the birth of our son when I was unable to get to my computer. I cannot thank my editor, Susan Fletcher, enough for giving me such a massive amount of her time and advising me so wisely – I am truly grateful for her enthusiasm and encouragement.

I would also like to thank my agent, Jo Frank, for her unwavering support, and my friend, Kate Rock, for without them I would not be writing at all.

Finally, I thank my husband, Sebag, who devised the idea driving down the M3 at six o'clock in the morning after a sleepless night with our daughter. He is the engine behind my writing.

PART I

Chapter One

Spring 1945

Mrs Megalith stared down at the body and sighed heavily. What an unsavoury sight first thing in the morning. It was rigid and cold and looked like something one of her grandchildren might have made at school out of papier-mâché, except this wasn't a silly prank. She clicked her tongue at the inconvenience and struggled into her dressing gown. Grabbing her stick, she proceeded to prod the corpse. It was little more than a decaying carcass of flesh and bones and fur, rather mangy fur at that. She looked at death and thought how unattractive the body was, even the body of a cat, once the spirit had departed. She felt little, just annoyance. She had so many cats she had lost count. They kept on appearing, though, in spite of the fact that she gave them little attention and certainly knew none of them by name. From where they came and why she hadn't a clue, but they were drawn to her by a mysterious force. As Mrs Megalith was a gifted clairvoyant, this was commendable indeed.

She picked up the cat, wondering why it had chosen to die in her bedroom of all places, and limped down the corridor towards the staircase. It was an omen, a bad omen, of that she had no doubt. She found Max in the kitchen making himself a cup of Ovaltine.

'Dear boy, what on earth are you doing up at this hour?'

It was six in the morning and Max rarely emerged before eight-thirty.

'There was a dead cat in my bedroom,' he replied casually. He still spoke with a Viennese accent and if it hadn't been for the Jewish blood that careered through his veins Hitler would have considered him the epitome of Aryan man: thick blond hair, sodalite blue eyes, a noble though sensitive expression on a wide, intelligent face. In spite of his nonchalant air, he was a pensive young man whose heart was far more complex than anyone would have imagined, with dark corners and deep crevices where shadows lingered. He showed little of the emotions that simmered there, for his father wouldn't have wanted him to bare his fear or pain; he would have wanted him to be strong for his sister, Ruth. Max owed him that.

He chuckled at the sight of Mrs Megalith dangling the dead cat from her fingertips. He was used to the cats and considered them part of the furniture. When he had first arrived at Elvestree House in 1938 as a ten-year-old refugee he had been quite afraid of the solitary creatures that inhabited the place and watched him suspiciously from every windowsill and tabletop, but Mrs Megalith had given him and Ruth a kitten as a present. Although he hadn't known that he would never see his parents again, he missed the familiar smell of home. The kitten had given him comfort.

'You too? Oh dear.' Mrs Megalith shook her head. 'One dead cat is bad enough but two is very worrying indeed. It does not bode well. But what are they trying to tell me? We've won the war for God's sake.' She narrowed her eyes, the same milky grey as the moonstone that always nestled on the ledge of her large bosom, and clicked her tongue. Max took the dead cat from her and placed it outside the back door with the other one. When he returned she was sitting in the armchair beside the Aga.

'You are always reading meaning into everything, Primrose,' he said. 'Surely it is nothing but a coincidence that two cats die on the same night. Perhaps they ate rat poison.'

Mrs Megalith pursed her lips. 'Absolutely not. The omen is as clear as quartz.'

'The war is over,' said Max. 'Hitler isn't coming back.'

'Thank the Lord! And I've already had one near miss so it can't be me!' she said, recalling a night during the Blitz when she had stayed with her sister in London. A cat had died then too. But Mrs Megalith was irrepressible; a limp and a grudge but more alive than ever. 'No, the omen has nothing to do with the war. It's much closer to home,' she continued, rubbing her chin thoughtfully.

'George comes home today from France,' said Max, thinking of Rita and hoping the bad omen didn't have anything to do with her. George was another matter entirely.

'By God, you're right!' Mrs Megalith exclaimed. 'Old age is a humiliating thing. I once had a good memory. Now it's no better than anyone else's.' She huffed. 'Young George Bolton, it's nothing short of a miracle that that boy survived in those flying tin cans. It's because of young men like him that we're not all having to learn German and that I'm not having to hide you in my attic. Not very comfortable my attic. Though, you would have had an advantage over the rest of us, speaking the language as you do.' She turned her attention to her granddaughter. 'Rita hasn't seen George for three years.'

'That is a long time, isn't it?' said Max hopefully. Ever since he had first set eyes on Rita Fairweather he had been hopelessly in love. The infatuation of a child had slowly matured into something more profound, for Rita was three years older than him and her heart was no longer hers to give away.

'In the Great War I didn't see Denzil for four. Thought nothing of it.'

'But you're not like other people,' teased Max. 'You're a witch.'

Mrs Megalith's face softened and she smiled at him. Few dared tease the 'Elvestree Witch' and it was well known that she found most people intolerable. But Max was beyond reproach. Mrs Megalith could see what no one else saw, those dark and shadowy corners of his heart where he hid a great deal of suffering. She would never forget the day those two frightened little strays were brought into her care. She loved Max and Ruth intensely, more intensely than she loved her own privileged children who had never known fear. She was the closest they had to family and she cherished them on behalf of the mother and father who were no longer alive to give them what is every child's right.

'I might be a witch, Max dear, but I'm as human as the next woman and I missed Denzil. Of course I took lovers.' Max raised an eyebrow. 'You might laugh,' she said, pointing a long finger at him. 'But I was something of a looker in my day.'

'Why don't you go back to bed? You look tired,' she said, getting up stiffly, leaning on her stick.

'No point now. The day has begun. I might as well bury the dead,' he replied, making for the back door.

'Throw them into the bushes, dear boy.' She waved a hand and her crystal rings glinted in the sunshine like boiled sweets. 'I'm going outside to enjoy the early worm.'

Mrs Megalith's house was a large white building, fine-looking in both proportion and symmetry. One half was covered in a delicate pink clematis, its petals fluttering in the wind like confetti, the other half in climbing roses and wistaria. The open windows revealed floral curtains and potted geraniums and the odd cat asleep in the sunshine. Mrs Megalith also kept two cows for milk, chickens for meat and eggs, and five white Aylesbury ducks for the sheer pleasure of watching them swim prettily on her pond. Foxes especially loved Aylesburies because they couldn't fly so she kept a hurricane lamp alight all night long to scare them away. She was an avid gardener and planted without design, sowing wherever there was a space. With the help of Nestor, the ancient gardener, she had dug up half her lawn to scatter poppies, cornflowers and wild grasses, and under-planted the rose beds with forget-me-nots. These seeded themselves throughout the borders where she grew love-in-the-mist, campanulas and euphorbia. Hollyhocks were carried on the wind and by birds and thrived among the cracks in the York stone terrace and between the bricks in the wall that surrounded the garden. The air was filled with the sweet scent of cut grass and balsam poplar, and the rich smell of bluebells from the wood above the house drifted down on the breeze.

Elvestree House also had the advantage of overlooking the estuary, which was filled with every type of sea bird, from the soft grey herring gull to the black cormorant. Their clamour now resounded across the wide expanse of sand where the receding tide left sandworms and small crustaceans exposed in an enviable banquet. Mrs Megalith gazed into the mouth of the sea and to the horizon beyond and pondered on the dead cats and the omen that clouded an otherwise clear blue day. She knew that Rita was out on the beach, staring at the same view, willing George's safe return from France and reflecting on her future and the realisation of all her dreams.

Rita hadn't slept. The anticipation was too much. In her hand she held the letter George had sent from France specifying the date and time of his arrival. It was transparent, the words nearly worn away by the gentle corrosion of love. She sat on the cliff top, gazing out over the sea that swelled below the circling of gulls – the same sea that had divided them for so long and was now bringing him home.

Today even the sunrise seemed lovelier. The sky paler, more translucent, and the sunlight like the gentle brush of a kiss. She loved more than anything to watch the sea, for the sea had moods like a person, one moment calm and serene, the next displaying the full force of its fury. But those waters were far deeper than a person could ever be. In spite of its mercurial nature the sea was constant and dependable and capable of filling Rita with a lightness of spirit unmatched by anything else in her life. The sight of that vast expanse of ocean touched her at the very core of her being. Sometimes at dusk, when the sky reflected the golds and reds of the dying sun and the sea lay flat and almost still, as if awed by the heavenly scene being played out above it, Rita felt sure there was a God. Not the remote God she learned about at school and in church, but her grandmother's God: a God that was an integral part of the sea, the clouds, the trees, the flowers, the animals and the fish, and an integral part of her too. Sometimes Rita would close her eyes and imagine she was a bird soaring high above the earth, with the wind on her face and blowing through her hair.

Rita loved nature. As a child she had enjoyed only nature classes; all the others she had found difficult and pointless. While the rest of the children played rowdy games in the playground, Rita had lain on the grass watching ladybirds or a ball of dew on a leaf or taming a titmouse with a walnut from George's father's garden. She would sit and sketch insects, observing every minute detail with great curiosity. She had few close friends. No one else had the patience or the interest to sit for so long. But she was well liked, if considered a little eccentric, for she was a gentle child with a great deal of charm.

But today there was more on her mind than the fluid circling of gulls or the beetles that scurried about the grass in search of food, for George was coming home. She prayed for his safe journey, whispering her words into the wind as she had done throughout the war and especially during those painful moments when Reverend and Mrs Hammond's son had been killed and Elsa Shelby's fiancé lost in action. But her George had been spared. She was ashamed to speak of her gratitude in case it was somehow jinxed. So she thanked God in whispers that were lost in the roar of the sea and in the cry of birds that flew with their wings outspread on the back of the breeze. She extended her arms and ran along the sand in imitation, her heart inflated with joy and hope, and no one could hear her laughter and frown upon her childish exuberance.

Rita had known George for as long as she could remember. Their parents were friends and they had gone to the same village school although George hadn't been in her class for he was three years older. He would wait for her at the end of the day and walk her home before continuing his journey by bicycle for his father was a farmer and lived a few miles outside the village. He taught her how to play conkers and Pooh sticks, how to find shrimps and sea urchins in the rock pools on the beach, and in summertime he demonstrated how to start a fire with nothing but a pair of glasses. On her thirteenth birthday he had been the first to kiss her, because, he claimed, he hadn't wanted anyone else to. It was his responsibility to see that she was initiated with care because a nasty first experience could put her off for life. He had held her in the dark cave that had become their special place and pressed his lips to hers as the tide crept in to witness their secret then wash it away. Thus they had discovered a new dimension to their friendship and, with the enthusiasm of two children with a new toy, they had visited the cave as often as possible to indulge in hours of kissing interrupted only by the odd tern or sea gull that wandered unexpectedly into their cavern.

George had always longed to fly. He, too, loved to sit on the cliff tops watching the birds circling above the sea. He observed them closely, the way they glided on the air then swooped down to the water. He studied their take-offs and their landings and vowed to Rita that one day he'd fly like them in an aeroplane. When war came he grabbed the opportunity to make his dream happen regardless of the danger to his life. He was young then and sure of his immortality. He had set out on his big adventure and Rita had been proud and full of admiration for him. She had watched the sea birds in flight and thought of him. Then she had watched the pheasants and partridges his father shot down and feared for him.

She sat on a rock in their cave and remembered those kisses. She recalled the spicy scent of his skin, of his hair, of his clothes, all so familiar and unchanged over the years. She could picture him there, his presence so overwhelming that he dwarfed the small cavern. She imagined him lighting a cigarette, running his fingers through his curly brown hair, fixing her with those speckled grey eyes, grinning at her with only half his mouth as was his way – an ironic, mischievous grin. She recalled his wide jaw, the squareness of his chin, the lines that fanned out from his eyes when he laughed. She pondered the bond that held them together, excited at the prospect of a future that was so reassuringly a continuation of the past. They would grow old together here on this beach, in this cave, in this small Devon village imprinted with the indelible footsteps of their childhood.

When she returned home her mother was making porridge, her dyed auburn hair drawn into rollers and her strong matronly figure wrapped in a dusty pink dressing gown. 'My dear, Friday's arrived, I can't believe it. I never thought today would dawn. After all these years. I'm quite overcome.' She put down her wooden spoon and embraced her child with fervour. 'God has blessed you, Rita,' she added seriously, pulling away and fixing her daughter with eyes that were moist with emotion. 'You must go to church this Sunday with gratitude in your heart. There are many who have not been so lucky. Trees and Faye must be beside themselves with excitement. To think their boy is finally coming home. It brings a lump to my throat.' She turned back to the porridge, wiped her eyes and sniffed.

Hannah Fairweather was a deeply sentimental woman. She had a wide, generous face, eyes that wept easily, especially where her children were concerned, and a large, spongey bosom that had nursed each of her three daughters for well beyond their first year. She was one of nature's earth mothers whose sole purpose in life is to raise and love children, which she did with enormous pride. Like a magpie she kept everything: Rita's first pair of shoes, Maddie's first drawing, a lock of Eddie's hair. The mantelpieces and walls were cluttered with memories that would mean nothing to a visitor but which meant everything to Hannah; a veritable museum of her past.

The Fairweathers' rambling cottage was situated in the small seaside village of Frognal Point, hidden behind tall yew hedges and lime trees, surrounded by a manicured garden filled with birds. Hannah's youngest child was now fourteen and spent all day at school, so the birds that she tamed and cared for were like children to her. The nightingale who made her home in the tangled hedgerow, the dainty titmice who arrived in the autumn and ate crusts out of her hand, and the swallows, her favourite, who returned each spring to build their nests in the top corner of the porch. As mild and modest as the little hedge sparrows, Hannah had a good heart and a soft one – as is often the case with children raised by overbearing mothers.

'I wonder why our Rita is glowing this morning?' said

Humphrey as he entered the kitchen, drawn by the aroma of porridge and toast. Short and stocky in grey trousers with scarlet braces over a neatly pressed white shirt, he was almost bald except for the thick white curls about his ears. He bent down, planted a kiss on his daughter's temple and patted her back with a warm hand.

'She's been down on the beach,' Hannah replied. Humphrey took his seat at the head of the table and poured himself a cup of tea.

'Nothing to do with the fact that George is coming home then?' He chuckled and opened the paper, the *Southern Gazette*, which he edited. He grunted his approval of the front page, emblazoned with a large picture of a young woman kissing a soldier on his return from the war. If George had any remarkable stories of bravery and adventure Humphrey would be only too pleased to put them in his paper. That's what people wanted now, tales of heroism and victory.

'I'm so excited, Daddy, and yet I'm frightened too.'

Humphrey peered at his daughter over the paper. 'There's no reason to be frightened, Rita. He'll be delivered home safely.'

'No, that's not why.' She paused and nibbled at a piece of toast. 'You don't think he will have changed, do you?'

Hannah spooned porridge into a bowl for her husband. 'Of course he will have changed,' she said. 'He'll be a man now.'

Rita smiled and blushed. 'I hope he won't be disappointed in me.'

'Who could be disappointed in you, my dear?' Humphrey laughed and disappeared behind the paper again. 'You're home to George, like your mother was home to me. Don't underestimate that.'

'I remember when your father came back from the Dardanelles. He was so brown I barely recognised him, and thin too. I had to feed him up like one of Mother's chickens. But we soon got to know each other again. George will take a while to adjust, but he'll be home and reunited with his beloved. War teaches you that nothing matters but the people you love. You've been his lifeline for all these years, Rita.' Hannah's voice faltered and she coughed to disguise it, recalling the horrors of the Great War and the broken spirits who lived to return. 'Where's Eddie? She'll be late for school.' She bustled out of the room to wake her youngest daughter.

When Eddie wandered into the kitchen, clearly still half asleep, she mumbled a brief 'good morning' before remembering that today was the day of George's return. 'You must be excited, Rita,' she said, waking up. 'Are you going to let him make love to you now?'

Humphrey's startled face popped up over the paper and Hannah swivelled around and stared in horror at her fourteen-year-old daughter.

'Eddie!' she gasped. 'Humphrey, say something!'

Humphrey pulled an exaggerated frown. 'What do *you* know about making love, Eddie?' he asked, wondering who had polluted her mind.

'Elsa Shelby's fiancé got back a week ago and they made love that very day. I know because Amy told me.' Elsa Shelby's little sister was as indiscreet as Eddie.

'What does little Amy know?' said Hannah, hands on hips, nearly shaking the curlers out of her hair.

'Elsa told her. She said it was like bathing in a tub of warm honey.' Eddie grinned mischievously as she watched her father's face extend into a wry smile.

'My dear child,' said Hannah severely, ignoring her husband's obvious amusement, 'physical love is for the procreation of children within the union of marriage.'

'They *are* engaged,' Eddie protested, beaming at her sister who had suddenly grown hot and fidgety. 'After all, she thought he was dead!'

'They still should have waited. What are a few months?' Hannah argued.

'George and Rita will be engaged soon.' Eddie turned to Rita. 'You will tell me what it's like when you do it, won't you?' Rita let her long, brown hair fall over her face in thick curls and wriggled in her chair in embarrassment.

'Edwina, eat your breakfast. You'll be late for school,' said Hannah, changing the subject. She was used to Eddie's tendency to say exactly what she thought, without reflecting on whether it was appropriate. *That* she had inherited from her grandmother. Eddie watched her mother spoon large dollops of porridge into a bowl then caught eyes with her father. His expression was indulgent.

'Eddie, dear, do you have to bring Harvey to the table?' said her mother, noticing the little black bat that clung to the sleeve of Eddie's woollen cardigan.

'I told you, Mummy, he doesn't like being left on his own. He's used to me now.'

Hannah sighed and picked up her cup of tea, which was as weak as dishwater. 'The fighting might have stopped but it's going to take a long time for this country to get back on her feet again. Oh, for a decent cup of tea with a healthy serving of sugar!'

Maddie was nineteen, a young woman of single mind, so there was no need to get up at such an unsociable hour. Although her parents encouraged her to get a job, she felt there was no urgency. Besides, she'd find a husband and then she wouldn't have to work. She watched Rita leave in the morning to toil away as a land girl on Trees Bolton's farm; how she'd come home in the evenings with her hands dirty and her hair full of dust, smelling of cows and manure, and was grateful that she had managed to avoid that kind of manual labour. There were enough people keeping the home fires burning for her not to have to add to their numbers. It was a shame the men on the farm were so old and ugly for if they had been as young and handsome as those GIs she might have found something worth doing, like boosting morale in the haystacks. She rolled over and contemplated doing her hair and perhaps painting her nails. Then she remembered that today was the day George was coming home from the war.

Throwing on a dressing gown she padded downstairs to find Rita and her father on the point of leaving. 'Good luck, Rita,' she said. 'I'll be thinking of you. Four, isn't it? Leave in good time so that I can do your hair,' she added, noticing her sister's unkempt appearance. But she knew it was useless. Rita was as natural as the sea she loved and her locks would always be as tangled as seaweed. 'I'll help you. You must look your best for George.' Then she turned to her mother and seemed to wilt with emotion. 'Isn't it simply the most romantic thing in the world, Mummy?'

Rita departed on her bicycle, Humphrey in his Lee Francis, and Eddie wandered reluctantly off to school with Harvey so that Maddie was left alone with her mother to eat what was left of the porridge, now cold beneath a thick layer of skin. Hannah hadn't had the heart to tell Rita to tidy her room and had overlooked her scruffy appearance on purpose. She turned to her middle daughter. Rita might be untidy but at least she wasn't idle like Maddie. 'What are you going to do today?' she asked, wondering how she could encourage her to do something useful with her time.

Maddie sighed and pulled a face. 'I'm going to do my hair,' she said, nibbling a piece of toast like her sister had done.

'My dear, is it really necessary?'

'I want to look nice for George too!' she insisted, knowing full well that George had absolutely nothing to do with it. 'I thought I could do my hair like Lauren Bacall. Besides, it's George's welcome home party tomorrow night. You never know who'll be there. Maybe I'll meet the man I'm destined to marry. I want to look my best for him.'

'Why don't you come to Megagran's with me?' Hannah said. Mrs Megalith had been rather rudely nicknamed Megagran by Humphrey many years before. 'The bluebells are out in the wood and her garden's looking lovely. We can have lunch. Make the time go faster.'

Maddie screwed up her nose. 'She'll only insist on giving me a reading.'

'And tell you to get a job.'

Maddie rolled her eyes. 'She never tells me what I want to hear,' she complained.

'That's because she would never lie.' Hannah began to clear away the breakfast. 'You know Megagran. She takes those cards very seriously.'

'Tools for Spirit,' said Maddie, imitating her grandmother's deep voice. 'All right, I'll come, but only because there's nothing better on offer.'

Maddie wished those GIs hadn't gone back to America. She smiled secretly to herself as she thought of them all returning to their wives and girlfriends with her Polyphotos in their breast pockets.

Hannah and Maddie cycled up Mrs Megalith's drive as petrol was still scarce. Spring had thrown the countryside into flower and painted the trees and bushes with a fresh palette of colour. The pink hawthorn and white apple blossom glistened among the phosphorescent green of leaves and grasses. The sky shone a cerulean blue upon which small white clouds floated like foam on the sea. Hannah breathed in this delightful scene, feeling God's presence in the beauty and power of nature.

*   *   *

'Isn't this rose quartz glorious?' said Mrs Megalith as her daughter and granddaughter appeared through the kitchen door. She raised her eyes above her spectacles and smiled at them warmly. Maddie looked at the crystals of every colour and size placed in rows on the kitchen table and grimaced at the strong stench of cat.

'What are they for?' she asked, scrunching up her nose at her grandmother's eccentricity. Ever since Megagran had visited India between the wars she had been obsessed with the strangest things.

'This, for example,' she replied, holding up the rose quartz, 'is the stone of gentle love. Its energy is soft and silky and calming. It restores harmony and clarity to the emotions. But the poor little fellow needs a good clean. I'll wash him with salt then leave him in the garden for twenty-four hours so he can soak up the elements. He'll feel a lot better after that.' She patted it affectionately. 'Still loafing around, Madeleine?'

Maddie rolled her eyes. 'I'm going to marry someone very rich so I won't have to work,' she said, raising her eyebrows provocatively at her grandmother.

'That might be harder than you imagine. There's been a war, in case it's escaped your notice,' Mrs Megalith replied, digging her chins into her neck. 'How's our Rita?' she asked Hannah.

'She needs a rose quartz, I should imagine,' said Maddie, picking up a fulgurite absent-mindedly.

'So excited,' enthused Hannah. 'I doubt she's been much use on the farm today.'

'Dear girl. I hope young George marries her this summer. She's been a paragon of patience. Pass me my stick.' She waved her bejewelled hand at her granddaughter then struggled to her feet. Her sky-blue dress fell about her legs like a tent, supported by the ledge of her large breasts and her thick shoulders. 'Now, come and see the garden. It's like heaven out there.' They walked down the corridor where cats draped themselves across the sunny window ledges. Maddie sneezed. She didn't much like cats. Mrs Megalith thought of the two dead cats. 'Tell Rita to come and see me tomorrow. I want to do a reading. I feel something in my bones. Don't ask me what it is, I don't know. But now George is coming back I think she needs a bit of guidance from an old witch.'

'They would have burned you at the stake a few hundred years ago, Grandma.'

'I know, Madeleine, my dear. I was burnt during the Spanish Inquisition and it wasn't pleasant. But I bounced back to live again, many times. Truth withstands flames and one day people won't be afraid of the power that lies in all of us. Even sceptics like your Humphrey, Hannah. Even him.'

They strolled around the garden, admired the 'clever little fellows' that seeded themselves and popped up in such unforgiving places as walls and terraces, and fed the ducks that swam contentedly beneath weeping willow and poplar trees. They sat on the terrace and drank elderflower cordial that Mrs Megalith had made herself. The war seemed not to have touched Elvestree House where eggs, milk and cheese were bountiful. She bartered butter for meat and fish, and managed to buy coupons on the black market for £1 each. She even grew bananas in her greenhouse, giving all the credit to the crystals she placed among them. Everything thrived at Elvestree and, much to Hannah's chagrin, Megagran's garden was a rich playground for every possible bird, even those like the puffin and wagtail who weren't supposed to stop off in England. For some reason, Elvestree was a paradise for migrating birds, even when they had to fly miles out of their way to get there.

They lunched on a succulent chicken and home-grown vegetables, then Hannah and Maddie helped Mrs Megalith clean crystals. By the time they had laid them outside, the air had changed and the light grown mellow. One by one they looked at their watches. It was 3.30p.m. They had barely noticed the passing of time.

'Good God, Hannah,' Mrs Megalith gasped, fiddling with the string of beads she had tied to her glasses to avoid losing them. 'George!'

'And I promised I would do her hair!' Maddie lamented, feeling guilty. But her grandmother turned on her, berating her dizziness.

'George isn't going to notice her hair, Madeleine. He loves her just the way she is.'

Chapter Two

Rita stood at the bus stop biting her nails. She was surrounded by George's family and yet she felt totally alone, isolated on a small island of fear, excitement and hope. She watched Trees and Faye Bolton and knew that they felt much the same as she did. There was always the possibility that he wouldn't be on the bus, that some misfortune had struck on his way over from France. Anxiety showed in the tautness around their eyes and behind their smiles as they waited with their daughter, Alice and her two small children. George wasn't the only young man returning from the war; other families waited too, all cautiously optimistic but wary of celebrating too soon. The air vibrated with apprehension, uniting them all.

'It is agony, isn't it?' said Faye to Rita. 'I'm so nervous I don't know what to do with myself.'

She cast a motherly glance at her daughter whose husband Geoffrey was yet to be demobilised, and felt sorry for her. Alice had always been an uncomplaining child, standing aside for George, who was impulsive and impatient. Always the centre of attention. She had never had to worry about Alice and still didn't. She was serene and philosophical and seemed to drift along on life's current, avoiding the rocks and whirlpools with ease. She promised herself that she would give her daughter due attention when Geoffrey returned from France. But today belonged to George.

Faye had a beautiful face. She seemed not to have aged at all: her skin was free of lines and as soft as brushed cotton.

She wore her blonde hair scraped back into a chignon, which accentuated the fine lines of her jaw and cheekbones. Her eyes were the colour of the sky on a misty morning and used to weeping over beautiful music, a lovely painting or a sad story – she adored Tolstoy, Pushkin and Oscar Wilde. Only her hands betrayed her craft, for they were rough and ragged. But they could fashion anything out of clay as her talent lay in sculpture. She always intended to sell the objects she made – they could do with the money – but she grew too attached to them. 'I create them with love, they're a part of me now,' she would say and so they were placed about the farmhouse among the books, pictures and scores of music she played on the upright piano: a chaotic kaleidoscope of all that she loved.

Trees put his arm around her waist and said nothing, a man of few words. Tall and thin with long arms and legs, he was nicknamed Trees on account of the walnut trees that were his passion. He spent his days on the land, looking after his animals, with his favourite sheepdog, Mildred, at his side. He had a noble face, handsome like a Roman bust, with an aquiline nose and deep-set eyes of a rich, honey brown. Faye leaned into him instinctively. She loved Trees but had never been able to reach him. He was detached and distant and more obsessed with his walnut trees than with any living creature. She didn't feel in the least bit guilty that she had a lover. A woman needs to be loved and Faye needed affection more than most. For her, love was an inseparable part of music and art and, because she poured all her love into creating sculpture and playing the piano it was only natural that she should require something back.

She touched Rita's arm. 'The waiting will soon be over. You will come back with us, won't you? George will drive you home after tea.' Rita nodded then caught her breath, for there she saw, over Faye's shoulder, the bus approaching in a stately fashion down the road.

They all turned and silence fell. The bus seemed to move in slow motion and they craned their necks to look through the windows, but all they saw was the mist in their eyes as they anticipated the faces of the young men they loved and longed for. Finally, the sound of squeaking brakes pierced the silence, then the thud of the door as it opened. A roar of joy burst from one family whose son was the first to descend. They swelled forward like a wave, then retreated, taking him with them so that only his blue hat could be seen bobbing above flapping arms and hands. Then another young soldier jumped out to a similar reception and finally, just when Rita was beginning to believe the horrors of her nightmares, George stood at the top of the steps, a broad smile stretching his face to the limit.

He leapt from the bus into his mother's arms. He was much taller than she, so had to bend down in order to bury his face in her neck and smell the familiar scent of his childhood. His father patted him on his back, a little too hard, and his eyes glistened with joy. Alice lifted her two-year-old daughter into her arms and George embraced them both, then crouched down to kiss the little boy he had met only once. Awed by the unfamiliar man in a starched blue RAF uniform the child wrapped himself around his mother's legs.

George stood up and cast his eyes over the heads of the crowd. It was then that he saw the pale face of his sweetheart. He felt his throat constrict. She stood quite still. Only her long hair blew in the wind, catching in her mouth and around her neck. He gazed on her intently and waded through his family to reach her. Then with great tenderness, as if he were picking up a wild bird, he took her in his arms and held her against him. He closed his eyes and nuzzled his face against her hair, murmuring 'my Rita' over and over again. Rita's tears cascaded down her cheeks, but she felt no shame, just an overwhelming sense of relief.

George pulled away and took her chin in his hands, then kissed her fervently on the lips. Rita was stunned. It felt different, more ardent, more passionate. His face was rough with bristles and his hands dry and calloused, even the smell of his skin had changed into something more animal. She knew then that her mother was right, he had left a boy and returned a man. With that thought the blood grew hot in her veins and caused her skin to prickle with something basic and primitive.

Trees had driven into town in his truck, so he, Faye and Alice sat in the front with the children, and Rita and George were left alone in the back with the wind racing through their hair and across their faces. George leaned against the cabin with his arms around her, his chin resting against her head. 'I've dreamed of this moment for years,' he murmured.

'Pinch me, George,' she laughed. 'Show me it's real.'

He squeezed her hard and kissed her neck. 'I carried your photograph with me and looked at it whenever I felt sad. I missed you all the time. Your letters kept me going.' He squeezed her again and sighed. 'It's like paradise here. England looks more beautiful than I remember it.' He paused a moment, then added quietly, 'And so do you.' They were both aware they were separated from his family only by a pane of glass, so they contented themselves with chaste kisses and soft whispers.

'You smell of violets,' he said, sniffing her. 'I want to kiss you all over.'

She laughed nervously, not recognising the strange shadows in his eyes. He ran a hand down her naked arm to hold her hand, then over the thin fabric of her dress, which billowed about in the wind revealing slender calves and ankles. She had grown plumper, he noticed, her breasts had swelled, but her open face and sherry eyes were still full of childish brightness. She hadn't changed, but he had and suddenly he recoiled in the presence of such purity and innocence.

What had he become? To what levels of depravity had he sunk? How many lives had he taken? He felt soiled right down to his very soul as if he had handed it over to the devil and was now asking for it back. It wasn't possible. The devil didn't work that way. He could never erase the unspeakable things that he'd done. The war had changed him irreversibly and he longed for the boy he had once been.

Not only had he taken life, but he had witnessed the brutal killing of those who had become brothers to him. He had dwelt in his own private hell, mourning the loss of his friends, fearing his own destruction and the inevitable void of death. His values had changed too. Love and life were all that mattered and to forget . . . but how could he expect Rita to understand? He gazed into her trusting eyes and resolved to marry her and secure his own immortality with a large number of children. He had risked his life to save his country from Nazi Germany. In the process he had lost his boyhood and the innocent expectations of his youth.

As they drove into the farm the sweet smell of cows mingled with the fertile scent of awakening fields. George leapt out to embrace Mildred who barked behind the gate. Trees parked the truck beside a pink hawthorn and helped his wife and grandchildren down. Rita watched as Cyril, the farm manager, appeared with the other farmhands to welcome home the man they had known since he had been a small boy. Mildred jumped up at George as he opened the gate to let her through, panting and crying with excitement. He ruffled her fur and kissed her wet nose, then turned to shake hands with Cyril who patted him firmly on the back. Rita watched from the truck. She was so full of admiration and pride. George was so handsome in his uniform. She found herself thinking of Elsa Shelby and wondered whether it really did feel like bathing in warm honey.

Faye and Alice walked into the house with the children. A weather-beaten red-brick farmhouse with small windows into rooms with low ceilings and wooden beams, it was typical of the 17th century. Trees was loath to spend money on repairs which he believed he could do himself, so in wintertime there were buckets to collect the rain that seeped through broken roof tiles, and rugs were placed over the stains in the carpets caused by the damp or mice. Classical music always resounded from either the gramophone or Faye's own piano playing, and flowers spilled over vases in order to distract from the questionable decoration and chaos.

George held out his hands for Rita and she jumped down from the truck. They were both aware of the sexual tension that now quivered between them and their faces burned with anticipation. 'Come with me to the beach after tea,' he hissed into her ear. 'I want to be alone with you.' She felt his breath on her skin and nodded eagerly.

George was happy to change out of his uniform and to find his room exactly as he had left it. His mother had made sure it was clean and tidy, the only room in the whole house that remained unaffected by her chaos. He took a moment to sweep his eyes over the place that had once been his boyhood sanctuary and felt saddened, for the things it contained now seemed to belong to somebody else. To an innocent boy who had not yet grown into a man. He blinked away his wistfulness and pulled on a pair of slacks and a shirt, then remembered they were going to the cave later and wriggled his feet into a pair of brown boots.

Faye had prepared a cake especially for her son's home-coming. They were fortunate enough to have fresh eggs from their chickens and butter from their cows, and the children had covered the icing with small sweets that Trees had acquired on the black market in exchange for a pig. There was a pot of steaming tea and china cups from the set they had been given as a wedding present, handed down from Trees' parents. They sat in the sitting room, surrounded by the homely chaos of Faye's artistic life. Little Johnnie tinkled the keys of the piano until Alice told him to sit down and eat his Marmite sandwiches.

'Come on, sweetie,' she said. 'We can't hear Granny's nice music if you're clanking around over there.'

'I'll teach you how to play it properly when you're a little bit bigger,' suggested Faye, watching him reluctantly slide off the stool. The child gazed at George with wide eyes full of curiosity.

'I don't want to play, I want to be a soldier like Uncle George,' he whined and wandered over to help himself to a sandwich.

'You can play soldiers with me any time,' said George.

'Do you have a gun? Grandpa has a gun and shoots rabbits. We ate a rabbit, didn't we, Mummy?'

Alice smiled at him indulgently. 'Yes, we did, Johnnie. It was delicious, wasn't it?'

'Do you shoot rabbits, Uncle George?'

'Sometimes.'

'Will you teach me how to shoot rabbits? Grandpa says I'm too little.'

'Why don't you go and fetch Granny's box of toys,' interrupted Alice, pushing him gently in the direction of the cupboard. 'You know where they are.' And Johnnie skipped off to find them.

There was a moment of silence as they all wondered what to say. George had been away for so long they didn't know where to begin. Rita was speechless with love and admiration, and Faye was overcome with happiness marred by anxiety. She noticed something strange in her son's countenance, something dark and unfamiliar. George knew that he could never describe to them the unspeakable horrors of war, that he could never share them with anyone. They were beyond any decent person's comprehension. Only Trees knew how much he had changed for he had lived through the Great War. 'So, son, how do you find your home?' he said, and everyone looked at him with surprise for it wasn't like him to indulge in small talk.

'Nothing's changed, Dad,' he replied. He suddenly looked sad. He was sitting on the long stool in front of the grate, his knees apart and his arms resting on his thighs. The china teacup looked ridiculously tiny in his large hands. Shaking his head he gazed into the tea leaves. 'Nothing's changed. Everything's just the way I remember it.'

How could he describe his sense of loss, his sense of guilt? He had survived when so many had perished. How could he explain the feeling of displacement that came from suddenly finding himself in his mother's sunny sitting room, drinking tea out of pretty china cups, in a place untouched by conflict. The war may as well not have happened for them. They could never understand.

'We had a good crop of winter barley,' Trees continued, much to the astonishment of his wife who looked anxiously from him to her son.

'Good,' George replied. 'And the livestock?'

'Not bad. Everyone needs milk, don't they?'

'They certainly do.'

'Ray retired, which was a great sadness. But those early mornings were doing him in, especially in winter.'

'Who'll do the cows now?'

'Barry's stepped in.'

'Good.'

'Ray wasn't happy, though. It's for his own good.' Trees' voice trailed off and he put his cup to his lips.

Once again there was a long moment of silence. Rita wanted to speak, but she felt shy. Finally George spoke.

'This cake is good, Ma.' He bit into the sponge and nodded at her appreciatively. Faye blinked back tears for she sensed why her husband was overcompensating. It was because of the strange shadows in her son's eyes that only Trees recognised and understood.

'Faye bakes terrible cakes,' said Trees suddenly, putting down his plate. 'Let's all admit it. It's a terrible cake.'

Faye stared at her husband then put her hand up to her lips and laughed nervously. 'Oh, dear Trees. You might not speak much but when you do, you're straight to the point.'

George threw back his head and laughed too, and suddenly the atmosphere cleared, like humid air after a heavy rainfall.

'It's a shocking cake,' agreed George, who was now laughing so much he could barely speak.

'But the eggs were fresh,' Faye protested.

'What else did you put in it, Ma?'

'It's not *that* bad,' said Alice loyally, her shoulders shaking as she tried to control her laughter. 'What do you think, Rita?'

'Don't ask Rita, she'll just be polite,' George interjected.

Rita smiled and bit her lip, blushing at the sound of his voice articulating her name.

From that moment, George was able to tell them some of his stories. Faye's tears dried up and Trees retreated into silence again. Normality was resumed. Once George started talking he was unable to stop and they listened with interest and delight, for he was a natural storyteller. Rita didn't once take her eyes off him and he felt her attention like the warm rays of the sun. But as he recounted his experiences he was aware of the minutes passing and of his desire to be alone with her in their secret cave. Finally, he stood up and put down his teacup.

'I could talk all night, but it's getting late and I must drive Rita home,' he said.

Rita felt the palms of her hands grow damp at the prospect of being alone with him. Nervously she pulled her hair behind her ears and stood up.

'Thank you for tea,' she said to Faye.

'Don't mention it, Rita. I gather Trees doesn't need you on the farm over the weekend.'

'He's got George to help him now,' Rita replied, imagining the fun they were going to have working alongside each other.

'I suppose you'll be too busy with George to continue your sculpting lessons.' Faye had been only too happy to see those feminine hands put to better use than farm work. Besides, she had enjoyed the company, even though Rita wasn't a natural artist.

Rita shook her head enthusiastically. 'Not at all. I dearly love to sculpt. I'll always make time for that.'

'Good.' She touched Rita's arm affectionately. 'Then we'll see you tomorrow night at the party. Thank you for helping Trees clean out the barn. I hope the weather's good.'

'I'm sure it will be.'

'Take the truck,' said Trees to his son. George nodded and slipped his hand around Rita's waist, leading her away.

Finally they were alone. George changed gear and then, when they were on the main road, he threaded his fingers through hers. 'Let's go straight to the beach.'

'It'll be high tide,' she said.

'Then we'll just have to get our feet wet.' He took his eyes off the road to smile at her. His smile was wide and reduced his face into lines around his mouth and eyes where they extended into crow's-feet. 'It's good to be home.'

'Your mother went to great trouble to make that cake,' she said and laughed lightly. 'It wasn't that bad.'

'It was terrible. I dream of your mother's walnut cake. Ma's a hopeless cook. She's better at sculpture.'

'My mother couldn't sculpt anything, even if her life depended on it.'

'How is Hannah?'

'As you said, nothing's changed.'

'Good. I'd hate to think of dear old Hannah changing. I imagine Megagran is still going strong.'

'As ever.' They both laughed at the thought of Mrs Megalith.

'Still reading those damned Tarot cards?'

'I'm afraid so.'

'I'll remember to cover myself with garlic before I see her.'

'She's not a vampire!'

'Well, how do you repel witches then?'

'I don't know about witches, but she hates dogs because they chase her cats.'

'I'll bring Mildred.'

'And risk a nasty spell? I don't want to kiss a frog.'

'You know what they say about frogs?'

'That if you kiss one it might turn into a prince?'

'Yes.'

'I don't want a prince. I just want you.'

He parked the car above the cliffs beneath the darkening sky.

'I can't walk in these shoes,' she said, climbing out. Besides, the stockings were a gift from an American GI she had befriended. A rare luxury she wasn't prepared to sacrifice to the sea.

George lit a cigarette and watched through the dusk as she bent down to unstrap her shoes. Then she leaned back against the truck and coyly lifted the skirt of her dress in order to release the stockings from her suspender belt. She was aware that his eyes were upon her and her face burned with shyness. He so unsettled her that her fingers fumbled with the catches. She laughed nervously.

'These damned things!' she exclaimed. George put his cigarette between his lips and strode over to assist. He knelt down and ran his hands appreciatively up her legs. She laughed again and attempted to push him away. 'I can do it, really,' she protested.

But his fingers were already unfastening the first stocking. His hands were warm against her skin and she knew he was taking longer than he needed to. She held her dress up for him and hastily looked around, afraid of being seen in such a compromising position. George didn't seem to care. He dealt with each catch deftly then slowly slid the silk down her thigh and calf and over her ankle and foot as if he were admiring them at the same time. She took the gossamer silk from him as he began on the other leg. He was aware that his touch was pleasurable for he deliberately stroked the skin above the silk with soft fingers. Then he threw his cigarette to the ground and kissed her there. She flinched and gasped in surprise, pushing her dress down modestly.

'A bit late for that, isn't it?' he teased, slipping the final stocking over her foot. He stood up. Her face was so pink he took it in his hands and pressed his lips to it before pulling away and smiling at her affectionately. 'Let's go to our cave.'

They walked hand in hand down the path to the beach. The sun hung low in the western sky, reflecting copper in the rise and fall of the waves. Rita stopped talking as they landed on the sand, aware that she was only minutes from being alone with him once again in the secrecy of the cave. The sand felt wet and cold beneath her feet as the rough grains oozed between her toes with every step. When they reached the rocks, George swung her into his arms, lifting her over the little pools full of sea urchins and crabs where they had played as children and across the narrow strip of sand that was now under four inches of water. His boots weren't impervious to water but he splashed through regardless and into the cave where the land rose enough to protect the sand at the back from the encroaching sea. There he put her down and, before she could utter a word, he was upon her, his mouth kissing hers deeply and urgently.

She closed her eyes and responded willingly, wrapping herself around him and kissing him back. How different it was from those teenage kisses. That had been the innocent exploration of children. Now George was a man. His face was rough and his touch firm and strong. She could feel the excitement straining his trousers as he pressed himself against her.

'My God I want you,' he breathed into her neck. 'I've wanted you for so long.'

She was desperate to please him yet remembered her mother's words. In spite of the many girls she knew who had eagerly given themselves to their men before they left for war, she had held back, saving herself for her wedding night. George had understood. He had never pressured her. But today she felt a desire far stronger than before and it frightened her.

His hand found her breast and he felt the nipple through the material with his thumb. His mouth was on her neck and the rough sensation of his stubble combined with the warm, wet feeling of his lips and tongue caused her whole body to tremble. She wound a leg around him and pulled him towards her with her knee, but he raised his hips to allow him room to run his hand up her calves and over her thigh. He looked into her eyes and she noticed that his were wild and feverish and unfamiliar. He remembered the French girls he had slept with after the liberation of Paris and yet none was as sweet as Rita or as pure. His lips found hers again and she lost herself momentarily until his fingers traced her inner thigh and then her knickers. She flinched and clamped her legs together.

'I want to make love to you, Rita,' he groaned. His brow was moist with sweat and his breath hot against her skin.

'I want you too,' she whispered. But she hesitated.

'You're going to marry me one day,' he said, understanding her reticence. He pulled away and chuckled. 'My darling Rita. I've never considered anyone else but you. You're already my wife in my heart.'

'And you're my husband in mine. I've saved myself for you,' she replied, remembering the glamorous American officers who had relentlessly courted her.

'When we're married I'm going to kiss you all over, every inch of you,' he said and kissed her forehead, sighing heavily and reining in his ardour.

Rita wrapped her arms around him and nuzzled her face against his. She belonged to George as surely as she belonged to this small Devonshire village and, with that sense of security, she lost herself in his kisses, glad to have him home.

Chapter Three

When Rita arrived home her parents and sisters were in the kitchen with her grandmother who had changed into a long dress of deep purple over which she had draped a turquoise shawl. They all stopped talking as Rita appeared round the door. In spite of having scrambled back into her stockings and shoes, her hair was wild and her skin covered in a rash caused by George's stubble.

'Well, my dear,' said Mrs Megalith with a sniff. 'I needn't ask if young George arrived back safely. Your face speaks volumes!' Eddie grinned, noticing at once that one of the buttons on her sister's dress was undone. Such a detail hadn't escaped the scrutiny of their grandmother either. 'Dear me, men are such animals. Surely he could have given vent to his lust on some random stray before mauling you.'

Rita followed the line of her gaze and her hand shot straight to the offending button. Maddie sat in silence, recognising the glazed expression in her sister's eyes because she had seen it in her own reflection after she had given herself to Hank Weston in the back of his jeep. Not even Megagran's powers of clairvoyance had been able to detect that secret.

'How is he?' Hannah asked, ignoring her mother. 'Dear child, you're frozen. Where on earth have you been?' She took Rita's icy hands in her large warm ones and led her to the rocking chair. 'Sit down and tell us all about it.'

'We went for a walk along the beach,' she replied dreamily,

avoiding Eddie who stared at her in fascination. Surely they had made love.

'Ah,' Mrs Megalith snorted. 'That would account for the hair, it looks as if a sea gull's been in it.'

'Did he kiss you lots and lots?' Eddie asked.

'Eddie, really, that's not the thing to ask a young woman,' her father chided. He was in his usual place at the head of the table, a glass of Scotch in his hand, watching the women in his family with amusement.

'You don't need to be clairvoyant to answer that question,' said Mrs Megalith, but her face softened and she smiled. 'There's nothing better for the health than kissing. It's a real tonic!' She smacked her lips and limped over to the table. 'Here, Edwina,' she thrust her stick out for her granddaughter to take. 'Now, pour me a sherry, dear girl, the excitement is wearing me out.'

'I'm sorry I wasn't around to do your hair,' said Maddie apologetically.

'Don't worry. I barely had time to change.'

'You should be grateful you didn't waste your time, Madeleine,' said Mrs Megalith, sitting back regally in her chair. 'You should put it up like mine, Rita, that way you wouldn't have to do it at all.'

'Well, Rita?' persisted her mother. 'Do tell us from the beginning. You waited for him at the bus stop?'

'Yes, with Trees and Faye and Alice and the children.'

'I don't imagine they all went to the beach with you,' said Mrs Megalith wryly.

'We went back to Lower Farm for tea and then George drove me home via the beach.'

'Has he changed?' Hannah asked.

'He's grown up. He's definitely stronger physically.'

'Oh, he would be, of course. He'll be a man now.'

'A summer wedding would be most welcome,' said Mrs

Megalith, taking the glass of sherry from Eddie. 'You can have it in my garden.' Rita was unable to conceal her excitement. Mrs Megalith raised her eyebrows and added exuberantly, 'Good God, he's proposed. About time too!'

'Has he?' Humphrey asked.

'He's proposed?' Hannah exclaimed.

'Not exactly,' Rita replied carefully. 'But he said we'll marry soon.'

'Words are cheap,' said Mrs Megalith, knocking back her sherry.

'Give him time, poor lad, he's only just got back,' Hannah interjected.

'I think a quiet celebration is in order,' said Humphrey happily. 'Hannah, let's open that bottle of wine we've been saving up.'

'Oh, do let's,' she agreed, bustling over to the cupboard. 'Maddie, hand out the glasses. Now where's the corkscrew?'

Hannah had cooked a large shepherd's pie, which she served with carrots and turnips from her vegetable garden. Rita soon warmed up although her feet remained as cold as a couple of frozen fish, reminding her of walking back up the beach with her toes in the sea. In fact, she could barely join in the conversation, so distracted was she by thoughts of their kisses in the cave.

'Rita, come for tea tomorrow, I want to give you a reading,' said Mrs Megalith darkly, watching her granddaughter with a perplexed look on her face.

Humphrey rolled his eyes. 'Primrose, is it absolutely necessary?' he asked, shaking his head and frowning with impatience. He didn't want her frightening his daughter at this happy time.

'Absolutely,' she stated firmly. No one ever opposed Mrs Megalith.

'I want one,' chirped Eddie. 'You never read cards for me.'

'My dear child,' replied her grandmother, 'you're too young to think about anything other than schoolwork. I don't need to consult the Tarot to tell you that.'

'But I might be about to die. You'd want to save me from death, wouldn't you?'

Mrs Megalith dug her jaw into spongey chins. 'Well of course I would, but the tarot has no death card, Eddie. That sort of thing comes to me in the form of intuition and I'm glad to say I've already looked into your future and am in no doubt that it's going to be a long one — and a hot one!' She grinned knowingly.

'Well, I'm delighted by that,' said Humphrey drily. 'We wouldn't want a funeral *and* a wedding, that would dampen everyone's enjoyment.'

'Really, Humphrey, sometimes your sense of humour is quite inappropriate,' retorted Mrs Megalith.

'Can I bring George?' Rita asked.

'No, you must come on your own. I want to talk to you in private.'

'You haven't seen something awful, have you?' Rita was suddenly gripped with panic.

'You see, Primrose, you're filling the poor child's head with unnecessary worry.' Humphrey's voice was crosser now.

'It's all right, Daddy,' said Rita diplomatically.

'Grandma wants to tell Rita about the birds and the bees,' said Eddie with a giggle.

'By the look in her eyes I think she knows enough about that already,' said Mrs Megalith, draining her glass. Rita blushed and looked to her mother for support. 'That really is very good wine, Humphrey.'

'Yes, isn't it?' he agreed, holding up his glass. 'It was water this morning.'

Hannah gasped and turned on him. 'Humphrey!'

'It's even better if you dine on snails and spiders' legs,' he continued, chuckling.

Mrs Megalith's mouth curled up at the corners and she looked down her nose at her son-in-law. 'You may mock me, Humphrey Fairweather, but believe me when I say that I will have the last laugh.' She turned to Rita. 'Don't blush, my dear, there's no need. One should enjoy the attentions of a man without shame, after all it's perfectly natural, isn't it?'

Hannah tut-tutted and changed the subject. She knew her mother's opinions and believed her an unhealthy role model for her impressionable daughters. She certainly wasn't representative of her generation and Hannah was anxious for her to keep her dubious sexual history to herself.

Rita was tucked up in bed when Maddie knocked on the door. 'Can I come in?' she whispered, poking her head through the gap. When Rita nodded enthusiastically, Maddie walked in and sat on the end of the bed. 'Was it wonderful?'

Rita smiled happily. 'Oh Maddie, I'm so in love,' she said, sitting up. 'I only just managed to stop myself.'

'What held you back?'

'Well, you know. We're not married.'

Maddie laughed. 'For goodness' sake, Rita, you're not the Virgin Mary.'

'But what if I get pregnant?'

'You won't if you use French letters. Or "rubbers" as Hank used to call them.'

Rita considered it for a moment then grimaced at the unromantic thought. She gazed at her sister longingly.

'I so want to.'

Maddie suddenly looked guilty. 'I have a confession to make,' she began slowly. 'I wasn't going to tell you because I thought you'd disapprove.'

'I'd never disapprove of you, Maddie.'

'Well, I made love with Hank.'

'You didn't!' Rita placed a trembling hand over her mouth.

'I did! It was lovely,' Maddie giggled. She was happy she could now talk about it with someone.

'But where?'

'In his jeep, at the Inn near Muddyhole. Goodness, that wasn't a problem.'

'Weren't you worried you'd get caught?'

'Not at all. Besides, it was worth it.'

Rita's eyes were wide and shining. 'But Megagran can see everything.'

'Obviously not. Look, other girls do it all the time. We just happen to have a very old-fashioned mother. Nothing's as sexy as wartime.' Maddie grinned suggestively. She thought better of confessing about the others. Rita would have been appalled.

'George looked so handsome in his uniform. He's big and strong and manly. But I'm going to wait until our wedding night. We're practically engaged, after all. It won't be long.'

'Don't be a fool, Rita, he'll lose interest in you unless you let him. There are plenty of girls around who won't think twice about giving themselves to him and you wouldn't want him running off with one of them, would you?'

'Of course not!' Rita was horrified. She swept a hand through her hair and swiftly changed the subject. 'Are you sad that Hank's gone back to America?'

'Goodness no! It was fun and romantic but I'm too young to tie myself to one man. They're all coming back now from the war, I want to keep my options open.' Maddie had discovered the forbidden pleasures of the flesh and was keen to enjoy as much of them as she could.

The following morning George drew up in his father's truck

and leapt out in time for breakfast. It was Saturday so Humphrey was reading the papers as usual but wearing slacks and a sleeveless green sweater instead of his grey suit. Hannah was knitting in the rocking chair. She had knitted so much for the war effort that she now found herself unable to stop. She looked forward to knitting little bootees for a grandchild some day. Eddie was still in bed and Maddie was enjoying a long bath. Rita saw George from her bedroom window and hurriedly slipped into an old summer dress and blue cardigan for, although the weather was warm, it was windy by the sea. She wished she had something new to put on for him. She hadn't had a new dress for years.

'Good morning, Hannah, Humphrey,' he said, smiling because he knew he had surprised them.

'Good gracious, if it isn't our own hero, George Bolton!' Hannah exclaimed, putting down her knitting and getting up to embrace him. 'Dear boy, what a lovely surprise. You look so well.'

'It's a pleasure to see you back, George. Come and join us. The tea's still hot. How about some of Hannah's home-made bread?' said Humphrey, patting George firmly on the back.

'Thank you. The bread smells delicious.'

'Rita will be down in a minute,' said Hannah, anticipating George's next question. She watched him sit at the table, his long legs spreading out in front of him, dwarfing the chair. How handsome he looked with his ruffled hair and light eyes. The war might have made a man out of him yet he still had the same boyish expression on his face, as if he were about to tell one of his stories. He always used to tell wonderful stories and, oh, how they'd laugh.

'We're all having a picnic on the beach today. Will you join us?' he asked, slicing himself a piece of bread. Hannah tore her eyes away and returned to the rocking chair, picking up her knitting needles.

'What a splendid idea. The girls will be thrilled,' she said and at that moment Rita's radiant face appeared at the kitchen door.

Humphrey watched his daughter as she walked buoyantly over to George and bent down to plant a kiss on his cheek. Her eyes sparkled like Megagran's glass of sherry and she reminded him very much of Hannah at the same age, for they had been young when they had married. George grinned bashfully, the way he always did with half his mouth and, as he looked up at her, his face softened into an expression of tenderness and pride. He patted her appreciatively on her lower back and with a sweeping glance took in her long curly hair and thin summer dress. Humphrey sat back in his chair, unaware that his face had been transformed by such a gentle scene.

When Eddie managed to drag herself out of bed she saw Trees' truck parked outside and knew that meant George was there. With great excitement she leapt down the stairs, two steps at a time and, without stopping, ran into the kitchen and into George's arms, throwing herself onto his knee. He laughed heartily as she pressed her warm face against his and kissed him passionately. 'I'm so pleased you're home. I missed you so much. More than Rita, I'm sure.'

'I missed your monkey face too!' he chuckled.

'You're a hero. Did you kill lots of Germans?'

'Eddie, why don't you let poor George eat his toast,' said Hannah. 'We're spending the day all together on the beach, you can plague him with your questions then.'

Reluctantly, she slipped off his knee and pulled out a chair. Rita wished they could spend the day alone and she linked eyes with George. He grinned, and her body trembled, for in his gaze she recognised the physical longing that she felt too, and the memory of the evening before returned to singe her cheeks with desire.

Maddie emerged from her bath to the sound of a man's voice downstairs that didn't belong to her father. It was deep and grainy like sand and unmistakably George's. She hastily dressed and did her hair in the mirror, rubbing a touch of rouge into her cheeks. Pleased with the result and with the doll-like prettiness that smiled back at her, she made her way downstairs to the kitchen.

She was surprised by the change in George. He exuded an animal vigour that now replaced the boyish exuberance of before. She felt momentarily envious of her sister, and couldn't help but imagine what it would be like to lie beneath him. She had to avert her eyes and concentrate on something else in case the lasciviousness in them betrayed her thoughts. She had always liked George; he was witty and funny and charismatic, but she had never looked on him as a *man*. Now, having experienced physical love she could barely think of anything else. It had been so pleasurable she wanted more. Instinctively, she sensed the sexual tension between George and her sister like a hound smelling the blood of a fox and she wished her American hadn't left so that he could satisfy her longing in the back of his jeep.

Hannah took pleasure in preparing the picnic. Hard-boiled eggs from Elvestree House, cold chicken and salad, turkey sandwiches, Spam and cheese. She packed the boot of the car with rugs and took an extra cardigan for herself in case the weather changed, which it often did, quite unexpectedly. While she cooked she looked out of the kitchen window and watched Rita and George talking on the swing chair while Eddie lay on the grass hanging onto their every word. Maddie was on the terrace flicking through a magazine. She adored gazing at photographs of the Hollywood stars like Lauren Bacall, Jane Russell and Rita Hayworth, and spent much time in the bathroom trying to cultivate the same looks with lipstick and curlers.

At eleven George drove the truck home with Rita by his side and Eddie and Maddie in the back, lifting up their hands to catch leaves from the trees that hung over the road.

'God, it feels good to be back,' he said, placing his free hand on Rita's upper thigh. 'It's good to feel you too,' he murmured.

'Careful, there are little spies in the back,' she replied, glancing through the window behind her.

'Only one little one, and one rather knowing one,' he said with a smirk. 'Maddie's lost more than her innocence in the war.'

'How can you tell?'

'A man knows these things.'

'Do I look so naïve?'

'Yes, but I like you that way.' He squeezed her thigh.

'Maddie gave herself to an American called Hank.'

'He would be, wouldn't he?'

'What?'

'Called Hank!' They both laughed.

'She's wicked. She's only nineteen. Nice girls aren't supposed to behave that way. Mummy and Daddy would be appalled.'

'Sex and war go hand in hand, Rita. You can't have one without the other. People know they could die at any minute so they lose themselves in each other.'

'It's terribly romantic.'

'In war a man has to love, if only to assert that he's very much alive in the face of possible death. Girls like Maddie serve a vital purpose, but you don't work in that department,

my love. You're special.' She smiled at him, reassured that
Maddie's advice had been wrong. 'I kept your photo with me
all the time and imagined making love to you,' he continued.
'You kept me going when little else could. Hank was probably
the same. Maddie made him feel alive.'

'I only had eyes for you,' she said quietly, her face flushing
with pride. 'I had loads of offers. The Americans were
everywhere. But I turned them down. All I could think of
was you.'

'You're a very special girl, Rita, and I love you for it,' he
said tenderly. He pulled his cigarette packet out of his breast
pocket. 'Here, light me one, would you?'

Rita liked the smell of smoke, it reminded her of those
early evenings on the cliffs when they'd both smoke together
after school, and of her father, who always lit up in the car
on his way home after work. Now she lit the cigarette for
George, took a drag herself, then handed it over. He held
it between his thumb and forefinger and placed it to his lips.
She attempted to put the packet back in his breast pocket
but it was obstructed by a thick piece of paper. She pulled
it out. It was her photograph. She was young. Not more than
Maddie's age. It was black and white and faded somewhat due
to so much handling.

'I think this needs replacing,' she said, slipping it back.

'Absolutely not. I'll carry that picture until I die.'

'There won't be a picture by then,' she replied with a
chuckle. 'It's faded already.' He couldn't tell her that he had
taken to kissing it after each flight. Such a sentimental ritual
seemed trite with hindsight.

They pulled up at Lower Farm and tooted the horn. The children ran out of the house and hung onto the gate, squealing in
delight at the prospect of a picnic on the beach. Alice emerged
with Faye, carrying baskets and rugs which they loaded into

the truck, and Mildred scampered out of a barn followed by Trees whose hair was white and fluffy and dancing on the wind like goose down. George and Rita joined the girls in the back and pulled the children up with them while Faye and Alice climbed into the front with Trees at the wheel. As the truck pulled out into the road they all broke into song while Mildred wagged her tail in time, pleased to be included.

They parked on the cliff next to Humphrey's Lee Francis and proceeded to walk down the little path to the beach. The sky was choppy like the sea and buoyant with feathery clouds and sea gulls that glided on the fresh westerly wind. George and Trees carried the picnic while Rita took little Johnnie's hand to guide him down the hill. The salty air was sweetened by the fertile smell of new grass and wild flowers, and Rita turned her eyes to the left where they had walked the evening before and her thoughts were once again drawn away from the present.

Humphrey and Hannah had set down the rugs near the bank where they'd be protected from the wind and while he stood smoking, gazing out across the ocean, she was carefully laying out the containers of food and thermos flasks of tea and hot cocoa. When they saw the approaching group they waved enthusiastically.

'What a jolly idea, Faye,' said Hannah happily. 'Pity about the wind, but at least it's sunny.'

'We just thought it would be nice to spend the day all together.'

'With dear George,' Hannah added, smiling fondly. 'Hasn't he grown into a handsome young man?'

'I know, I'm very proud,' replied Faye, turning to make sure that he was out of earshot.

'To think we may share grandchildren.' Hannah sighed. Then she added hastily, 'God willing.'

'Oh, wouldn't that be nice. Grandchildren are such a

blessing. Johnnie and Jane give us so much pleasure. I'd like to see George settling down with a family. He's been through so much.' Her face suddenly darkened with anxiety. 'Well, I'm sure he'll talk to Trees. After all, he served in the Great War. He understands.'

'What a brave young man. Our fighter pilots were the heroes of the war. You must be so proud.'

'I am,' she said. She couldn't begin to explain how grateful she was that he had survived and dared not speak of her fears to anyone, not even Trees. 'Now, let me help you. I've got some leftover rabbit stew, the farm is literally hopping with rabbits. Trees takes Johnnie up to the woods in his truck and they spend long evenings shooting them. Johnnie's riveted. He worships his grandfather. I can't cook much,' she said, remembering the welcome home cake, 'but I can cook a good rabbit stew thanks to your mother's recipe. Did you invite Primrose?'

'Goodness no! We want a little peace, don't we?' They both laughed and looked at Trees, who was sitting on the rug talking to Humphrey. Of all of them, he was the one person who truly appreciated Mrs Megalith, for she was just as passionate about walnut trees as he was, and for such a taciturn man he was remarkably verbose when talking to her.

After lunch George set up a treasure hunt for the young by drawing trails into the sand with a shell, then burying a bag full of boiled sweets at the very end of one trail. There were many red herrings and it took him half an hour to complete for the lines he drew weaved around rocks, into caves and for long distances across the beach. Finally Johnnie and Jane set off with the help of Eddie, Maddie and Alice. Their laughter and squeals of delight resounded across the bay, carried on the wind with the cries of gulls and the roar of waves. The grown-ups drank cider, smoked and talked so that George and Rita were able to sneak over the rocks and across the strip of sand to their secret cave without being noticed.

It was warm and damp inside and quiet out of the wind. He swung her around and kissed her. 'Careful, they might find us,' she said, pulling away.

'Not in here they won't. Believe me, it'll take them hours to find the treasure.' He grinned at her triumphantly and kissed her again. He smelt of smoke and tasted of cider. His hands ran over the skirt of her dress, against her thighs and over her bottom and she felt a warm wave of arousal wash over her. 'They can leave us here and we can walk back to your house later,' he mumbled, burying his face in her neck and tasting the salt on her skin. But to her dismay, Rita remembered her grandmother.

'I have to go to Megagran's for tea,' she said with a heavy sigh.

'Can't you go tomorrow?'

'You know Megagran.'

He pulled away and frowned impatiently. 'There's no one like Mrs Megalith to dampen one's ardour.'

'I'm sorry,' she said, running her fingers through his hair.

'Well, no point wasting time,' and he bent his head to kiss her again.

Chapter Four

'Ah, Rita,' said Mrs Megalith as Rita appeared through the arch in the garden wall. 'You can help me with these crystals.' She picked up a large amethyst and handed it to her granddaughter. 'Careful, it's heavy. Now, that one goes in the drawing room, on the table as you go in, you'll see the gap. It's my favourite so don't drop it.'

Rita obediently put it in its place then helped with the others. There were many, of every shape and colour, and Mrs Megalith took great pleasure in telling her the properties of each as they placed them all over the house. 'Just feel the energy in them now they've soaked up the elements. Nothing like a good clean.' She stood on the terrace, clasped a large blue sodalite to her bosom and closed her eyes. She breathed deeply while Rita stood quietly, waiting for this moment of spiritual ecstasy to end. A ginger cat slipped sinuously between Mrs Megalith's ankles, rubbing his fur on her thick stockings. Rita picked it up and held it against her until her grandmother finally opened her eyes. 'Magical, simply magical,' she breathed enthusiastically. 'Nature never ceases to delight one.'

Rita followed her into the kitchen and was given a tumbler of elderflower cordial and a biscuit. At that moment the ginger cat sprang out of her arms. A couple of black ones dashed out from under the kitchen table and three or four jumped off the windowsills and disappeared outside in pursuit of something beyond the senses of human beings.

'Cats never cease to delight one either,' said Mrs Megalith, watching the last, very fat cat amble lazily through the door. 'I seem to attract them. Every time I count I have more than the time before. God only knows where they all come from.'

'Cats are most unaffectionate creatures,' said Rita, thinking of Mildred and how much she loved to be petted.

'There you're quite mistaken, my dear. They obviously sense that you don't like them.'

Mrs Megalith was wrong for Rita loved all animals, even antisocial cats but she knew better than to contradict her grandmother. Biting her tongue, she followed her outside again and took a seat at the table on the terrace. The garden looked splendid, full of colour and the scent of spring.

'You know a damned fox had a go at my Aylesburies last night. The wind blew the lamp out. What a wind there was last night! I found feathers all over the place. Fortunately my ducks escaped with little more than a fright. One's missing but I suspect she's sitting on her eggs. So Rita,' she said, fixing her granddaughter with an intense stare. 'How are you?'

'I'm happy, Grandma,' she replied, averting her eyes, sure that her grandmother could see her innermost thoughts.

'You look well, if slightly apprehensive. What's on your mind?'

'Nothing. I'm just happy to have George back.'

'And how is he?' she asked. Rita wondered where her questions were leading.

'Happy too. He wanted to come and see you with me,' she lied, cringing as the colour in her cheeks exposed her.

'Good gracious, there's plenty of time for that. I wanted to see you on your own. I feel turmoil and uncertainty.'

Rita shook her head. Mrs Megalith's eyes darkened. They often changed colour, which unnerved those who didn't know her.

'Not at all. I'm very certain about George.'

'No dear. Not you. In George.'

Rita frowned and lowered her eyes. She wished she hadn't come. 'George and I are going to be married. We love each other.'

'I know. You always have. But George will need you to love him more than ever.'

'What do you mean?' Rita was very confused and a little frightened. She looked up to see a large black cat, almost the size of Mildred, staring at her from the roof.

'He will need you to listen to him, Rita. He's lived through a terrible war. He will need to talk about it. He's suffered, my dear. He's seen his friends killed and faced death himself. It will all seem like a horrible dream that he can't communicate to anyone because they won't understand. You have to try to understand him. I know, because my Denzil was never quite the same after the Great War, all that mustard gas and mud, a terrible business. The greatest casualty of war, my dear, is marriage and young people like you who are ripped apart by it. Give him time, but then talk to him. Don't forget that the only relationship he has been able to rely on in the last five years is the one between him and his Spitfire. He has to learn to trust human beings all over again. Don't let him become estranged to you.'

Rita listened carefully to her grandmother. She might be an old witch but what she was saying made sense.

'I want to understand him, Grandma, and I want to make him happy.'

'And you will.' Mrs Megalith smiled and her moonstone eyes softened to a gentle grey. 'Now where did I put my cards?'

While her grandmother limped into the drawing room Rita noticed a swallow dancing on the warm evening air. The sunlight was behind her and catching the tips of her wings as she flew. The bird was so light and buoyant she seemed to reflect Rita's sense of optimism. She remembered how she used to watch them with George. 'One day I'll fly like a swallow,' he had said and she had believed him. She recalled that the swallows returned to Elvestree every year to build their nest, and hatch their young in the top corner of the drawing room. Mrs Megalith enjoyed them so much she didn't mind the mess they made and curiously they seemed to have grown accustomed to the cats and weren't bothered by them. Rita raised her eyes to see that the scary black cat had slipped off the roof and disappeared. There was something eerie about Megagran's cats.

Mrs Megalith emerged from the dark drawing room just as the swallow flew in. She was shuffling the twenty-one cards of the Major Arcana. She only required her granddaughter to pick three for she had a specific question in mind. She sat down and settled her glasses on the bridge of her nose. Then she handed the pack to Rita, looking at her over her lenses.

'Shuffle these for a while. Did you see the swallow?' Rita nodded. 'What a delight they are and what a privilege it is to offer them a home, year in year out.' Rita shuffled the cards. 'When you're ready, think of George and pick three, giving them to me as you choose them.'

Rita did as she was told. She visualised George's face and remembered how cross he had been that their afternoon had been interrupted. Then she chose three cards from different parts of the pack. Mrs Megalith took them in her jewelled fingers, placed them on the table and turned them over one by one. The cards were brightly painted with elaborate pictures and Megagran always referred to them as 'tools for spirit communication'. 'They're not magic in themselves,' she would explain to a new sitter. 'Spirit will lead you to pick the cards that will answer your question and guide you. My job is simply to interpret them and for that I follow my intuition for it is never wrong.'

She stared at the cards for a long while then tapped the first one with her finger. 'Temperance. My dear, this card is about you, at this present time. It is a card of emotional indecision. You see a woman in a virginal white dress, with a red cloak that represents the base vibration and a blue one – that represents a higher vibration – pouring water from one golden goblet into another. This represents a battle between sexuality and virtue. I don't need the cards to tell me that, it's written all over your face. My dear Rita, let it go and enjoy him. There is nothing wrong with making love as long as it is with love.'

Before Rita had time to blush her grandmother tapped the next card. 'The Fool,' she stated, then sniffed knowingly. The card depicted a man at a crossroads, looking backwards with a grave face. 'This is the card that reveals the circumstances that surround you.' Rita looked at it. She wondered whether the white cliffs and the sea were representative of Devon, but Mrs Megalith continued stridently. 'You will have a choice to make. It will not be an easy one. In fact, it will be life changing. You will not want to let go of the past for the past is your security. But trust your instincts and follow them for they never lie. I sense that the sea is literal; one path leads to it and to the horizon beyond. That is the road that I feel you should take. You see the dog who accompanies this man?' Rita nodded and thought of Mildred. 'You won't be alone. George will look after you.' Rita didn't think George would appreciate being the dog in the picture. He was a small white dog with short hair, not a big shaggy one like Mildred.

'Ah, The Moon.' Mrs Megalith picked up the third card and nodded knowingly. 'A man gazing to the moon with his back to a woman who sits on the step looking up at him sadly. My dear, this is the card of illusion. The man is chasing the moon, which he will never attain. Don't let George leave you behind, holding the cup of love like this poor girl.'

'Thank you, Grandma,' said Rita, relieved that it was over and nothing dire revealed. The only part that she remembered was the fight between her sexuality and her virtue. Her mother would be appalled to know that her own mother was encouraging sex outside marriage although she had heard it said that Megagran had enjoyed quite a colourful past before Denzil had made an honest woman out of her. Rita looked at her watch and wondered whether it would be rude to leave. After all, she had to prepare herself for the party.

Mrs Megalith was aware that her granddaughter hadn't paid much attention. She had watched her eyes glaze over for the second and third card. Unfortunately, the first card had diverted her attention from the two other more important ones. She took off her glasses and stood up. 'I suppose you need to slip into your glad rags for the party,' she said with an impatient sniff.

Rita nodded. 'I'd love to stay, but it's getting late.'

'Yes, yes. Quack quack jabber jabber and all that. Well, if you must. But don't disregard the cards, Rita, or you'll make a grave mistake.' Mrs Megalith wondered why she bothered with such an unenthusiastic sitter. 'If you ignore my advice, my girl, it will be at your peril.'

'I won't. Look there's the swallow again.' Megagran was suitably distracted so that they talked about the swallows all the way round to the front of the house where Rita had left her bicycle.

'I'll see you tonight,' she said, waving at her grandmother, pedalling as fast as she could up the drive and out of sight.

Trees wandered into the house at the same moment as his wife alighted at the foot of the stairs in a pretty blue dress printed with cornflowers. His hands were dirty from handling the sticky leaves of his precious walnut trees. One of his favourites was the large Juglans Negra that had been planted beside the house about three hundred years before with the intention of catching the summer flies in the leaves before they flew inside. It was tall and majestic and produced the sweetest nuts in the autumn. He had planted forty-seven varieties in the last thirty years and, although most took at least twenty-five years to produce fruit, he was excited at the recent discovery in France of a variety that produced fruit in only three years. Sadly, the war had thwarted his plans to investigate further.

'Our guests will be here very soon and you haven't even bathed,' said Faye. She looked at the chaos in the hall and was glad the party was in the barn. The hall table was covered with papers, books and the laundry she had intended to take up to her bedroom before she got distracted by Johnnie standing on a chair removing all her scores of music and photograph frames from the lid of her piano. Trees nodded at her and rubbed his hands together purposefully. 'Is everything ready in the barn?' she asked.

'Yes, I'll go and change.'

'The barbecue lit?' she added as he passed her. He nodded again. 'Good. It's not much, only twenty or thirty people at the most. I've asked the village and who knows, maybe some of George's old friends will turn up. It's just a gesture to welcome him home. I want him to feel appreciated. We can all raise our glasses, there's plenty of cider.'

It was a windy evening. The sun had disappeared behind heavy clouds and it looked as if it might rain. Faye raised her eyes to the sky and hoped that it would at least stay dry for the party. Her attention was drawn to a flock of starlings that flew across it like a waft of black smoke, diving and dancing their aerial evolutions, and she thought of George in his Spitfire. She walked over to the barn, which stood on the periphery of the farm nestled among a cluster of apple trees. It was used for storing hay at harvest time. When George and Alice were little they used to climb the stacks like mountains, hiding from their parents at bedtime. How innocent life had been back then, she reflected.

It was warm and sheltered out of the wind and smelt of cut grass and smoke from the barbecue. She had set up two long tables that they had improvised with logs and planks, made a tablecloth out of sheets, and borrowed cutlery, plates and glasses from Mrs Megalith who had enough for a banquet. She had offered the use of her garden, which would undoubtedly have been a prettier setting, but Faye had declined. It was George's homecoming party and nowhere else would do but home. She lit a candle and proceeded to light all the hurricane lamps on the tables. It felt surreal that he was home, that the war had ended. She tried not to think about the dangers he had been through. He was still her little boy and she couldn't bear to imagine how much he had suffered. She lit the lamps and silently said a prayer of thanks and another one for the future. She sensed he might need it.

As the sun waned people began to arrive armed with food and drink to contribute to the party. Reverend Elwyn Hammond strode in with his wife and two grandchildren carrying bags of bread buns; old June Hogmier, who ran the village shop, brought potatoes for baking which she had scrounged from the chuck basket, being too mean to bring fresh ones; and Cyril and his sweet wife, Beryl, brought vegetables and baked apples for pudding. The farm labourers came with chickens, and a boisterous group of George's old friends, the few who had survived the war, carried bottles of beer. George mingled beneath the large banners that the children had painted with Alice that spelt 'Welcome Home George'. He was touched by the effort his parents had gone to, if a little self-conscious. He didn't feel he deserved so much attention. He was unable to shake off the feeling of guilt that had gnawed at him ever since he had come home. So many men hadn't lived to see victory.

He was talking to Reverend Hammond when Rita arrived with her family. He excused himself politely and made his way through the people to greet her.

'How was Megagran?' he asked, putting his hand in the small of her back and pulling her against him so that he could kiss her.

'She didn't tell me anything I didn't already know,' she replied.

'Losing her touch, is she?'

'No, I'm just improving mine. She's coming tonight.'

'On her broomstick or will she be jumping out of a cake?'

'I hope neither. I don't think your mother is up to making a cake that size.' They both laughed.

'Hello, Eddie. How's my favourite girl?' He grinned down at her and ruffled her hair.

'Don't lie. I'm not your favourite. Rita is.'

'My second favourite then.'

Eddie sighed melodramatically. 'One day I'll be someone's number one!' And she strode off into the crowd with Harvey the bat clinging to her sleeve.

When Mrs Megalith arrived the crowd seemed to part like the sea before a big liner. No one dared stand in the way of the Elvestree Witch. She had stuck peacock feathers into her hair and draped herself in her favourite purple dress over which she had thrown the green tasselled shawl her late husband had bought her in India. She wore the heavy moonstone around her neck on a black cord and her fingers were laden with crystals.

'Hello George, remember me?' she said, tapping him firmly on his shoulder. He swivelled around.

'Mrs Megalith, how nice of you to come.' He ran his eyes up and down her eccentric costume. 'You look glorious!'

'One mustn't disappoint. These good people expect me to dress like a witch,' she said with a wink.

'Don't witches wear black?' he asked. Rita put her hand to her lips to suppress nervous laughter. Her grandmother was notorious for her unpredictable nature. Only Max could get away with teasing her about being a witch. To Rita's surprise Mrs Megalith narrowed her eyes.

'Not this one,' she replied with a grin and George raised his eyebrows. Was it possible that she was being flirtatious?

'You're a bright star shining through war-torn Britain, Mrs Megalith.'

'Thank you, George. You certainly know how to flatter an old girl. Now where's your father? I hear he's had some more information on that rare variety of French walnut.'

'What is so special about walnut trees?' Rita asked. Then when Megagran launched into a lengthy explanation she wished she hadn't asked.

'Dear girl, how much time have you got? They are very special trees with a fascinating history. Really, I'm surprised George hasn't already told you. Walnut is so precious it was believed to belong to the Gods, that they ate it! The Persians referred to the nuts as "Royal Nuts" and it was a crime to touch them. The Greeks brought the tree to Rome in about one hundred BC where they grew at the time of Christ and the Romans brought them to England. It's the most beautiful timber, deliciously rare and expensive. You have to guard your mature walnuts with your life, like Trees does, bless him. The one that overlooks your house, George, is a real corker! There's nothing batty about your father, he's a genius, a wonderful, much misunderstood genius. I bet he has one of the largest collections of walnuts in the country. Oh, and squirrels love them and we love squirrels, don't we?' Rita nodded, remembering how she used to feed them as a child in Megagran's garden. 'Especially barbecued with a little bacon,' she added, smacking her lips.

'Pa's over there,' said George, pointing to his father, towering at least a head above everyone else. When she moved regally on, Rita rolled her eyes.

'Why did I get her going? I was simply humouring her.'

'You need never humour a witch. They humour themselves. It must be a hoot to live like she does, with cats and cards and crystal balls.'

'I don't know. Perhaps she gets lonely,' Rita said. 'Even with all those cats.'

'Not with Max and Ruth. They must be saints to live with her.'

'They have no choice, poor lambs,' said Rita with a smile.

'But she's never dull. The world has enough dull people in it. She's a spark of colour in a grey world.' For a moment his face clouded and he looked sad. She touched his arm and remembered her grandmother's advice.

'I'd like a glass of cider,' she said. 'I want to toast your homecoming more than anyone.'

'Right, follow me,' he said, smiling once again, and they weaved their way to where the drinks were set out at the far end of the barn.

Max and Ruth had arrived with Mrs Megalith but had got left behind in her wake and swept to one end of the barn where the barbecue was cooking. After a moment of hesitation, Ruth was dragged off by Eddie and her friends, leaving Max alone with a glass of cider. He watched his sister and felt heartened by her happy face. He was aware that, although Mrs Megalith was like a mother to them, they were very much alone in the world and he felt desperately protective of her. She was still a child and he was now seventeen. He ran a hand through his hair and surveyed the room. His eyes settled on Rita who was nuzzled up against George, and he suffered a pang of jealousy. He was ashamed that he had hoped George might not come back from the war. Shocked that he was capable of such a thought. He took in her long wild hair and pale face scattered with freckles like a thrush's egg and wished that she would look at him with the same devotion she reserved for George. He wrenched his eyes away for the sight only caused him pain and observed with amusement the rapacious eyes of the Elvestree witch.

Mrs Megalith had the rare ability of being able to concentrate on many things at the same time. While she listened to Trees telling her about the French walnut trees he hoped to import to Devon, she noticed Maddie in the midst of a group of young men at the other end of the barn. She was sitting in a very unladylike fashion on the knee of one of George's friends. She had her arms around his neck and her legs slightly apart, roaring with laughter with her mouth wide open. Hannah was too busy talking to Reverend Hammond's wife, Vera, to notice, and Humphrey was discussing the continuing war in Japan with Mike Purdie, his neighbour. Eddie had found Ruth and a few other young people to entertain and was running through the barn like the pied piper of Hamelin, making a frightful din. She looked back at Maddie. Suddenly in her mind's eye she had the vision of her granddaughter in the arms of a GI in the back of a jeep. She blinked the image away; it was most distasteful, not to mention intrusive, but it certainly made sense of Maddie's lack of motivation. 'She has discovered the forbidden pleasures of the flesh, God bless her,' thought Mrs Megalith to herself, remembering her own first taste of it many moons ago. She hoped the girl's desire wouldn't get the better of her.

The party was jolly, a veritable celebration of George's homecoming and victory. The atmosphere was carefree and vibrating with excitement. Years of conflict had united everyone in fear and purpose and now liberation united them again in festivity. Yet they didn't forget those who had given their lives in service and held a moment of silence to honour them. During that moment Max thought of his parents and suppressed the dull ache that came on the occasions that he allowed himself to remember them. Reverend Hammond took his wife's hand and silently prayed for the soul of their son Rupert, killed at Dunkirk. Then Trees toasted George, too overcome to say more. Rita looked up and noticed that Max was staring at her, his eyes glazed and sad. She smiled at him but he seemed not to see her. Then the dancing began and the sound of feet tapping caused the whole barn to shudder and the record on Faye's gramophone to skip.

Faye watched her son as he swung Rita off the dance floor and out into the night.

It was raining now, a light drizzle on a strong wind. The air was fresh and smelt heavily of damp earth and foliage. George took her by the hand and they ran through the farm to an old shed that stood low and squat beside a large chestnut tree. He pulled the bolt and opened the door. They crept inside to where it was pleasantly warm and dry and full of newborn calves. When George closed the door behind him, the soft shuffling of hooves on straw and low mooing rose out of the silence as the animals strained their senses to observe them. The place was illuminated by a dim light and Rita was enchanted by the shiny-eyed calves who pushed their faces through the bars of their pens to look at her. Without saying a word she crouched down and stroked their silky faces and wet noses. The mooing grew louder as they all demanded to be petted. George took her hand and raised her to her feet. She followed him up a ladder to the hayloft, where it was cosy and sweet smelling.

They could hear the wind whistling over the roof of the shed but the hay was soft and warm to lie on. The rustling from the pens diminished as the calves settled down again and only the odd moo disrupted their peaceful breathing.

George kissed her. It wasn't the fevered kissing of their cave but slow and tender and full of significance. 'I can't cope with the crowd. I just want to be alone with you,' he said, burying his face in her neck and running his lips over her damp skin.

Her dress was wet from the rain and clinging to her body like seaweed. She smelt of violets and her own brand of innocence and George was reminded, by the contrast, of the loose women he had bedded during the war in order to feel human again and to forget the carnage of combat. But it felt strange. Familiar, comforting, but strange, as if he had come home expecting to fit into his old mould, surprised that he had grown out of it. Rita seemed unaware of the difference, which made it somehow harder to make sense of and certainly impossible to communicate. He looked down at her flushed, still childish face and realised that, as much as he enjoyed her, he didn't want to mar her purity by making love to her. Everything about the war had been sordid. Rita remained untarnished. He wanted to preserve it for as long as he could.

She looked at him quizzically as if aware of the turmoil of his thoughts. 'Forget the war, my love,' she whispered, smiling up at him timidly. 'It's over. You're home and I'm here to comfort you.'

'Thank God for you, Rita,' he mumbled, burying his face in her neck again. 'Thank God for you.'

Chapter Five

The following day Rita sat in church next to her mother and Maddie. Hannah wore a simple beige hat beneath which her face assumed an expression of intense piety as she stared solemnly into her prayer book, unable to read a word because of her poor eyesight. If she had known that one of her daughters sat before God tainted and unashamed and the other entertained thoughts of a sexual nature, she would have sunk to her knees in horror.

But Maddie was careful to keep her voice low. 'So, what was it like?' she hissed into her sister's ear.

Rita blushed and lowered her hat to hide from her mother. 'Lovely,' she replied with a contented sigh.

'Where did you go? You didn't get back until dawn.'

'I know!' Rita stifled a yawn. 'We went to the shed full of newborn calves. They were adorable.'

'You made love in a cowshed?' Maddie gasped in horror.

'No, we were in the hayloft, not the cowshed. And we didn't make love.'

'You didn't?'

'No.'

'Why on earth not?'

'Because we're not married.'

Maddie shook her head. 'You foolish girl!' she exclaimed. 'Don't say I didn't warn you.'

'Shhh,' silenced their mother. 'Don't forget that this is God's house and you, Rita, have much to thank Him for.'

Rita nodded and glanced across the aisle to where Faye and Trees sat with Alice, the children and George. They, too, had much to be thankful for. She caught George's eye and he grinned back at her discreetly, the intimacy of the night before still shining in his speckled grey eyes.

As Reverend Hammond strode into the centre of the nave, dignified in his long black robe and white dog collar, only his long grey curls rebelled against the studied perfection of his demeanour. Like Hannah, he assumed a different guise in church. He seemed taller, broader, more imposing in his role as vicar than when he was Elwyn Hammond, the husband and grandfather buying vegetables from Miss Hogmier's village shop. In God's house he was God's spokesman. A man of vocation whose duty it was to be God's shepherd, to lead His sheep home, to show that the way to heaven was through suffering and repentance. Reverend Hammond knew suffering better than most, having lost his only son, and he knew love and compassion too, for his daughter-in-law had brought his grandchildren to live with them in Frognal Point. Every day he saw his son in the faces of those two children and every day he mourned him, but he took comfort that Rupert was with God now. He had found his way home and was at peace.

The congregation fell silent as Reverend Hammond's deep voice resonated through the church like the low moan of a double bass. He spoke slowly, articulating his words with care so that even the old and partially deaf could hear him at the back. Rita looked past her mother to Eddie, who sat doodling on a small notepad. She was careful to draw patterns of crucifixes in case her mother took her eyes off Reverend Hammond to see what she was doing. Humphrey sat beside her, his small round glasses perched on the end of his nose, flicking through the hymn book. He wasn't a religious man and found Reverend Hammond extremely tedious and self-satisfied. But he liked to come to support Hannah, who never missed church, even when she was sick.

Suddenly the door burst open and Reverend Hammond's voice trailed off in surprise. There was little that could silence the good Reverend so every head in the congregation turned to the door to see what kind of demon stood there. Rita craned her neck, then nudged Maddie urgently. Mrs Megalith paused a moment at the entrance while the fresh coastal wind blew in and caused her long blue dress to billow about her ankles. She sniffed as her moonstone eyes surveyed the scene before her. It had been years, literally, since she had last been to church, but only a matter of weeks since she had last clashed with Reverend Hammond over the corruption of the word of God by organised religion. Reverend Hammond found he could not continue. Mrs Megalith had reduced him to a gasping fish floundering on a riverbank.

She proceeded to walk up the aisle, slow and stately, the tapping of her stick echoing ominously off the walls. No one spoke. Only Eddie giggled mischievously into her hand to be silenced by a sharp nudge from her mother. Hannah was aghast. Megagran was famous for hating church, the vicar and for finding the very institution of religion dogmatic, not to say mercenary. She claimed she felt the presence of God in her garden and didn't need to pay good money for the privilege of sitting in His house and hearing the vicar speak of Him as if he knew Him more intimately than anyone else. 'It's a bloody con,' she would say. 'If people knew they could talk to Him in the comfort of their own kitchens they wouldn't bother going to church and listening to that old bore lecture them about suffering.' Now Hannah cringed as her mother forced them all to squeeze together so that she could sit at the end of the pew. Reverend Hammond watched the large crystals around her neck glitter as they caught the light and nervously fingered the simple cross that hung about his own. He seemed to have shrunk and, when he finally managed to speak, his voice was little more than a croak.

'We are *all* welcome here in God's house,' he began and tried to ignore the loud 'tut' from Mrs Megalith and the challenging expression in her eyes. Hannah wondered what on earth had possessed her mother to come. What's more, thanks to her, they were all exceedingly uncomfortable squashed together like cans on the kitchen shelf. 'Let us sing hymn number three hundred and twenty-five, *I Vow To Thee My Country.*' The congregation rose to its feet and sang in hearty voices the hymn they all knew and loved so well. Reverend Hammond was only too happy to hand the service over to Miss Hogmier and her uncertain organ playing.

As the service progressed Reverend Hammond began to relax. He avoided looking at Mrs Megalith's tight face and reasserted his authority. Then just when everything seemed to be back to normal a large black cat, the size of a dog, appeared from nowhere and jumped onto the altar. Reverend Hammond was the only person who didn't see it for he was facing his congregation. Johnnie and Jane pointed at it excitedly.

One cat might not have caused a commotion, two might have been allowed to roam the nave in peace, but five, six, seven, eight cats could not be ignored. One by one the cats appeared at the altar, slid up against the white cloth with their backs rigid and their tails high in the air, then sprang up to pad across the top, carefully avoiding the candlesticks and silver. Reverend Hammond noticed that the eyes of his congregation were not on him as he delivered what he felt to be a brilliant sermon. When he allowed his gaze to succumb to the magnetic force of Mrs Megalith's awesome personality, he found that she was looking as surprised as everyone else.

No longer able to contain his curiosity he turned to see what had diverted their attention.

Cats of every colour and size played about the altar. He was in no doubt that the Elvestree Witch had something to do with it for she was well known for keeping a house full of cats. Wearily he turned back to his congregation. 'As I said, we are all welcome in God's house,' he quipped lamely. Then he focused his attention on Mrs Megalith. 'Legend has it that cats are good luck. God has blessed this house today. Let us pray.'

Mrs Megalith leaned over to Maddie and hissed loudly in her ear. 'It is also legend that if you keep a black cat you will never be short of lovers. I bet he doesn't know that.' Maddie wanted to retort that if such a legend were true her grandmother would have more lovers than time, but she wisely kept her thoughts to herself.

When the service finally drew to a close the entire congregation waited for Mrs Megalith to hobble back down the aisle with Maddie and Rita followed by Hannah, Eddie, Humphrey and the eight cats. They watched her pass, more sure than ever that she was indeed a witch. Out in the sunshine Hannah turned on her mother. 'Why did you come?' she demanded.

Mrs Megalith smiled smugly. 'Didn't the good vicar say that we are all welcome in God's house?'

'But you don't like church,' she argued.

'It's important to ruffle the old goose's feathers every once in a while, otherwise he gets too big for his boots.' She snorted with laughter. 'No, I came because I felt it was appropriate. George and all that.'

'Really?' Hannah was astounded.

'Elwyn says that the way to Heaven is through suffering. Well, after today's débâcle I'm one step closer.' She smiled triumphantly. 'Got him going, though, didn't I? The fool!'

Reverend Hammond was barely able to conceal the trembling in his hands as he conversed politely with all the congregants. 'It is also legend, Reverend,' said Miss Hogmier darkly, 'that after seven years cats become witches. Imagine the number of witches we'll all have to deal with in the future if that is true.'

'Really, Miss Hogmier, you don't believe in all that nonsense, do you?'

'I most certainly do, Reverend Hammond. Trust me, Mrs Megalith is an evil woman!'

That afternoon George and Rita sat on a blanket on the cliff top watching the birds as they had done since childhood. The storm had passed, leaving a perfect blue sky without a cloud in sight. It was still windy, especially up there on the cliffs, but it was a warm and pleasant wind. Rita had packed Marmite sandwiches and hot cocoa for tea. Her mother had made biscuits for them and added slices of cold ham for George.

'Everyone's talking about your homecoming,' said Rita happily.

'They can't have much else to talk about if that's the case,' he replied, gazing out across the sea to where the horizon quivered enticingly with the promise of adventure.

'They say you're a hero.'

'Do they,' he replied flatly. 'No, Rita, the heroes are the boys who gave their lives. I'm not a hero.'

'And I don't want to fly any more.' His comment was unexpected. She didn't know how to respond, so she said nothing. 'I don't want to remember the war. I want to forget it ever happened and lose myself in you.'

But George wasn't able to forget the war. He could suppress the memories during his waking moments but at night, when his resistance lay dormant, images penetrated his psyche and plagued his dreams. So real, he could smell the petrol and cordite, feel the sweat forming on his forehead and nose, dripping into his eyes, misting up his oxygen mask. Back in his Spitfire he relived that sensation of immediacy, of living intensely, of cold, nerve-shattering fear . . .

The sky is dark with German bombers, Heinkels mostly, like a swarm of black wasps, moving towards him at great speed. Suddenly he's in the thick of it. Planes coming out of nowhere, one hundred and fifty at least, not to mention the ME 109s covering them. *Bloody Krauts!* The sound of gunfire like tearing calico, the raw hiss of passing tracers, then a flash and a loud explosion. More gunfire. Spraying the sky with bullets. *Black smoke, not me, not my Spitty? Not this time. Near miss. Some other poor sod.* A Heinkel dives out of control. A man bales out but his parachute gets caught in the propellers, taking him down with it. What a horrific way to die. Then, gripped with an icy calm, his training takes over, fear freezes into concentration, *it's either them or me and I've got too much to live for*. He presses the boost override, opens the throttle and narrows his eyes as he picks up speed. *Take control for God's sake. Don't lose it, George, you fool. Blast the buggers out of the sky.* Once again he's fighting for his life. Again and again. How much longer can he go on like this? Oh, to sit up on those cliffs and watch the birds. Now he's flying higher than any bird and into the ugly face of death. No one told him it would be like this.

To keep those images at bay George helped his father on the farm, slipping off to kiss Rita at every opportunity. Love was a sure way to forget. It burned away the guilt and the pain. If he didn't keep busy he was apt to remember his dead friends: Jamie Cordell, shot down during a sweep over Northern France; Rat Bridges, killed in a sortie over Dunkirk; Lorrie Hampton, dead at the bottom of the sea and many many more. He had to block them out or he'd go mad.

Rita was patient. She indulged him and loved him and never pressurised him to marry her. She was sure he would when he settled down again. She instinctively understood that he had been through a great deal and needed to acclimatise. Faye discussed the future with her while they sculpted. The two women took it for granted that they'd be one big, happy family. They talked about doing up one of the farm cottages and the fun Johnnie and Jane would have with small cousins to play with. Faye recalled the old haunts that Alice and George had so enjoyed as children, chasing rabbits out of the stooks and feeding the livestock, and imagined the next generation in the same places, doing the same things. But at the back of her mind there were gnawing doubts that she tried to ignore. She watched her son. She watched him closely. When he wasn't occupied his face looked much older; the face of a disillusioned old man.

The summer passed. A new Labour government came in. The war in Japan ended. Rations continued as Britain struggled to get back on her feet again. George lost himself in Rita, in the farm, in the White Hart with his friends. But he couldn't ignore his restless soul for ever.

Faye awoke with a sinking feeling in the pit of her stomach. She turned over and lay staring into the darkness for a while, thinking about George and his future, worrying about Rita and hers. She sighed heavily and tried to go back to sleep but she could not. Something was chewing on her gut, telling her to get up and go down to the kitchen. It wasn't the first time that she had awoken with this feeling. When her children were young she'd sense when one had suffered a nightmare, or felt unwell, unhappy or simply couldn't sleep. She was used to padding along the creaking corridors, feeling her way in the dark.

She crept downstairs and turned on the light in the kitchen.

She opened the ice chest and helped herself to a glass of cold milk and a slice of bread. She nibbled at it in silence, wondering what to do next. Then something drew her attention outside. She walked onto the terrace to find George sitting alone, smoking. He looked forlorn there in the dark and she could feel his unhappiness reach out to her with leaden arms and pull her down too.

'Do you mind if I join you?' she asked in a soft voice, hovering in the doorframe. He looked up, not at all surprised to see her.

'I'd like you to,' he replied, exhaling the smoke into the fresh autumnal air. She wrapped her dressing gown about her and sat down beside him on the bench.

'Are you all right, darling?'

'Just couldn't sleep,' he replied, recalling his nightmare with a shiver.

'Me neither. Perhaps it's the cheese. They say cheese gives you nightmares.'

He chuckled cynically. 'I don't think so. My mind doesn't give me any peace.'

'Darling, don't be disappointed.'

He took a hard look at her for a moment and the corners of his mouth twitched with misery. 'But I am,' he said finally and his voice was little more than a deep groan.

She put a gentle hand on his arm. 'You were a boy when you left, George. You can't get him back, or his life. You have to try to adapt to your changed circumstances.'

'But it's too quick. I come home and everything seems the same. Rita's the same, you and Pa, even the old vicar. Nothing has changed. The sea is the same, the beach, the birds, the sky. Only rations, coupons and empty shops are different – and me.' He dropped his head and stared at the flagstones. Then he continued in a very quiet voice. 'You don't know what it's like to lose so many friends. The best, the brightest.

Like brothers they were. I miss them. You don't know what it's like to see the whites of your enemy's eyes, knowing that he's just doing his job like you, he's not much more than a boy, with a mother and a girl at home, to shoot him down and watch his plane spiral to the ground. Black smoke, knowing he's suffering like hell. You can't feel pity because if it's not him, it's you.

'Every time that telephone rang, ordering us to scramble, I wondered whether I'd ever hear it again. But somehow I survived to do it again – and again and again and again. You see, Ma, when I close my eyes at night that is what I see. That is what I dream of: fighting for my life and feeling fear. That terrible fear. And feeling afraid of feeling fear. You see, I'm a coward really.'

'You're not a coward, darling. You're human,' said Faye, blinking through her tears. Not wanting him to see. He shook his head and took another drag of his cigarette.

'In a funny way I miss it. I miss the camaraderie, the sense of purpose. I feel like a drifting kite. My string's been cut.'

'Why don't you become a flight instructor or something? Surely there's a place for you in the Air Force?'

He chuckled cynically. 'Of course. But I can't . . .' His voice trailed off. She stroked his hand. 'I want to settle down, work the land like Pa, marry Rita and raise my children. But I just can't. Not yet. I feel my life has peaked and I'm only twenty-three. There's got to be more for me out there.' He wanted to tell her how he hated what the war had done to him, the level of depravity to which he had sunk. How could he feel comfortable in his own skin when it was stained with the blood of German youth?

'What is it you want to do?' Faye asked, wanting so desperately to chase away his shadows.

'I don't know,' he groaned.

'You're not worrying that you'll disappoint your father and

me, are you? Because whatever you do we will support you. We're proud of you, but we're not your keepers.'

George dragged on his cigarette. 'I want to go away for a while,' he stated finally.

'Where to?'

'I don't know. America, the Argentine.'

'With Rita?'

He shook his head. 'Possibly. I don't know. This place is stifling me. Too many memories, too much nostalgia. I don't fit in any more.'

'Why don't you go and visit my sister and Jose Antonio in the Argentine? You could work on their farm in Córdoba, gain some experience and then, when you're ready, come home and work with your father. It will do you good to get away for a while. How does that sound?' His unhappiness lifted like autumn mist when the sun burns through.

'Good,' he said, his voice full of relief. He rested his head on his mother's shoulder. She hugged him to her, this great big son who so easily dwarfed her. 'You're the only person who really understands me.'

'What about Rita?' Faye asked after a while.

'I love Rita,' he said, sitting up. 'She's part of all that is home to me. I'm just not ready for home yet. I'll ask her to wait for me. Then, when I return, we'll marry. Rita is the only thing I'm sure of.'

Chapter Six

'Eddie, where have you been?' Maddie asked as Eddie ran into the house, flushed and giggling. Eddie skidded to a halt and grinned guiltily. She couldn't tell her sister that she had spent the whole summer holidays spying on Rita and George kissing in the cave. Love fascinated her. Or rather the physical aspect of it did. She had confessed to her best school friend, Amy, that she had seen Maddie making love to her American in the back of his jeep. They had created such heat the windows had steamed up. She couldn't tell Maddie that, either.

'Nothing. Just playing with Harvey,' she replied innocently.

'Well, where is he then?'

'Hunting now. A bat's got to eat, you know.'

Maddie's eyes narrowed. 'You've been down on the beach.'

'Haven't.'

'Have, I can tell.'

'So what if I have?'

'You've been spying again. They'll catch you one of these days.'

Eddie laughed. 'They're much too busy for that.'

'Really?' Maddie tried not to look too interested.

'They do it all the time.'

Maddie thought of George making love to Rita. She knew he'd be a good lover. Passionate, masterful but sensitive. She envied Rita. She had it all.

* * *

Rita lay in George's arms, listening to his breathing and the roar of the waves in the distance. It was warm in the cave but the air had changed. Their innocence had gone and so had their playfulness. George had been distracted for weeks. As if he were slowly drifting away from her. Perhaps Maddie was right after all, that he was bored with her because she wouldn't sleep with him. She hadn't said anything, preferring to pretend that nothing was wrong. Although he kissed and caressed her with tenderness, she couldn't help but feel that he did so in order to hide from something. He looked into her eyes but didn't see her. He talked to her but didn't listen. They laughed less, or rather, less from the pit of their bellies. There was no doubt about it; the war had changed George in more than just his physique.

'Rita, we need to talk,' he said at last.

Rita stiffened. 'We're all right, aren't we, George?' she asked, feeling unaccountably apprehensive.

'Of course we are, my love.' They sat up and he put his arm around her. But she wasn't reassured.

'I'm going away.'

'Where to?' she asked, shocked that he would want to leave Frognal Point.

'I'm going to the Argentine and I want you to come with me.'

Rita's lips began to tremble.

George lit a cigarette and blew the smoke out in rings. 'I can't stay here,' he continued, staring out of the mouth of the cave. 'The war has changed me, Rita. I need to shake off the last five years and I can't do that in Frognal Point. I'll go to the Argentine, work on my uncle's farm for a year or so and then come back.'

'Do you really want me to go with you?'

'Of course,' he replied, but his voice sounded flat.

'As your wife?'

In the lengthy pause that followed he dragged on his cigarette, wondering why her question made him feel so uncomfortable.

'We can get married out there,' he replied weakly, cringing because he knew he sounded less than enthusiastic. He could feel her disappointment as if it were lead fibres in the air.

'I have to think about it,' she said in a small voice.

'As long as you need.'

'When do you want to leave?'

'I don't know. Soon. I hadn't thought.'

Rita sighed, then looked at him with eyes that glittered with tears. 'Do you love me, George?'

'Of course I do.' He tried to kiss her but she resisted him.

'Or do you just love the idea of me?'

'What do you mean?'

'It doesn't matter. Let's go back, I'm cold.'

They walked up the beach in silence. Rita looked about her at the sea she loved, at the gulls that wheeled and spiralled above them, their plaintive cries echoing the helplessness she felt inside, and wondered whether she had the courage to leave. They held hands and yet they both felt miles apart. Estranged and sad and, for the first time in their lives, uncertain about one another.

George kissed her goodbye then climbed into the truck he had parked in the driveway and reversed out into the road. She watched him go, then broke down and sobbed. Before anyone spotted her she made her way through the village to the cliffs, where she sat until dark, watching the sun turn the sea to molten copper as her heart splintered into pieces.

She would have the courage to leave Frognal Point if she could be sure of George. She loved him enough to follow him to the ends of the earth, enough to embark on a new adventure in a strange country. She could do it in spite of her fear of the unknown. But she couldn't do it without his full commitment.

When she returned home it was dark. She could see her mother and Eddie through the kitchen window, Eddie at the table painting while Hannah, in her blue apron, kneaded dough. She desperately needed to talk, but her mother was obviously busy. Without further thought, she grabbed her bicycle and pedalled as fast as she could to Elvestree. The little light on her bicycle wouldn't have been sufficient, but the moon was bright enough to show her the line of the road. Choked with despair and chilled in her thin cardigan and dress, she arrived dishevelled and shivering.

She burst into the house to find Max on the sofa, reading poetry. When he saw her he blanched. 'Are you all right?' he said, jumping up and striding towards her.

'Is Grandma around?' she asked, wiping her eyes with trembling fingers.

'She's out. But she will be back very soon.'

'Oh,' she groaned. Her whole body seemed to sag with disappointment.

'Why don't I make you a cup of tea, or Ovaltine? You look like you will freeze to death.'

'Yes, thank you,' she stammered, following him into the kitchen. 'Where has she gone?'

'She took Ruth to tea at your Aunt Antoinette's house. I didn't want to go. I don't much like your aunt.' He opened the ice chest to reveal a large container of milk. Taking a ladle he filled a saucepan, which he placed on the Aga. 'A hot drink with a dash of brandy will do you good.'

'Rather luxurious making Ovaltine with brandy?'

'Primrose won't have it any other way.'

Rita pushed a cat off the armchair and sat beside the Aga, her shoulders hunched and shivering.

'Is George all right?' He couldn't help but ask. Rita's eyes welled with tears again.

'He wants to go to Argentina,' she said. Max's hands began to shake and he sunk his eyes into the hot milk.

'Will you go with him?' he asked, trying to sound casual.

'He wants me to.'

'But you don't want to leave Frognal Point?' She nodded. She felt foolish. Max had been driven out of Austria to start a new life with strangers in a foreign country. How could she speak of such a fear to him?

He handed her the mug of hot Ovaltine, rich with a thick froth on the top. It looked and smelt comforting. After taking a sip she felt a little better. It was warm there beside the Aga.

'Do you feel part of the place, Max?'

He sat on a stool and smiled down at her. She noticed how much he had grown up in the last year. He was now tall and strongly built with earnest blue eyes that revealed a surprising depth and compassion for a boy of his age. She had never really taken much notice of him before because he had seemed such a child compared to her. A rather shy, solitary child. But to her surprise she felt better for his company.

'Yes, I do feel part of the place,' he replied. 'Thanks to Primrose. I feel I belong here with her.'

Rita frowned. 'How can you live with her? She's so strange.'

'A witch?' He chuckled and shook his head.

'In the nicest possible way.'

'She's a generous and kind woman. I know she is outspoken and offends people easily. But she has a heart of gold.'

'Yes, she does,' Rita agreed. 'But still, I don't think I could live with her.' She took another sip of Ovaltine and felt the heat spread through her body, easing the emotional knots little by little. Then Max told her something he had never told anyone else, not even his sister.

'When I arrived here as a little boy I was frightened of her but that first night I lay awake. I heard her come into our bedroom. It was late. Very dark. I closed my eyes because

I did not want her to see that I was not sleeping. She stood over me for a long while. I don't know what she was doing but I felt a very strong feeling of warmth and love. Then she drew the blanket over me and tucked me in. She bent down and kissed my forehead. When she left, after doing the same for Ruth, I cried. Not because I was frightened but because I was grateful. My own mother had never been so tender.'

Rita blinked at him in amazement. Suddenly she appreciated the enormous impact that losing his family must have had on him She had always known that he had no one, that Megagran had adopted him, but not once had she really considered the tragedy of his past.

'Oh, Max. That is the nicest story. Have you ever told her?'

'No. You know what she's like. I think she would feel uncomfortable.'

'She'd be touched to know that it meant so much.'

'I'm sure she knows that.' There was a pause while Rita watched him carefully and, because he felt the intensity of her scrutiny, he took a big gulp of Ovaltine, which burnt his throat.

'Do you miss your family dreadfully?' she asked softly, knowing that this was probably one of the only moments of real intimacy Max had ever had with anyone besides Ruth and Megagran.

'Yes, sometimes. I wonder how different my life would be if I had stayed in Austria. If they had survived.'

'What a bloody thing this war has been!' she snapped, thinking of George. 'It's destroyed so many lives and I don't just mean those who died!' Max looked at her quizzically.

'Ruth and I are lucky.'

'And unlucky too. I still have my family.' She fixed him with an intense stare, then her face crumpled. 'But I'm losing George,' she added in a small voice.

Max, against whose nature it was to show much emotion, hopped down from the stool and crouched beside her chair. He took her hand in his and looked at her with tenderness. 'Why do you think that?' he asked and his sympathetic look made her cry all over again.

'The war has changed him. He's unhappy and restless so he wants to leave behind his old life and start afresh. I'm part of his old life.'

'He loves you. He's always loved you.'

'I don't think he does any more,' she whispered and allowed herself to be drawn into his embrace. She rested her face on his shoulder and sniffed. 'I was so sure of my future. Now I don't know any more.'

They remained in silence, both alone with their thoughts until the sound of the kitchen door opening interrupted the moment. Reluctantly Max pulled away. Mrs Megalith hobbled in with Ruth.

'Now, my dear, put the kettle on immediately, it's blasted chilly out there.' When she saw her granddaughter sitting beside the Aga with a tear-stained face she feared the worst. 'Those damned dead cats. I knew it!' she muttered, closing the door behind her.

'Rita, come into the drawing room. Ruth will bring me a nice cup of tea, won't you dear?' Rita caught eyes with Max and pulled a rueful smile. He smiled back, full of energy and happiness for he had held her close and she had confided in him. Rita followed her grandmother down the corridor.

'I knew this would happen. Felt it in my bones. They may be old but they are most sensitive. Never let me down.' She entered the drawing room to find cats draped across the sofas and on the window seats. She waved her hand to shoo them away, but it was as if they hadn't seen her. 'Now, let's sit comfortably and you can tell me all about it. What the devil is going on?'

Rita told her everything. She also disclosed the advice that Maddie had so carelessly given her. 'I'm worried that he's grown tired of me because I haven't slept with him.' Mrs Megalith was unshockable. She frowned irritably and shook her head.

'Absolutely not. What a foolish girl your sister is. There's nothing wrong with making love as long as it is with love. The trouble with Madeleine is that she gives it away to any Tom or Dick who'll have her. I'm afraid she's turning into a slut. But we're not discussing Madeleine, we're discussing you. Sex has nothing to do with it, Rita, my dear.'

'I don't think he wants to marry me any more, Grandma,' said Rita, feeling less tearful since she had opened her heart to Max.

Mrs Megalith clicked her tongue. 'Of course he does. He's confused, that's all. Give him a year in the Argentine and he'll come to his senses. Don't forget, he's been through a terrible time. He's been tied up in the RAF for the duration of the war. I imagine the thought of tying himself down again, here in Frognal Point, is a somewhat daunting one. He's young, let him go.'

'Are you suggesting I stay here and wait for him?'

'What choice do you have?'

Mrs Megalith was right. She couldn't go without marrying him and he was wary of committing himself at this stage. She had waited three years for him, what was one more?

'If it means he'll come back as the George I grew up with, then he can go for as long as he wants.'

'Quite right, my dear. That's the spirit.' Mrs Megalith nodded her approval. 'Now, how long can it take to boil a kettle?' she said impatiently, looking towards the door.

★   ★   ★

When Rita cycled home she felt much lighter in spirit, although apprehensive about her decision. Megagran was right. If George put a great distance between himself and Europe for a while he might settle down. She thought back over the last ten years and reminded herself of the depth of their friendship. She remembered those short leaves he had taken at the beginning of the war. He had been posted at Biggin Hill then, before he was sent abroad. They had walked up and down the beach and reminisced about the way things were before fighting broke out. He hadn't wanted to talk about the battles. He had found his security in the past. What halcyon days they were. She remembered how bitterly they had cried the night before he was due to sail for Malta. He had told her that it was she who kept him going. It was her photograph he kept in his breast pocket. Hadn't he told her that he would keep it there until the day he died? Surely it wasn't so easy to break a bond as strong as theirs?

'You're looking a little peaky, Rita,' said her mother when she arrived home. 'Are you all right?'

'I'm fine,' she replied. Eddie and Maddie grinned at her mischievously.

'What's everyone looking at me for?' she complained.

'How's George?' Eddie asked, barely able to contain her giggles.

Rita narrowed her eyes. 'Have you been spying on me, Eddie?'

'No,' she lied.

Rita suddenly felt irritated. 'Typical,' she snapped. 'One simply can't be private here. No wonder George wants to go to Argentina.' Hannah put down the chicken she was preparing and turned around. The smirk slipped off Eddie's face and Maddie put her hand to her mouth in horror. 'Yes, he's going to the Argentine to work.' Her statement was met with a shocked silence.

'Are you going with him?' Eddie asked finally.

'How can I?'

'Surely he'll marry you, dear.'

Rita's voice cracked. 'He doesn't want to.'

'My dear Rita . . .' began her mother, walking towards her with arms outstretched.

But Rita stiffened. 'I'm fine, really. I'm going to have a bath.' And she hurried out of the room.

The moment she had gone, Maddie burst into commentary. 'What do you think has happened? They were quite happy this afternoon, ask Eddie!' Hannah looked at Eddie hopefully.

'They were kissing in the cave on the beach,' said Eddie.

'Which cave?'

'You know, the one on the left as you walk down the path.'

'I know the one. The swallow cave. They always used to build their nests there when I was growing up. Year in, year out. But what of it?' she waved her hand dismissively and shook her head. 'I wish Humphrey were here. He'd know what to do. I hope she's all right. Should I go up and talk to her?'

'Do you think he really doesn't want to marry her?' Maddie asked. 'How dreadful. She's waited years for him. What a bastard.'

'Maddie, don't use that sort of language please,' Hannah chided gently. 'I'm sure they've just had an argument or something. It's probably nothing serious.'

'But why's he going all the way to Argentina when he's only just got back?' said Maddie, biting her bottom lip.

'I don't want Rita to leave,' said Eddie in a small voice. 'I don't know what I'd do without Rita.'

'Dear child, if Rita goes to Argentina we will all miss her, but we will all support her choice. Besides, they won't stay there for ever, I'm sure.' She picked up the chicken unenthusiastically. 'When she comes down I think it would be better if we don't talk about it. Unless she wants to, of course.'

When Humphrey returned from the office Hannah briefed him discreetly in his study. His face turned the colour of the plums in the garden and he knocked back a swig of Scotch. 'He'll marry her, by God,' he said in a quiet voice. 'She's not going out to Argentina without that ring on her finger.' Hannah felt more confident now her husband was back. Besides, when Humphrey spoke in such low tones he meant business. When the girls were growing up he never shouted at them when they caused trouble, just spoke to them with that icy calm and they trembled right down to their toes.

'Have you talked to her?' he asked.

'No. Not yet.'

'Well, let's not make a mountain out of a molehill. After all, the boy's just come back from the war, he needs time to adjust.' Then just before he left the room he turned to her and added, 'But I'll tell you one thing, he's not leading our Rita a merry dance and then not marrying her.'

No one mentioned George Bolton at dinner. Rita was aware that Eddie and Maddie were longing to discuss it, but she kept her thoughts to herself. She didn't even tell them that she had been to see Megagran. When things got bad, Rita liked to lick her wounds in private.

Unable to sleep, she sat on the window seat and stared up at the moon. She wondered whether George was staring up at it too and thinking of her.

★   ★   ★

Max wandered across the garden and down to the estuary, his path illuminated by the bright, phosphorescent moon. In his hand he held a worn book of poetry that had once belonged to his mother. He thought of Rita and their conversation in the kitchen. At times like this he missed a mother's advice. He'd like to tell her about Rita. He imagined she would have approved his choice, in spite of the fact that Rita wasn't Jewish.

His mother had been an actress, a bohemian in long flowing dresses and soft fur stoles; his father a wealthy banker, ennobled by the last Emperor Charles for giving the imperial house its final loan. Max could remember hanging around the Imperial Theatre which his father had built especially for his mother after he had first seen her perform as a young girl. He used to relish telling them how he had lost his heart to her the moment she first floated onto the stage. So bright was the light that shone about her it had penetrated his very soul and dazzled him to the point that he was aware only of her presence and of his desperate need to have her. So he had built a small theatre with crimson velvet curtains and glittering chandeliers, commissioning the best craftsmen in Vienna to mould the ceiling with golden roses and swans, then knelt down on one knee and asked her to marry him. That was before he lost his fortune in 1918, when the empire fell apart leaving his mines in the newly independent Czechoslovakia. As a little boy, Max had loved hearing stories of his mother's celebrity, how she had been the toast of Vienna. Great figures from Court had graced the gilded boxes to admire her, but none had given her as much pleasure as seeing her husband every night in the small, private box he had furnished for himself, not even the Prince of Wales who had insisted on attending to witness with his own eyes the legendary beauty of Vienna's secret jewel.

Max pulled his coat tightly about his chest and gazed up the beach. Shallow pools shone silver in the moonlight for the tide was out and the sleeping birds of the sea were now silent.

The breeze was strong and fresh and smelt of marshland. He cast his eyes to the sky, to the vast glowing sphere that hung suspended among glimmering stars, and thought how often he must have looked up as a child to see the same display of wonder. His heart ached for Rita. He couldn't tell Primrose or Ruth of his secret; all he could do was read his mother's poetry and try to derive comfort from others who had suffered as he did the pain of unrequited love.

Trees slept soundly, unaware of the anxiety that kept his wife up, sculpting in her small studio to the reassuring notes of Strauss's *Alpine Symphony*. Her hands worked away at the clay, moulding and smoothing, but her mind churned, worrying about her son, unable to bear the thought of him leaving her again. She couldn't help but resent her husband for his ability to rise above domestic strife. The only things that animated him these days were his walnut trees. Her thoughts drifted to Thadeus Walizhewski.

People in the village dismissed Thadeus as eccentric. He kept himself to himself, went about his own business, never spoke about himself. But he had invited Faye into his secret world and she had discovered a man of education, poise and dignity. He played the violin with the sensitivity of a man who has loved and lost and survived terrible times. He read Voltaire, the plays of Molière and the erotica of Count Mirabeau, and cried over the stanzas of his countryman, the great Polish poet, Adam Mickieiewicz.

Thadeus had fled to England in 1939 when the Russians arrived at his ancestral home, and had drifted on the wind of Fate to this sleepy corner of Devon. He had always vowed he'd return one day to reclaim his home, but he was older than his sixty-two years and had suffered enough. In Faye he found a soul mate, a woman who understood him, and slowly love had flowered between them. He had captivated her with his pale, liquid eyes and unrestrained passion. Together they played music, read books and talked. Unlike Trees, Thadeus listened. He didn't just listen with his ears but with his whole body, touching her hand every now and then to show compassion, understanding or when he laughed, which he did in loud, infectious guffaws. At first it had been an affair of the mind. She hadn't contemplated sleeping with him. But one afternoon he had told her of the horrors suffered by his family at the hands of the Russians and she had given herself to him for comfort. Their lovemaking had been both tender and ardent, like the music they played together or the poetry he read to her. It enabled him to escape his past and she the war and her fears for her son. But since George had been back she hadn't visited him.

Faye's fingers worked away as if by remote control while she wondered what advice Thadeus would give her. Even if he had none to offer, he would hold her and listen and she would inevitably feel better for his support. Unable to bear the aching loneliness a moment longer, she looked out of the window, at the large, luminous moon that beckoned her to throw her reservations to the wind and yield to her longing.

George stood at his bedroom window. He knew he had hurt Rita and he hated himself for it. He felt under pressure to marry her, but he wasn't ready. He couldn't take her to the Argentine unless they were married. The wheels were now set in motion. His mother had already sent a telegram to her sister in the northern province of Córdoba. George knew he was running away. From his grief, from the memory of his lost friends in the squadron, from the echoes of his past and the boy who used to live there.

His eyes were suddenly drawn to a shadowy figure leaving the house by the back door, just below his bedroom window. It was his mother. She disappeared a moment then returned with a bicycle. He watched, intrigued, as she cycled out of the farm.

Chapter Seven

When Rita arrived at Lower Farm for work the following morning, her eyes were red from crying and her face taut. She wondered how much longer she would be needed as a land girl now that the army was now demobilising and returning home. She enjoyed the open air and loved the animals, especially the calves and lambs.

The sun blazed down but the air was fresh and autumnal. The nightingale had gone and so had the swallows, taking their twittering song and sanguinity with them. But the titmice had arrived. She had noticed them sitting playfully on the washing line, as happy upside down as the right way up. Her mother tamed them with walnuts and pretty soon they'd be eating out of her hand.

When she appeared at the door of the workshop Cyril and the boys were already talking with George and Trees. She smiled tightly and joined them, avoiding catching eyes with George who looked as anxious as she did. She felt the tension in the air and barely heard a word Cyril said. Mildred sensed it too for she lay at Trees' feet blinking uneasily.

'Right, Rita, you come with me,' said Cyril when he'd finished explaining the jobs for the day. George managed to tap her on the shoulder before she left.

'I need to talk to you,' he hissed.

'Later,' she replied, hurrying after Cyril. Her voice sounded unfriendly.

'I imagine a Spitfire's easier to manage than a woman,' Trees quipped, looking at his son.

'And so are trees.' George grinned, but he felt dead inside.

Rita set to work sweeping out the cowsheds. She tried to concentrate on the rhythm of the brush on concrete, focus her eyes on the old pieces of straw that she was clearing away, anything but think of George. She felt anxiety strain the muscles in her throat and neck, making them ache. She was so absorbed in her work that she didn't notice George who had left his job on the tractor to find her, so she jumped when he appeared.

'George, you shouldn't creep up on people like that!' she chided, then began to brush again, this time with more vigour.

'Stop working for God's sake. I want to talk to you.'

'What about?' She paused and straightened up.

'Us. I'm sorry I was offhand with you last night.'

She immediately felt guilty for being so unfriendly. 'That's all right. I know things aren't easy for you at the moment.'

'Come. Let's go and sit down somewhere,' he suggested, taking her by the hand.

She followed him outside and they sat on the grass in the sunshine. A few dry leaves blew about in the breeze and a dark brown thrush playfully hopped among them.

'I hope Cyril doesn't catch me shirking off,' she said.

'I'm the boss's son, I can do what I like and I want to talk to my future wife.' His mouth curled up at one corner and something in Rita's stomach fluttered with happiness. He took her hand in his and sandwiched it with his other hand. 'I love you Rita and I don't want anyone else but you. We've grown up together. We're made for each other. I don't need to tell you that.' He studied her face for a long moment, eager not to offend her. 'But I'm not ready to get married. I'm only twenty-three years old. The only life I've seen is from the cockpit of an aeroplane. I can't settle down yet. I'm too young. You understand, don't you? Part of me feels I've reached the pinnacle of my life. I'll never be so challenged or have such purpose again, ever. The other part feels like I've been robbed of something. My youth, my innocence, I don't know. It's as if someone has taken me apart and put me back together all wrong.' His voice was calm but there was an undertone of desperation which made her heart buckle with compassion.

'I understand,' she said, pulling his hand to her mouth and kissing it softly. 'Darling George, I'll wait for you for as long as it takes. Go to Argentina, explore the world, stretch your wings and let the wind blow through your feathers.'

He settled his eyes on her face and his expression was so tender and full of affection that she caught her breath and blushed.

'I don't deserve you, Rita,' he choked. 'You've supported me with love and letters through years of war and now you're willing to suspend your life a little longer. You're one in a million.' His words made her swell with pride. 'When I come back we'll marry at once and start a family. We'll make beautiful children, you and I.' She laughed lightly and let him draw her to him so that he could kiss her temple, close to her hairline.

'Megagran has always threatened to lend me her wedding dress.'

He chuckled, content to indulge her female whim and discuss their wedding. 'Surely you'd get ten of you into it.'

'She claims she was slim when she was young, and a smasher too!'

'I can't envisage that, even with a long stretch of the imagination.'

'I don't mind what I wear on our wedding day. I just

want to be your wife and make you happy. I feel so hopeless. I know you're suffering but I'm ill-equipped to help
you.'

'No you're not. Just being with you makes me feel better.'

'I'm glad you came to see me last night, although I would
like to have held you until morning,' said Thadeus, stroking
Faye's hair. She rarely wore it down, but Thadeus insisted on
it. Said she looked severe with it drawn into a chignon.

'Me too. I've missed you,' she replied.

'Everything always seems so much worse at night. The light
of the sun melts away one's anxieties whereas the light of the
moon simply magnifies them.'

She nuzzled against him. It was warm there in the garden. It
wasn't only Thadeus' presence that filled her with tranquillity
but the atmosphere of the garden itself. Shaped in an oval,
it was surrounded by trees, rhododendron bushes and a tall
yew hedge. A vibrant green paradise where Faye felt secure
and detached from her own life. By virtue of being situated
up a remote little lane there was no fear that their affair might
be discovered by prying eyes or unwelcome visitors. Thadeus
had no close friends. He was a big bear of a man. His hair
was wild and grey, framing a long, weather-beaten face. He
wore a soft beard, which retained some pale yellow tones –
the only indication that he had once been flaxen – and thin
round glasses. Faye loved to press her cheek to his beard and
nestle against it. She had never kissed a bearded man before
Thadeus.

'How one worries about one's children. It's the curse of
motherhood,' she said and heaved a sigh.

'You can only do your best. You bring them into the
world then you set them free. George has to find his own
way. Destiny is a river you cannot control. It sweeps them
off, around rocks, down waterfalls, then into quiet, peaceful

waters for a while. You cannot swim after them so you have to surrender yourself to the greater force and put your trust in God.'

'But how will I cope without him?'

Thadeus pulled her close. 'The same way you coped when he was flying those planes.'

'He may never come back.'

'That is something you will have to deal with when the time comes. Don't fear things that might never happen.'

'It's hard not to.'

'Live in the moment, Faye. Unhappiness comes from trying to put up resistance. Let the current take you too, don't swim against it. What will be will be. Life is a long time.' She took his hairy face in her hands and kissed him.

'Darling Thadeus, what would I do without you? You're so strong and wise.'

'Do you know why I'm wise?' he asked, looking at her with pale, sensitive eyes. 'Because I have made a point of learning from every experience that life has thrown at me. No experience is worthless, however small, however painful. Everything that happens to you is for your own higher good. Don't ever forget that. Through pain we learn and through happiness we celebrate our learning.'

'I shall try to let George go with gladness in my heart. He doesn't belong to me. I will remember that.' Then she smiled at him timidly. 'It won't be easy, though.'

'If things are too easy you are in the wrong class of life. After all, if we are not stretched we don't learn.' He stood up. 'Come, let us play some music together. There is nothing like the magic of music to soothe the soul.' She followed him inside and watched him pick up his violin. He placed it under his chin and poised the bow above the strings. 'Let us play Chopin. It reminds me of my childhood. Not even the Russians could rob me of that.' And he played while Faye sat and listened, her chin in her hands, her eyes misted with admiration.

When Faye returned home for lunch Trees was washing his hands while Mildred sniffed the boots that reminded her of walks in the woods and picnics on the beach.

'How is George?' she asked, hovering at the door. Her hair was once again drawn into a tidy chignon. Nothing about her appearance would give her away, only the rosy hue in her cheeks and the languor of her gait, but she knew her husband's mind was on the farm and his walnut trees. He looked up and nodded thoughtfully.

'I think his future with Rita is secure again,' he replied.

Faye's spirits rose. 'Oh, I am pleased. Thank God. Is he going to take her to the Argentine? Did he tell you anything?'

Trees shook his head. 'He hasn't said a word.'

'Are they coming in for lunch?'

'That will be them now,' he said, turning off the tap.

Light, happy voices signalled their approach at the back door. Faye left her husband drying his hands and went to greet them. She was delighted to see the colour had returned to their cheeks and they were teasing each other and laughing again.

'What's for lunch, Ma?' George asked, taking off his boots.

'Cold meat.'

'A man needs a good lunch after a hard morning on the land.'

'So does a woman,' said Rita, putting a hand on his back to steady herself as she too removed her boots.

While Faye laid the table and set out the food George told her of their plans. 'So we'll marry the moment I return. You'll look after Rita while I'm away, won't you, Ma?'

Faye smiled at Rita with admiration. 'You are a good girl,' she said. 'George is very lucky to have you.'

'I'll wait for him as long as he wants,' she replied, enjoying the attention her self-sacrifice awarded her.

'You have the rest of your lives to be married,' said Faye, recalling with wistfulness Thadeus' wise words. 'Life is a long time.'

It was only during lunch, when Faye stifled a yawn, that George remembered his mother's midnight parting witnessed from his bedroom window. A secret rendezvous, perhaps. With whom he did not know and he instinctively sensed not to ask. He watched his father tuck into the cold ham, his thoughts far away as usual. If his mother was having an affair his father would be the last to notice. Then he looked at Faye. Her eyes sparkled and her cheeks glowed but her expression was innocent, as innocent as an angel's. He dismissed the idea as preposterous and felt ashamed for having entertained it. Faye was a devoted wife and mother and a good Christian besides. He took Rita's hand and thought no more about it.

In the evening George drove Rita home, stopping on the way as they often did to sit on the cliff top and watch the sunset. It was breezy up there, a chilly northern wind that signalled for certain the end of summer. They both looked out across the sea and in the golden light of the dying day they felt the warm afterglow of an enchanted season.

'Rita and George love each other again!' squealed Eddie, running into the house to tell her mother the good news. 'They're sitting on the cliff kissing.'

Hannah continued to knit. She didn't want to encourage her youngest to put her nose into other people's business, even though Eddie's news was heart-warming.

'What were you doing down there?'

'Collecting shells with Amy. I wasn't spying, I promise.' Eddie flopped into an armchair. 'So does that mean Rita will be leaving us?'

'I don't know. We'll have to wait until she gets back.'

'She's always down on the beach. She should have been born a sea gull!'

'What would that make you, then?' Hannah laughed and paused her knitting needles to give full attention to her most amusing child.

'A bat like Harvey.'

'They're rather ugly little things, bats.'

'Not Harvey, he's beautiful. Daddy always says that beauty is in the eyes of the beholder. I think he's adorable.' She pulled him off the sleeve of her jersey and held him in her hands. 'Look at his little nose and shiny eyes. I swear he smiles at me.'

'I thought bats were blind.'

'He can sense me, though. We're real friends.'

'Then you're most certainly not a bat, my dear, for you see far too much for your own good.'

Rita returned home with the good news. Humphrey poured himself a whisky and Hannah telephoned her mother.

Mrs Megalith put down the receiver and shook her head ominously. 'That was Hannah. George is going to Argentina and Rita is going to wait for him here,' she said to Max and Ruth. 'It'll come to no good. I feel it in my bones.'

'For how long is he going?' Max asked, putting down his book.

'He has no plans. He's just going to fly out there and take it as it comes. Damned casual if you ask me.' Mrs Megalith sat down at her card table and plunged her hand into a bowl of small crystals. She breathed deeply, dragging the energy up her arms and into her tense shoulders. When she opened her eyes there were five cats sitting at her feet, licking their fur. 'Rita should go with him,' she said, ignoring the cats.

'It's not proper to go as an unmarried woman,' said Max, not wishing to encourage Rita to leave Frognal Point.

'Damned convention. She should flout it and leave or she'll lose him.'

'He might fall in love with someone else,' said Ruth, who said very little but listened to everything.

'He might well, Ruth, dear.'

Max rubbed his chin. 'Poor Rita,' he muttered.

'She's young, young people recover very quickly. A broken heart is a heart ready to be put together again. She's far more resilient than Humpty Dumpty, I assure you.' She touched her moonstone pendant thoughtfully.

Max recalled the night before when Rita had cried in his arms. She wouldn't notice him now that she was happy. He stepped over the cats and out into the dark. He lit a cigarette, the way George did, holding it between his thumb and his forefinger. How he wished that he had been old enough to fight in the war, to wear a smart blue RAF uniform with wings. George was a brave and glamorous man. A hero. How often had he heard it said that it was because of men like George that the Nazis hadn't occupied Britain? Where would he be now if Hitler had won? Dead like his parents? He would have liked to have blown some Nazis out of the sky. But he was still a boy and boys didn't impress girls like Rita. He wandered around the garden, illuminated by the lights of the house. It was quiet, except for a cooing pigeon and the odd cough of a pheasant. If the war had continued he could have signed up. Now he'd never be a hero. But one thing was certain, he'd make something of his life, for his parents, for Rita, and then, when he had made his fortune, he'd buy back the Imperial Theatre his father had built and restore it to its former glory.

The autumn passed and winter set in. The day of George's departure arrived and Rita was reminded of the day he left for Malta. She felt the same hollowness inside, the same wrenching of the gut, the same dread of being left on her own again with nothing but letters to connect her with the man she loved. But she told herself the sooner he left the sooner he would return and the sooner they would marry and begin their life together.

It rained all morning. George picked her up in the truck and they drove to the beach one final time. They hurried down the path and across the sand towards the cave. The sea was tempestuous, the sky grey and dark. There were few birds, black-headed gulls mostly, their barking banter carried on the wind with the salt and sea spray. It was a mournful sight. Looking at the desolate bay Rita felt spring would never again flower on this shore.

It was cold and damp inside the cave. They sat huddled together at the far end, where the sea had not encroached to wash away the love that they had left there. He ran his hand down her face and brushed away her tears with his fingers. He kissed her, tasting the salt on her lips and the unhappiness on her skin and promised that he would be home again soon.

'One day we'll sit here while our children are at school and we'll remember today.' Rita sunk her face into his chest and cried quietly. 'I think you had better get Megagran's dress out of the cupboard and start taking it in. It'll need a hell of a lot of work. I want it ready by the time I get back.' Then he thrust his hand into his pocket and pulled out a little black box. 'I want you to wear this always,' he said, placing it in her hand. She sat up and wiped her face on her sleeve.

'What is it?' she asked, opening it. Set firmly into velvet a small diamond solitaire ring sparkled.

'I was going to give it to you on my return, but I want you to have something to assure you of our engagement.' He took the ring out himself and slipped it on the third finger of her left hand. 'There, it fits like it was made for you.'

'It's beautiful,' she sighed happily. 'Really beautiful.'

'Every time you look at it I want you to remember how much I love you,' he said solemnly. She threw her arms around his neck and kissed him.

'And I want you to remember, every time you look up at that moon, that I love you too.'

They stayed in the cave as long as they could, then walked back to the truck. Rita was unable to take her eyes off the ring and moved her hand around in the light to watch the diamond sparkle. They held hands all the way back to Lower Farm, where Trees and Faye, Alice and the children awaited them. It was a grim parting. Faye tried to hold back her tears, remembering the wise advice Thadeus had given her and Alice, who was saddened by her brother's decision to leave again, held Jane in her arms and watched Rita with sympathy. Her husband Geoffrey had been lucky to survive the war like George. She didn't think she'd cope very well if he announced on his return that he was leaving her again, for the other side of the world. Besides, she suspected what none of them dared to admit – that George wouldn't be coming back.

George kissed his family, then held Rita in his arms for the last time, breathed in the scent of her skin and felt her tears on his face as he pulled away. He couldn't express what was in his heart so he just gazed upon her with tenderness before climbing into the truck with his father who was to drive him to the station. He rolled down the window and waved. They all waved back, but his eyes clung to Rita until the very last moment when the truck turned the corner at the farm entrance. Only then did he look away.

Later that day Faye sat at her sculpture and tried to keep her mind distracted from her grief. She reminded herself of Thadeus' words, that she didn't own George, she had simply brought him into the world and loving him meant setting him free to make his own mistakes and learn from his experiences. It was a comforting philosophy.

Alice went for a walk with the children, returning later to her cottage to brood. When Geoffrey finally came home from France she was going to hold onto him.

Rita sat in her bedroom watching the drizzle through the window, allowing her misery to engulf her. She played with her ring and relived their most intimate moments. After a while she noticed a robin alight on the windowsill and proceed to peck at the glass with its small beak. It seemed to want to make contact. Slowly Rita stood up and with great care, so as not to frighten it away, opened the window. To her astonishment the robin flew in and, after circling the room for a while, landed on the bookshelf. It hopped from book to book then perched on the edge of a pottery bowl Eddie had made her at school, and danced about the rim before flying out in search of materials with which to fashion its nest.

Chapter Eight

George sat on the deck of the *Fortuna*. The harbour was shrouded in damp, grey mist out of which the cranes of cargo ships rose up like dinosaurs from a bygone age. It was noisy too, voices resounding through the drizzle accompanied by the low rumble of engines and the distant bugle of a parting cruiser. He was numb with sadness and more alone than he had ever felt. A wheeling gull flew above the harbour, its melancholy cry echoing his own inner discord and reminding him of the cave, of Rita, and the youth he had lost up there in the sky. He felt like an old man. Burdened with guilt and resentment, weary of life. He wanted to iron out all his feelings. Remove them one by one and sort them into colour and shade. They were so jumbled up he sensed nothing but turbulence.

He smoked into the fog, taking comfort from the one thing that had been consistent throughout the war. Smoking relaxed him, made him feel better as it had done in the mess after an offensive sweep or an escort over northern France. With his squadron around him he had enjoyed that sense of belonging, of achievement and purpose. A peace of sorts came later when he was reconciled with his fear of dying, but he would never get over the deaths of his friends: Jamie Cordell, Rat Bridges, Lorrie Hampton – he'd never forget. Having conquered his own fear of death he now battled against his fear of living. He had no purpose, no drive, no sense of belonging. He felt adrift.

The boat shuddered and slowly began to move away from the dockside. He cast his eyes to the sea and the foam that now frothed on the surface, then took a final look at the bleak coastline. *Goodbye England, goodbye war. When I return I'll be a different man.*

George kept himself to himself for the first couple of weeks. He barely noticed the people around him, and discouraged conversations with strangers he had no desire to know. He sat on the deck, smoking into the wind, lost in the past. He didn't think too much about the future. Having never been to South America he had no idea what to expect. There were plenty of passengers on the boat who would have been only too happy to share with him their experiences of Argentina, but he deliberately kept away. They busied themselves with deck quoits, chess and bridge. Put on plays with the children, danced the nights away, made friends in the bar. They were too occupied to notice him, or perhaps they had seen his scowl and told their children not to approach.

The boat stopped along the way, in Lisbon, Madeira, Rio and Santos. He was able to spend those days stretching his legs and seeing the sights. It was good to step onto solid ground for a few hours and smell the scents of the earth and nature. Small boats drew up alongside the *Fortuna* and tradesmen clambered aboard to lay out their wares. George thought of Rita when he saw the silver bracelets and cheap Brazilian gold. He wanted to buy her something to show that he was missing her. Something special. He searched through all the jewellery, some of it fine, some badly made and sure to fall apart in the post by the time it got to England. Then his eyes alighted on a pendant. It was of a bird with its wings outstretched, crafted in silver with eyes of turquoise. The moment he saw it he knew he had to have it. The skinny salesman with black hair and a long, brown face smiled crookedly when George said he would buy it. He thought of a price and doubled it, delighted when George paid without hesitation. The man wrapped it in brown paper and handed it to him. 'Bird, good luck,' he said in broken English, pointing to the packet. 'Good luck.'

'He means,' interjected a fellow passenger who was also browsing through the jewellery, 'that birds symbolise good luck. In fact, in ancient times they were considered magical because they could fly. Each breed has a different meaning. What is your bird?' George unwrapped the paper and showed the old scholar his purchase. He studied it carefully, much to the bewilderment of the salesman who thought they were scrutinising it for faults. 'It appears to be a dove. The dove symbolises love, happiness and wedded bliss. It features in the flood stories of the Babylonians, Hebrews and Greeks as a symbol of peace and reconciliation. The dove carrying the olive branch in his beak to Noah in his ark has become an international symbol.' George thanked him. It must have been Fate that he should find such an appropriate gift for his sweetheart.

It was not until the beginning of the third week, just off the coast of Brazil, that his curiosity was roused by one of his fellow passengers. It was early evening. He was sitting alone watching the sun set and remembering how he and Rita used to sit on the cliffs as children and watch the sun sink into the sea. A very different sea from this tropical ocean. His eyes were drawn to a woman who stood leaning on the railings, gazing out towards the horizon. She was quite still. Only the skirt of her pale dress billowed about in the wind, revealing with each gust slender ankles and fine, shapely legs. She had blonde hair, almost white, that was scraped back into a chignon at the nape of an elegant long neck. The angles of her profile were thus accentuated to her best advantage. Straight nose, high cheekbones and a well-defined chin and jaw. She looked haughty, confident, a little disdainful. George wondered who she was with, whether she was married and, if so, to what sort of man. She had great beauty and poise. A real handful, no doubt, he thought with a chuckle. She didn't seem to sense his eyes on her for she continued to stare out without flinching. As he scrutinised her, he realised that there was something wistful and sad about the way she stood. Perhaps because she didn't move. A happy person would surely move every now and then, look around, smile. But she just stared as if she wasn't concentrating on the sunset after all, but on pictures in her own mind.

She remained there a long time. George finished his cigarette and the sun descended deep into the earth, leaving a pink glow where the sea joined the sky. Finally she dropped her hands and stepped back from the railings. As she turned towards him he was stunned to see that down the left side of her face ran a large, ugly scar. He gasped in horror and pity that this exquisite woman could be so cruelly disfigured. She met his eyes but didn't allow them to linger for more than a moment. Before he could stand up she was gone. Now his curiosity was thoroughly roused. Who was she? What had happened to her?

He wandered inside and scoured the public rooms for her. How could she have been dealt such a cruel blow? In a man such a wound would enhance his masculinity and appeal, but in a woman it was a curse to have one's beauty so maligned. Drawn out of himself by compassion he suddenly became aware of the world around him and felt a renewed desire to be a part of it.

After dinner, exasperated that the mystery woman hadn't appeared in the dining room, George wandered into the bar. He placed himself on a high stool and ordered a Scotch. No sooner had he taken a sip than the old man two stools away leaned towards him and said, 'You escaping the war too?'

'The war is over,' George replied.

'Brigadier Bullingdon.' The man extended his hand.

George shook it, noticing at once that the brigadier's eyebrows were so large and bushy they appeared ready to crawl off his face at any moment. 'It might be over, young man, but the cloud still hangs over the country. I played my part in the Great War, wounded on the Western Front, hence the gammy leg, damn it. Would have relished the opportunity to serve in this one. Bloody Huns.' He shook his head and knocked back his whisky, neat and warm the way he liked it. 'You did your bit. I can tell. It's in the eyes. You change and that never leaves you.' He raised those furry eyebrows at George.

'Flight Lieutenant George Bolton,' he replied automatically. The brigadier nodded his approval.

'Brave man,' he said and his voice was thick with admiration. 'So what takes you to this part of the world?'

'Nothing more than the promise of adventure.'

'You'll get plenty of that,' he chuckled. 'Where?'

'The Argentine, Córdoba.'

The brigadier nodded and stuck out his lips thoughtfully. They were fleshy, the lips of a young man. 'My wife and I went there before the war. Very green. Mountainous. Lovely. You on your own?'

'Yes,' he replied, remembering Rita and wondering whether she'd survive on another continent. The brigadier leaned towards him unsteadily.

'Between you and me, wish I was on my own. Argentine women are a juicy lot. Can't get a look in with the little lady. She keeps a sharp eye on me, as well she might.' He coughed and chuckled into his glass. 'Few pretty young fillies on this boat.'

George thought of the mystery woman and wondered whether the old brigadier would know anything about her. But before he could open his mouth a small, shrivelled woman appeared and tapped the brigadier on the shoulder.

'I think you've had enough of that, dear.'

'Ah, the lovely Mrs Bullingdon. Esther, let me introduce you to my new young friend. Flight Lieutenant George Bolton at your service.' She gave him her hand. It was limp and dry and dappled with liver spots.

'Ah, one of the boat's loners,' she said in a high, quavering voice. 'I've just seen the other one on deck. Strange girl. So disfigured. What a pity. It's no wonder that she keeps herself to herself. Poor child.'

'Do you know who she is?' George heard himself asking.

'She's an American, Susan Robertson. I took the liberty of introducing myself at the start of the trip. She was rather aloof. Of course, I forgave her. With that ghastly scar on her face. She's not married,' she added, indicating the small sapphire ring on her own hand. 'A woman notices these things.'

'What a waste of a good-looking girl,' the brigadier commented.

'No one will have her now. Every woman deserves a husband and children. After all, what else is there for a woman to do?' George didn't like Mrs Bullingdon's tone. She was clearly delighting in the younger woman's misfortune.

'It's been nice meeting you. Will you excuse me?' he said, slipping off the stool.

'I'm being dragged to bed by matron,' said the brigadier with a snort and a wink. 'Like being back at school being married to Esther.'

'You'll only have yourself to blame when you wake up with a hangover, dear,' she said. Then she turned to George. 'I'm glad you're not unfriendly. Perhaps you'd like to join us for dinner tomorrow night?' George nodded reluctantly, hoping they'd forget by the morning. Then strode out of the room towards the deck.

It was a clear night. The sky shone vast and eternal above them, illuminated by stars and a large phosphorescent moon.

All was quiet except for the low rumble of the engines and the sound of the bow cutting through the water. The air was balmy and a warm wind blew over the ship, carrying with it the fresh smell of the sea. George walked out onto the deck by the same door as before. The woman was standing in the same place, staring out into the darkness. He hesitated a moment, uncertain how to ignite a conversation. He didn't want her to think his attentions were motivated by pity. He pulled his cigarette packet out of his breast pocket and tapped it onto the palm of his hand. While he played for time the woman remained oblivious of him. He cupped his hand round the cigarette to light it, then exhaled into the wind. For a moment he thought she had noticed him because she lifted her hand to curl a wisp of hair behind her ear and turned her head in his direction. But she didn't see him. The wisp of hair danced disobediently about her cheek, reluctant to be restrained.

He stepped lightly across the deck and leaned as she did on the railings. 'May I join you?' he asked, turning to look at her. She straightened and glanced at him with an imperious look on her face.

'Oh, it's you,' she replied in a soft American drawl. Then, in response to his quizzical frown, she added. 'I noticed you watching me earlier.'

'I'm sorry if I was intrusive.'

She shrugged. 'You couldn't possible have been. I was deep in thought.'

'You just looked sad,' he ventured boldly. She was clearly irritated by his compassion.

'What do you know?' She glanced at him disdainfully. 'You're just a boy.' George was affronted. She couldn't have been that much older than he was.

'A boy who has lived more than most men.' He returned her stare with the same arrogance.

'Really?' She sounded intrigued. 'Now you're inciting my curiosity as I have incited yours. That is why you have come to talk to me, isn't it?' He was lost for words. 'Don't worry. You're not the first.' She chuckled bitterly. 'I have a funny effect on men. At first they look on my face with admiration. It is truly beautiful when one only sees it from this side.' She touched her flawless cheek. 'But then their admiration dissolves into horror when I turn. It's a game I often play. It amuses me.'

'Does it?'

'Oh, please, spare me the pity. I'm a grown woman,' she snapped. George wouldn't usually persevere with such a rude person, but his instincts told him that her fury was not directed at him personally, but at life or whatever had done that to her. However, that was the one question he felt he couldn't ask.

'Have you come on your own?' he said instead.

'You should know the answer to that yourself. After all, you've been watching me, haven't you?'

'Only this evening. I hadn't seen you before then.'

'How funny. I saw you on the first day. In a world of your own. If anyone looked sad, you did.'

'To tell you the truth, I am a bit lost. I'm starting a new life in Argentina.'

'The war's been too much for you?'

He nodded. 'Something like that.'

'I know how you feel. I suppose I'm the same.' She sighed. When she looked at him her expression softened. 'I'm running away, too.'

'What are you running from?' he asked, pleased that he had managed to warm her up a little.

'Oh, life. My old life, that is. Shame I can't run away from this.' Her fingers ran across the scar. 'It's there as testimony of something I'd much rather forget.'

'Do you want to talk about it? After all, I'm a complete stranger. You know, in the war I opened up to people because I knew I'd never see them again. Told them my innermost secrets. Dead now, most of them.'

'So your secrets are safe then?' She smiled and George noticed she had a lovely, warm smile.

'Some of them.'

'You don't look old enough to have so many secrets.'

'Neither do you.'

'Oh, you'd be surprised. Anyway, if I were to tell you my secrets you'd have to jump overboard afterwards. You look like a mighty fine swimmer to me, so I think I'll keep my secrets to myself, if you don't mind.'

'What were you doing in England?'

'I can't tell you that. That's part of my secret. You don't want to die, do you?' She grinned at him, the brittleness in her expression now completely gone.

'Where are you going? You'll tell me that, at least.'

'Let's talk about you a little. A girl must retain her mystery.'

'What do you want to know?'

'Do you have a sweetheart?'

'No,' he replied without hesitation. What harm would it do to lie to a woman he was sure never to see again? He threw his cigarette butt into the ocean.

'So why are you so sad?'

'I lost many friends in the war. Good friends. People I'd grown attached to. They died but I survived. Why me?' He shrugged.

'I see,' she said gently. 'Where were you in all this fighting?'

'In the air.'

'Oh, a pilot. That's very glamorous, you know.'

'Not when you're in the middle of a bloody battle it isn't.'

'No, I suppose not. You must be a very good pilot to have survived.'

'Perhaps just lucky.'

'So you're leaving all those memories behind. The funny thing is that memories are like my scar, you can't run away from them.'

'But one can try.'

'I suppose we both will and then, one day, we'll wake up and find that we can only be happy by confronting our demons. The thing is, I'm not quite ready for that yet.'

'Neither am I.'

'Who would have thought that you and I had so much in common?'

'I don't even know your name,' he lied. He didn't want her to know that he had been discussing her with the unpleasant Mrs Bullingdon.

'Susan Robertson.'

'George Bolton.'

'Mind if I steal one of your cigarettes?'

'Not at all. Please.' He pulled the packet out of his breast pocket.

'Oh, Lucky Strike. There's an old familiar friend,' she said, taking one.

She had slender white hands with long nails painted red. She placed the cigarette between her lips and fixed George with pale shiny eyes, probably blue but he couldn't see well enough in the darkness. He flicked his lighter but the wind blew it out at once. She cupped her hands around it, lightly brushing his with her fingers and he tried again. This time it worked and she inhaled deeply.

'Where in America are you from?' George asked, intent on drawing more information out of her.

'You don't give up, do you?'

He laughed. 'I'm just curious.'

'Like a child who is denied a toy.'

'Or like a man in the presence of a strikingly beautiful woman. Isn't it natural that he should want to know everything about her?'

'Are you flirting with me, George Bolton?'

'I wouldn't be so presumptuous,' he retorted and grinned crookedly as was his way.

'Very well. I'm from all over. My father was a diplomat. I was brought up in Washington. Then we lived for a while in Buenos Aires. My fondest memories are of that time. After that we moved to Europe. Paris, London, Rome. I consider myself a child of the world. I don't really belong anywhere.'

'But you consider yourself American?'

'But of course. That's different. That's in my blood. Have I satisfied your curiosity?'

'Marginally.'

'That's better than nothing.'

'But we have three more days before we arrive in Buenos Aires.'

'And you think you'll wheedle it all out of me in three days? I'm not a pushover, George, and I'm not in the mood to be romanced. You've had your opportunity.' She smiled at him indulgently and added in a soft voice. 'You've been good company, though, and I don't feel sad any more.'

'Me neither.'

'Good night, George.' She patted him on the hand before walking away.

George remained for some time on the deck. It irritated him that she considered him little more than a boy. The idea of being romanced by him was obviously preposterous to her, like being courted by a child. He wanted her to look on him as a man. After all, she couldn't have been more than twenty-eight or nine. Hardly in a position to patronise him.

He returned to his berth and decided to write to Rita. He

recalled the letters he had written her during the war. He had never recounted his experiences in the air. They had seemed somehow too harsh for Rita's gentle sensibility. Besides, he hadn't wanted her to know the dangers he was in. So he had dwelt on their past. On the cliffs and the beach, in their cave and on the farm. He had written long, nostalgic paragraphs recalling their games and their innocence, without really realising that when he returned it would all be gone for ever. This time he simply told her that he missed her.

Before he slept he thought of Susan. He tried to think of Rita and felt guilty when Susan's face eclipsed hers. He recalled their conversation from beginning to end. The brittleness of her expression and the way it had softened. She was abrasive and sharp, quick-witted and dry. A woman in control of herself but one who shut out people as a form of self-defence. She was distrustful and cynical and yet he sensed she was capable of great tenderness. He wondered whether they would see each other again once they arrived in Argentina. He would disappear up to Córdoba on the Rayo del Sol train, miles and miles from the city, and she would be lost amongst the millions of faceless inhabitants of Buenos Aires.

Chapter Nine

The following morning George awoke feeling light spirited, unlike the previous mornings when it had been a trial just to drag himself out of bed. He realised, too, that it was the first night in many that he hadn't relieved the war in his dreams. He lay in bed for a while staring up at the ceiling, delighting in the novelty of such cheerfulness. Now he awoke to the promise of a new beginning in a new country and he was tickled with excitement.

He splashed his face with water and brushed his teeth. His thoughts were far from Frognal Point and the letter to Rita lay discarded on his bedside table. Written out of guilt and a sense of duty. He took a while deciding which shirt to wear and ran a comb through his hair. He didn't shave. Felt he looked more like a man with a shadow of stubble on his chin. Satisfied with his appearance, he stepped out into the corridor.

To his dismay, Susan wasn't in the breakfast room but the brigadier and his wife were. When she saw him, Mrs Bullingdon waved furiously before leaning into the table to whisper to her friends. He approached and greeted her politely. 'George, dear, let me introduce you to Mr and Mrs Linton-Harleigh and their daughter Miranda,' Mrs Bullingdon exclaimed in her reedy voice. 'Flight Lieutenant George Bolton. One of our young heroes. Do join us, George.'

George swept his eyes over the eager red faces who beamed enthusiastically up at him. He shook their hands graciously, reluctantly, accepted Mrs Bullingdon's invitation, and noticed at once the sexual hunger in the eyes of their daughter. Like a predator who hadn't fed for weeks.

'Miranda's going to set Buenos Aires alight,' twittered Mrs Linton-Harleigh, nervously playing with her teaspoon. 'We're going to be staying with cousins in Hurlingham. You must come and visit. So many parties. We'll have to go shopping the minute we get there, no pretty dresses in London with all that ghastly coupon business. Such nice people the Anglo-Argentines.'

'You will come, Mr Bolton?' Miranda asked, and George shuddered at the steely resonance in her voice.

'I'm afraid I'm going to be up country.'

'Oh dear, how frightfully dreary.' Miranda sniffed her contempt. 'You know, Buenos Aires is the centre of all things. If you're not there, you're nowhere.'

'Then I shall be content to be nowhere,' he stated impassively. Miranda stared at him in disbelief, not knowing what to make of him.

'The Ambassador is giving a party next week. A charming man, the Ambassador. Do you know him?' Mrs Linton-Harleigh asked, raising her plucked eyebrows.

'This is my first visit to the Argentine,' George explained, wondering why the hell he was spending time with these obnoxious people. Miranda's shoulders relaxed for she was now able to forgive him his ignorance.

'If I were you I would spend some time in the city. It's a delightful place. Proper people,' she said with emphasis on 'proper'.

'When one's fought in the war one thinks very little of the social ambitions of the likes of you, my dear,' said the brigadier to Miranda, in a patronising tone. 'Ambassadors and princes, who gives a damn? We're all flesh and blood, aren't we?'

'Perhaps,' said Mr Linton-Harleigh. 'But in order to get on in the world one has to know the right people. It's all very well pretending you're above it all, but it's not about what you know, it's about *who* you know.'

'It's most unfair, but it's life,' his wife added breezily. 'In that respect the war has changed nothing.'

George watched her pick at a piece of toast and thought they were the worst kind of English people to represent his country abroad. He shuddered to think what the Argentines thought of the British if they were epitomised by the Linton-Harleighs and Bullingdons.

'Look, Mama, there's that poor American lady again.' Miranda looked over George's shoulder to Susan who was taking a small table on her own. Mrs Linton-Harleigh's face twisted into mock sympathy.

'Poor thing. What a shame,' she simpered. 'She must have been quite a beauty once.'

'She's called Susan Robertson,' said Mrs Bullingdon with an air of authority. 'I spoke to her on arrival.'

'What's she like?' Miranda asked, licking her lips. George was sickened.

'With such an unfortunate face she was in no position to be arrogant,' sniffed Mrs Bullingdon. 'She was most unpleasant with a tongue that could slice through marble.'

'Oh dear. What sort of life must she lead, poor woman? Fate has been so unkind.' Miranda's words were disingenuous. George could tell from the cold glint in her eye that she took great pleasure from Susan's disfigurement.

'You see, looks, like class, will never diminish in importance,' Mr Linton-Harleigh stated heavily. 'Anyone who says they don't matter doesn't know what they're talking about.' His wife nodded enthusiastically.

'Isn't it lucky our Miranda's so pretty and charming?' she said, pulling a saccharine smile.

When George felt pressure on his ankle he assumed there must be a dog under the table. When it persisted he realised to his horror that it was Miranda's foot nudging his. He looked at her to find her discussing Susan with Mrs Bullingdon, relishing all the details that the elder lady was expressing with delight. For a moment he thought he must be mistaken, she appeared too engrossed in her conversation. But it couldn't be Mrs Linton-Harleigh's foot, for she was sitting next to him, and surely not that of the brigadier's wife. The foot crept up his leg and rubbed against his shin. Pretending to drop his napkin, he bent down and poked his head beneath the tablecloth. To his relief the foot belonged to the girl. He was vaguely amused to think that her parents no doubt considered her a paragon of virtue. Hastily he tied the napkin around her ankle and attached it to the leg of the table. Then he pushed out his chair and got up.

'Surely you're not leaving us, George,' Mrs Bullingdon exclaimed, put out. 'You haven't had any breakfast.'

'I'm afraid I am.'

'Lady friend?' the brigadier asked, one bushy eyebrow shuffling off into his hairline.

George smiled bashfully. 'How right you are, Brigadier. A very beautiful and classy one at that.'

Mr Linton-Harleigh sniggered. 'Now, here's a lad who knows what's good for him.'

Miranda pouted.

'Bring her with you to dinner?' Mrs Bullingdon suggested. Then she turned to her friends. 'He was a bit of a loner before I found him.'

George turned on his heel and stopped at Susan's table. She looked up and smiled at him. 'Do you need rescuing?' she asked.

He shook his head in exasperation. 'May I join you?'

'Please do.' George pulled out the chair and sat with his back to Mrs Bullingdon's table. 'You seem to have caused a bit of a commotion by leaving them to breakfast with me.'

'Good. They're possibly the most unpleasant bunch of people I've ever met.'

'You were better off on your own.'

'I was. But they jumped on me in the bar.'

'I know the sort. Leeches. Once they've met you they want to suck you dry.'

'Well, I'm backing out before I'm totally depleted. How are you this morning?'

She took a sip of her coffee. She was beautifully dressed in an ivory-coloured skirt and blouse, a simple pearl necklace around her neck. Her nails were perfectly manicured and her make-up carefully applied. Her hair shone with health and vitality. Only her eyes betrayed a certain weariness of spirit.

'I enjoyed last night,' she said, much to George's surprise. 'Oh, close your mouth before something flies in. It was nice to talk to someone.'

'It was nice for me too. Shame we didn't meet earlier.'

She lowered her eyes. For a fleeting moment she looked like a young girl and George suddenly felt protective of her. He poured himself a cup of coffee and ordered some more toast from the waiter.

'Two breakfasts! Isn't that a little greedy even for a growing boy?' she teased.

'They put me off my food,' he replied, buttering a piece of toast. 'I'm suddenly very hungry.'

'I think you've upset that rather sour-looking child,' she said, referring to Miranda. 'She hasn't taken her eyes off you once.'

'She's far more curious about you.'

'You think?'

'Just a hunch.'

'I imagine she's wondering how a good-looking young man could possibly prefer the company of a disfigured old maid to hers.'

'Beauty is skin deep.'

'So the saying goes.'

'But it's true, and you're no old maid.'

'You're very sweet.' She was clearly delighted by his flattery for her cheeks flushed. She struggled to compose herself. 'What are you going to do today?' she asked, folding her napkin.

'Spend it with you. You don't think I'm going to leave you on your own, do you?'

'You obviously think I'm incapable of defending myself.'

'On the contrary. However, I'm incapable of defending myself against the likes of Mrs Bullingdon and Mrs Linton-Harleigh. If you leave me on my own, I'm bound to be set upon again.'

'Well then, I have no choice but to give you my protection. But I better warn you, I've brought out a pile of classics to read. I won't be good company.'

'I love the classics. My mother introduced me to the likes of Dickens, Austen and Thackeray at a very young age.' She raised her eyebrows, impressed.

'I was weaned on *Winnie-The-Pooh* and *The Wind in the Willows*. You know something, they're far more delightful to read as an adult.'

'Like *Alice in Wonderland* and *The Wizard of Oz*.'

'Exactly. Very clever to write on two levels like that.'

Suddenly, there was a shriek from the table behind as Miranda tried to stand up but was held down by the napkin George had tied around her foot. Her parents looked at her in bewilderment while Mrs Bullingdon's face flushed with embarrassment as the girl's loud cries drew attention to their small party.

'Good God child, what is the matter?' Mr Linton-Harleigh exclaimed irritably. Miranda pursed her lips and dived under the table. She wrenched her foot free and emerged red-faced and scowling.

'Nothing,' she snapped. 'Don't look at me like that, Mama. And I'm not a child!' As she passed George she stuck her nose in the air and glowered at him.

'What was that all about?' Susan asked him as the party left the room.

'An offending foot that strayed where it shouldn't,' he replied with a grin. 'Fortunately, it's a big boat. I'd better keep well clear of her or I'm likely to find myself thrown overboard.'

George spent the day with Susan. They walked up and down the decks in the sunshine, lay on deckchairs sipping lemonade, and quietly read their books, commenting every now and then on something that amused them. They lunched together and gossiped about the brigadier and his wife and their ghastly friends who now considered him traitorous. In the evening they swam in the pool and drank cocktails on the deck watching the sun slip towards the sea as it sank beneath the surface to alight upon another continent the other side of the world.

A couple of days later, when the ship anchored just off the coast of Uruguay, they took a small boat into the port to wander among the shops and up and down the beach. It was soft and fine, quite unlike the sand in Devon.

'Isn't it beautiful here? Gone are the grey clouds and drizzle of England,' said George, enjoying the sapphire-blue sky and bright sunshine.

'The smell is what delights me,' said Susan. 'It's thick and sweet like honey.'

'I grew up by the sea. I've always loved it.'

'It pulls at you, doesn't it? Right here.' She placed a hand on her chest. 'It makes me feel my own immortality and question what there is beyond. I suppose death is like the sea. The horizon is only the limit of our sight. You have to have faith. I like to think heaven is there, beyond our senses.'

'Will I see you again?' George asked suddenly.

She laughed. The same laugh that a mother might give a child in order to indulge him. 'Oh, George,' she said and sighed.

'Tomorrow we arrive in Buenos Aires.'

'Let's live that long first, shall we?'

'Oh, we'll live that long, I assure you,' he replied tightly.

'I know, you survived the war.' She took his hand in hers. He held it reluctantly.

'Don't patronise me, Susan.' His voice was angry but she still smiled which infuriated him all the more.

'I'm not patronising you, George. You're asking me something I don't know the answer to. It's easier not to think about these things. To avoid them.'

'Are you married?'

'No.'

'Are you meeting a lover?'

'No.'

'Don't you want to see me again?' He stopped walking and withdrew his hand, putting it into his pocket defensively. She put her head on one side and looked at him gravely.

'I don't know. Perhaps we are just destined to meet and part on this boat.' Her fingers traced the scar absentmindedly, running up and down her cheek.

George swallowed hard. 'Is it because you think I'm a boy?'

'You're certainly much younger than I am.'

'Does that bother you?'

'Age is like beauty, George, irrelevant.'

'Then what is the problem?'

'I'm not ready for you,' she said, and her eyes dimmed once again with sadness. She shook her head. 'I'm sorry.'

Instead of sulking, which is what a boy would have done, he made a conscious effort to behave like a man. He shrugged off her rejection, knowing that he had the rest of his life to brood on it if he so wanted, and tried to behave as before. At dinner they discussed the history of Uruguay and Argentina, of which she knew a great deal, and afterwards they stood where they had met, leaning on the railings looking out into the darkness. George felt suffocated, as if the air was too thick to breathe. He was suddenly afraid of being without her.

'What are you thinking, George?' she asked.

'I'm staring into the void,' he replied, feeling that familiar sense of loss engulf him. 'I can't accept that I won't see you again.'

'Who knows what destiny holds for us?'

Overcome by desire and desperation, he swung her around and kissed her. Her body went rigid and she pushed him away in terror. 'I can't,' she said, her cheeks aflame. Then her voice wavered. 'You don't understand.' But her eyes betrayed her longing. Ignoring her protests he kissed her again. She felt frail in his arms, vulnerable even. For the first time since they had met, she let down her guard. Slowly the tension in her body subsided and she sank into his embrace. He held her tightly, knowing she would be lost to him in the morning, and kissed her deeply. She smelt of the sea and lily of the valley and of something sweet, entirely her own, that he would never forget.

Finally, she pulled away and looked at him with eyes brimming with regret. 'That wasn't the kiss of a boy,' she quipped. 'I must go.'

'Spend the night with me?' he groaned, the world falling away from him.

'No, George. I'm going to my own bed.'

'So this is it?'

'Don't be sad. You're young, you have your whole life ahead of you. You're only just beginning.'

'Don't say that, Susan. I feel as if it's the end.'

'Good night.' She pressed her lips to his and kissed him tenderly. Then she was gone.

George wanted to run after her but he knew it was useless to beg, not to mention undignified. Besides, she would think less of him for it. He lit a cigarette and inhaled through a constricted throat. He wanted to cry. What the hell was wrong with him? He had been on the brink of tears waving farewell to Rita only three weeks before. He put his head in his hands and listened to his breathing and the clashing of his thoughts.

When he finally sank into a troubled sleep his nightmares resurfaced to torment him again.

The blackness dissolves like mist and there he is, flying high in a clear blue sky. The vibration of the plane rattles his bones. The thunder of the engine is an urgent battle cry. The oxygen mask is hot and he's finding it hard to breathe, but his eyes are focused on the cloud of German Messerschmitt 109s moving ominously towards him. He's not alone. Lorrie's on his right, and Tony? He turns. Yes, Tony's there on his left. Just knowing they're there boosts his confidence. *We'll show you buggers.* The MEs loom large and menacing and suddenly he's in the thick of it. So many planes he doesn't know where to start. Fear takes hold. An icy fear that once again forces his concentration and steadies the turbulence in his mind. Sometimes fear is a good thing. This battle's going to be a bloody one. *Focus, George, keep your wits about you.* The voice on the R/T articulates with urgency: *109s at 4 o'clock, 3,000 feet above, eight at 6 o'clock. Watch out. They're swooping down.*

For God's sake, break! Gun button to fire, press emergency
boost override, straps tight, focused. Very focused. Calm as
never before. He looks about for a target. Dorniers below.
One of those will do. He casts a glance about him. It's chaos
out there. Planes everywhere. Spitfires lost in the swarm
of German gnats. He swoops down to the Dornier, never
takes his eyes off him. The sound of a tracer whizzes by,
then gunfire behind. But nothing deters him from his target.
I'll get you, you bastard. You'll be sorry. He presses the gun
button and fires. *Got you.* The Dornier takes a dive. Black
smoke coming out of her tail. Loads of it. Too busy to watch
her crash into the sea. Too busy to wonder who will mourn
him back at home. He's quick to spot a Heinkel III, he fires
in short bursts but the enemy turns away and breaks for the
sea. George is hot on his tail. He's aware that they've left the
battle. It's just the two of them and one will surely die. Sweat
trickles down his forehead and into his eyes. He's hot and
uncomfortable. The sea lies shimmering in the early evening
light. It looks hypnotic, alluring even. The final resting place
of so many brave men. The Heinkel is below him so he has
the advantage and swoops down, gaining on him fast. Goes
for the quarter attack. Eases back the throttle and settles just
off his port side. Short bursts of fire. Black smoke. He's hit.
God, I'm good at this, he thinks triumphantly. Too slow to
avoid the counterattack. Sound of bullets on metal. *Damn,
he's got me!* Uneasy relief when he realises that it's only the
wing. But it was close. He pulls up on his starboard side and
fires in long bursts this time. Determination and controlled
fury. Never takes his eyes off his target. He's sure he can see
the fear on the face of the enemy. The German rolls away.
He's like a slippery eel. How he avoided those bullets George
will never know. Suddenly he's out of eyeshot. George looks
around, a strange feeling of anticipation strains his nerves. *A
bloody 109 on my tail. How did he get there?* George flies for

his life. Flies all over the sky. This way, that way, anything but straight. He knows he's a hard target. Then a streak of red passes his cockpit. More gunfire, an explosion, the smell of cordite and his own terror. Then it dawns on him. He's been hit. He blinks to get the sweat out of his eyes. They're sore and his head hurts. *Pull yourself together, George, for God's sake. You're not ready to meet your maker.* The 109 pulls away, leaving him for dead, no doubt. But to George's amazement he's still flying. Must be the fuel tank. He turns on his back and now he's above the enemy. The pursued is now the pursuer. *Bloody arrogant sod*! Gaining speed as he swoops down after him he fixes his target and fires. Long bursts. The last of the ammo. *I don't care if you take me with you, but you're going down*, he shouts, firing like a crazed man. Grey smoke puffs out of the fuselage. The propeller slows down and the nose dives. More black smoke and, like a winged bird, the 109 falls away, trailing oil and despair behind him. George watches as the plane crashes into the sea, swallowed up at once in a thick froth of white foam. Then all is still and quiet. He looks about him. He's entirely alone. With his heartbeat slowing down he throws open the hood and loosens his mask. With his head in the slipstream he begins to calm down. He's wounded, but he'll make it home. That was a close shave. Nearly copped it. Then he's overcome with a sudden feeling of loneliness. Where's everyone got to? He sees the coastline. Scans the sky for planes. But there are none. Where's Lorrie and Tony? He knows they didn't make it. He can feel it. He's alone. Quite alone.

Chapter Ten

George awoke in a sweat. His heartbeat raced and his body trembled with fear. It took him a while to shake off his dream and remember that he was aboard the *Fortuna*, bound for Argentina. Then he thought of Susan and he was suddenly thrown back into his dream, feeling lonelier than ever.

As he dressed he could feel the vibrations of the ship as it docked in Buenos Aires. He raced up the corridors and out onto the deck, hoping that by some small miracle he would catch a final glimpse of her as she disembarked. It was hopeless. He stood against the railing watching the passengers walk down the ramp onto the dockside, his eyes scanning them for that familiar blonde hair, neatly combed into an elegant chignon. The port was teeming with uniformed officials but, unlike England where they exuded efficiency, here the atmosphere was languid. Although still early morning, the heat of the sun was intense. The flow of passengers dwindled and he resigned himself to the fact that she had long gone. One more face in the millions of unfamiliar faces of Buenos Aires.

He returned to his cabin and threw his things into a bag. He hesitated when he came across the letter he had written to Rita and the dove pendant he had bought her. He fingered it thoughtfully before placing it at the top and clipping shut his bag. Then he left the ship and its sweet memories. He had nothing to remember Susan by: no photograph, no letter, no small token to mark their meeting and their parting.

Nothing. Once he left the ship it would be as though they had never met.

Buenos Aires was a fragrant, romantic city. He imagined Susan in the small cafés and beneath the violet jacaranda trees that had burst into blossom with the unexpected flowering of his own fragile heart. He envisaged her walking down the wide, tree-lined avenues, perhaps residing in one of those pretty Parisian buildings, with their high roofs and ornate façades. He had time to kill before his train to Córdoba so he wandered into a plaza that was ablaze with flowers and trees in bloom, the air thick with the heady scent of gardenia and the happy twittering of birds. It was peaceful there beside a fountain.

The delicate trickle of water soothed his spirit and he was able to appreciate the change of scenery and the promise of something new that this country offered him. He lunched alone in La Recoleta, at a table that looked out from under sinewy rubber trees onto the wall of the cemetery. A flower stall was set up at the entrance and the smell of spring mingled with the aroma of cooking meat and diesel. He ate Argentine beef, a steak that spilled over the sides of the plate, juicy such as he had never tasted. He drank wine and allowed it to numb the sense of rejection that still gnawed at his heart, and watched the scenes play out around him through lazy eyes.

This was a country untouched by war. People sat in the sunshine, sipping cocktails, chatting happily and eating luxuries that were a rarity in Britain. It felt good to be a part of this carefree world. It made it easier to forget. He shook off the winter and let in the spring. But as much as he tried to think of Rita, Susan's face still invaded and lingered in his mind. He was too drowsy with wine to fight it. So he looked upon her with wistfulness and longing, his eyes staring ahead but focusing on nothing. He realised with a shudder that if he had really loved Rita he would have married her there and then and brought her with him. But she was tied to Frognal Point, to his past, to the ghosts from which he was running. He was running from her too.

This thought disturbed him. Surely he had loved Rita for as long as he could remember? Besides, Susan was gone. He would never see her again. He paid the bill and took a taxi to Retiro station. The driver was a jolly man with a large belly and a keen sense of patriotism, for blue and white Argentine flags were stuck in every possible place in his cab. Disappointed that George didn't speak Spanish, he chattered away regardless, sure that the young foreigner would pick it up after a while. George let him talk on, nodding and saying *si* and *no* in agreement, depending on the driver's tone. When he was dropped at the station he was amused to see that it was a replica of London's Waterloo, built by the Victorians in the same cast iron as the original. Even the details of the ticket windows were identical. He felt a sudden nostalgia, remembering the trains he had so often taken at the beginning of the war when coming home on leave.

When he found a seat on the Rayo del Sol train bound for Córdoba it was strange to look out of windows free of black-out fabric, to sit comfortably in an uncrowded carriage, to find himself opposite a brown – skinned woman with a parrot perched contentedly on her shoulder. He watched the city for a while, the buildings becoming shabbier the farther they travelled until they were little more than shacks with corrugated iron roofs. He must have drifted off to sleep for when he awoke countryside had replaced the concrete of the city.

As they cut across the pampa, flat plains of long grasses extended as far as the eye could see, interrupted only by clusters of trees where there were dwellings. The odd ombu tree sat proprietorially, squat and weathered but undeniably the king of the pampa. Occasionally herds of shiny ponies, the colour of rich honey, grazed in the sunshine or gathered under tall plane trees. They tossed their heads lazily, too hot to canter around. He passed terrain dotted with small towns, and huge fields planted with corn, wheat and sunflowers. The sky was vast, as if the earth had fallen away exposing the gateway to heaven, and occasional fluffy clouds, drifting across it, like angelic chariots. They stopped at quaint, old-fashioned English stations that once again reminded him of home. The lady opposite him nodded off to sleep unaware that her parrot, so beautifully behaved during her waking moments, now snatched the opportunity to hop about the carriage. He used his claws to climb up the seat, over the luggage rack and down the other side. George watched him with interest, wishing he had something he could offer him to eat.

George dined alone. He remembered his last dinner with Susan on the *Fortuna*, the way she smiled, the dreadful scar on her face, which he found so endearing, and the stony blue eyes that had softened for him. He recalled little about their conversation. The history of Uruguay and Argentina, what did he care? But he could envisage her as if she were opposite him now. He could even smell her. The sweet scent of lily of the valley and her own, unique perfume. He didn't desire the company of anyone else. He was content to be left alone with his thoughts. After dinner he retired to his berth to sleep. Although he had the compartment to himself the man next door snored so loudly the dividing wall shook. In the morning, having slept fitfully, he emerged to discover, to his horror, that the snorer was the woman with the parrot.

Finally the terrain changed. Hills appeared on the flat plain like giant waves breaking on a beach and he remembered that Susan had told him how those mountains were home to condors, coral snakes and pumas. They were rich in vegetation and waterways as well as heritage, for colonial monasteries and churches remained as testimony of a once-thriving Jesuit culture. At last the train drew up at Córdoba station. He was pleased to get out, stretch his legs and cool down in the shade of the awning.

'George, is that you?' He turned to see a stout, determined-looking woman striding purposefully towards him. 'Yes, by God, you've grown!' Aunt Agatha's face was weathered and brown like an old leather shoe. She held out her arms and pulled his face down to her level to kiss him. He was at once engulfed in a fog of perfume. *'Carlos, traiga el equipaje, por favor,'* she said, waving at the skinny youth who hovered awkwardly beside her. Even with George's little knowledge of the language he could tell that his aunt spoke it badly. 'George, what a delight it is to see you after all these years. Yes, you were little more than a boy when I married Jose Antonio. Of course, you probably don't remember me. But I remember you. Oh yes, you may have grown but that cheeky face of yours hasn't changed a bit!' She linked her arm through his and led him out into the sunshine. 'Isn't it hot? Lovely. Bet you haven't seen sun like this in all your life. And Faye can't understand why I haven't set foot in England for fifteen years! Well, you can tell her now, can't you. How is Faye?' George did not remember Aunt Agatha and usually switched off when his mother spoke of her. He wondered for a horrible moment if he had made the right decision coming to stay with her. Perhaps he would have been better off remaining in Buenos Aires, searching for Susan.

'Mother is well. Sculpting, looking after Father,' he replied, suddenly feeling very weary.

'Good. Trees is keeping the country fed, no doubt. And how is Alice? I gather she's waiting for Geoffrey to come home. Shouldn't be long now. Thank God the war is over. What a dreadful business. Faye wrote me wonderful letters. I gather you're something of a hero. I'm very proud of you.

Told all my friends. Very glamorous flying those planes. What fun it must have been!' George didn't have the energy to disagree with her.

Agatha climbed into the front seat of her canvas-top Ford, leaving the young boy to load the luggage in the boot before scrambling into the back. 'Only an hour to Jesús Maria, we're not far from there,' she said, squeezing his leg enthusiastically. 'Now tell me, how is Rita and when will she be joining us?'

'She's not coming out, Aunt Agatha. It wasn't appropriate. After all, we're not married.'

'Oh, pooh to that.'

'I'm too young to settle down.'

'Jose Antonio was your age when we married. I'm a little older than him. He's always liked the older woman.'

George began to take interest. 'How much older are you?'

'Five years, I think. He still looks like a boy, whereas I look like an old hag. That's what the Argentine sun does to a woman's skin. No good at all. Not that I'm bothered. Faye was always the pretty one. I'm strong on personality.' He looked across at her forceful profile and silently agreed with her. She might have been small in stature but she was built like a Panzer tank, with thick wrists and ankles and a generous girth. 'So you've left that poor girl in England pining after you. You brute!' She gave a deep, throaty laugh.

'I asked her to come. She didn't want to. She loves Frognal Point. I can't imagine her ever leaving it. I'll return in a year or so and marry her.'

Agatha snorted. 'Don't be ridiculous, George. You won't marry Rita. It's all about timing, you see. Perhaps if you were a little older I'd say it had a chance. But you're young. You'll fall in love out here. The Argentine girls are famous for their beauty and femininity. Don't know why Jose Antonio chose me when he could have had any of them. Don't think we're out in the sticks here,' she continued. 'I travel down to BA every now and then, and friends visit us up here. Some stay for months. Jesús Maria is very sociable. Nice people. You have to learn Spanish, you know. I'll get someone in the town to come and give you lessons. You simply won't survive without it. Jose Antonio will take you around the farm this evening, show you how things work. You ride, I presume?' He nodded. 'Good. We go everywhere on horseback. Tracks not good enough for cars. It's the rain, you see. Rains a lot here in summertime, that's why it's so green. They say the climate is like Spain. I've never been to Spain so I wouldn't know. The children will love you. You'll be a hero to them, flying planes in the war. Told them all about it.'

George listened with half an ear to her ramblings. She told him about her children, the education in Jesús Maria, how they were contemplating sending them to school in Buenos Aires. His mind wandered to Rita, out of guilt; he felt duty-bound to remember her. He would post his letter and gift to her as soon as possible, and felt a stab of pain when he envisaged her pining for him on those cliff tops, the wind whipping through her wild curls.

Finally the car left the highway and rattled along a dirt track for what seemed miles and miles. It was bumpy and dusty and the sun burned through the glass windows causing him to sweat. Unlike the pampa, Córdoba was thick with trees and vegetation and undulating with hills. He felt his stomach rumble in protest for he hadn't eaten breakfast. At last they turned into a driveway lined with leafy trees.

'Home sweet home,' said Agatha. 'Welcome to *Las Dos Vizcachas*, The Two Hares.'

George sat up and paid attention. Agatha drove slowly down the shady drive in order to give her nephew a good look at her beautiful home. She was immensely proud of *Las Dos Vizcachas* and ran it with military efficiency. Of course

George would never appreciate the work she had done for he hadn't seen it when she arrived.

At the end of the drive the house stood as squat and sturdy as its mistress. Built around a courtyard, it was painted white with a roof of green tiles, rising into two towers at either end. The windows peeped out from behind green iron bars to deter intruders, and the shutters were closed from within to keep it cool. At the back a wide veranda shaded a tiled terrace that faced an ornamental lake and then beyond, across those seemingly interminable plains. Borders spilled over with flowers and large bushes of gardenia and bougainvillea dazzled in the sunshine. Eucalyptus trees rustled in the breeze and filled the air with the smell of camphor, reminding George of Malta. Carlos carried his bag inside, receiving a scolding on the way from a woman with a shrieking voice. She ejected her words like bullets, raising her hands in the air and waving them madly.

'That's Dolores,' said Agatha. 'As you can see, she is quite unable to control her temper. She was here when I arrived and there was no way I could get rid of her. One tolerates her as one tolerates an aged relative.'

'What does she do?' he asked, following his aunt into the house.

'She's the maid. She cooks, but she's far too superior to clean. Agustina sees to that. She's a younger woman, more agile and, thank the Lord, as docile as a cow.'

The house, although very colonial, betrayed Agatha's English upbringing by the paintings that hung on the walls and most notably the two large dogs who lay on the cool tiles in the hall. They barely lifted their eyes when George walked over them, so he gathered they were not there to guard. 'They're meant to be Great Danes, but didn't quite make it. They answer to Bertie and Wooster,' said Agatha. At the sound of their names their long tails thumped happily.

He followed his aunt down a dark corridor and into a bedroom at the end. 'I thought you'd like this room, it looks over the park,' she said. 'It's also the other end of the house from us, so you'll have some privacy.'

George was delighted with his room. It was large and cool with dark wooden floorboards, white walls and a queen-size iron bed imported from England. The light fell in through a tall open window, its shutters ajar and the linen curtains pulled back. George stood in front of it admiring the view and feeling rejuvenated by the fresh, sugar-scented air and the peaceful song of birds.

'When you're ready I'll be outside on the terrace. You'll need a drink I should imagine.' Before she left the room, George unzipped his bag.

'I have a letter to post,' he said, pulling out the small package in brown paper and the letter. 'It's for Rita.' Agatha raised a knowing eyebrow.

'I'll see to that for you,' she said with an air of efficiency. Nothing was ever too much for Agatha. 'Any washing put in the basket. Agustina will do it and return it to you in the morning.'

George unpacked, bathed, shaved, and dressed in light trousers and a short-sleeved shirt. He splashed his face and neck with cologne then walked through the house to the terrace. Agatha was standing beneath the veranda talking to one of the gardeners. She had her hands on her hips and her feet akimbo, like those old portraits of Henry VIII. George was sure she could be just as terrifying if she so wanted. The gardener held his hat deferentially and listened to everything she said with a bowed head. When she saw George she dismissed the man without so much as a thank you and turned her back on him. He shuffled away, wiping the sweat from his brow with a filthy handkerchief.

'That's Gonzalo. As strong as an ox and just as stupid,'

she said, pulling out a chair and sitting at the round table. 'Lemonade?' She poured him a glass, which he drank gratefully, then continued boisterously, articulating her words in that old-fashioned aristocratic way, barely opening her mouth as she did so. George thought she would have made a very formidable colonel in the army. 'When I arrived here I barely spoke a word of Spanish and this place was a wreck. Jose Antonio grew up here. His grandfather built it and at one time he lived here with his parents, grandparents and two sisters. The grandparents died, then the father, and his two sisters buggered off. One married a Mexican, the other lives down south.'

'What happened to his mother?' George asked, though he wasn't really very interested in Jose Antonio's family history.

'She lives in Buenos Aires. Mad as a hatter, though. Never comes up, the journey's too much for her. I can't say I'm sorry. She always was rather hard work.'

'You've made this into a paradise,' he said. Agatha was pleased.

'It wasn't easy. Coming here, not speaking the language. It wasn't Jose Antonio's money, either. They lost it all, the fools. I had a bit, enough to get the place up and running. Didn't know much about farming. Had to learn all that as I went along. We're comfortable and labour is cheap. We live off the land. You'll see. There's plenty of meat and vegetables. We're self-sufficient. Come, I'll show you around. Bring your glass with you.'

They walked to the lake, where birds nested in the reeds and wild duck swam on the water. Beyond, across a park of carefully planted trees, was the *puesto*. Here the gauchos looked after the horses. A couple of brown ponies rested in the shade of an ombu. A dark-skinned youth sat shirtless, scrubbing down a saddle and bridle, and another, much older man, leaned back against the fence, sipping *mate*, the traditional herb tea, out of a gourd through an ornate silver straw. A number of skeletal dogs sniffed the ground beside the logs where a barbecue had been the night before. They looked wild and mangy and no one took any notice of them. When the gauchos saw their mistress approach they stood to attention and bowed their heads. George wondered what Jose Antonio was like and whether Aunt Agatha was the one wearing the trousers in the marriage. She certainly took all the credit for everything at *Las Dos Vizcachas*.

'Jose Antonio will take you off this afternoon. He'll want to show you the farm. I suggest you relax for a couple of days, settle in, then get to work after the weekend. Jose Antonio could certainly use an extra pair of hands.'

With Aunt Agatha George barely had a moment to think of Susan, or Rita for that matter. She talked without pause, often finishing her sentences with 'isn't it?' or 'don't you think?' so there was no way he could let his mind wander. Perhaps it was better that he forgot them both for the time being and concentrated on getting settled into this new country.

They sat once again at the table on the veranda, now laid for lunch. The smell of cooking meat wafted out from the kitchen. George's stomach rumbled continuously and he longed to grab one of the bread rolls that lay enticingly in a basket in the centre. Finally, just when George was beginning to feel nauseous with hunger the low, gravelly voice of Jose Antonio bellowed through the hall. 'Gorda! I smell food. Let's eat!'

Chapter Eleven

Jose Antonio was a giant of a man: over six feet tall, with a broad frame, a wineskin stomach and thick curly black hair. When he saw George his face widened into a beaming smile. 'George! Welcome to *Las Dos Vizcachas*.' His English was good, though he retained a strong Argentine accent. Instead of extending his hand he slapped George firmly on the back and gave a loud belly laugh. 'I'm sure Agatha has shown you around the *estancia*. She is very proud of her home.'

'Yes, it's a beautiful place,' George replied, overwhelmed by the magnetism of the man.

'I'm glad you like it. It will be your home for some time, I hope.' He shifted his deep brown eyes to his wife. 'Let us eat!'

Agatha tinkled a little silver bell that was placed next to her on the table and Agustina came scampering out with a large oval plate of meat, potatoes and salad. A high-pitched shrieking resounded from the kitchen. Jose Antonio chuckled as he poured himself a large glass of wine. 'I see Dolores is at war again,' he said, raising his glass to George. 'And you thought the war was over.'

'She's in a particularly filthy mood today. Though I have to say in all the years I've been here I've only ever seen her smile once,' said Agatha, serving herself some lunch.

George filled his plate as much as he could without appearing greedy and took a generous mouthful. It tasted as good as it looked.

'You know they say people become their names. Dolores means "pain",' said Jose Antonio.

'She's not in pain!' Agatha exclaimed.

'No, Gorda, she gives pain to everyone else!' He roared with laughter.

'If what you say is true about names I've certainly become mine,' she said with a smile. Then turning to George she added, 'Jose Antonio's nickname for me is Gorda, which means fat.'

George wanted to reassure her that she wasn't fat but felt he could not do so without looking foolish, so instead he said, 'You're a fine figure of a woman, Aunt Agatha.'

'I have to be to run this place; Jose Antonio lives like a king.'

It was true. Jose Antonio was waited on hand and foot by his wife and even Dolores, who had known him since he was a boy. George was surprised to see that with her husband Agatha seemed to suppress her personality. She didn't talk so much and she laughed at all his jokes, however lame they were. She was quite clearly cleverer than he was and so capable that he had no idea how much work it took to run their home. Everything was just as he liked it. The meals were served on time, the food was always fresh and delicious, the horses were always ready, the *puesto* was organised and efficient, and the small band of helpers toiled away quietly so that Jose Antonio was aware only of the perfection of the stage and not of the sweating behind the scenes. Guests came and went, and the bedrooms were always clean with linen sheets, cut flowers and new bars of soap. Jose Antonio received them warmly but never thought to thank his wife for all her hard work. Only Dolores screeched and wailed, totally out of anyone's control. But he tolerated her for she was part of the place. She had screeched all the way through his childhood so he had grown used to it.

After lunch Jose Antonio slept a siesta. Sometimes he would ride into town and visit his mistress, Molina. He'd roll around with her for a while, then fall asleep on her large, foamy breasts. Unlike Agatha, she was young and slim with skin the colour of burnt sugar. Best of all he liked her bottom, soft and round like a peach. Today, however, he was tired. Showing off in front of their new guest had required more wine and the wine had made him drowsy, so he fell onto his bed and snored for two hours, dreaming of Molina's firm buttocks. George dozed off in a hammock that belonged to the children. It was hot and he had barely slept the night before. Fortunately, Jose Antonio's room was up in one of the towers on the other side of the house, so George was able to rest undisturbed by his uncle's snoring and the churning sound of his digestion.

In the afternoon George accompanied Jose Antonio on horseback to survey the farm. The sun still burned, but it was less intense. In spite of his uncle's coarse nature George found his company enjoyable. They rode across the plains where wheat and maize grew in fields of gold and sunflowers turned their faces to the light. Brown cows roamed among wild grasses and flowers in vast herds, their coats thick and shining with health. Jose Antonio had an army of labourers who seemed to do most of their work on horseback. They were dressed in the traditional gaucho attire: baggy trousers tucked into leather boots, and woven sashes tied around their waists, upon which rested elaborate belts decorated with silver coins. They looked flamboyant with their wide-rimmed hats, hide chaps, glittering spurs and the all-important knife, tucked into their belts. But Jose Antonio was much more interested in talking about George.

'La Gorda tells me you have a woman in England,' he began. But before George could reply he added, 'What good is a woman you cannot make love to, eh?' He laughed boisterously. 'If you want a whore I know a good, clean place

in town. A man has to fuck like he has to eat and shit, no?'
George was speechless, not that Jose Antonio would have
noticed. 'A wife is for children,' he continued. 'She organises
your life and takes care of you. A whore is for pleasure. If I had
wanted to spend the rest of my life making love to my wife I
would have married Molina. But Molina is only good for that.
Every man should have a woman for love and a woman for
lust, no?' George had been quite happy to engage in bawdy
talk in the mess, but it seemed inappropriate to discuss such
things with his aunt's husband. Jose Antonio fixed him with his
mahogany eyes and said with a smirk, 'I see you are in love.'

'I'm going to marry Rita,' said George, feeling gauche. He
pulled out a cigarette and lit it.

'Then what you need is a woman to keep you occupied,'
Jose Antonio suggested, obviously an authority on the subject.
'A year is a very long time and you are young. When I was
young I made love whenever I could because, as you get older,
you no longer have the energy or the time to indulge so often.
You will see that I am right.' When George said nothing, Jose
Antonio added thoughtfully, 'Rita must be a very beautiful
woman.'

'She is,' George replied, envisaging her face, wondering
what she would make of Jose Antonio. He rather looked
forward to telling her in his next letter.

'I have always liked women. Young girls lack the experience. They are like green fruit on a tree. They get better once
they have been exposed a little to the elements. They need
to ripen.'

George thought of Susan and felt a wave of regret. He
should have asked for her address at the very least. The
knowledge that he might never see her again made her all
the more enigmatic and intriguing.

'There is something very attractive about a woman who has
seen a bit of the world,' George agreed.

'And who has tasted the forbidden fruit. Young girls are naïve, trusting, adoring. They lack personality. I was attracted to La Gorda because she knew her own mind. She is a strong and capable woman. It does not matter that she speaks Spanish like a tourist.'

'I must say, Jose Antonio, your English is admirable,' said George truthfully, wondering how on earth he was ever going to learn Spanish.

'I had an English nanny who left when I was twenty. No, no,' he was quick to add, once again roaring with laughter, 'I was potty trained by then, I assure you.'

When they returned to the *puesto* two brown children sat on the fence waiting for them. Seeing them approach they jumped down and ran up to the ponies. Pia was eight, Jose Antonio, nicknamed Tonito to avoid confusion, was ten. Their father leapt to the ground and gathered both children into his arms. They giggled excitedly and Pia placed her small hands on his rough face and kissed him. 'Come and meet your cousin George.'

They clung to him shyly, watching George with the same dark eyes as their father's. Neither resembled their mother. Pia was destined to be a beauty and Tonito a giant. They belonged to the Argentine as the ombu belongs to the pampa. George was surprised to discover that neither spoke good English for their parents talked to them in their native tongue, more out of laziness than intention.

'*Vamos a casa a tomar el té*,' said Tonito. He turned to George and translated in pidgin English. 'Teatime.'

Tea was laid out on the veranda, the silver and china neatly placed on a clean white tablecloth. The children drank their milk and told their parents what they had done at school. Jose Antonio was indulgent, Agatha mindful of their manners and deportment.

'Children, we must all speak English now we have an

English guest,' said Jose Antonio, running a large hand over his son's hair. 'Show us what you have learned in school.'

'Monday, Tuesday, Wednesday, Thursday,' said Tonito with a giggle.

'Surely you know more than that?' Agatha exclaimed, unimpressed.

'I don't want,' Pia complained, looking up at her father beneath thick black lashes. She had already mastered the art of flirting.

'George flies aeroplanes,' said their mother, attempting to engage them. 'He fought in a war.'

'Like a bird,' said Pia, pointing to the sky.

'Just like a bird,' George agreed, smiling at her. 'But once I crashed. Fell to the ground. Not like a bird!' The children giggled, clearly understing more than they let on.

'Good God, George. Did you?' Agatha's eyes widened.

'Damned nearly killed me,' he said, then added softly, 'Saved by the grace of God.'

Suddenly the sound of breaking china, scraping chairs and Dolores' inimitable screech alerted them to trouble in the kitchen. They all stiffened and strained their ears, looking at one another in bewilderment. Pia giggled nervously into her hand. Jose Antonio got to his feet, still chewing on a piece of cheese and *membrillo*, and walked unhurriedly across the terrace. He entered the kitchen to find the old woman standing in the middle of the room wielding a knife at an invisible aggressor. Like an angry crow she was dressed in her usual black gown and sensible black shoes, her hair pulled up into a severe bun. 'Out! Out!' she shouted, rigid with fury. When she saw her boss she turned on him too. 'Señor, if you have come to take me away I ask God in advance to forgive me my actions.'

'Dolores, why would I want to take you away? No one cooks *empanadas* like you do!' His voice was calm but forceful.

'I have a melon growing in my stomach. For that they have come to take me away.' Jose Antonio looked at her quizzically. He towered over her and it wouldn't have been difficult to wrest the knife from her, but her eyes shone with terror more than rage.

'Who has come to take you away?' he asked patiently. 'I see no one there.' She stuck out her jaw and nodded to the wall.

'Spirits. They come when your time is up, to take you on to the next world. But I tell them I'm not ready yet. *Váyanse, váyanse!*'

Jose Antonio's face darkened and he frowned. This wasn't the ranting of a crazed woman for he knew of spirits and had seen them himself. 'Who is there, Dolores?' he asked. His voice was barely a whisper.

'Mama and Ernesto.'

'Put down the knife. You cannot harm spirits with knives.' He walked a few paces towards her. She raised her eyes, now bloodshot and moist, bit her thin lip and placed the knife in his hand. 'By all means tell them to go, but politely,' he said, placing the knife back on the table. This she did. He watched her wave her hand as if to dismiss a tiresome dog. Then she turned, patted her grey hair and nodded at him gravely.

'My time is near, señor,' she croaked.

Jose Antonio put his hands on his hips and sighed ponderously. 'A knife and a few obscenities cannot delay your meeting with God, Dolores. No, they come with a warning. I will call la señora.'

When he returned to the table Agatha was busy telling George all the famous Dolores stories. The time she was nearly killed by a wild pig, the fight she had had with a whore in Jesús Maria, and the discovery that her husband, Ernesto, had been leading a double life with another family in La Cumbre. 'Of course he died shortly after,' Agatha was

saying. 'She made life impossible for him as you can imagine.'
When she saw her husband approach her voice trailed off and
she raised her eyebrows enquiringly.

'What the devil is wrong with her now?'

'Gorda, go and see her. She says she has a melon growing
in her stomach. I don't believe it is a real one.' He turned to
George. 'This is women's business.'

'Is she going to die?' Pia asked as she watched her mother
fold her napkin neatly and place it on the table.

Jose Antonio patted her shoulder. 'Of course not, *mi amor*,'
he replied.

'*Qué pena!*' said the child to George's astonishment. He
knew few phrases in Spanish, but there was no doubt in his
mind that she had just said 'pity!'.

'Pia, have more respect, please!' Agatha chided irritably.
She hated getting involved in the personal lives of her staff,
much less in their bodily functions. The idea of a melon in the
woman's stomach made her head swim. She didn't want to
know any more about it. But she did as her husband asked.

She found Dolores slumped in a chair sipping *mate*. She
looked like a benign old lady, hardly the fiend who had ruled
the kitchen for the last forty odd years.

'Are you all right?' Agatha asked in Spanish. She tried
to soften her tone but was aware that she sounded uncon-
cerned.

'What does it matter?' Dolores groaned. 'I'm on the way
out.'

'Don't talk such nonsense,' Agatha replied, wanting to add
that she'd been trying to get rid of her without success for the
last two decades. 'Señor Jose Antonio tells me that you have
something growing in your stomach.' The melon sounded too
absurd to mention.

'He should mind his own business,' Dolores snapped.

Agatha dropped her shoulders. '*Bueno*, we shall all mind

our own business then,' she replied with equal briskness, and left the kitchen, relieved that she didn't have to take the matter further.

George knew he would be happy in his new home. He took a swim in the evening then sat on the flagstones watching the gnats and flies dance upon the smooth surface of the water and allowing the scents of eucalyptus and gardenia to flood his senses. He felt blissfully detached from England. Both physically and mentally he was thousands of miles away and, for the first time since the war, he was at peace. The gentle mooing of cows accompanied the clicking of crickets and the light twittering of birds, and the setting sun brushed the plains with amber.

That night they ate in the courtyard beside a sprawling tree whose red flowers burst into the air every now and then with a loud pop. Dolores appeared to have recovered from her haunting and could be heard shouting at poor Agustina and Carlos. The children drank wine and conversed with the adults. George, weary from his trip, retired before they did. He slept a dreamless sleep, lulled by the sweet night air and the gentle snorting of ponies.

A couple of days later he started work. It felt good to ride out across those plains and there was much to learn. Another cloudless day to lift his spirits and sharpen his sense of freedom. With the wind in his hair and the sun on his face he rode with the gauchos, rounding up the herds and surveying the thriving fields of maize and wheat. He was keen to belong and watched them carefully, copying their casual way of riding, their backs slouched, reins in one hand, their hats pulled over one eye. They only spoke Spanish and George wished he were able to communicate in more than gesture. But they smiled at him roguishly and sensed that he was a good sort. They chuckled at his enthusiasm, the reckless way he rode and the endless cigarettes he smoked. When they offered him a sip of *mate* he gagged and choked at the sharp taste in spite of the honey they added to sweeten it. Consequently he filled a flask with orange brandy and drank that instead. Jose Antonio told them he had been a brave fighter pilot in the war and so they named him El Gringo Volante – The Flying Foreigner – and for once he was grateful for his inability to communicate because it saved him from having to tell them about the war.

Agatha sent him off to Jesús Maria to learn Spanish with a languid young woman called Josefa. With raven hair and moist brown skin she was plump and fragrant and as idle as a sloth in sunshine. She had a couple of textbooks she had obviously retained from her school days and a fondness for conjugating verbs. Fortunately she was blessed with an easy nature and limitless patience. She corrected George's errors over and over again without irritation and listened to his first faltering attempts at forming sentences. That she grew fond of him there was no doubt. She splashed herself with cologne, braided her hair, applied make-up and adorned her sensuous body with lotions and jewellery. The heat allowed her to wear as little as was decent, exposing more and more cleavage with his every visit. But George was too busy learning to notice. His heart was locked to her endeavours in spite of her heaving breasts. She sensed the ghostly presence of another woman and resigned herself to the impossibility of her desires.

November passed quickly, overshadowed by Dolores' increasing wrath and by Agatha's declining patience. George was now able to communicate in Spanish and was riding like the gauchos, although his lasso-throwing left much to be desired. He joined them around their camp fires at night and had even picked up the words and tunes to some of their songs, accompanied by the skinny lad they called El Flaco who played the guitar like an angel. He insisted that he would never grow to love *mate*, but killing and skinning an animal was well within his capability. Pedro, the white-haired gaucho who kept his age as secret as the names of the mistresses he visited in Jesús Maria, gave George a silver knife as a gift, telling him proudly that it was to use on the occasion of his first castration.

Whenever George looked up at the moon he thought of Rita. He wondered how his family was, Mrs Megalith, his friends in town. But he knew for certain that life at Frognal Point would always remain the same. How tired he had grown of the sea and those cliffs and how refreshing the fertile plains and hazy mountain range of Córdoba were to him. He thought of Susan too. When his mind wandered free, when he was caught unawares, when his thoughts were let loose to do as they pleased in dreams. Always the same image of her leaning against the railings, curling a stray piece of hair around her ear, her reluctant smile and those sad blue eyes that hid secrets he would now never know.

But then the winds of fate, so often blowing an unfavourable course, blew to his advantage. It all began with the melon. Agatha had dismissed the problem as another warped turn in the never-ending drama that was the life of Dolores. The old woman ranted and screeched and berated poor Carlos for the smallest oversight. Agustina was at her wits' end and often tearful. George grew accustomed to the shouting and, like Jose Antonio, he ignored it. The food she cooked was always good. Then one day in early December Pia ran out onto the terrace during tea shouting for her father. '*Papa, Papa, Dolores está muerta!*' George now spoke enough Spanish to understand that the child had declared Dolores dead. Agatha pushed back her chair with such vigour one could have been forgiven for thinking her impatient to see with her own eyes the evidence of the fiend's demise. Jose Antonio strode through the house with the same haste.

Even George, who rarely dared enter the kitchen, followed them.

Dolores lay inert on the floor but, much to Agatha's disappointment, her pulse still throbbed and her lungs still sucked in air, albeit weakly. The doctor was called and Jose Antonio lifted the woman into the sitting room as if she were nothing more than a bundle of twigs. He placed her on a sofa and George noticed at once her distended stomach. He thought of the melon and felt his own stomach heave. She was not a pleasant sight. Old and wrinkled like one of his father's walnuts. He thought of Trees and smiled inwardly.

The doctor declared that Dolores did indeed have something vast and uncomfortable in her stomach. Not a melon, he added hastily after one of the children mentioned it, but a tumour. It had to be removed without delay. Agatha had no choice but to drive her to Buenos Aires for the operation. The idea of spending hours in a car with the fiend, tumour and all, made her dizzy with repulsion. But she knew it was her duty. Jose Antonio didn't acknowledge the degree of self-sacrifice this trip involved. But she had to vent her frustrations to someone, and was swift to complain to George.

'Good God!' she exclaimed, throwing clothes into a suitcase. 'What a bloody nightmare. I've spent all the years of my married life putting as much distance as possible between me and that ghastly creature some see fit to call a woman. I call her a ghoul or a monster, there's very little evidence of anything human. And now she goes and develops a tumour. Why God didn't just take her when he had the chance, I don't know.'

'How long will you have to stay in the city?' George asked.

Agatha huffed furiously. 'A lot longer than I would like, of that I am sure. I don't know, ten days, two weeks. It's a bugger.'

'Where will you stay?'

'That isn't the problem. We have enough friends in Buenos Aires to populate an entire town. Not a word of gratitude from Jose Antonio. Never was very quick with the thank yous! Not that I'm complaining. He's a good man, just not very sensitive. He considers the domestic side of life my responsibility entirely! That I understand and don't mind. It's just a bugger that Dolores falls into that category.'

'Why don't I take her?' George heard himself suggesting, somewhat rashly. 'Or at least let me accompany you.'

'No, no. That's not necessary. Thank you so much, dear George, for offering. What a selfless young man you are.' Of course there was nothing selfless about his offer. He couldn't help but hope that, perhaps, if he were in the same city as Susan, their paths might, by some miracle, cross.

George watched the two women depart for the city and felt suddenly deflated. He consoled himself with the fact that he was hardly likely to bump into her in a city of millions. He was naïve to have even imagined it.

Twelve days passed. George longed for Agatha and Dolores to return because, while they were in Buenos Aires, he couldn't help but imagine Susan was close by, unknown to his aunt. Perhaps they took tea in the same café, or stood side by side in a shop somewhere. If only he had gone with her he might have chanced to see her. Even if Agatha did find herself beside the woman with the dreadfully scarred face, she wouldn't know how her nephew's heart pined for her.

Eventually Agatha returned with Dolores. George was out with the gauchos, but Jose Antonio was quick to bring the good news. 'Dolores is cured,' he beamed, expressing his delight by gesticulating wildly with his large hands. George wondered how his aunt felt about that. 'What's more, the melon contained poison that infected her whole body, her very nature. She is much changed. She smiles!'

'And Aunt Agatha?' George enquired.

'La Gorda seems to be incapable of going to the city without returning with some human token of her visit.'

'I think she deserves a reward for driving all that way with Dolores,' George suggested diplomatically.

'One woman cured, another scarred. It doesn't rain then it pours,' he exclaimed jovially, shrugging his shoulders. George's heart froze. 'She's invited a woman to keep you company, gringo. But of course,' he joked, slapping his thigh, 'you have eyes only for Rita.'

'What?'

'She's now running a sanctuary for recovering women. I might as well move in with Molina. Think nothing of it, gringo. She's not for you. God has cursed her beauty by slicing through it.' He ran a rough finger down the side of his face. 'Come, we have work to do!'

Chapter Twelve

In little more than a dressing gown and slippers, Rita ran outside to meet the postman, as she did every morning, with a hopeful spring in her step and a silent prayer on her lips. Today, surely, there would be a letter for her. It was a frosty November morning. Another Christmas without George, she thought gloomily. Mr Toppit, the postman, smiled broadly and waved a fat brown envelope in the air. He recognised George Bolton's handwriting from all the letters he had sent Rita during the war. Why the young man had gone away again he didn't know, but he thought it a mighty silly thing to do to leave a pretty girl like Rita Fairweather on her own. 'A love letter for you from overseas,' he exclaimed, watching his breath curl on the air like smoke. Rita took it from him and pressed it to her lips. Her whole body seemed to inflate as if she had trouble keeping her feet on the ground. Mr Toppit felt proud, as though he were the cause of her happiness.

'Oh thank you, Mr Toppit. You've made my day!' she replied with a laugh, feeling the lumps with her fingers, trying to guess what the envelope contained. He noticed her eyes shining in the cold and thought how happiness enhanced a girl's looks. If he weren't married, if he were a young man again, if arthritis hadn't begun to knot his joints, if he had the confidence of young George Bolton, he could lose his heart to Rita Fairweather. George was a lucky man, he mused. There was something about Rita that placed her out of reach, as if she belonged to the sea, like a mermaid. Not only was George lucky, he was blessed.

'Would you give these to your mother?' he said, rousing himself from his daydream.

'Of course,' she replied, taking the letters and turning to walk back into the house. 'I'm going to open this all by myself on the cliff top. That's our special place, you see. Up there on the cliffs.'

'Mind you don't fall off,' he teased.

'I won't fall off. Life's much too good!' With that she skipped lightly into the house.

When she returned to the kitchen, her family could tell by the smile on her face that she had finally received a letter from George. 'About time too!' exclaimed Humphrey, who vehemently disapproved of George's decision to leave Rita for another year. If it hadn't been for the engagement ring would have taken the boy aside and had strong words. As it was he had doubts that George would return. He was a bag of contradictions. An old man of the war in the body of a boy. Emotionally immature, yet wise and jaded, cynical even, disillusioned perhaps, keen for novelty and adventure but most of all for freedom. Why would he want to settle down to a quiet life in Frognal Point? Of course the war had changed him. It was inevitable. But it hadn't changed Rita.

'What is it?' Hannah asked, while Eddie sprang up from her chair, spluttering questions through a mouthful of toast.

'Open it. Go on!' instructed Maddie, sipping her tea. Fully made up in scarlet lipstick and black mascara, with her hair combed in the style of Lauren Bacall, she looked like a movie star herself.

Hannah had tried to dissuade her from making such an exhibition of herself, but she was nearly twenty now with a personality of steel. There was no job either. She wouldn't hear of it. And she spent far too much time with the boys in the White Hart pub. Hannah turned a blind eye. She had to accept that her child was now a grown-up.

Only Eddie was still at school and biddable. Hannah often wandered around the house, picking up relics from their childhood, taking pleasure from the memories they triggered. Time raced and children grew up and away. Thankfully her birds remained. Some migrated, but they always came back and seemed happy to see her.

'I'm going to open it on the cliffs. I need to be alone,' Rita announced to everyone's disappointment. But before they could object she rushed out, her footsteps disappearing up the stairs.

'What do you think it is?' Eddie asked her mother.

'He's already given her a diamond ring,' said Maddie sulkily.

'I'm sure it's a souvenir from Buenos Aires,' said Hannah. 'I don't think it matters much. The fact is, he's thinking of her.' She caught eyes with her husband and nodded at him triumphantly. She was well aware of his doubts, but this letter simply proved that Rita had done the right thing. 'Absence makes the heart grow fonder,' she added pointedly. Humphrey grunted behind his paper.

'Don't forget we're going to Megagran's for lunch,' Hannah shouted up the stairs. 'Aunt Antoinette will be there with Emily and William.' It was Saturday and on Saturdays Rita was apt to spend all day on the beach, by herself. What she did there Hannah didn't know. Probably daydreamed. At least she now had a job at the library in town otherwise she'd disappear altogether into those fantasies of hers. Working on a farm was no life for a girl. She eyed Maddie, dressed up as if she were going to a party, and wondered what she was going to do with her day. Not that she dared ask. Maddie would only snap at her. She was growing more and more like Aunt Antoinette, which wasn't a compliment.

*   *   *

Rita walked through the village towards the sea, clutching the brown envelope to her chest. She was unable to contain her smile or the bounce in her step. Spotting Reverend Hammond in the village shop talking to Miss Hogmier she quickened her pace in case they saw her and came out for a chat. She didn't much like Miss Hogmier, a sour old lady with disappearing lips and protruding nasal hair, and did almost anything to avoid having to go in with her mother's shopping lists. When she reached the cliff top she sat with her legs dangling over the edge, in the exact spot where she always sat with George, and tore open the brown paper.

It was windy and bitterly cold. She was wrapped in an old sheepskin coat of her father's and almost hidden beneath a woolly hat pulled low over her head. She had to take her gloves off to open the envelope, but it was worth the discomfort for, to her joy, she discovered the little dove pendant George had bought her aboard the *Fortuna*. She held it in her hand while she unfolded the letter. It wasn't long. George never wrote long letters, not like hers that went on for pages and pages. But she was sure it contained words she needed to hear. Oblivious of the worsening winds and the tempestuous sea that crashed against the rocks below, she devoured his words hungrily.

My darling Rita. I write this aboard the Fortuna, *just off the coast of Brazil. It is night-time and I find my mind wandering once again to you. I hope you like the pendant. I bought it from a wizened old man who came aboard to sell his wares. I'm sure he tripled the price. I would have bought it for ten times as much because you are worth it. The dove symbolises love, happiness and wedded bliss. I send it to you as a lucky charm and hope that it brings you all those things and more. I miss you, my darling, and sometimes wonder why I'm doing this, whether there's any wisdom in it. But we will both be richer for it for I will come back settled, I am sure, having found inner peace. I will make a better husband and father because of this experience. You are a wonderful girl to let me go, certain that I still hold your heart. You have mine too, for ever. All my love, my sweet Rita. George.*

Rita read it again and again. Unlike previous letters this one didn't dwell on the past. He didn't mention the summer, the cave or their picnics on the cliffs. It was also very short. But she couldn't complain. He loved her and missed her and that was all that mattered. She opened her hand and studied the pendant. It was very pretty. She would always wear it. Eager to put it on straightaway she fumbled with the catch, still holding the letter. But her fingers had grown numb in the cold, and suddenly the flimsy page of paper caught in the gale and was whisked out of her grasp. She gasped in horror as it flew into the air where it danced about, blown this way and that like an autumn leaf. She scrambled to her feet and watched helplessly as it floated towards the sea. She ran down the sandy path to the beach. She looked up at the sky, sure that it would fall within reach. Not a single bird braved the weather. Only George's letter hovered and dived like a gull as if grateful to have been set free. For a moment it looked as if it would indeed fall onto dry land, but then an unexpected gust swept up the beach, causing it to soar over the sea where it finally fell. Lost for ever in the water.

Rita was desperate. She shed tears of fury and frustration. Having waited a month for such a letter it was now gone. Mortified, she touched the pendant with gratitude and consoled herself that at least the wind hadn't taken that. She walked slowly back up the path downheartedly, her head bowed low to protect her face from the icy gale. She sniffed miserably and tried to remember exactly what George had written. She decided to write it down the minute she got home so that she wouldn't forget.

As she walked back through the village, her eyes lost on the road in front of her, she bumped straight into the mad Pole, Thadeus Walizhewski. He too had his focus fixed on the ground. He rarely met anyone's eyes for he hadn't the need or desire to make friends. 'Sorry,' she muttered. He noticed at once her tear-stained face and blue lips and was filled with compassion.

'Are you all right?' he asked, and his voice was so deep and gentle it took her by surprise. She felt an expanding lump lodge itself in her throat.

'Yes,' she replied unconvincingly.

'You look cold. Come.' He took her elbow and led her up a narrow lane and through a small gate almost hidden in a thick hedge. 'Let me make you a cup of something hot. You are in no state to be walking alone on a day like this.'

For an instant, when she gazed up at him with her large, sad eyes, he was reminded of his daughter. He felt a stab of pain in his chest, but was quick to dispel the memory. It was not healthy to dwell on those moments of fear and anguish for they were past, and only became present in the mind if one allowed them to.

Thadeus' cottage was warm and vibrated with a strange tranquillity which gave Rita the feeling that she had been there before. It smelt familiar. Even the clutter of manuscripts and books was reminiscent of somewhere else. Then she made the connection. Lower Farm had the same sense of cosy chaos. The same scent of burning wood in the grate, of kindness and hospitality. She felt she could throw off her boots and curl up on the sofa. That Thadeus wouldn't mind. She had never really spoken to him before. If she hadn't been so utterly miserable she probably wouldn't have now, but he had sounded so understanding and it was dreadfully cold out there in the wind. She took off her coat and settled into an armchair beside the fireplace. She breathed in the smoky air and found it pleasantly comforting. Thadeus came back with a pot of tea on a tray. None of the china matched and the teapot was chipped. Without saying a word he walked over to the gramophone and put on a record of Strauss's *Alpine Symphony*. At once the notes filled the room, injecting her with the cheerfulness that she had lost out there on the cliff top.

'"*If music be the food of love, play on,*"' he said, sitting down on the armchair opposite.

'Shakespeare, *Twelfth Night*,' she replied with a smile.

'You see, you are already feeling better.' He nodded gravely. 'Only love can make a woman weep so.' Rita poured herself some tea.

'You have a lovely home,' she said, stirring in the milk.

'I am very happy here,' he replied. 'You must be Rita Fairweather.'

'Yes, I am.' She laughed because it seemed absurd to be sitting in his house having never been properly introduced.

He looked at her thoughtfully for a moment. Then his eyes fell onto the pendant that hung about her neck.

'That is a very pretty necklace,' he said admiringly. 'Did George give it to you?'

'Yes, I received it today. I was out on the cliff and the wind blew away his letter.'

'Had you not read it?'

'I had read it. Several times.'

'But you are a sentimental woman and like to keep all his letters to read over and over, am I not right?' He chuckled. 'I thought so. I don't imagine you ever found the letter?'

'It's at the bottom of the sea,' she replied forlornly.

'Imagine how much worse it would be had you not read it. Besides, I'm sure there will be more.'

'I feel so foolish.' She sighed and drank her tea.

'But the dove is much more valuable. Words fade, but that is made out of silver and will be with you for always.

You know, the dove speaks its own language if you listen to it.' Rita laughed at the ridiculous thought, but Thadeus was serious. 'You may think me a little eccentric but it is true. The dove speaks of peace, of love and reconciliation. It speaks of forgiveness, serenity and joy. In fact, George has sent you a message in a symbol. Much more original than a letter, don't you think? When you are up on the cliff next time, when it is not so windy, take a good look at it and listen.'

'I will,' she said in order to humour him. He scratched his grey beard and watched her with his pale, watery eyes. 'Do you play the violin?' she asked, noticing the instrument languishing on top of the piano.

'Yes, I play to soothe my soul. Music is a wonderful healer.'

'The piano as well?'

'It is old and not well tuned, but I suffer it, yes.'

'I sculpt,' she said. 'Badly. Faye, you know, Faye Bolton, she's giving me lessons. She's incredibly talented.' Thadeus' face softened as if the light in the room had suddenly changed from white to amber.

'With practice I'm sure you will be as good as she is,' he said in a quiet voice.

'Oh no, I won't be. But I don't expect to be that good. Like you said, music soothes the soul, sculpting is the same. I'm able to lose myself in it.'

'I know exactly what you mean.'

'Like the sea. I lose myself in that too.'

'As well as George's letters.' His eyes twinkled.

'Yes. Silly, really.'

After about an hour she thanked him for the tea and for his company. She felt much better having talked to him and promised that next time she was on the cliff she would listen to her pendant. Before leaving she asked if she could use his lavatory, and hurried upstairs, aware that she was due at Megagran's for lunch. As she opened the door she turned to cast a quick glance into his bedroom. She was struck immediately by a large sculpture of a bear, which sat on the mantelpiece, all on its own. This was strange, for every other surface was scattered with objects and curiosities. There was no doubt that it was one of Faye's, her style was so distinctive. She wondered what had possessed her to part with such a masterpiece, but knew instinctively not to ask.

Thadeus helped her into her coat and watched as she pulled the hat over her head; her hair fell out of it like seaweed washed up on the beach. 'I hope you will come and have tea with me again sometime,' he said.

'I would like that very much. Perhaps then you can play the violin for me.'

'It would be my pleasure.'

Thadeus watched as she disappeared through the garden gate. Faye had spoken so highly of her and she was right. She was a sweet-natured child and if he hadn't bumped into her, literally, he would never have met her. Sometimes it wasn't good to walk around with one's head bent, avoiding people's eyes, hiding from the world. He closed the door and picked up his violin.

When Rita arrived home she crept in through the garden and tiptoed up the stairs to her bedroom to write out what she remembered of George's letter. The little robin had made a fine nest out of moss and grass in the pot that Eddie had made her at school. Rita loved her new friend, the way it watched her from the bookshelf without fear, its small black eyes unblinking. It flew in and out as it pleased, for Rita always left the window open. Hannah often came in to observe it and to offer it food out of her own hand but the robin would accept nothing from anyone but Rita. Hannah found this hard to accept for she had always had a special relationship with the feathered creatures that made their homes in her garden.

Rita decided to keep the fact of the lost letter to herself. She was ashamed that she had been so clumsy. Instead, she would show off her pendant. A symbol of love, happiness and wedded bliss.

They all piled into Humphrey's car at twelve and drove to Elvestree for lunch. Eddie was fascinated by the silver dove but Maddie sniffed rather dismissively.

'Sweet,' she stated flatly. If the eye had been studded with something worthwhile, like a diamond, she would have been more impressed. 'What did the letter say?' she asked.

'I want to keep the letter to myself. Besides, the dove speaks if you listen to it,' Rita replied.

Maddie screwed up her nose. 'Love is turning your mind to sawdust, Rita. If that dove speaks I'm the Queen of England.'

'Thank goodness you're not, Maddie. You'd be a frightfully bossy queen,' said Eddie. 'I want to hear the dove speak.'

'It speaks of love, happiness and wedded bliss,' Rita said. 'George has sent me a symbol, much more original than a letter.'

'My dear, I think the pendant is charming,' said Hannah. 'What a thoughtful young man he is.'

Humphrey snorted and shook his head, but only Hannah was aware of his scepticism.

When they arrived at Elvestree the drizzle had turned to hail. Tiny balls of ice were blown about on the wind, and the trees, so lush and green in the summer, now stood twisted and tortured and bare. They hurried into the hall, which was warmed by a large log fire and adorned with cats. There were cats on every surface. Five curled up together on the sofa, three on the old oak chest where Denzil's tennis rackets rotted away in the dark, and another six or seven beneath the table, stretched out on the shabby Persian rug. There were ginger ones, sleek black ones and petulant white ones. Hannah was used to her mother's house being full of these creatures but every time she visited there seemed to be more.

Mrs Megalith simply shrugged when asked where they came from. 'I'll bet there are some very sad families out there missing their little friends. I don't know why, but they're drawn to Elvestree. It's not my place to turn them away.'

Max's heart suffered a tremor of longing when he saw Rita enter with her family. Her hair was wild and her cheeks rosy from the coastal winds and salty drizzle. Although her dress was pressed and her cardigan clean, she appeared dishevelled. Max smiled to himself, Rita always looked as if she had dressed in a hurry and left something behind. He swivelled the ice around in his glass and quietly watched from the sofa.

Antoinette sat on the club fender with her daughter Emily, who was the same age as Eddie and Ruth. She was a beautiful woman, slim and painted like a china doll with glossy red hair combed into sleek waves. She smoked through a long ebony holder, which balanced between elegant fingers dripping with shiny burgundy talons, always perfectly manicured. Her skin was luminous and damp with eau de cologne and rose water, her eyes a harder version of her mother's grey ones. She hated cats because their fur stuck to her clothes and because they smelt and she had no time for her sister's feathered friends either. 'I would rather sit in a field and watch cows than waste my time studying birds,' she once said. 'They fly, so what? So can George but I don't want him crashing about in my garden.' This of course made no sense, but Antoinette cared little for logic or for truth. She was a born liar and a show off. Her tidy little nose was a mystery to her sister who was sure that with every lie it would grow like Pinocchio's, and her ageless skin was the envy of many. Well aware of her beauty and the strength of her personality, she had brought up her daughter in her own image, in spite of the lengths to which poor Emily went in order to rebel. Emily was not blessed with either beauty or strength of character, but she was clever like her father, and kind. The only person capable of silencing Antoinette was, of course, her mother.

Maddie adored her aunt and longed to be exactly like her. 'Aunt Antoinette,' she cried when she saw her and rushed past her grandmother and cousin William, an arrogant twenty-year-old she didn't much like, to embrace her.

'Darling girl, you grow prettier every day,' enthused her aunt who saw the loveliness of her own features reflected in her niece. 'I've bought you some nail varnish and eyelashes I found in a charming little shop in Portobello Road. Just the thing for a girl like you.'

Rita felt her stomach cramp with anxiety for her aunt always patronised her. She represented everything that Antoinette despised: a love of nature and animals, an aversion to make-up, and a quiet, submissive nature that her aunt interpreted as weakness of character. If there was one thing Aunt Antoinette abhorred it was weakness.

'Hello, Rita,' she said tightly, pressing her cheek to her niece's but not even bothering to make the sound of a kiss. 'I hear George has left you again.' Rita nodded and mumbled something inaudible. Her obvious fear was irresistible to Antoinette who added in a low voice, 'I hope you're not hanging about for him like a lap dog. Men have no respect for doormats.'

Rita felt humiliation rise in her face and, as she went to sit next to Max, she heard her aunt turn to Emily and add in an intolerant tone that surely if he loved her he wouldn't have turned on his heel and left her again. Antoinette greeted her sister and Eddie, recoiling at the sight of Harvey like a vampire in the face of the cross. She let out an ugly yelp, more a gurgle than a cry, before shouting at the child to 'Take the ghastly winged rat outside and drown him before I throw you both into the pond!' Eddie, who had inherited her candour from her grandmother, retaliated in the same tone.

'It's a shame you're so big, Aunt Antoinette, because Harvey and I would like to throw *you* in the pond. That would see off Megagran's foxes, to be sure, *and* probably poison the water.' Antoinette gazed down at the precocious child in horror, took a long drag of her cigarette then replied in a strangled voice.

'Eddie, hasn't your mother told you how to speak to your elders and betters?'

'Yes, but you're not better, just older,' And she swivelled around, grabbing Emily by the wrist, and led her and Ruth out into the hall to play with the cats.

'I hear you got a letter from George,' said Max when Rita reached him. Rita smiled, though her eyes revealed the hurt she had just suffered at the hands of her aunt.

'He sent me this pendant,' she replied quietly, holding it out for him to see. His heart plummeted.

'It's lovely,' he said, but he felt sick with jealousy.

Hannah, noticing her daughter showing off her gift, turned to her mother.

'Do look, Mother. George sent Rita a pendant. It's a lovely silver dove. A symbol of love, happiness and wedded bliss. Isn't that delightful?'

'Charming,' enthused Mrs Megalith, hobbling over to take a better look. Antoinette followed her.

'Sweet,' she said. Then her scarlet lips extended into a wicked grin and she cocked her head on one side and said in a loud whisper for all the room to hear, 'Surely the action of an unfaithful man.'

Chapter Thirteen

Rita fled the room in tears, Max following her, leaving Hannah speechless with shock and Humphrey the colour of a ripe tomato.

'Was it absolutely necessary to be so wounding, Antoinette?' he said in a very quiet, steady voice. He wanted to remove the smug expression from her face with a healthy slap.

'Oh, come on Humphrey, where's your sense of humour?' she retorted, sighing melodramatically.

Mrs Megalith slowly removed her glasses and looked at her younger daughter with a dark and serious expression. Antoinette felt the hairs on the back of her neck bristle with uneasiness.

'There is nothing clever about wounding someone weaker than yourself. Pick your equal before you launch into battle. Now, apologise before I lock you in the pantry with every cat and bat in this house.'

Antoinette was thoroughly humiliated. Nursing her dented pride, she strode out of the room in search of Rita. But her niece had disappeared with Max, placing as much distance between herself and her aunt as possible.

'Here we are again,' said Rita, seated beside Max on his bed. 'Why is it I'm always crying on to your poor shoulder? Really, you deserve better.'

Max smiled, delighted to be given another opportunity for intimacy. 'Antoinette is a bully. Bullies are cowards. They prey on those weaker than themselves.'

'No, I'm the coward. I should have retaliated like Eddie.'

'You're not Eddie. You're lovely just the way you are.' Max lowered his eyes bashfully. Rita put her hand on his knee.

'That's so sweet,' she said in a soft voice. She hesitated a moment then swallowed hard. 'Tell me something, Max. You're a man.' Max straightened up, pleased that she considered him a man, not a boy. 'Do you think I've made a mistake letting George go away again without me?'

Max loved her too much to jeopardise their blossoming friendship by telling her the truth. That yes, she had made a terrible decision. That he believed, and hoped, that George would never come back.

'You have done a very brave thing. A coward wouldn't be so bold.' He took her hand in his. 'Trust him. Loving someone is all about trusting.'

'I do trust him,' she replied quickly, ashamed that she had voiced doubts. 'I miss him, that's all.'

Max longed to kiss her. He had imagined countless times what it would feel like and now, sitting so close to her, he realised how easy it would be to lean over and press his mouth to her lips. She had pretty lips, pale pink and perfect like the lips of a shell. Overcome by desire and encouraged by the compassionate expression in her eyes, he inclined his head and planted a lingering kiss on her cheek. Her skin was still damp from her tears and she smelt of violets. He felt her stiffen and pulled away. Anxious that he might have ruined the tenuous balance of their friendship, he said hastily, 'I feel you're like a sister to me. Perhaps I can be the brother you never had.' Rita's face relaxed into a smile and she bit her bottom lip shyly.

'Of course,' she replied. 'I've always wanted a brother.'

There was a long pause, during which Max felt the mortification of having so nearly declared himself singe his cheeks with shame. Rita cast her eyes about her until her gaze settled on a faded green book that sat on the small table by his bed. It was smaller than a hand and almost threadbare, its pages coming away from the binding.

'What an enchanting book,' she commented, relieved to change the subject.

He leaned over and picked it up. 'It belonged to my mother. It's a book of poetry.'

'May I have a look?'

'It's in German. A collection of her favourite poets.'

He handed it to her, wanting to add that the poems about love he now knew by heart. She opened it with care and ran her fingers over the yellowed paper that was thick and coarse like parchment. Rita wondered whether he could feel his mother reaching out to him through the pages and hear her voice, perhaps, whispering softly across the years to comfort him when he missed her. It was an unbearably romantic thought. She lifted her eyes and rested them on Max's sensitive face.

'Megagran says that your mother was once a famous actress. Was she very beautiful?'

'I think so.'

'I imagine you look a lot like her,' she said, handing back the book.

Max's mouth twitched and he shrugged. 'I don't know,' he replied, not wishing to conjure up his dead mother's face. It was better if he didn't focus his thoughts too intensely on his past. 'Are you ready to face your aunt?' he said instead.

'As ready as I'll ever be,' she chuckled. 'Come on, they'll be wondering what on earth has happened to us!'

Eddie scowled at her aunt all the way through lunch. Megagran had told her to put Harvey in the car but she had rebelled, stuffing him up her sleeve instead, where he could peek out every now and then and squeak at Antoinette.

Antoinette had apologised to Rita, laughing off her remark by insisting that it was nothing more than a joke. 'How would I know if he was unfaithful or not?' Rita knew she wasn't sincere and made sure she sat at the other end of the table with Max, William and her father. Humphrey had never liked his sister-in-law and admired David, her husband, for putting up with her. David was as elusive as the Scarlet Pimpernel and just as crafty, but then one would have to be, being married to Antoinette. He was rarely seen by anyone, including his wife. He paid the bills, enabled her to live a grand life, and kept a discreet mistress in a mansion flat in west London. What he did for MI5 was top secret, but it gave him the perfect excuse to shut Antoinette out of his life.

Megagran held court at the other end of the table, watching Antoinette with a weary look in her opaque grey eyes. She noticed Harvey, but said nothing, and she pitied Rita, who looked crestfallen in spite of the pretty dove from George that hung about her neck. She had a strange sense of foreboding. It curled up her spine like a cold eel, causing her to bristle with uneasiness. Something wasn't quite right about the dove. She chewed on her roast lamb and considered it. A symbol of love and all that, of course, but there was more to it. Wasn't the dove a symbol of forgiveness and peace, too? Now why would Rita need to forgive?

After lunch she took Rita to one side. 'What did George say in his letter?' she asked, placing her glasses on her nose in anticipation of being allowed to read it.

'I've left it at home,' Rita lied. Megagran frowned. It was no use lying to her grandmother. 'I was reading it on top of the cliff,' she whispered, afraid that someone might overhear her. 'And it was blown out of my hand by a gust of wind. I ran down to the beach to retrieve it but it floated into the sea, where it is now. Lost for ever.' Mrs Megalith nodded gravely.

'I see. That explains the pendant and the significance of the dove. Interesting,' she pondered darkly.

'What do you mean?'

'Absolute nonsense, I'm sure,' she said with a deep chuckle. 'Don't worry about losing the letter, dear. After all, there will be more, won't there? And Antoinette's a brute sometimes. We all have an ugly side to our nature; the trouble with Antoinette is that the balance is all wrong. It'll start showing on her face soon and then she'll change. She's far too vain not to and I shall be the first to tell her.'

'I'm reading a wonderful book at the moment,' Antoinette was saying to anyone who would listen. 'About the tsars of Russia. What a colourful history.' She ran her hand across the bindings of her mother's books squashed chaotically into old mahogany bookshelves. Antoinette considered herself something of an intellectual. 'Humphrey, what are you reading? One must always have a book on the go, don't you think? In my case, several. Depends on my mood. I do so enjoy reading the classics again and again. I loved *Anna Karenina*. Many women find *War and Peace* hard-going, but honestly I enjoyed that the most. But then I have always relished a challenge. If something is too easy I bore of it.'

Humphrey smoked a cigar and didn't bother to reply; Antoinette had no interest in what he was reading, only in boasting about herself.

'I love reading!' exclaimed Maddie, who had only read at school because she had been forced to. She decided that she would read *Anna Karenina*, whoever she was, because she wanted to be just like her aunt.

'Good girl, Maddie,' said Antoinette admiringly. 'There's nothing more undesirable than a stupid woman. You catch a man with your beauty but hold him with your mind. Make your mind rich, like mine, and you will marry well,' she advised. Humphrey rolled his eyes and looked at his watch.

'Hannah, we really should be getting back,' he said to his wife, who was sitting with Eddie, browsing through old family photograph albums.

'Do we have to?' she protested, enjoying the pictures of her childhood.

'I really think we should,' he repeated. 'Rita, Maddie, we're going home.'

Hannah recognised the impatience in his voice and dutifully closed the book. She stood up and followed him out into the hall where Megagran was on her hands and knees with Emily and Ruth, playing with the cats.

As Humphrey and his family were on the point of leaving, a loud shriek erupted from the drawing room. 'Good God, what's that?' he exclaimed, marching back into the house. Hannah, Rita and Maddie ran after him for the cry was that of a woman in mortal danger. However, the sight of Antoinette besieged by at least twenty cats was an amusing one for Humphrey and Rita who couldn't have thought of a more appropriate revenge themselves. 'Get the buggers off me!' she cried hysterically. They clawed at her nylons, jumped on her dress and one was astride the crown of her head, pawing her hair into a terrible mess. 'Mother!' she wailed, but there was nothing Mrs Megalith could do to stop them. Only Eddie knew why they had set upon her aunt and she wasn't telling.

'Eddie,' demanded her father, trying hard to contain his amusement. 'What did you do to those cats?'

'How do you know it was me?' she asked innocently, hanging up her coat, happy to be home. She wandered over to the kitchen cupboard and opened the biscuit tin.

'Because of the mischievous look on your face,' he replied.

'What did you do?' asked Rita, wishing that she had thought of it first.

'I didn't do anything,' she protested. 'How on earth could I control all those cats?'

'Exactly, the idea is preposterous, Humphrey,' said Hannah, taking the biscuit tin from her daughter. 'It's not tea time yet, dear.'

'Just one biscuit. I'm hungry. That lamb was disgusting.'

'Oh, all right,' she sighed. 'Just one then.' Eddie plunged her hand in and drew out three oatmeal biscuits with a large grin.

'Well, whatever happened to Antoinette, she thoroughly deserved it,' said Humphrey, taking the papers to the sitting room.

'I think you're all horried to Aunt Antoinette,' Maddie said sulkily, sticking out her bottom lip. 'I like her.'

'We all like her, dear. But she was unkind to Eddie and Rita.'

'No one likes Harvey!' Maddie argued to Eddie's fury.

'That's not true, is it Mummy? You like Harvey?'

'Of course I do. From a distance.'

'Rita's just oversensitive,' Maddie continued. Rita rolled her eyes and followed her father down the corridor and into the sitting room. Maddie stomped upstairs to reapply her lipstick and flick through her magazines. Hannah turned to Eddie.

'What did you do to those cats?' she asked in a quiet voice. Eddie narrowed her eyes and made sure that they were alone.

'All right, I'll tell you. As long as you don't sneak to Megagran.'

'I promise I won't.'

'I asked them to.'

Hannah screwed up her nose. 'You asked them to?' she repeated incredulously.

'Yes, I just spoke very clearly to the big black one. I think he's the king, you see.'

Hannah nodded slowly. 'I see.'

'He understood and immediately went to tell the others. Megagran always says that if one bothers to talk to animals telepathically they will understand. I was so cross with Aunt Antoinette, I tried it.'

'Well, it worked,' said Hannah, not knowing whether to believe her. She had grown up with a witch for a mother, but she couldn't quite reconcile herself to the fact that she might have one for a daughter.

'No one speaks ill of Harvey and gets away with it,' Eddie added menacingly. Hannah was taken aback, for when she spoke in that tone the colour of her eyes changed, just like Megagran's.

'Good God!' she exclaimed. 'I've bred a witch!'

Eddie's face crinkled into a wide smile. 'I'd love to be a witch then I could fly. Do you have a broomstick?'

'Not one that flies,' her mother replied, running a gentle hand down Eddie's hair.

'But can I try?'

'If you want. It's in the cupboard. Why don't you see if you can sweep the kitchen at the same time?'

Eddie shook her head and giggled. 'Nice try. It's flying or nothing,' she replied, skipping off to fetch it.

Maddie was irritated by Rita. She moped around like a lovesick puppy, walking up and down the bleak and windy beach, and refusing company. Aunt Antoinette was right. If George really loved her he wouldn't have left her again, not for a year. She doubted he would return. He would most probably fall in love with someone out there. Latin women were famous for their beauty. Rita was weak. She should have told George to marry her or else. There were plenty of other men around. Maddie could vouch for that.

Maddie was currently sleeping with two different men. One was the son of the local builder, Steve Eastwood. He was strong and muscular with thick blond hair and brown eyes as soft as suede. His hands were rough and calloused but he knew how to caress a woman without scratching her. He spoke with a strong country accent and his smile was wide and confident and deliciously boyish. Maddie enjoyed making love to him. In his arms she felt feminine and vulnerable. The other, Bertie Babbindon, was rich and grand but boring. With sleek black hair and a Jensen he considered himself something of a playboy, sent her flowers, gave her expensive gifts and kissed her like a wet afternoon on the beach.

Maddie had never been in love. She didn't understand her sister's pining for George. She only understood lust. Until Harry Weaver arrived in Frognal Point.

'Who's Harry Weaver?' Maddie asked her mother, screwing up her pretty nose. 'Do we have to stick around for lunch? I was going to spend the day with Bertie.'

Hannah stiffened. She didn't much like Bertie Babbindon. He was arrogant, selfish and flash at a time when ostentatious wealth was considered tasteless. He had done nothing to help with the war effort, hiding away at the family schloss in Switzerland until it was safely over. He had probably learned German just in case the Allies lost. She looked out of the kitchen window at the thin sprinkling of snow that glittered in the early morning sunlight. A couple of shiny cock pheasants strode across the lawn, scratching the snow with their claws. They had probably flown over from Elvestree where Megagran put corn out for them all winter.

'I would very much like you all to be here. He's a charming man and knows no one. He's bought that dear little white house on Bray Cove.'

'What does he do?' asked Maddie. She caught Rita's eye and pulled a face.

'He's a writer.'

'What's he had published?'

'Oh, I don't know. But he's a bird-watcher. That's how I met him.'

'How boring!' Maddie sighed. 'As Aunt Antoinette would say, birds, what's the point of them?'

'Is he married?' Rita asked.

'Divorced. I just think it would be nice if we adopted him. Poor thing, he's all alone in the world.'

Maddie slouched in the armchair and sulked. Sundays were just like every other day for her, whereas Rita enjoyed having the day to herself. It had been a couple of weeks since she had lost George's letter to the sea, since Aunt Antoinette had bullied her, since Max had kissed her on the cheek. She had written a four-page letter to George, telling him about Antoinette and the cats, Eddie's unnatural interest in witchcraft, her new job at the library in town and her father's campaign to prevent a site of virgin land, not far from Frognal Point, being destroyed by developers. In her large flowery handwriting she reminded him of the summer, those balmy evenings up on the cliff watching the gulls, and their secret trysts in the cave. She confessed that she missed him more than she could express in words. She adored the pendant and the diamond ring, which she looked at every day, and remembered that he loved her. She would wear both on her wedding day. She had asked to borrow Megagran's dress, by the way, and her mother was going to take it in for her. Not that it needed much altering – her grandmother had been true to her word – and the dress was so much more beautiful than she had imagined, with embroidered vines and pearls and lace. She sealed the letter with her tears and sent it with love. She hoped it would have the power to keep him faithful.

Bertie's Jensen arrived at ten, scattering a trio of pigeons fighting over a crust of bread on the gravel. Maddie agreed to go for a drive with him as long as he got her back by lunchtime.

'Mummy wants me to meet an old bird watcher,' she

explained, rolling her cool blue eyes and flicking her hair off her shoulder. 'Says he doesn't know anyone. That's no surprise; bird-watchers are a lonely bunch. He's a writer, apparently, but has never had anything published so he can't be very good.' Bertie was disappointed. He had hoped to take her into Exeter for lunch.

When Harry Weaver arrived at the house in a rusty old banger, Maddie was being kissed and pawed by Bertie in the back of his Jensen in a lay-by five miles outside Frognal Point. Hannah was furious. At least Rita and Eddie hadn't let her down. Humphrey shook Harry's hand firmly as if he were an old friend. Harry had that effect on people. He was woolly, affable and ungainly with an easy, natural charm. He smiled and his rugged face folded into lines and creases. He looked weather-beaten, as if he'd been exposed to the elements. His hair was greying at the sides and receding at the front but it rebelled on top and stuck up in triumphant tufts. His eyes were a soft grey fanned by long, dark brown lashes, the envy of many a woman to whom nature had not been so generous.

Hannah hung up his coat, noticing at once that it was moth-eaten and thinning at the elbows, and led him into the sitting room where Eddie was playing with Harvey and Rita was sitting in front of the fire reading the papers. 'These are two of my daughters,' she said, her voice thick with pride. 'Eddie and her bat Harvey, I'm afraid they're inseparable, and Rita, whose fiancé is in the Argentine. He was in the RAF, you know.'

Harry shook their hands, smiling diffidently. Rita warmed to him immediately. He had that quality so often found in men who have been through life's mangle that made women want to mother him.

'Ah, a Microbat,' he said, extending his hand and stroking the animal's furry black head with his forefinger. 'Shouldn't he be hibernating?'

Eddie's eyes sparkled. No one had ever taken such an interest in Harvey. 'He doesn't hibernate.'

'Well, most bats hibernate during the winter months. I suppose your sleeve is so nice and snug he wants to be awake to enjoy it. What do you feed him?'

'In the summertime he flies about and catches his own insects. But there aren't any now so I give him berries and bread.'

'Try a little fish,' Harry suggested. 'They love fish.'

'Oh, I will,' she enthused, her face extending into a wide smile. Harry sat down on the sofa and chuckled as Eddie placed herself beside him, so close they were pressed together, leaving half the sofa unoccupied.

'Don't suffocate our poor guest,' said Humphrey in amusement. 'I'm afraid you've made a new friend,' he added to Harry. 'Or should I say two new friends!'

'Bats are fascinating creatures. They're the only mammals that fly and are more closely related to humans than mice. Look at their hands, they have four fingers and a thumb, forearms, elbows and upper arms.' He turned to Eddie. 'Their scientific name is in fact *Chiroptera* which means "hand wing". It's thanks to bats that night-blooming flowers are pollinated and they're nature's best insect control. I've always enjoyed bats.'

Eddie sat gazing up at him with eyes full of love. 'My Aunt Antoinette hates Harvey. He was so hurt when she said she would throw him in the pond,' she said, blinking up at him. He put his arm around her and patted her gently.

'You must forgive her, she was just frightened of him. She doesn't know him like you do.'

At that moment a horn tooted outside. Hannah looked at her watch. *About time too*! she thought. They all looked at the door in anticipation.

'That will be our other daughter, Maddie,' she said to Harry. 'She's been out all morning with a friend.'

Humphrey raised his eyebrows at his wife, for he didn't much like Bertie either, although the boy and Maddie had an awful lot in common.

Maddie strode into the sitting room. She'd much prefer to be lunching in Exeter. Already scowling, she hovered by the door with her arms crossed defensively in front of her. 'Sorry I'm so late,' she said.

'That's all right, my dear. Come and meet Harry Weaver. Harry is an expert on bats.'

'Not an expert. Just curious,' he replied, standing up to greet Maddie.

He was tall and lean like Trees but hunched a little as if uncomfortable with his stature. Maddie stared at him in wonder. To her embarrassment she felt her face burn and her heart accelerate. She shook his hand, which was soft and warm like dough, and was aware that an uncharacteristic grin, which she was quite unable to control, tickled the corners of her mouth. His gentle eyes settled on her, took in her immaculately painted face and sunset-coloured hair and felt, as she did, the invisible force of attraction vibrate between them like the quivering strings of a violin. He smiled back and shook his head slowly, awed by the unexpected allure of this young woman. Maddie blinked out of her daze and hastened to a chair where she was relieved to be able to rest her trembling legs. Everyone could feel the change in the air, subconsciously hearing the music of love that danced about the room, but no one was more surprised than Maddie. She lifted her eyes to look at him again and noticed, to her embarrassment, that he was still watching her, as if she were a rare and lovely bird.

Chapter Fourteen

George rode out across the plains, squinting in the sunlight and blinking away the mist of dust kicked up from Jose Antonio's horse galloping furiously in front of him. But all he could think about was Susan. What strange coincidence was at play? Could some fortuitous twist of fortune have made their paths cross once again? Her face surfaced in his mind and this time he didn't will it away but allowed his inner vision to dwell on it, hoping with all his heart that he had understood his uncle correctly, that the 'token' his aunt had brought back from Buenos Aires was Susan.

The afternoon seemed interminable. He was too distracted to be of any use on the farm. The gauchos teased him, certain that a woman was to blame for scrambling his brain. They gesticulated to him with their hands, suggesting all sorts of unspeakable sexual acts then laughed raucously, nudging each other in amusement. He was a handsome man; it was unthinkable that he wasn't taking advantage of the whores in Jesús Maria. Finally Jose Antonio dismissed him.

'Go and entertain the women,' he said, grinning at his newphew. 'The sun has obviously penetrated your skull.'

George protested. He didn't want the gauchos to think him faint-hearted.

'I'm a little tired,' he explained. 'But nothing I can't handle.' If they only knew what he had been up against in the skies over Britain! His uncle slapped him on the back and winked at him affectionately.

'There's nothing more for you to do today, gringo. La Gorda will be happy to see you. Have tea, a swim, a rest. Take the afternoon off. You deserve it.'

George knew he didn't deserve it at all, but did as he was told. He knew better than to argue with Jose Antonio.

He turned his horse around and galloped back to the *puesto*. He hastily removed the tack and brushed his horse down before tying him up in the shade with a bucket of water. His legs felt weak as if he had borrowed them from someone else and was having trouble getting used to them. As he walked unsteadily through the trees to the house he prayed that it was Susan and not some other woman with a scarred face who had come to stay at *Las Dos Vizcachas*.

As the house came into view he was able to make out two women sitting on the veranda taking tea. He squinted to see them better. The woman facing him was without doubt his aunt. Her large form was unmistakable. She sat holding a teacup with her arms on the table, her solid bosom resting heavily on the tablecloth. The other was at an angle, talking to her. Her hair, tied into a neat chignon at the nape of a long and elegant neck, was pale yellow, almost white, and shone with health. With graceful fingers she curled a stray wisp around her ear then stroked the skin of her neck absent-mindedly. He felt his heart stumble. It was Susan. It couldn't be anyone else. As he got nearer he saw that she was wearing a white dress imprinted with blue flowers and he was sure he could smell lily of the valley, carried above the scents of the park on a warm breeze. He wondered whether he should go and change first – he imagined he looked grubby with dust and smelt of sweat and horses – but, before he could decide, his aunt spotted him and began to wave at him vigorously. He had no choice but to walk over.

Susan turned around and smiled at him. She extended her hand and greeted him formally. 'Hello,' she said in a polite voice. 'It's a pleasure to meet you. Your aunt has told me so much about you.' George understood at once that she was pretending they had never met. He took her hand and held it for a little longer than was necessary. He gazed into her pale eyes, silently questioning her. But she looked away and said to Agatha, 'He's obviously settled in well, one could almost mistake him for a gaucho.'

'My husband is delighted with him. A quick learner with a good sense of humour. Jose Antonio is very hard to please.' George was irritated that they were discussing him as if he wasn't there. He felt gauche standing like that while they appraised him. His excitement drained away, leaving an aching disappointment.

'How was your trip, Aunt Agatha?' he asked, trying his best to act casually, as if Susan meant nothing to him.

'You won't believe the difference in Dolores. She's been transformed into a placid human being. She even smiles. In all the time I've lived here I have not once seen her smile.'

'She sounds like she's making up for lost time,' said Susan.

'Well, she's got a lot of making up to do!' Agatha laughed. 'I found Susan languishing in the heat in Buenos Aires. Thought she would enjoy spending Christmas with us. More the merrier and all that.'

'It really is stifling in the city in December,' Susan agreed. 'It's lovely up here.' George noticed that Susan didn't really look at him. Her eyes might settle on him every now and again as they conversed but they seemed not to see him.

'George has learned Spanish,' said Agatha. 'He learned much faster than I imagined he would.'

'Enthusiasm is the best incentive,' said Susan. 'Does he ride like a gaucho too?'

'I think he even castrates like a gaucho!' Agatha replied with a snort.

George felt the irritation rise in his chest and clenched his fists. Defeated he put his hat back on.

'Please excuse me, I would like to clean up,' he said, resting his eyes on Susan once again. She smiled up at him, but her smile was remote as if she had forgotten their intimacy on the *Fortuna*.

'Have a swim, George,' Agatha suggested. 'Then come and join us for tea.'

George closed the door to his bedroom and stood leaning against the wall, breathing through his nostrils like a furious bull. Once again she had treated him like a little boy. He was maddened by her and frustrated. If his aunt hadn't been there he would have confronted her. What was she doing at *Las Dos Vizcachas*? If she hadn't come for him, why had she come? He didn't believe for one moment that it was a coincidence. She knew he was there and had been expecting him, for her reaction was flawless. As cool and impenetrable as she had been the first time they met on the deck of the ship.

He scrambled out of his trousers and shirt, leaving them on the tiled floor in a pile of dust for Agustina to pick up. He wrapped a towel around his waist, grabbed his packet of cigarettes and strode back up the corridor and out of the back door to the pool. He was so angry he didn't notice the light clamour of birds, the lucid sunspots that danced about on the grass at his feet, or the intoxicating scent of gardenia. At the edge of the pool he shed his towel and stood a moment contemplating the limpid water. The afternoon sun bathed his skin, now brown like the gauchos', and caught on the newly formed muscles that swelled beneath his flesh. He'd show her how much of a man he was.

He dived naked into the water, which was deliciously refreshing against his warm skin. It seemed to wash away all his fury. He swam energetically up and down, kicking with his feet, splashing the water into the air. After a while he draped himself over the edge, gazing across the park. He was reluctant to return to the veranda. If his aunt were there he wouldn't be able to talk to Susan. The idea of pretending they had never met now seemed tiresome. He decided to spend the evening in the pool, that way he would avoid tea altogether. Perhaps he would have a chance to talk to her alone before dinner.

He pushed himself off the edge and began to swim lengths again. He did backstroke, front crawl, breaststroke and one or two entirely underwater. He was a beautiful swimmer and recalled for a moment those summer evenings in the sea at Frognal Point. Finally, exhausted, he paused at one end and raised his eyes. To his surprise Susan was sitting patiently on the bench watching him. She smiled when he looked at her. This time her smile was warm and full of affection. He swam slowly to the other end and rested his arms on the tiles in front of her.

'How long have you been here?' he asked.

'For some time,' she replied, amused. 'I knew you were a fine swimmer. I was right not to tell you my secrets.'

'What have you done with Aunt Agatha?'

'Dolores was calling for her. I thought I would take a walk. I could hear your splashing from the other side of the park.'

'Good.' He grinned up at her. His crooked grin that had haunted her dreams ever since she had left him on the *Fortuna*. 'Will you throw me my towel?'

She stood up and held it out to him, unable to tear her eyes away as he climbed naked up the steps. His body was honey-brown and perfectly proportioned and toned as she had imagined it would be. He took the towel and wrapped it around his waist, pushing his curly hair off his forehead with his hand.

They sat on the bench and George lit a cigarette. He offered her one but she declined.

'I think I have some explaining to do,' she ventured.

'Yes, you do,' he replied. She tilted her head and frowned.

'I'm sorry I was so cold. I was nervous.' George had thought her incapable of feeling nervous. She was always so composed and in control. 'I met your aunt at a dinner party. She spoke about you. I'm afraid I engineered the whole thing.' She turned and looked at him with the same sad eyes that had gazed out across the ocean and said in a quiet voice, 'I haven't stopped thinking about you since we parted.' George's spirits lifted. He felt his whole body tremble, but this time with joy.

'I haven't been able to stop thinking about you, either,' he replied. 'I didn't think I would ever see you again.' She chuckled, and touched his arm with nervous fingers.

'Neither did I. But fate interceded.' He put his hand on hers and squeezed it.

'I'm so glad you're here, Susan.' She visibly relaxed as if she had needed confirmation that he still wanted her.

'I think your aunt took pity on me when she saw my face. It has its advantages, you know.'

'I like your scar because it's you,' he said and watched as she fingered it with her other hand. 'To me, you're more beautiful because of it.' She turned her eyes away and blinked uncomfortably.

'If you're lucky your scars are on the inside,' she said with a sigh. 'Still, it got me here with you so I'm grateful.'

'So we're pretending to Agatha and Jose Antonio that we've never met?' She blushed.

'I know it's absurd but I didn't know what to do. By the time your aunt asked me up here I had feigned ignorance about you. It was then too late to tell her the truth. Besides, perhaps she would have suspected I had ulterior motives and not invited me.'

'You're a better actress than I am,' he said with a smile.

'Only when my future depends on it.'

He looked at her steadily for a long moment. She turned and settled her eyes on his. He felt a sudden urge to trace his fingers down her scar but Agatha's loud, booming voice resounded across the park, causing them both to sit up with a start.

'George! Susan! Your tea's getting cold!'

They stood up and George stubbed his cigarette into the grass and threw it beneath the bushes. 'Act one, scene one,' he said, grinning happily and taking her hand. They walked towards the house but George, overcome with impatience, suddenly pulled her behind a tree and kissed her ardently on her lips. She giggled like a young girl and wound her arms around his neck, pressing her body against his. She kissed him back, without inhibition. 'That will keep me going, but only for an hour or so!' he said, stroking her smooth cheek. She put her hand against his chest and gazed up at him with eyes that no longer looked sad.

George had a quick bath and changed into clean clothes, washed and pressed by Agustina. When he reached the terrace Susan was already there, talking with Jose Antonio, Agatha and the two children, recently returned from school. 'Gringo, have you met Susan?' Jose Antonio asked, gesticulating towards her. She sat beside him like a fragile bird in the shadow of a bear.

'Yes, we've met,' she replied, her eyes twinkling at George. 'I found him in the swimming pool.'

'I do hope you were wearing something, George,' said Agatha. 'Like Jose Antonio, George thinks nothing of throwing himself into the water naked. Even I've found myself blushing once or twice.'

'Don't worry, Agatha, he was very proper,' said Susan, picking up her teacup and taking a sip.

'So what brings you to the Argentine?' asked Jose Antonio,

slicing off a large piece of cheese, which he ate with *membrillo* on a dry biscuit. 'There's no war in America.'

'I was in England, actually,' she replied coolly. 'I lived here as a child. My father was a diplomat.'

'Are you staying long?'

'I don't know. I have no plans.'

Jose Antonio frowned. There was something very mysterious about her. She answered in short sentences in a tone that suggested she was uncomfortable talking about herself. He longed to know how she was so horribly scarred but knew it would be impolite to ask. He would get Agatha to ask her later.

'She was suffocating in the city. I thought a bit of country air would do her good,' said Agatha. 'Nothing like life on a farm. You can take her riding, George, or into Jesús Maria. If you're interested in old colonial churches, Susan, there was once a thriving Jesuit culture here.'

'Oh, I know,' Susan replied enthusiastically, happy to change the subject. 'My father was very interested in history and took us up here as children. We visited Santa Catalina, Las Teresas, Alta Gracia, Colonia Caroya, Estancia La Candelaria. But I would love to go and see them again. I was very small and don't remember a great deal.' She turned to Jose Antonio. 'Can you spare George?' He threw his head back and laughed boisterously.

'I think the gauchos will manage without him!' Then he raised his teacup to George. 'What do you think, gringo?'

'I'd like to see those places myself. Since I arrived I haven't had a chance to be a tourist.'

'Working you too hard, eh?'

'You must go into the sierras,' suggested Agatha.

'Hay pumas en las sierras,' said Tonito, making his hands like claws and growling.

'If there are pumas, George will be there to save me

from them,' Susan replied in perfect Spanish. George was impressed.

'Gringo, you had better practise your Spanish. Susan speaks like a native,' said Jose Antonio.

'I do have the advantage,' she replied tactfully. 'We lived all over.'

'Then you speak Italian and French too?' Agatha asked enthusiastically. Susan nodded. 'How lucky you are.'

'I should go and check on Dolores,' said Agatha, getting up. 'Jose Antonio, why don't you come with me?'

'If she shouts at me I'm sending her straight back to Buenos Aires,' he replied in a gruff voice, following her into the house. Once inside he took his wife's arm, looked behind him to check that they were alone then hissed in Spanish, 'What the devil happened to her face?'

Agatha shook her head. 'She wouldn't tell me.'

'But you asked?' He raised the palms of his hands to the sky.

'Of course, I asked. What do you think I am? I'm as curious as you. I felt sorry for her. She looked so sad. I think she's alone in Buenos Aires. I liked her. We talked all the way up in the car and yet, as much as I tried, she gave nothing away.'

'Was she married?'

'Why do you ask?'

'She has that wounded look in her eyes.'

'Not as far as I know. She has no ring.'

'That means nothing. Why has she come out here all alone? Doesn't it strike you as odd?'

'Not if she grew up here. Besides, she's an independent woman with a very strong character. Very American. She's got money. I don't think she's in need of protection.'

Jose Antonio narrowed his eyes. 'Don't be fooled by what is on the outside. Still waters run deep.'

'Maybe, but she doesn't want to talk about it.'

'I put money on a man. It's either a man or a lion and I lay my bets on the former.'

Agatha chuckled. 'We will probably never know.' She sighed and folded her arms. 'What a shame. She would be a beautiful woman. She's young too. She should be married with small children.'

'She's come to the wrong place if she is looking for a husband. What Latin man would marry her with a face like that?'

'Jose Antonio, may the devil strike you down,' Agatha gasped, appalled. But she knew he was right. The men she knew were all much too obsessed with physical perfection.

'Perhaps she doesn't want a husband.'

'Don't believe it, Gorda, every woman wants a husband.'

Agatha shook her head and marched through the hall and up the stairs to where Dolores sat in bed in a baby-pink nightdress, waited on by Carlos and Agustina. When she saw Jose Antonio she smiled coyly, the smile of a flirtatious young girl.

'May God's blessings rain down upon you,' she said in a velvet voice.

'I am glad to see that you are well again,' Jose Antonio replied politely. He noticed that she wore her grey hair down over her shoulders and thought how grotesque she looked in pink frills with her wrinkled old skin spilling over the lace collar. She smiled at him, a toothless smile full of gratitude and affection.

'I remember when you were a little boy,' she began. Agatha looked at her husband and raised her eyebrows. 'You were a dear little thing. Not the big man you are now. How proud your father must be of you.' Jose Antonio didn't want to remind her that his father had run off with a girl half his age and settled down south in Patagonia. 'He would have done what you did. God rain his blessings down on him too.'

'You are being well looked after?' he asked, edging back out of the room.

'La señora is a generous-spirited woman. I knew that from the first moment I saw her. When you invited her to *Las Dos Vizcachas* to meet your family.' She sighed with nostalgia. 'May God rain his blessings down on her too!' She smiled again and her eyes filled with tears. 'Mama and Ernesto are watching over me, señor. I know because without their warning I would have died. What would you and la señora have done without me? God be praised.'

'God be praised,' said Jose Antonio drily, stepping out of the room and down the stairs as fast as his long legs could carry him.

They had dinner in the courtyard, beside the popping red tree. The food wasn't as good as Dolores', which was a shame because Jose Antonio was now unsure about employing her.

'She's crazy,' he said, shaking his head. 'I could cope with her better before.'

'At least she doesn't mope about in that ghastly black all the time,' said Agatha.

'Baby-pink on a woman of her age is monstrous!' Jose Antonio exclaimed in distaste. 'Let's face it, Gorda, she's a hag who has suddenly discovered her dried-up sexuality. It is too late to revive it!'

He laughed boisterously at his own joke. The thought of Dolores' sexuality put George off his food. It wasn't until later, when the children and their parents had gone to bed, that George and Susan found themselves alone.

They sat on the swing chair on the veranda, holding hands in the darkness, watching the flickering candle in the hurricane lamp attracting moths and flies. The gentle clicking of crickets rang out across the park and a large, luminous moon lit the plains in a pale green light. They had retained their glasses of wine and George was smoking. Both of them felt the night was enchanted and that they were lucky to be there. With their memories of home temporarily forgotten they only had eyes for each other.

'I'm thirty years old,' she said, staring out in front of her. 'I had a right to call you a boy.'

George blew smoke into the humid air. 'You don't look thirty,' he said truthfully.

'I felt like forty until I met you.'

'What does age matter? I'm twenty-three now. My birthday passed without a murmur.'

'That's what happens when you travel, those at home forget you.' George suddenly thought of Rita and hoped that she would be able to forget him. Somehow he doubted she would. But he dismissed the thought. He didn't want to ruin this moment with Susan.

'When is your birthday?' he asked.

She laughed softly. 'March the twentieth. I'm Aries.'

'What does that mean?'

'I don't know. I'm not really into that sort of thing. I can tell you what I am without consulting the stars.'

'So what are you?'

'In love with you, George. Very much in love with you.'

George was once again surprised by her directness. Having been so cagey on the boat her candour was disarming. He put his arm around her and drew her to him.

'I have dreamed of hearing you say those words. I never thought I would. What changed?'

She sat in silence for a while, deliberating how to answer his question. He was longing to ask her about her scar, he knew there was more to it than simply a slice of violence through her skin. He knew she would satisfy his curiosity when she was ready and not a moment before.

'I was confused, George,' she replied carefully. 'I didn't expect to fall in love. I kept myself to myself deliberately. I needed time alone.' He kissed her temple and breathed in the scent of her hair.

'I didn't expect to fall in love, either,' he said, enjoying holding her so close, scarcely able to believe that she was really there, in his arms. 'I also needed time alone, that's why I came out here in the first place.'

'Oh dear. We've really messed it up for each other, haven't we?'

'No. We've made it better. You don't look so sad any more.'

'I only realised when it was too late that I had met someone special. I thought I had lost you. I've been given a second chance and I don't want to blow it.'

'You won't blow it, Susan. I won't let you.' He kissed her tenderly, sensing that she had been deeply hurt by someone and not wanting to frighten her.

After a while he pulled away and held her face in his hands. He gazed into her eyes, searching for the hidden truth. They glinted in the light of the candle like impenetrable spheres of glass. He frowned at her in bewilderment, then slowly moved his right hand towards her scar. At first she flinched. No one had ever touched her there, not since the doctors had stitched her up. Her eyes suddenly looked fearful and she recoiled like a startled swan. But he shook his head and smiled at her encouragingly, with compassion, and she became still and allowed his fingers to gently trace the bumpy surface of a wound that had only healed on the outside. The skin was soft and smooth but lined with scar tissue like a railway track. He pulled her face towards him and kissed her there, tasting the salt of her tears as she blinked away emotions that had lain unexpressed for almost two years.

'Who did this to you?' he asked, cradling her against his chest. 'What bastard did this?'

But Susan was unable to reply. Not yet.

Chapter Fifteen

Susan lay in bed, staring out into the darkness. It was quiet, but for the crickets and a dog who barked somewhere, far away in the distance. The room smelt heavily of gardenia and cut grass, smells that since childhood she had always associated with the Argentine. The sheets were soft, the bed comfortable and the darkness cool and soothing, a familiar friend, for during the year after her disfigurement she had hidden in it as much as possible. She was acutely aware that George was in the room next door and strained her ears for a sound to confirm his presence there. The closing of a door, the running of a tap. But the walls were thick and she heard nothing. She wanted to climb into bed with George and wrap herself in his strength and confidence: she knew the only way to rid herself of her past was to create new memories, forged out of love. She loved George. She had loved him from the moment she had left the *Fortuna* knowing that she had let someone very special slip through her fingers. But she hadn't trusted him. For how could she trust anyone to love her now?

Something light and winged fluttered in her stomach as she recalled the moment he touched her scar. She put her hand up to her face and felt the wound, trying to convince herself that it wasn't so grotesque, it wasn't so big, that George really had kissed her there. It had been an unimaginable moment. A sudden stepping out into sunlight after months and months of shadows. She had been right to come. She had been right to trust him.

To escape her recent past she recalled her childhood. When she concentrated she could still remember her mother's smell. Sweet like bluebells in springtime. She could still remember what it felt like to be embraced so totally, pressed so tightly against her body, wrapped in her love. She was used to being adored. She was beautiful, flawless, blessed. She had dazzled wherever she went, from the parties in Washington to the races in Paris, her loveliness had been celebrated. Perhaps she had been too arrogant; perhaps this scar was a punishment for narcissism. She was now used to the stares. The whispered comments and the small children pointing or laughing at her.

Why George had seen beyond the scar, she didn't know. Why, when so many other men had recoiled in horror, did George run his fingers down it and kiss her there? With those thoughts she drifted into an untroubled sleep. The first in many months. And when she awoke the sky was clear and blue and full of brightness.

George was already beneath the veranda having breakfast with Agatha and the children. Jose Antonio had risen early to ride out with the gauchos. For him the farm wasn't work, it was a way of life. He liked to use his hands, feel the horse beneath him, gallop across the plains rounding up the herds of cows. The sun cracked his skin and the palms of his hands grew rough and calloused, but he felt part of the land and the land was where he belonged. If he weren't the boss he'd be just as happy as a gaucho. He could even play the guitar like one but Agatha hated it when he sang. Said he sounded like a strangled bull.

When George saw Susan his face lit up. She was wearing a pair of beige slacks and an open-necked white shirt with short sleeves. She looked refreshed and happy.

'How did you sleep, Susan?' Agatha took great pride in the comfort of her guest bedrooms. Susan smiled and sat down next to George.

'Very well, thank you. What a lovely room it is,' she replied, turning to look at George. He pulled a lopsided grin and his eyes twinkled, taking pleasure from their secret. The children seemed to pick up on the invisible vibrations that quivered between them for they wriggled in their chairs and giggled behind their hands.

'The perfect day to go to Santa Catalina,' said Agatha, referring to the old colonial Jesuit church a few kilometres outside Jesús Maria. 'Take the truck, George, and a picnic. Spend the day there. Make the most of it.' She picked up the little silver bell and rang it vigorously. A few moments later Agustina hurried out.

'*Si señora?*' she asked, rubbing her hands together in a gesture of servitude. Agatha instructed her to make a picnic for two, then dismissed her with a wave. As she retreated inside, Carlos loomed out of the shadows holding a letter. He whispered something to Agustina then handed it to her. 'Señora,' she said in a meek voice, stepping onto the terrace again. 'Here is a letter for Señor George.'

'Ah, George,' Agatha exclaimed jovially. 'News from home. But not from Faye.' She studied the handwriting as George felt the shame burn his cheeks. 'A young woman, no doubt. Must be Rita.' Susan's face blanched and she turned enquiringly to George. 'George has a fiancée in England,' Agatha continued, oblivious of the discomfort she was causing. 'I'm afraid I'm not putting any money on the marriage actually happening. He'll have given his heart to someone else by the time the year is out, mark my words.' Susan disguised her concern with a tight smile. Agatha handed him the letter.

'I'll read it later,' he mumbled, tucking it into the pocket of his shirt. He caught Susan's eye and tried to reassure her by shaking his head. To his surprise she didn't look hurt as he had expected.

'Do tell me all the news though,' said Agatha. 'I'm longing

to know how they are.' Then she turned to Pia and Tonito and said in Spanish. 'Think of all those poor children in England next time you decide you don't want to eat your lunch. They could do with a few beef steaks, I can tell you.'

Pia and Tonito screwed up their noses. They were tired of being told of hungry English children. Not having enough to eat was beyond their comprehension.

The letter was quickly passed over and they resumed their conversation about the Jesuits of Santa Catalina. The colour returned to Susan's cheeks and George breathed easily again. He hadn't wanted to tell her about Rita. He had decided to sort it out in his own good time in the kindest possible way. After all, there was no need for Susan to know. As far as he was concerned, Rita was the other side of the world, part of a past life that bore no relation to the present. A life that he had chosen to leave behind. Susan was his future. He felt sorry for Rita. But she was young, she would find someone else.

Carlos put the picnic basket in the back of the truck and Susan appeared at the door with a sunhat on her head and a thick book in her hand. George climbed in at the wheel and revved up the engine. They drove in silence up the drive, beneath the avenue of lofty plane trees, and out onto the dirt road that led to Jesús Maria.

'I have some explaining to do,' he began. Susan put her hand on his knee and smiled at him in understanding.

'Now isn't the time, George. Let's get to Santa Catalina and spread out the blanket in the shade of some big tree. Then you can tell me about Rita.'

'It isn't what you think,' he began.

'It never is,' she replied drily with a slow shake of her head. He chuckled, feeling foolish.

'You have an answer for everything,' he said. 'The day I strike you dumb I will know I've got the upper hand.'

'I'm an American woman. We're taught to answer back.'

'They taught you too well. What do you think of Aunt Agatha?' he asked, changing the subject. Now it was her turn to chuckle.

'What an extraordinary couple they are. She's short, stout and rather fierce in a very English way. I imagine she would make a formidable headmistress in one of those cold English boarding schools of yours. He's coarse and rough and bombastic, but not without charm. He's got a mischievous twinkle in his eye and a good sense of humour, though I wouldn't want to cross him. I wouldn't want to cross either of them.'

'They're unlikely, aren't they?'

'As a couple, yes. But he's probably got a beautiful mistress tucked away somewhere. He's Latin after all.'

'Not like us Englishmen.'

She glanced at him sidelong. 'I should hope not.'

The route to Santa Catalina was no more than a dirt road that rose and fell as it cut across undulating plains and thick woodland. The snow-capped sierras soared out of the mists on the horizon to touch the sky with their jagged peaks, and George could imagine the condors riding the winds in search of prey. It was already hot and they drove with the windows down, taking in the scenery, happy to be there in this remote place where only the most persistent memory could find them. The church of Santa Catalina stood proud and magnificent, the two bell towers and dome rising high above the ancient trees that gave it shade. There seemed to be no one else there. It was peaceful and quiet, almost eerie. They could very well have stepped back across the ages to the eighteenth century when it was built by the Jesuits in the flamboyant style of German baroque. The building hadn't changed and neither had the air it breathed.

George parked the truck in the shade and walked around to open the door for Susan. She left her book on the seat and stepped out into the sunshine. George took her hand

and helped her down then lifted the picnic basket and blanket from the back. They found a cool spot beneath a cluster of plane trees not far from the walls of the church and spread the blanket on the ground. A couple of doves settled nearby, eager to see what delights lay in the basket and determined to be the first to seize upon any crumbs.

Susan leaned against the trunk of the tree and sighed happily as she surveyed the surroundings. 'Oh, it's so pretty here,' she said with a smile. 'It's peaceful. Churches always give off an unearthly serenity, don't you think?'

'They never change, we do and the cities we build around them. They're timeless and that in itself gives them a certain poise.' George lay on his side, propping up his head with his elbow, barely able to believe that the woman he thought he had lost for ever was sitting with him now, as naturally as if they had known each other a lifetime.

'Are you going to read your letter now?' she asked coolly. George looked up at her and his brow furrowed.

'I wish she hadn't sent it,' he said with a sigh. 'I wish it wasn't full of her hopes and dreams, all of which rely on me.'

'Tell me about her. She's the reason you needed time alone, isn't she?'

'I'm sorry I didn't tell you before,' he began, but Susan simply silenced him with a soft laugh.

'You owe me nothing, George. Besides, if you were intending to return to England to marry her you wouldn't have declared yourself to me, nor would you have looked so forlorn on the boat. In fact, if you were in love with her, you wouldn't have left her in the first place.'

'You're right on every count, Susan. I'm a cad.' He sighed and his face seemed to sag with misery. Susan shuffled across the rug to lie next to him, resting her head on her elbow as he did. She touched his forearm tenderly.

'Tell me about her, then let me decide if you're a cad.'

So George told her everything. 'You see, I'm a cad because it would have been kinder to have finished it there and then. This is worse. She's in England pining for a man who doesn't want her.'

'But you do care, George. I don't think a cad is capable of caring.' George looked into her eyes and was grateful for her compassion and understanding.

'I do care for Rita. You can't love someone all your life and then turn it off like a tap. I love her like a sister. I just don't want to marry her.'

'So what are you going to do?'

'I'll have to write and tell her.'

'Would you mind if I give you a bit of advice?'

'I would welcome it.'

'Don't tell her about me, George. That will hurt her more. Tell her what you have just told me. You can't make an omelette without breaking eggs, George. This is going to cause her pain whichever way you put it. But it will make the blow less hard if you tell her that you still love her but not enough to marry her.'

George chuckled bitterly. 'I've been putting it off. When I met you on the *Fortuna* I was ready to write to her and break it off, but when I thought I'd never see you again, I decided to avoid the issue altogether.'

'Avoiding things doesn't make them go away. Rita will certainly be crushed by your rejection but people heal in spite of themselves. She's young. With good fortune she will find someone else and a new happiness. If you no longer love her then let her go.'

'I've never hurt anyone like this in my life. I've always been mister nice-guy. It's not a pleasant feeling.'

'Sometimes one has to be cruel to be kind. In this case, you're being kind to yourself. Don't you deserve to be happy?'

He fixed her with his speckled eyes and the intensity of his stare weighed so heavy that she had to look away.

'You make me happy,' he said simply. When she raised her eyes again he was still looking at her.

'You barely know me,' she whispered gravely.

'There's much I don't know about you. But I do know for certain that I love you and I trust that, when you feel ready, you'll tell me about yourself.' She patted his arm and smiled, though her eyes seemed to shrink with apprehension.

'Let's take a look around the church before we eat,' she suggested. 'We can leave the picnic here, we seem to be alone.'

'Except for a couple of doves,' said George with a chuckle, getting up and stretching his limbs.

'If they manage to open the basket I'll be most surprised,' she said, putting on her sunglasses and striding out of the shade.

Holding hands, they entered the church. It was cool inside and smelt of the ages mingled with incense. The sound of their shoes on the stone floor echoed off the walls and they spoke in whispers, although there was not a soul in sight, just the silent presence of God in the paintings on the gilded altarpiece and in the air that still vibrated with the echo of centuries of worship.

'I've never understood the catholic need to confess,' said Susan in a quiet voice when they found themselves standing before the black confessional.

'Confessionals make me think of perverted priests,' George replied, drawing back the red curtain to peek inside.

'I object to the idea that one can only communicate with God through a priest. It's the church's way of controlling people.'

'Now you're sounding like Mrs Megalith,' said George with a chuckle. 'She's Rita's grandmother, they call her the Elvestree Witch because she's psychic. She says God's in everyone's kitchen and if they knew that they wouldn't bother going to church.'

'She sounds quite a character,' mused Susan, running her hand over the wooden banister that ran up to the pulpit. 'Though church has a restorative effect on many people. Sometimes it's good for the soul to share things. I'm not a crowd person. I like to stand back, to have my own space, to watch from a distance. But some would find it very lonely talking to God in their kitchens on their own.'

George walked up behind her and put his arms around her waist, nuzzling his face into her neck.

'Do you talk to God?'

'Sometimes. At my lowest ebb. I don't know what He is, or if He is at all. But it feels good to reach out to someone.'

'Oh, I know He exists. I felt Him up there in the skies. I felt Him very close. I could even feel His breath on my neck.' Susan turned around to face him.

'You must have been very frightened,' she whispered and ran her fingers softly down his cheek. He took her hand in his and held it there.

'I had terrible dreams. I was afraid to sleep,' he said, shaking his head and frowning solemnly as the faces of Jamie Cordell, Rat Bridges and Lorrie Hampton surfaced in his mind. 'But since I met you, they've gone.' She smiled and withdrew her hand.

'I'm glad I'm frightening those demons away,' she said.

'I wish I could frighten yours away,' he ventured. She shook her head.

'Only I can do that,' she replied. 'But with your help, I will.'

They walked out into the light to find a group of brown-faced children playing on the steps of the church. They were jumping up and down, laughing and shouting, their voices ringing out across the silent grounds. When they saw the two strangers they stopped what they were doing and stared. George took Susan's hand as they walked down the steps. One by one the children gazed at Susan. Their mouths dropped open and one or two pointed. Then, like a pack of animals who all understand each other without having to speak, they ran around her, holding their hands up to her, asking to touch. George was seized with fury. In a bid to protect her he waved at them and shouted in Spanish as he would to the stray dogs that roamed the farm. 'Get away! get away!' But to his astonishment, Susan simply smiled, let go of his hand and crouched down. As she did so the children recoiled and fell silent as if suddenly afraid.

'She's an angel,' said the smallest.

'Is it real?' asked another.

'I'm not an angel,' said Susan with a laugh. 'Go on, touch it.' And George watched as one by one their grubby brown hands touched her hair. Susan looked up at him and grinned.

'Children are a law unto themselves,' she said.

'I'm sorry,' he replied, feeling foolish.

'You don't need to apologise. To these children my face is not nearly as exciting as my hair.'

Susan clearly loved children. She talked to them, stroked their hair, their dusty faces, she did up the buttons on the shirt of one, brushed down the shorts of another, commented on a grazed knee and a bruised forehead. Once she had kissed the knee and the forehead they all rushed at her, inventing ailments for her to kiss away and she laughed as she tried to satisfy them all, a laugh so natural and so happy that George stood transfixed by her joy. He realised then that part of her sadness must come from her longing for children.

It took her a long time to break away. They hung onto her like little monkeys, giggling in their efforts to keep her, determined to have their way. Finally she retreated into the shade where they had left the picnic in the care of the doves and the children returned to their games, though their eyes wandered over to the trees every now and then, hoping she'd come back.

George opened the bottle of wine and poured her a glass. Agustina had packed beef sandwiches and potato salad.

'You have a magical way with children,' he said, before biting into a sandwich. She suddenly looked sad.

'I love children so much,' she replied, taking a sip of wine. She looked over to the steps where they played, and smiled because she recognised that their voices were louder and their games more exaggerated for her benefit.

'You will be a wonderful mother,' he said, then wished he hadn't as her cheeks flushed and she sighed heavily.

'Let's drink to that,' she replied, raising her glass. And George was more aware than ever of the secrets of her past that lay hidden from him, and bit his tongue to restrain his impatience.

They remained under the trees until the sun had descended behind the church, casting them in shadow. The air was sugar-scented and balmy and crickets had replaced the chatter of children. Susan's eyes were sleepy with wine and pleasure and shone from her laughter. Yet, as the shadows of evening crept across the grass into nightfall, her thoughts turned to the shadow of war that was the weight on George's soul.

'You think about them all the time, don't you?' she said, watching him carefully. He understood her at once.

'Yes,' he replied. 'All the time.'

'You feel guilty that you survived when they died.' He returned her gaze with dark and troubled eyes. He shook his head slowly and sighed.

'My brain tells me that some gamblers win and others lose. It's logical and inevitable. I just can't help but feel I don't deserve to have been a winner. I wasn't the bravest pilot or the best.'

'It wasn't your time.'

'That's what I keep telling myself.'

'But it doesn't make you feel any better, does it?'

'Not really. Guilt sticks to me like clay.'

'They were young, like you. It's so senseless.'

'Lorrie had a girl at home he was going to marry and Rat was his mother's only son.'

'Rat?'

'Short for Humphrey.'

'Of course, silly me!' she quipped, grinning back at him.

'We grew closer than brothers and yet, in the end, only Brian and myself remained out of the original squadron. The others dead.' He drew his lips into a thin line. 'Dead, at the bottom of the sea or in pieces. Jamie, Rat and Lorrie, their names are engraved on my heart and on my conscience.'

'Give yourself time, George. Time has a way of ironing these things out.'

He looked at her intently and his expression lightened as if the sun had defied the force of nature and risen above the towers of the church.

'You really understand, don't you, Susan?'

She reached over and placed her hand upon his. 'A little, and the little I don't, I try to.'

He shuffled across the rug so that he could wrap his arms around her and kiss her. With Susan he could muffle the insistent scream of war, the nagging of his conscience and the small, plaintive voice somewhere deep inside his heart that was Rita's.

Chapter Sixteen

Max was unable to concentrate. He lit the small candle and began slowly to ignite the eight flames of the menorah, the symbol of Hanukkah. From the moment he and his sister Ruth had arrived at Elvestree, Primrose had resolved to practise their Jewish festivals and customs as they had done in Austria, before Hitler had set out to extinguish the very soul of their people. Ruth's face was solemn. She never spoke of the family they had lost but it was impossible not to think of them at such a time. Some memories never fade. Mrs Megalith's glasses were perched on the bridge of her nose and she dug her chin into the folds of flesh on her neck. Her face was serious too, in spite of the cats that circled her ankles and rubbed their backs against her calves. Max's thoughts were far from Vienna and the small dining room where his mother had nodded at him across the table to indicate the moment to light the candles and say the accompanying prayers. They were with Rita. Since the day he had kissed her in his bedroom they had spent evenings together playing chess, reciting poetry or writing their own prose to read out to each other beside the fire in Primrose's drawing room. She had finally noticed him.

Ruth watched her brother's hand tremble as he lit the candles. She wondered whether he was remembering, as she was, the dimly-lit dining room in Vienna where their father presided over the family gathering of uncles and aunts and cousins to celebrate the festival of Hanukkah. She could almost smell the smoke from his cigar and taste the wine in the air. She shook away the invading sense of nostalgia with a toss of her head and focused her now glittering eyes on the flame in her brother's hand. Mrs Megalith felt the contradicting vibrations in the room, Ruth's heavy sadness and Max's light excitement, and sent one of the cats scurrying out from under the table with a firm kick of her foot.

'That'll teach the little rotter!' she exclaimed as Max lit the eighth candle. Then she raised her glass. 'To absent friends, that we may always remember them.' Max thought of Rita, Ruth of her mother, and Mrs Megalith cast her mind momentarily to Denzil. He wouldn't have put up with all these cats and they wouldn't have dared intrude if he were still alive. She felt a cold nose against her knee and sent a fat ginger cat flying out from under the table to join the other. Ruth felt tearful and sunk her eyes into the steaming soup, silently fending off the memories that now threatened to swamp her. Mrs Megalith launched into a story about her late husband's disastrous tiger hunt in India and Max began spooning the soup into his mouth with relish. Neither seemed to notice her anguish.

Then, just when Ruth's tears threatened to spill, Max's spoon hesitated before his lips. Mrs Megalith was laughing raucously at the thought of Denzil being chased by a tiger when he had been told very firmly to remain still. Max was no longer listening. He looked down to see a small white cat sitting quietly at his feet staring up at him with large, unblinking eyes the colour of the peridots on Mrs Megalith's earrings. Max shifted his eyes to his sister and felt his heart, a moment ago as light as a soufflé, now slump with compassion. Without further thought he swept the cat into his arms, stood up and walked around to the other side of the table where Ruth sat hunched over her cooling soup. Mrs Megalith's laughter faded into a chuckle as she watched him place the cat onto his sister's knee where it proceeded to nuzzle her face affectionately. The old woman understood the boy's gesture and gazed at him with admiration. When she turned back to Ruth, the cat was licking up her soup with her neat pink tongue and Ruth was giggling, her tears settling into her eyelashes, her misery forgotten.

Maddie was unable to think of anything but Harry Weaver. She had been struck by love, slapped around the face, kicked in the gut and, to her shock, it really hurt. Now she knew what Rita went through.

'I so admire you!' she wailed to her sister. 'Love is the most painful thing in the world. I feel as if my heart is being pulled and torn. I long for him with every nerve in my body!'

'What about Bertie?' Rita asked, unable to take Maddie's dramatics too seriously.

'Bertie?' Maddie spat the name as if the very sound of it was detestable to her. 'I never loved Bertie. He made the time pass. Now I've met the man I want to spend the rest of my life with and if Megagran is right, the many lives I have to live after this one.'

'I thought you were going to marry a movie star. Cary Grant at the very least.' Rita found it hard to contain her amusement.

'Love strikes when you least expect it. I don't care that he's old, forty at least, don't you think?' She screwed up her nose. Forty was definitely the beginning of old age.

'Mummy and Daddy would die if they knew. He's divorced.'

'Don't remind me. Not only is he divorced and old but he's a poor, unsuccessful writer. What am I going to do?' Rita sat on the edge of her sister's bed and stroked her hair.

'That's not your only problem. You've got serious competition.'

Maddie gasped in horror as yet another obstacle raised its ugly head. 'Who?'

'Eddie's lost her heart to him too. He's the only person other than Mother and Megagran who has taken an interest in Harvey.'

'Thank God for Eddie!' she burst with relief. 'You really scared me, Rita.'

'At least you can see him as much as you like. Mummy's always at Bray Cove bird-watching. I suggest you begin to take a keen interest in birds and books.'

Maddie sat up and looked at her sister with eyes that sparkled. 'You're right. I'll go with her, then a romance will surely blossom. I'll win him in the end, you'll see.'

Suddenly Maddie's life had a purpose. She rose early to sit in the garden, hunched in her father's sheepskin coat, with a sketchpad and pencil of Eddie's, drawing the birds which fed from her mother's many bird trays. She braved the snow and the cold and didn't mind that her breath froze in the air and her fingers lost their mobility, so determined was she to convince her mother that her interest was genuine. She asked her about their habits, about migrating birds and domestic birds, birds of the sea and birds of the mountains. Hannah was only too happy to discuss her feathered friends, surprised and delighted that her most difficult daughter was at last showing signs of growing up. Her knowledge was vast and, to Maddie's delight, she discovered a colourful new world that coexisted with hers but which she had never noticed before. By Christmas she had not only persuaded Hannah but had managed to cultivate a real hobby for herself.

'I've asked Harry to join us for Christmas at Elvestree,' said Hannah over dinner one evening in mid-December. 'He's

all alone and there's nothing more miserable than spending Christmas on one's own.' Maddie's face throbbed with
excitement but so overwhelmed was she that she temporarily
lost her voice.

'That's good of you, my dear,' said Humphrey who was
only too keen to dilute Antoinette and Megagran.

'Mother's happy. More the merrier is her motto. He loves
animals so he won't mind all those ghastly cats. I would like
to embrace him into our family. He's such a nice man,' she
continued. 'He's made a very warm home in Bray Cove and,
do you know, the birds there are fabulous. So many different
breeds. It's a veritable paradise, even in wintertime.' She
settled her eyes on Maddie and smiled. 'Maddie, you must
come with me one of these days with your sketchpad.' Maddie
nodded and nearly choked on her stew.

'Me too!' Eddie's voice rose. 'Harry says that he has bats
in his attic. Harvey could do with a few friends.'

'I'm sure Harry won't mind if we all descend on him. He'll
probably be grateful for the company,' said Hannah.

'I doubt he's ever inspired such devotion,' mused Humphrey
with a smile. 'Will you go too, Rita?'

'No,' she replied.

'Not still pining for a letter from George?' he commented
tactlessly. 'It seems like only yesterday that you received the
pendant.'

Rita lowered her eyes to hide the sadness in them. 'I know.
I shouldn't complain. Besides, I'm sure he's written. It's just
that the post from overseas is so unreliable.'

'Quite. The Royal Mail is most efficient these days, but I
wouldn't say the same for the post in Argentina.'

'I write to him weekly,' she said in a small voice. 'At least
he knows I'm thinking of him.'

'Of course he does,' her mother exclaimed encouragingly.
'And you have that lovely pendant.' Rita fingered it fondly.

'I'm sure a letter will arrive soon. It will be worth the wait. Every good thing in life is worth the wait.' Rita hid her apprehension behind a smile.

Maddie could scarcely wait for Christmas. She decided she would paint a picture of a bar-tailed godwit for Harry's present. The godwit was a superior wader by virtue of its large size and slender, slightly upcurved bill. In summer its plumage was chestnut-red like her hair and it had long, elegant legs. There was a framer in town who could frame it for her and perhaps Harry would hang it above the desk where she presumed he wrote, so that it would remind him of her whenever he looked at it. Eddie, in turn, set about crafting him a little house for the bats in his attic with the help of Nestor, her grandmother's ancient gardener.

Rita sat in her bedroom reading, watching the robin who had nested in her bookshelf, going over George's old letters dating back from the outbreak of the war or pacing the cliffs, gazing anxiously out to sea. She continued her sculpting lessons with Faye, cycling over after work even in bad weather. She felt closer to George when she was with his family and their affection for her did much to relieve her doubts. Her sculpture was improving. There was nothing like the aching of the heart to enhance one's creativity. Faye was impressed. She understood love and longing and how they fine-tuned the soul. Since Thadeus, her work had moved into another dimension and taken on an almost unearthly quality. The birds really seemed to fly, the animals to breathe, and the bust of Thadeus that she kept locked in a cupboard looked at her with such tenderness her heart stumbled every time she gazed upon it.

Christmas morning dawned with a heavy snowfall. Maddie and Hannah rushed out into the garden to break the ice on the water in the birdbath and scatter the ground and bird trays with breadcrumbs. Rita slept in for there was nothing to get up for, no post on Christmas Day. Eddie, for whom Father Christmas' visit was an exclusive occurrence, awoke to the heavy weight of the bulging stocking on the end of her bed. Her excitement, however, was suddenly dashed when she discovered the lifeless body of Harvey, like a small toy, inert in the middle of the floor. Cradling him in her hands she rushed downstairs to where her father was in his usual place at the end of the kitchen table. 'He's dead!' she wailed. At the sight of his daughter's devastated face Humphrey first thought Harry Weaver had died, but then his eyes settled on the little black bundle she held in trembling hands.

'Oh, my dear Eddie!' he exclaimed, jumping to his feet. Gathering the snivelling child into his arms he carried her to the rocking chair and sat down with her. She was inconsolable.

'What am I going to do?' she cried. All Humphrey could do was hold her tight and stroke her forehead. He wasn't very good at this sort of thing. When Hannah came in with Maddie, clad in her dressing gown and a pair of boots, she was horrified.

'Harvey has gone to the great bat attic in the sky,' he said gravely. Hannah's shoulders dropped.

'Oh, Eddie. I am sorry,' she said, swapping at once with her husband and dragging a by now very soggy Eddie onto her knee. Eddie stroked the dead bat, which looked even more revolting than when it had lived.

'What will I do without him, Mummy? How will I go on?'

'You will, my dear. Because life does go on. You're going to have to be very strong. For Harvey's sake. He won't want you crying your little heart out over him, will he? That would make him very sad and heaven is meant to be a happy place.'

On hearing the commotion downstairs, Rita appeared with

her hair in knots, her face pale and her eyes cast in shadows. 'What's happened?' she asked anxiously.

'Harvey's died,' said Maddie. Then added in a whisper. 'You'd have thought it was Daddy the way she's carrying on!'

'We must give him a proper funeral,' said Hannah, kissing Eddie's forehead. 'Where would you like to bury him?'

'In the garden,' she sniffed. 'In a box.'

'I'll make a little headstone for him if you like,' said Rita. 'You can choose what you want it to say.'

'Why don't we find a nice box to put him in now, then we can all have breakfast. We mustn't be late for church,' said Hannah, patting Eddie dismissively and getting up. Eddie followed her into the larder where she emerged a moment later with a small box. With much ceremony, she placed Harvey inside.

'I want to bury him with my blue cardigan,' she said gravely. Hannah put her hands on her hips, uncertain of whether to indulge such an extravagant whim just for a bat.

'Eddie, I really don't think that's necessary,' she began lamely. Eddie sensed the weakness in her mother's voice and immediately seized upon it.

'Oh, there's no question, Mummy. I have to or he won't rest in peace. In fact, he won't rest at all.'

'But you don't have many cardigans and that one will fit you for years.'

'I am willing to sacrifice it for him. After all, it's only a piece of clothing. Harvey was a life!' Her eyes bulged as she said 'life'.

Hannah was silenced by her daughter's logic and mumbled, 'We'll see,' before turning around to make the porridge.

Maddie made such an effort for church that she looked as if she had stepped right off a Hollywood set. Her hair was beautifully groomed and fell onto her shoulders like shiny curtains, her eyelashes were thick with mascara and she had painted her nails blood red. Her skin glowed with radiance and was as pale as the petals of an orchid. Her lips were glossy with scarlet lipstick and curled into a permanent smile for today she would see Harry Weaver again. She stood in front of the mirror in the hall, arranging her hat and smoothing down her olive-green suit. When Hannah saw her she couldn't help but gasp in admiration at the beautiful creature she had produced.

Humphrey drove to church. If the weather had been better they would have all enjoyed the walk. The road was wet with slush but the sun was out, doing its best to melt the snow. The trees and bushes glittered as if festooned with diamonds and from the roofs of houses hung icicles which caught the light and twinkled like silver. It was bitterly cold and the girls huddled in the back to keep warm. Only Maddie was hot, her heart aflame in her chest like a burning coal, anticipating Harry.

Humphrey parked the car on the green and was cheered to see Trees and Faye Bolton walking up the path with Alice, her husband Geoffrey, recently returned from the war, and the children, immaculately dressed in little navy blue coats and hats. Maddie looked out of the window, anxiously scanning the faces for Harry, but to her disappointment he was not yet among those now filing into the church.

They settled into a pew, smiling graciously at their friends as they passed. Aunt Antoinette sat looking bored alongside her husband David, who was making a rare appearance in Frognal Point. Emily winked at Eddie but William sat with his nose in the air as if he was too good for such a provincial little place. When Harry Weaver strode in, dressed in a moth-eaten tweed suit, everyone seemed to turn to stare at this gangly stranger. Maddie sat up at once and beckoned with her gloved hand for him to come and sit with them. Harry was grateful. He walked hastily down the aisle, his shoulders hunched and his head bowed, embarrassed to be the centre of so much attention. He nodded formally as he greeted Hannah and Rita then smiled at Eddie.

'Harvey is dead!' she hissed melodramatically.

Harry sat down and mouthed, 'I'm so sorry,' before smiling rather more broadly at Maddie.

'She's lost without Harvey,' Maddie whispered into his ear.

'I can imagine, poor child,' he whispered back and she shivered as she felt his lips brush her skin.

The church was ablaze with holly and bright red berries. The village children had decorated a fir tree with shiny gold balls and little figurines of Santa Claus. Illuminated by candles and the bright sunlight that tumbled in through the windows it looked festive and suitably heavenly. 'Merry Christmas one and all!' Reverend Hammond's voice silenced the low rumble of chat and everyone shuffled in their seats to find the most comfortable position. They knew the service was going to be a long one.

Reverend Hammond surveyed his congregation and was relieved the Elvestree Witch had not decided to grace them all with her presence, or her cats for that matter, and he shuddered as he recalled that spring Sunday, forever engraved on his memory. As he launched into a lengthy welcome, Maddie sat pressed up against Harry, the coal in her chest burning her body more intensely than ever. Harry was aware of his own burning coal and realised to his embarrassment that the hymn sheet in his hand was shaking. He didn't notice Maddie slip hers into her handbag so that when the organ began to play she had to ask to share his. Rita felt tearful. She looked across at Faye's sensitive profile and knew that she was also missing George. Trees sung loudly and out of tune. If he was missing his son he didn't show it. But then Trees rarely showed emotion. The last time she had seen him upset was when someone had sneaked into the farm and stolen a rare black walnut.

Reverend Hammond gave a very long sermon about the meaning of Christmas. Hannah was sure that it was identical to the one that he had given the year before, just longer. The congregation began to cough and stir in their seats. Only Maddie and Harry sat as still as the Christmas tree figurines, more aware than ever of the parts of their bodies that touched.

At the end of the service, after greeting their friends, Humphrey and Hannah gathered their family together to drive to Elvestree for Christmas lunch. The boot of the car was stuffed with presents, all neatly wrapped in brightly coloured paper.

'Maddie, why don't you go with Harry,' suggested Humphrey, climbing into the car. 'That way he won't get lost.' Maddie hurried over to Harry's car, tottering slightly on her high heels, her breath rising into the air like steam.

'Wait for me!' she shouted as he started up the engine. 'I'm coming with you.' Harry barely had a moment to sweep the pages of manuscript and old newspapers off the front seat before she got in. 'Daddy thinks you might get lost,' she explained breathlessly. Harry looked flustered but delighted.

'Good.' He looked at her and a shy grin crept across his face. Then he turned his attention to the road ahead.

'Is this your latest book?' she asked, pointing to the typed manuscript strewn all over the floor.

'No,' he said. 'I'm afraid I haven't had time to clean out the car. It ends up as a general dumping ground for things I should throw away but can't bear to.'

'What do you write?'

'Novels.'

'Are they any good?'

Harry found Maddie's directness slightly disconcerting. He wasn't used to such bluntness.

'My publishers think so,' he replied.

'Are you famous?'

'No.'

'Do you want to be?'

'No.'

'Why not?' She looked at him sidelong, unable to understand why he wouldn't want to be famous.

He smiled indulgently. How could someone so young appreciate the pitfalls of fame?

'Because famous people lose their anonymity and in most cases their dignity too, not to mention their sanity. I don't want people to know who I am.'

'Really?' she gasped.

'Do you want to be famous?'

'I wanted to be a film star like Lauren Bacall, but I don't any more,' she said hastily. She couldn't tell him that since meeting him she wanted to be a simple bird-watcher in Bray Cove.

'You're very wise.'

'I want to paint birds,' she said proudly.

'Are you any good?' he asked, imitating her bluntness of tone.

'Quite. There's plenty of room for improvement, as Daddy would say. But I like birds. You like birds, don't you, Harry?'

'I love all animals. Bray Cove is a delightful place for birds. In fact, Devon is a haven for both animal and bird. I'm very happy I moved here.'

'Where is your wife?'

Harry remained silent for a moment, amazed that she knew he was divorced.

'In Scotland,' he replied after a while.

'Why Scotland?'

'Because she married a man called McInty,' he said with a wry smile. 'He has a castle and she likes big houses.'

'She wouldn't like Bray Cove, then, would she?'

'No.'

'But you don't have children?'

Harry shook his head and Maddie breathed a heavy sigh of relief. She didn't like the idea of stepchildren at all. Harry stole a quick glance at her while she was staring out of the window, but she turned and caught his eye before he had time to look away. He felt the blood rise to his cheeks and tried to change the subject.

'Tell me about your sister's fiancé.'

'He's in the Argentine. He's promised to marry her when he comes back. But I don't think he will come back.'

'Oh dear.'

'As my aunt Antoinette says, if he loved her he wouldn't have gone in the first place.'

'Well, there's some logic in that,' Harry agreed.

'But Rita is hopelessly in love. I sympathise with her. I know what love is and how much it hurts.' She looked across at him and sighed melodramatically. 'How old are you, Harry?'

Harry shook his head and laughed. 'For a young woman you ask very strange questions,' he said in astonishment.

'Is it wrong to ask?' She looked hurt.

'Of course not,' he replied gently. 'Only unexpected.'

'You can ask me how old I am and I won't take offence. I'm nineteen,' she said with a broad smile, as if she expected praise for the achievement of reaching such an advanced age.

'I'm thirty-six,' he stated. Maddie's jaw dropped.

'Only thirty-six! That's not so old,' she exclaimed cheerfully, clapping her hands together.

'I hope not,' said Harry in bewilderment.

'Not old at all. You're only . . .' she squinted and mumbled. 'Seventeen years older than me.' She sat back in the seat, content that at least one of the obstacles in the way of her future happiness was surmountable.

They swept up the long drive lined with trees, naked and crippled by the frost, and parked on the gravel outside Elvestree House. In spite of the winter bareness the house exuded an inviting warmth. The windows blazed with light and life. The sun had melted Jack Frost's flamboyant sketches and the snow on the roof was now only in patches where there were still shadows. The chimneys choked out smoke and the sweet smell of burning wood reminded Harry of autumn, when his father had set fire to mountains of leaves on Saturdays. A robin played with a crust of bread on the steps that led up to the porch and didn't bother hopping away when he saw them approaching. Harry followed Maddie through the front door, decorated with a wreath of holly tied up with a red velvet ribbon.

The sound of animated voices rang out from the drawing room and the scent of cinnamon and orange mingled with the overpowering smell of Aunt Antoinette's perfume. Eddie was telling everyone about Harvey and inviting them all to the burial, which would take place at six in the garden at home, beneath the apple tree he had so loved for all the insects it attracted. Antoinette knew better than to speak ill of the dead, especially a dead Harvey, and bit her tongue as she almost stumbled into asking Rita about George. *Family politics*, she thought wearily, *are so trying*. Her husband, the mysterious David, was standing by the window seat with Humphrey, discussing with indignation the nearby unspoilt land under threat from developers.

'What will become of the countryside, I ask you?' exclaimed Humphrey hotly.

'Buildings go up with much too little thought,' David

agreed. 'I suppose the poor buggers have to be housed. But what will people think fifty years from now?'

Maddie strode in with Harry close behind, hunching his shoulders in an attempt to look as inconspicuous as possible.

'Madeleine, come and help me fill everyone's glasses. This is not a dry house,' said Mrs Megalith in a booming voice, waving her becrystalled fingers at her granddaughter. 'Ah, you must be Harry Weaver, how jolly nice to meet you. Shoulders back, dear boy, or you'll develop a hunchback!' she added, handing him a glass of champagne. 'Had this in the cellar for years. My Denzil kept a bountiful cellar, but was loath to drink any of it himself. All the better for us, don't you think!'

Harry took the glass and straightened up. He was at least a head and shoulders above everyone else. Mrs Megalith hobbled past him. Dressed in a rich purple dress that fell from her breasts to her feet she looked every inch the witch of village legend. The shining moonstone swung hypnotically as she limped across the room and she had pinned her hair up with chunky square amethysts.

Suddenly she stopped in her tracks, blinked in amazement at the misty image that appeared before her eyes and very slowly turned around, her face a pale shade of pink.

'Good God!' she exclaimed under her breath, looking from Harry to Maddie. 'Well, I'll be damned!'

'Is everything all right, Grandma?' Rita asked, distracted a moment from her lonesome pining.

'Better than ever. I thought only cats had that kind of luck.'

Mrs Megalith smacked her lips together in satisfaction. Rita looked bewildered. Mrs Megalith shook her head dismissively.

'Just the ranting of an old woman whose gift still has the ability to surprise her. Think nothing of it,' she said before looking worriedly at Rita.

'No more letters from George, Rita?'

Rita shook her head mournfully. 'Not yet. I'm sure he's written. I don't doubt him, Grandma.'

'Of course you don't,' said Mrs Megalith with sympathy, patting her on the arm. 'Of all the people I know most deserving of luck, it's you.' She turned and narrowed her pale eyes at Maddie. Then she shook her head and pursed her lips in disapproval. 'Sometimes the least deserving win the lot.'

Chapter Seventeen

George wrote to Rita just before Christmas. He decided it was kinder if she received the letter after the celebrations were over. He sat in his bedroom in the early hours of the morning, when sleep resisted the summons of his weary body, having ridden out all day with the gauchos. He sensed Susan in the next-door room and strained his ears, as she did, for a sound. The last he had heard was the closing of the door and then his imagination stirred as he thought of her undressing and climbing into bed, reading perhaps and then turning out the light. He ached for her with every muscle in his body. Of course he wanted to make love to her. He wanted to kiss her all over, to stroke her, to give her pleasure. But more than that he just wanted to lie beside her and hold her in his arms all night long. He wondered how long he should wait. Susan wasn't an innocent like Rita but she had obviously been hurt. She commanded respect but, above all, she needed to trust. Only time and patience would banish the demon in her past that still haunted her.

Resisting the temptation to knock on her door he sat at the desk and began to write.

My darling Rita. This is the hardest letter I will probably ever have to write in my life. There is no easy way to put it, I only wish that I could say it to your face rather than on paper. Then I could hold you and we could part as friends, understanding one another. I don't think I've been entirely honest with you. I was afraid of hurting you, which is ironic as I'm hurting you more now. I cannot marry you. I still love you. I have loved you for as long as I can remember. But I love you more like a brother loves a sister. I'm no longer the George you knew. He died up there in the skies over war-torn Britain. I have decided to stay in the Argentine indefinitely. Frognal Point was stifling me and I needed to find my feet in a new place. I'm happy here. I cannot express how grateful I am to you for waiting for me during those years when your support meant more than you will ever know. It kept me alive. I'm sorry to let you down. I'm sorry to hurt you. To think of your sad face fills me with terrible regret. Please forgive me, Rita. I wish you happiness. You are young and beautiful and will no doubt find someone to replace me in your affections. I thank you also for giving me the very best of you, my darling. They were the most wonderful moments of my life. George.

He wiped his forehead with the back of his hand where sweat had gathered in beads. He read the letter over and over again. Agonised over one or two of the sentences. Tried to read it from her perspective, hoping he hadn't been too blunt, checking that she would understand beyond a shadow of a doubt what he endeavoured to communicate. He knew Rita so well. He knew this would break her heart.

The following morning he gave the letter to Agatha to post along with one to his mother, explaining what he had done. At breakfast Susan noticed that his face was taut around the eyes and grey beneath his suntan. She understood at once, but Agatha interpreted it as a bad case of lovesickness.

'The best cure for that, my boy, is to ride out hard. Take your mind off her. You won't last very long if you've such a soft heart. What you need is a nice Argentine girl. No point pining for a woman so far away. Never did anyone any good, long-distance love.'

George went along with it but at the end of the day, when

he was alone once again with Susan, he was able to voice his anxiety to someone who sympathised completely.

'I feel so cruel, Susan,' he said, sitting beside her on the swing-chair beneath the veranda. She took his hand and held it firmly. 'I did as you suggested. I refrained from telling her about you.'

'Good,' she replied. 'I would hate to be the cause of her heartbreak.' Then she added in a quiet voice. 'I know what it's like to have one's heart broken.' George turned and looked deeply into her troubled eyes.

'Do you know what it's like to have it mended?' he asked softly.

'Yes, I think I do,' she said, gazing at him steadily. 'To think I thought you were just a boy.'

'I'm glad I've proved you wrong.'

'Oh, I'm the first to admit when I'm wrong.' Suddenly, gripped with longing, he grasped her upper arms with both hands and held her gaze with the sheer force of his.

'I don't want you to go back to Buenos Aires after Christmas, Susan. I want you to stay up here and marry me.' He half-expected her to laugh. If he had delivered such an outburst on the boat she would have laughed at him. That condescending laugh that had so irritated him. But she didn't.

'You don't know anything about me,' she protested weakly.

'Then tell me. I promise you there is nothing in your past that could be bad enough to stop me loving you. My God, Susan, you've enchanted me. I love everything about you. I even love the things about you that I don't know.'

She looked away and her profile toughened. 'I'll tell you if you promise not to pity me.'

'I promise.'

'I hate sentimentality,' she warned. 'Far worse things have happened to people.'

'I promise,' he repeated. She sighed heavily and leaned back against the chair.

'I was engaged,' she began. 'To an Englishman called John Haddon. I was very much in love. We had known each other a number of years and with each year I loved him more. There was no question that it wouldn't lead to marriage. My future with him was settled and needed only to be legalised.' She hesitated a moment, staring out into the night as if her demons were there in the shadows beneath the bushes. 'Then I got pregnant,' she stated in a matter-of-fact way, but her voice grew thick and quiet. George couldn't help but silently pity her. No wonder she had looked so sad at Santa Catalina among all those adoring children. 'John was delighted and we brought forward the day of the wedding.' She placed a hand on her belly and gently rubbed it. 'I felt so sick. Lethargic with sickness. But it didn't matter because a child was growing inside me. A mother will suffer anything for her child. Then one day, playing golf, John got distracted. I can't remember exactly. But he must have swung his club for when he followed through it hit me in the face.' George was horrified. He put his arm around her, but remembered he had promised not to pity her and let his hand flop beside her rather than onto her shoulder.

'The next thing I remember is waking up in hospital with half my face throbbing with pain. It's a strange thing, pain. You can't imagine a person can hurt so much and live. But I did. They stitched me up and covered me in bandages. I was drugged to the eyeballs, but it still throbbed. John was distraught, as you can imagine. He felt terrible and was full of apologies. I was more concerned about my baby. To my relief he was fine. Of course, the wedding had to be cancelled, or rather postponed. I remember playing a lot of solitaire in my hospital bed.' She laughed bitterly. 'Then they removed the bandages and I was faced with the horror of a disfigurement that would be with me for the rest of my life. You see, George, I had been very vain. I had taken beauty for granted. I enjoyed people admiring me. Suddenly I looked like a monster. Beauty is a very fragile thing. I would have to learn to live all over again. It sounds foolish, but it was as if I had lost the use of my legs, an important limb, a vital organ. You can't imagine how much a beautiful woman relies on her looks. Then John broke off the engagement. He couldn't cope with an ugly wife.'

George gasped, sickened and furious. 'The bastard!' he exclaimed.

'Yes, he wasn't the man I thought he was after all. It was a difficult time.'

'What happened to the baby?' he asked gently. Susan's voice had been steady until that moment. It now quivered for he had plucked the most vulnerable string.

'I suffered a miscarriage,' she whispered. It sounded so much worse when said out loud.

'From the shock of the accident?'

'No,' she said with a sigh, then added dispassionately. 'From a broken heart, I think.'

'My God! I'm so sorry!' He groaned, his face crumpling with sympathy.

'You said you wouldn't pity me!' she protested angrily as he drew her into his arms and pressed his lips to her temple. 'I don't want your pity.' She tried to push him away, but he held her in a vice until she was forced to surrender to his superior strength.

'I don't pity you, Susan. I've just realised that I love you even more. I'm going to marry you and look after you for the rest of your life.'

That night the humidity brought on a torrent of rain. Susan slipped quietly into her dressing gown. Her skin felt damp to the touch and the blood pounded against her temples. With a trembling hand she opened the door of her room and stepped into the tiled corridor. The lights on the veranda swung in the wind as the downpour clattered against the glass in the hall, casting a mobile of shadows across the white walls like a cinema screen. She ran her fingers over her throat where her skin was hot and moist, straightened up and turned to face his door. She hesitated a moment. The sound of the gale whipping across the roof sharpened her resolve. It wasn't a night to be alone. She put her hand on the doorknob and turned it. It made no sound and opened easily, as if facilitating her purpose. She saw him lying on his back, a sheet thrown casually across his waist, exposing his torso. The smell of him mingled with the natural scents of the farm: wet grass, eucalyptus, jasmine, leather and horses. She breathed quietly and stepped lightly towards the bed. He opened his eyes to see her standing over him, her white dressing gown luminous in the moonlight, like a ghost. He didn't say a word. He simply pulled back the cover and made room for her.

She stood a moment beside the bed, encouraged by his smile. Slowly she shed her dressing gown then lifted the straps of her nightdress so that it, too, fell to the ground to form a white puddle at her feet. Her naked body was now lit up by the lamps that illuminated the veranda and George ran his eyes over the soft undulations of her breasts, hips and thighs, and Susan was confident that in this gentle, unassuming light she looked beautiful again. She climbed in beside him and let him gather her into his arms. He unclipped her hair and scrunched it in his hands so that it fell about her shoulders in disarray. His kiss was slow, exploratory, tender and she surrendered to the longing that had almost suffocated her. George surprised her. His touch was unhurried for he wanted to savour every inch of her body and he was masterful, the man she had fallen in love with, not the boy she had laughed at on board the *Fortuna*. Only his enthusiasm was boyish and that she was grateful for.

She kissed him fervently, intoxicated by the warm smell of him and the sensation of her flesh against his and he grinned at her in delight for she was a woman unashamed of her experience and the pleasure she could give to a man.

Depleted of energy they lay together talking until the storm passed and the wet plains were lit up by the early rays of dawn. Susan was pleased she had found the courage to let another man make love to her. It was a hurdle that had once seemed insurmountable. But George reduced all her hurdles to a size that she could kick down with her foot. Her ghosts now seemed to be made out of nothing more than cobwebs.

Rita watched the snow melt and with it her hopes for the future. The week after Christmas saw no letter from George, nor the week after that. Maddie was rarely at home; she spent her time in Bray Cove painting or organising Harry's office, having muscled her way into his life. Love had transformed her into an efficient secretary, which surprised her as much as her mother. She didn't ask to be paid; being close to Harry was more than enough. But, as much as she flirted and encouraged, Harry didn't so much as touch her.

Then one rainy morning John Toppit brought Rita George's letter. She accepted it tearfully, overwhelmed with relief and gratitude and at once feeling foolish that she had ever been so weak-hearted as to doubt him. She scrambled into her boots and raincoat and grabbed a large golf umbrella and set out for the cliffs, the letter folded into her pocket. With a buoyant heart she skipped through the rain, enjoying the light tap-tapping of the drops as they landed on the umbrella. In her altered state of mind she now saw beauty in the bare trees and heavy grey skies. She could hear the sea crashing onto the rocks in the distance and smell the salty scent of ozone and wet sand. It was windy up on the clifftops. Just the way she liked it. She sat beneath the umbrella, sheltered by a grassy knoll.

This time she held onto the paper with great care so as not to sacrifice another precious epistle to the sea. She savoured his writing on the envelope and shuddered with anticipation as she tore it open and pulled out the thin sheet of paper. As diaphanous as the wings of a butterfly. Slowly she read what he had written and slowly her throat constricted as if an invisible hand was wrapping its icy fingers around her neck, choking her to death. Her breathing became laboured as she struggled for air and understanding. The paper shook in her grip and tears blurred the words so that she could no longer make them out. All she saw was a gloomy future that stretched out before her like the grey sea and the grey sky. Bleak and cold and unfamiliar. She had no experience of living without George. She was afraid she didn't know how.

When she had read the letter enough times to know the words by heart she put it back in her pocket and drew her knees up to her chest where she hugged them inconsolably. George meant everything to her. She loved him more than she loved life. Without him there was no reason to go on. No reason to live. After sobbing came an empty feeling of resignation. A strange serenity. An unsettling calm. George had taken away his love and therefore the very oxygen that she needed to breathe. There would be no home, no children, no family Sunday lunches in a kitchen that smelt of freshly baked bread and stew. Only silence and sterility, like a vast, dry desert where nothing can grow.

Slowly, she stood up. Her legs were weak and trembling, but they carried her forward to the brink of the cliff. She held the umbrella in her hands until the wind blew it away. She didn't watch it crash down the rocks and disappear onto the beach below. She let it go willingly and simply stared out ahead as if in a trance. She saw a lone gull riding the gale and slowly extended her arms. She wished that she could fly like a gull. What tremendous freedom birds had. To swoop and dive at will. To ride the breeze high above the earth. If she were in the clouds the earth wouldn't hurt her. She'd be too far away to care. Detached and blissfully unaware of the minute detail of daily life. She'd see the green of the fields and the blue of the sea and the beauty of the forests and rivers, but not the ugliness of rejection and the hopelessness of the human struggle. What good was love? What a fool she had been to believe in it.

She shuffled closer to the edge of the cliff. She didn't look down. She looked out ahead at the solitary gull that still glided on the wind. A ray of light penetrated the thick cloud and seemed to catch the tips of his wings, igniting them like candles. To Rita heaven now opened up to her, promising her eternal flight and relief from devastation. She let the gale take her arms and lift them. Up and down, up and down, just like a bird. They felt weightless like wings, detached, as if they were no longer in her control. She closed her eyes and felt the gentle rain on her face and the comfort of the dark. The wind blew her hair across her cheeks and lips and she threw her head back, ready to let it take her to heaven. To peace and silence and oblivion.

Just then two arms grabbed her roughly around the waist and wrenched her back. Shaken from the tranquillity of imminent death she screamed and fell to the ground with a painful thud. Blind with shock and fury she began to wrestle with the stranger who had stolen from her grasp the only escape available to her. They rolled around on the grass, panting like dogs. She clawed at his face, at his hair, at his clothes, at anything that would release her from his clutches so that she could make one final run for freedom. She howled her torment into the freezing air. A strange howl, more animal than human. The clouds closed on the ray of light and the gull disappeared into the mist. Finally, being bigger and far stronger than she, her assailant managed to pin her to the ground. She blinked up at him and when her sight returned she saw Harry Weaver's strained, scratched features looming over her. He was struggling for breath and wet from sweat and mud, and covered in blood.

'My God, Rita!' he gasped in horror. 'What are you doing?' The sound of his voice penetrated her numb senses and she suddenly realised how close she had come to ending her life. She began to shake uncontrollably.

'George . . .' she wailed in a high-pitched voice that didn't sound at all like hers. 'George . . .' She was unable to get the words out. She tried to inhale but her throat and chest were now so tight with panic she could barely breathe. Harry pulled her into a sitting position and pushed her head between her knees.

'Come on, there's a good girl. Calm down. You're all right,' Harry encouraged gently and slowly her airways cleared.

'George doesn't love me any more,' she burst out the moment she was able to speak. Harry drew her into his arms and she sobbed into his soggy coat.

'I'm so sorry. Poor you. You'll be all right, I promise.'

But Rita knew she would never be all right. She had just stepped through the door to hell and only George could pull her back.

Bray Cove was only a short distance away. Harry helped her walk by supporting her around the waist with his arm. In the other hand he held the umbrella that had practically knocked him out while watching gulls on the beach below. He had sensed something was wrong and ran as fast as he could to the top. Rita had been only moments from falling. Her arms outstretched, her head back, her neck as white as death, she had been a frightening sight. What had she been thinking of? No man is worth dying for.

Back at his cottage he ran a hot bath and left her in his room to warm up. She was soaked through. He offered her his dressing gown until her mother arrived with dry clothes. He put the kettle on the stove, then telephoned Hannah. Hannah telephoned Humphrey at the office and commanded him to come home at once. Rita had tried to commit suicide. Eddie was at school, but Maddie was upstairs applying make-up ready for Harry Weaver.

'Maddie!' shouted her mother. 'We're off to Bray Cove now!' Maddie recognised the urgency in her voice and appeared at the kitchen door almost before Hannah had finished the sentence.

'What's happened?' she demanded, terrified that something had happened to Harry.

'Rita tried to throw herself off the cliff.' Maddie's face blanched with horror. 'Apparently George's letter broke off the engagement. He doesn't love her any more. Harry saved her life.'

'Oh, Harry's such a hero!' Maddie gushed, her voice heavy with admiration.

'We owe him everything,' said her mother, striding into the rain.

At last, thought Maddie happily, *they're so grateful they'll give me to Harry as a prize.*

Hannah arrived to find Rita sitting hunched in Harry's dressing gown in front of the fire. She looked painfully thin and fragile. 'My dear child!' her mother whispered, for she was almost too moved to speak. She rushed to her side and Rita dissolved into her arms, crying all over again.

'We are so grateful to you, Harry,' said Maddie, following him into the kitchen. 'What happened?' Harry was only too happy to talk to Maddie. He felt Hannah and Rita needed time alone together.

'What did George say?' Hannah asked, her heart buckling at the sight of her broken child. Rita drew the letter from the pocket of Harry's dressing gown and handed it to her. With a heavy sigh Hannah squinted to read what he had written. Then she closed it and handed it back.

'I just don't understand it,' she said, shaking her head. 'How could he let you down like this, after all those years of waiting?' She pushed Rita's dripping hair off her forehead then caressed her cheek with tenderness. 'What happened up there on the cliff?'

Rita's eyes welled with tears. 'I wanted to die,' she said and her voice cracked.

'Oh, my dear child. Nothing ever is worth dying for. You'll pull through this.'

'I don't think I can.'

'Of course you don't. Not now. But later, when you get over the initial shock of it, you'll begin to heal. We'll help you. Your father and I, Maddie and Eddie. We love you and we'll look after you.' Rita stared into the fire.

'George was all I wanted,' she said. 'I never wanted more than that. I would have waited decades for him. When did he stop loving me?'

'It's a mystery to me. He seemed so in love when he left for Argentina,' said Hannah angrily. She wanted to kill him for hurting her child.

'I should have known. I should have realised when he told me he wanted to go away again. As Aunt Antoinette said, if he really loved me he wouldn't have left me, would he? I think he stopped loving me during the summer. I felt him pulling away but I didn't want to face it. A life apart was so unthinkable. I couldn't bear to even imagine it. I pretended it wasn't happening. Do you think he left to get away from me?'

'Of course not. Absolutely not. No,' said Hannah firmly. 'He wanted to get away from Frognal Point. Not from you. I should imagine he doesn't really know what he wants. The responsibility of asking you to wait for him probably weighed too heavily on his conscience. He must have thought it better for you to let you go.'

'You don't think he's met someone else?' Rita asked, her eyes darkening with anxiety.

'He's only been out there a few months. I don't think this has anything to do with another woman.' Rita's shoulders relaxed a little.

'Maybe he'll come back after a year as planned . . .' she ventured hopefully.

'Exactly. Who knows? Don't give up, dear. But he's a fool. A pretty girl like you! You'll be snapped up by someone else in no time at all.'

'But I don't want anyone else.'

'Of course you don't.' Hannah patted her arm and raised her eyes to the window.

The sound of a car drawing up outside alerted them to Humphrey. He strode into the hall, patted Harry appreciatively on the arm and asked to see Rita.

'Good God, Rita, what were you thinking?' he demanded, standing in the middle of the room with his hands on his hips. His face was ashen and the white tufts of hair around his ears glistened with raindrops.

'It's all right, Humphrey,' interjected Hannah calmly. 'We've talked about it. It was a mistake.'

'A mistake? What if Harry hadn't been there?' he raged. 'It's a bit late for regrets once you're dead!'

'Harry *was* there,' said Hannah with forced patience, glowering at her husband to pull himself together. 'And Rita is fine. Let's not blow this out of proportion.' But she knew as well as he did how close they had come to losing their daughter.

'You silly girl!' he exclaimed, kneeling on the floor beside her chair. 'You frightened the life out of me.'

'I'm sorry, Daddy.'

'What were you thinking of?' he repeated. 'George isn't bloody worth it. He's quite clearly not the man we thought he was. You're too bloody good for him!'

'I agree,' said Maddie, who was now standing in the doorway with Harry. 'He doesn't deserve you. Thank God for you, Harry! We owe you everything for saving Rita. Everything. We'll never be able to do enough.' Humphrey stood up.

'Maddie's right, Harry. Without you I hate to imagine what would have happened.' Harry smiled diffidently and lowered his eyes.

'It was nothing, really,' he said bashfully. 'Anyone would have done the same.'

'Look at the scratches on his face,' said Maddie, reaching out to touch them. The blood had now dried along with the mud but his hair was still wet and full of grass. He cradled a cup of tea in his hands, aware that they were still trembling. He could still see Rita balancing precariously on the edge of the cliff. 'She must have fought like a wild cat,' Maddie continued, running her fingers down his cheek. But Harry was uncomfortable with all this praise and attention.

'She was just a frightened child,' he mumbled, shrugging her off. Then Rita got to her feet.

'I'll go and change now,' she said. 'I want to go home.' Then, as she passed Harry, she smiled weakly. 'I'm sorry if I hurt you.'

'Not at all,' he replied, watching her shuffle out of the room. She didn't know whether she was grateful to have been saved or not. Death had looked so inviting.

Chapter Eighteen

Faye read George's letter with a heavy heart. She had feared this would happen ever since that night on the terrace when she had suggested he go and work at *Las Dos Vizcachas* for a change of scene. She had hoped he would take Rita with him, but he had been struggling with his feelings for her even then, although he had been reluctant to admit it. Her first thoughts were for Rita. She knew she would be devastated. George was her future. She had waited patiently for so long. Faye was sad for herself too. She loved Rita like a daughter. How was this going to affect their relationship with Hannah and Humphrey?

She sighed in resignation and decided to ring Hannah. Perhaps Rita had received George's letter that morning too. With some trepidation she picked up the receiver and dialled Hannah's number. She was quite relieved when no one answered. It was pouring with rain. Angry drops crashed against her windowpanes and the wind seemed to shake the very foundations of the house. She thought of Thadeus and longed for his advice but she had made a resolution a long time ago never to telephone him from home. It was disrespectful to Trees. She shivered with a sense of foreboding. It was unlike Hannah to be out in this weather. She wondered whether they were at Bray Cove with Harry Weaver and decided to try there. When Harry answered, his voice sounded strange, heavy and grim.

'They left five minutes ago,' he said, reluctant to divulge

the terrible circumstances that had brought them to his house in the first place. Faye knew something wasn't right. She felt it. Scrambling into a raincoat she hurried out into the storm. Trees had driven off in the truck; her only option was the car, which Trees only took out of the garage on special occasions. It was clean and smelt of polished leather. She was sure he would understand. It was an emergency.

The rain was so torrential her windscreen wipers did little to improve her vision. She drove slowly, with great care, for the roads were narrow and winding and the fog dense. It took much longer than normal. She seemed to be driving for hours, her mind whirring with anxious thoughts. At least George was happy out there with Agatha and Jose Antonio. As well as his sad decision about Rita he had described his new life in Argentina with relish. For once she wasn't worrying about him.

Finally she turned into the driveway, the tyres of her car scrunching on the gravel. She emerged through the evergreens to park in front of the house. They had obviously just arrived for the windows of Humphrey's car were misted with condensation. The lights were on in the hall and the heavy door to the porch was ajar. Faye took a deep breath and climbed out, her indoor shoes sinking into the wet stones. She opened the door to the hall, poking her head round nervously.

'Hello?' she called. 'Is anyone at home?' She crept in, shutting the door behind her. She could hear voices in the kitchen. 'Hello, Hannah?' The voices hushed as she walked up the corridor, then Hannah's grey face appeared at the kitchen door.

'Faye!' she cried, blinking away tears.

'Oh, Hannah. I'm so sorry,' she gasped, embracing her friend. 'How is Rita?'

'She's gone up to bed. She's heartbroken.'

'I can't bear it.' Faye shook her head, desperately guilty that it was her son who had caused such unhappiness.

'Come in and have a cup of tea. We were just talking about it.'

Humphrey was sitting on the rocking chair beside the stove, looking hollow eyed. Maddie was in his usual chair at the head of the table, hugging a steaming cup of Ovaltine. Faye was unable to sit down. She stood with her back to the wall, leaning against the sideboard where Hannah chopped vegetables. 'I only heard myself this morning,' she explained. 'George said he had written to Rita so I assumed she received his letter today as well.' Hannah poured Faye a cup of tea with an unsteady hand.

'We've been at Bray Cove,' she began in a thin voice. 'Rita tried to throw herself off the cliff.' Faye gasped and covered her mouth with her hand in horror.

'Good God!' she groaned. 'What happened?' Hannah handed her the cup, then sat down next to Maddie.

'Harry saved her,' said Maddie. 'If it hadn't been for him she'd be dead.'

'I can't bear to think about it,' said Hannah. 'It's just too terrible.'

'What was she doing on the cliff on a day like this?' Faye asked, appalled that George's rejection had driven her to such extremes. She knew Rita was a fragile girl, but had never thought her capable of suicide.

'She took his letter to read at the spot where they always picnicked,' Humphrey replied tonelessly, staring into his tumbler of whisky. 'I don't know what possessed her.' He shook his head. 'Rita's a sensible girl. Bloody stupid thing to do. Scared the hell out of all of us.' Faye lowered her eyes. Maddie continued the story.

'Harry just happened to be on the beach below. When Rita dropped her umbrella it almost killed him. But he was clever enough to sense that something wasn't right. So he ran as fast as he could up the path to find her swaying on the very edge. He said one gust of wind in the wrong direction and she would have fallen like a leaf.'

Maddie relished the details of Harry's heroism. Faye noticed that she looked incredibly rosy in the face compared to her parents. It seemed quite inappropriate that she should glow so beautifully in the midst of such unhappiness.

'She's sleeping now,' said Hannah quietly. 'I tucked her in with a cup of Ovaltine. She didn't drink it though. She just put her head beneath the covers and hid from all of us. I think she needs to sleep off the shock. I don't think she meant to kill herself. It was a cry for help and, thankfully, Harry was there to hear it.'

'I'm so sorry,' said Faye. 'I feel utterly responsible.'

'Don't be silly, Faye,' said Hannah. 'This is between George and Rita. We can't be responsible for the actions of our children.'

'Let's not let it come between us,' Faye suggested hopefully, sipping her tea.

'Of course we won't,' Hannah agreed. Humphrey remained silent, lost in the golden mirror of whisky that reflected his twisted features.

'Rita is young, she'll find someone else to love,' said Maddie confidently. Hannah frowned at her flippant tone of voice.

'I hardly think that thought will be much consolation to her at the moment,' she replied sharply.

Maddie stifled a yawn and wondered when she would be able to slip back to Bray Cove.

'When Rita wakes up, will you ring me?' said Faye. 'I'd like to see her.'

'Of course,' Hannah replied, getting up to see her friend off.

'In the meantime, if you need to talk you know where I am.'

But Faye knew she wouldn't. Humphrey's silence was loud and resentful. She embraced Hannah again but her body felt stiff and unyielding.

Faye drove up the lane, but she didn't take the road to Lower Farm. Instead she turned towards Thadeus' house.

It wasn't long before Mrs Megalith appeared in the hall, having brought with her a cautiously optimistic Max and the stale smell of cat. Max, like an acolyte, stood beside her, assisting her out of her raincoat and hat, holding her walking stick while she brushed herself down. She had been incapable of driving through such a storm by herself and, as Max was languishing in the house with nothing to do, she had asked him to act as chauffeur, telling him all about Rita's suicide attempt on the way.

'Mother!' exclaimed Hannah. Rarely was she so happy to see her mother.

'My God, what a morning you've all had!' said Mrs Megalith, taking her stick from Max without so much as a thank you.

'Max, how nice of you to drive Mother over. Let's all go into the sitting room, the kitchen is making me claustrophobic,' suggested Hannah. 'Humphrey's devastated,' she hissed to her mother. 'I've never seen him like this before.' Mrs Megalith hobbled down the corridor and settled comfortably into an armchair beside the fire.

'Hello, Grandma,' said Maddie, striding in with an indecent smile spread across her perfectly painted face. 'Harry Weaver saved Rita's life!' Mrs Megalith looked over her glasses and frowned disapprovingly.

'So I hear,' she replied. 'Wipe that grin off your face, Madeleine, and fetch me a sherry. Make it a large one.' Maddie rolled her eyes at Max but continued to smile.

'What do you want, Max?'

'He'll have a cup of tea,' replied her grandmother. She waved a bent finger at her. 'Mind that sherry's a large one,' she repeated as Maddie disappeared. 'Maddie is a very silly girl,' she said, once her granddaughter had gone.

'I don't know what's got into her today,' said Hannah, bemused. Mrs Megalith raised her eyebrows.

'Really?' she said cynically. 'I think it's love, Hannah dear.'

'Love?' Hannah sighed wearily. She couldn't take another child in love.

'Yes, right under your very nose.'

'Not Harry?' She shook her head. Then it all made perfect sense. 'Oh dear. Why did I have three daughters?'

'That's the least of your problems, Hannah. Those cats died for Rita, not Maddie.'

'What cats?' Hannah would never understand her mother, but Max did. He nodded, remembering the bad omen.

'Maddie will sail through life. I don't know which star she was born under but it was a very large, shiny one, for sure.'

'And Rita?' Hannah asked.

'A fragile star, I'm afraid. But she'll live, thanks to the likes of the Harry's of this world!' Mrs Megalith chuckled and dug her chin into the fat folds of flesh around her neck. 'Where is she?'

'Asleep.'

'Then I'll wait until she wakes. We're not going back out into that storm until we have to.'

Max longed to see Rita, but just being in her home made him feel warmed by her invisible presence. He was appalled that she had wanted to throw herself off the cliff. He wanted to tell her that George wasn't worth it. That he wasn't the only man to love her. Max loved her, but his love went unnoticed in the glare of George's. George had been the driving force of her life. The air she breathed. The wind that enabled her to fly effortlessly like a bird. Max's love was a thin cry lost in that wind. If she could only give him time to prove himself. He could be more of a man than George.

Max was seventeen years old now. He had left school in the summer and was about to leave Frognal Point for the city. Mrs Megalith was full of encouragement. 'You can't stay at home fetching and carrying for an old bag like me,' she had said. 'You're a clever young man with a bright future ahead of you. Had they lived, your parents would have been very proud of you.' But Max didn't want success to please his dead parents but to win Rita. He had bigger ambitions than could be fulfilled in Frognal Point.

Maddie returned with a cup of tea and a large tumbler of sherry. Mrs Megalith clicked her tongue and eagerly took the glass. 'What are you all dressed up for, young lady?' she asked Maddie after taking a big gulp. She shivered as it slid down her throat to her belly.

'A girl should make the most of her assets,' replied Maddie with a smirk.

'You've certainly done that,' Mrs Megalith retorted. 'I hear you're making yourself useful at Bray Cove.' Maddie had the decency to blush.

'Harry needs help. He's chaotic. Besides, I've been sketching birds,' she said proudly.

'What? Dressed like that?'

'Of course not, Grandma. What do you think I am?'

'I'd better not say. I'll offend your mother.'

'Maddie's an excellent secretary,' interjected Hannah. 'She's also discovered a talent she never knew she had.'

'I don't wish to imagine,' Mrs Megalith commented drily.

'She paints beautifully.' Hannah turned to her daughter. 'Go and fetch your sketchbook, Maddie.' Maddie was only too happy to show off her paintings. She knew they were good. Mrs Megalith was pleasantly surprised.

'A talent inherited from me,' she said arrogantly. 'I was a

very good painter.' Then Rita appeared at the door like a shadow and Maddie reluctantly closed the book.

'Maddie, go and make Rita some Ovaltine with a dash of brandy,' Mrs Megalith ordered, appalled by the grey pallor of her eldest granddaughter's complexion. 'That's guaranteed to make you feel better, my dear,' she said softly. 'Come and sit down by the fire, you look frightfully cold.' Rita shuffled over to the fire and perched on the edge of the fender beside her grandmother.

'How do you feel?' Hannah asked. Rita shrugged.

'Empty,' she replied.

'It will get better,' her mother encouraged.

'Not today it won't,' interrupted Mrs Megalith stridently. 'Not tomorrow either. Broken hearts are hard to mend, but the healing process can only get going if you talk about it instead of bottling it all up inside. Nothing good comes from bottling up one's emotions, you just build up an awful lot of negative energy that weighs you down.'

'It was so unexpected,' said Rita. 'I thought we had a future together. I feel so bruised and let down. I can't believe he doesn't want me.' Her voice trailed off and she fixed her gaze on the carpet.

'I told her that I don't think George knows what he wants,' said Hannah. Mrs Megalith frowned for she knew better, but she pursed her lips.

'Give me my handbag, Max,' she said, holding out her hand expectantly. Max retrieved her bag from the hall. She placed it on her knee and delved inside. 'Ah, here we are.' She pulled out a black velvet bag of crystals. 'I want you to keep the rose quartz in your pocket, my dear. The others simply place beside your bed.' Rita took the bag, relieved that her grandmother hadn't brought her tarot cards. Weighed down by so much positive energy she looked outside longingly, but it was still too wet to go for a walk. Maddie appeared with a mug of Ovaltine. 'You didn't forget that dash of brandy, did you?' Mrs Megalith said, taking the mug from Maddie and handing it to Rita. 'This will do you good. You must keep your strength up. Life is a series of obstacles. The trick is to jump them, then let them go. Don't look back. No point crying over spilt milk and all that. You can come out of this stronger if you want to. You have a choice.'

'I don't feel I have any choice at all,' said Rita mournfully. She caught Max's eyes, surprised once again by the warm affection that shone through them. She turned back to her grandmother. Mrs Megalith chose an analogy that Rita would understand.

'Take two birds with broken wings,' she said thoughtfully, toying with her moonstone pendant. 'Shot down by huntsmen one fine spring morning. They scurry away to hide in the safety of bushes to nurse their wounds. Little by little their damaged wings heal. One bird decides not to let such misfortune ruin her life. With the sheer force of her will she trains herself to fly again. It's not easy. She has to practise and practise and some days she's nearly overcome with hopelessness, but in the end, her hard work and positive mental attitude pay off. She flies. She flies higher than ever before and such flight gives her more pleasure because she knows what it is to be grounded. The other bird, however, is too frightened to try. She hides in the bushes, in the shadows, where it is dark, where she can wallow in her own self-pity. Unable to conquer her unhappiness and let go of the past, she lets her broken wing dominate her life, until it destroys it, robbing her of the most precious thing of all – her freedom.'

Mrs Megalith took off her glasses and looked into her granddaughter's sad eyes. 'You have just been shot down by a huntsman, Rita. You can be either bird, it is your choice. You can't decide now, but later, when spring comes and you are able to see your situation from a distance, you will have to make that decision. Just remember the story and let it guide you. Ultimately, the choice is yours, my dear. Now drink up, you'll feel better with a bit of liquor in you!'

In the afternoon Faye returned to see Rita. The weather had cleared a little and Mrs Megalith and Max had finally gone home after a good lunch. Thadeus had been sympathetic, giving Faye strength by wrapping his large arms around her and listening to her relate the story of Rita's suicide attempt. He had been shocked. How a girl could throw away a perfectly good life for the simple rejection of a man was beyond even his understanding. 'She wouldn't have lasted five minutes in Poland during the war,' was all he had said, which made Faye feel much better. George was within his rights to break off their engagement. Much better to hurt her now than to regret marriage ten years down the line when there were children to think of as well as a wife. She understood her son and stood by his decision, however painful it was for Rita.

'I'm so sorry,' said Faye to Rita, who was sitting like a shrivelled version of her former self on the window seat of her bedroom.

'It's not your fault,' she replied, looking out of the window at the drizzle that now floated down in the wake of the storm.

'I know. But I'm George's mother. I love both of you.'

'I really thought we were going to be a family.'

'So did I. I would have loved you as a daughter-in-law.'

Rita turned to Faye. 'Do you think he'll come back, one day?'

'I'm sure he will. He didn't mention it in the letter he wrote to me. But when he left he was only planning to be gone a year or so.'

'That was when he had me to come back for.' Faye took Rita's hand.

'He was very confused when he left, Rita. He didn't know what he wanted. He just knew he had to get away. If you ask me, it weighs too heavily on his conscience to ask you to wait for him any longer. He doesn't trust himself and he probably doesn't want to feel that he has to come back if he's not ready to. Now he's in Argentina he's detached from home, from you and me, from his life here. You have to understand that he was hurting too. He lost friends in the war and he lived through a terrible experience that will be with him for the rest of his life. He's recovering out there. I hope when he comes back he will have found the part of himself he lost up there in the skies, or at least something of him.'

'I don't want to give up,' said Rita with a sigh. 'Am I wrong?'

'You must do whatever feels right for you,' Faye replied, knowing that the best advice she could give her would be to let him go. But she couldn't bring herself to look into this dejected child's eyes and tell her so.

Trees wasn't much help. He didn't see the seriousness of the drama. 'Oh dear,' was all he said, scratching his head. When Faye tried to explain to him that it could come in the way of their family friendship, he was adamant that it wouldn't. 'We can't be held responsible for George,' he said firmly. 'They know that.'

'They do know that,' Faye argued. 'But in their eyes George has hurt their daughter, they're bound to be protective of her. In their position I would resent George a great deal.'

'Be that as it may,' he said with a shrug. 'Only time will tell.'

So Faye had shut herself in her studio and sculpted a hideous, angry crow with a wide-open, screaming beak. It was grotesque, but brilliant. She wondered whether Rita would continue to bicycle over after work for her lessons. She doubted it.

Max stood outside in the drizzle, smoking. Mrs Megalith hated him smoking in the house. She said it was bad for his lungs but he just laughed at the absurd idea. In his opinion, the stench of cat was far worse for one's health. He looked about the sleeping garden, at the naked trees and rotting foliage, and thought of Rita and her wintry heart. Then he thought of his childhood and the part of his own heart that had frozen over. He had arrived at Elvestree as a little boy on a day like this. He remembered the cold and the grey, the heavy cloud and the heaviness of heart. He remembered saying goodbye to his parents, embracing them for what turned out to be the last time. They had told him he was going away for a while but that, when things quietened down, they would send for him and Ruth. Of course they never did. Pain was relative, he mused. Rita didn't know the pain of losing one's family and one's home. He didn't know the pain of losing a lover. To each one the pain was total. But experience had taught him that time numbs it. It doesn't cure it completely, but it takes away the edge of it, like wrapping a blade in cloth. He only suffered if he tried to remember the past in too much detail. It was the smell of it, the sound of it, the sense of it that destroyed him, the indescribable things that defined his childhood that debilitated him completely, not the pictures in his mind. He had a photograph of his parents and one of the baby sister, Lydia, who had stayed with them to perish with the rest of the Jews. His parents had at least lived, Lydia hadn't even been given a chance. He stubbed out his cigarette on a wet paving stone and extinguished thoughts of his family and his childhood with it.

Chapter Nineteen

The following morning Harry arrived at Hannah's kitchen door in bright sunshine, holding a little cardboard box and a book. There was still a fierce wind but the clouds had been blown away leaving a cerulean sky against which sea gulls wheeled, crying their plaintive song into the icy air. Hannah was still in her dressing gown having just fed the birds and broken the ice in the birdbath. She waved at him through the window. Maddie fled the kitchen to change before he laid eyes on her old nightdress and cardigan, and Eddie ran to the back door to open it for him, thrilled by his unexpected visit. She didn't suppose he had come for her; no one could talk of anything but Rita's suicide attempt. But Eddie didn't complain. She had convinced her mother that she should stay at home to comfort her, so Hannah had made two telephone calls, one to the library where Rita worked and one to the village school. Both the headmistress and the head librarian were most understanding.

'Good morning, Harry,' chirped Eddie happily. Then she mouthed secretively that Rita was very pale and quiet. Harry nodded and mouthed back that he had brought her a book to distract her. 'What's in the box?' Eddie asked, standing on tiptoe because the lid was punctured with air holes.

'A surprise for you,' he said. Eddie's face lit up.

'For me!' she gasped. 'Mummy, Mummy, Harry's brought me a present!' And she skipped into the kitchen to tell her mother. Harry strode in behind her, slightly bent, almost apologetic.

'Would you like a cup of tea?' Hannah asked.

'That would be nice, thank you.' Then he asked after Rita.

'She's still in bed. The first day of the rest of her life, I suppose,' she replied gloomily. Then she forced a smile. 'What's this you've brought for Eddie?'

'I've brought a book for Rita. It's an old favourite of mine. *Fables of La Fontaine.*'

'How good of you. She loves books and I'm sure that will take her mind off things for a while. Thank you.'

Then he bent down and handed Eddie the box. She took it with great care for she knew it contained something living. With shining eyes she gently lifted the lid. Her mouth dropped in wonder as she looked down at the little creature blinking nervously up at her.

'A rat!' she exclaimed in delight.

'An African gerbil,' Harry corrected. 'I've got a nice big cage filled with wood shavings and a bag of food in the car.'

'Oh, Harry! You're so generous. I love him already!' She took the opportunity to wrap her free arm around his hips and bury her face appreciatively in his stomach. He patted her back and chuckled.

'I'm glad you like him. What are you going to call him?'

Eddie didn't need to think about it. 'I'll call him Ezra Gunch,' she said proudly.

Hannah laughed and her heavy spirits lifted quite unexpectedly. 'Where did you find a name like that?' she asked in amusement.

'I made it up,' she replied. 'I was going to find another bat, like Harvey, and I decided that I would call him Ezra Gunch. But Harvey wouldn't like me to love another bat. He was very jealous, you know. An African rat is much more appropriate. He can't be jealous of a rat, can he?'

'Of course he can't,' Harry agreed. 'He'll like to live up your sleeve and play on the floor in your bedroom. We can make him a run outside, if you like?'

'Oh, what a good idea. He'll need fresh air and exercise,' she enthused, taking him out of his box.

Eddie swung around to introduce Ezra Gunch to Maddie who now stood in the doorway dressed in a tweed skirt and sweater, her hair neatly brushed, her lips shining crimson and pouting shamelessly.

'What's that? A rat?' Maddie asked, screwing up her nose in disgust at the furry little creature that wriggled about in Eddie's hands.

'It's a gift from Harry,' Eddie replied importantly.

'It's adorable,' Maddie replied silkily, restraining her natural inclination to grimace. She looked up at Harry from under thick black lashes and smiled.

'Good morning, Harry.'

'Good morning, Maddie.' Harry blinked in wonder at her beautiful face and sensual body that seemed to simmer beneath her clothes. He immediately felt awkward and couldn't think of anything to say.

Hannah handed him a cup of tea and indicated that he make himself comfortable at the kitchen table. Maddie followed him and placed herself in her father's chair. Humphrey had driven off to work at dawn without saying a word. He hadn't smiled or even said 'good morning', which was most unusual. He had spent a sleepless night devising elaborate plans of revenge on George, which was quite out of character, then imagined Rita's fragile body falling from the cliff like a stone. Her misery affected him in a way that he could never have imagined. He felt cheated, made a fool of but, more crucially, useless. His child was broken and he was incapable of putting her back together again.

Harry drank his tea, aware that Maddie watched him with

her sharp, alluring eyes. He knew she was infatuated with him. Even at his most unassuming he could sense when a woman was drawn to him. Not that women fell over themselves to seduce him – in fact, it had only happened on two occasions – but he instantly recognised that predatory, calculating look and the way they leaned towards him breasts first. However, he didn't dare contemplate a relationship. Maddie was like the forbidden fruit at the top of the tree. The juiciest, softest, most succulent of peaches, temptingly swelling with ripeness in the autumn sunshine. Not only was she forbidden but she was way out of his reach, like the apple in the Garden of Eden. He was not prepared to yield to temptation and pick it.

'What did you bring for Rita?' she asked, having overheard his conversation with her mother from her bedroom upstairs.

'A book. *Fables of La Fontaine*.'

'That's nice. When she's finished with it, I'll read it,' she lied.

Harry was eager to get back to his book. The one he had been writing for the last two years: an epic tale of love and betrayal in war-torn France. He was struggling with the love aspect of it. When he got up to leave, Maddie declared that she was going with him. Harry knew she wasn't intending to paint birds on the beach dressed like that and there was nothing more to do in his study, or his house for that matter. But Maddie was determined.

'Can I read what you've written so far?' she asked, deciding she'd tackle the problem of actually reading the book once she got there.

Harry was about to shake his head and explain that it wasn't nearly ready to be seen, but then he was struck with an idea. Maddie was young, intelligent and sensitive. Perhaps she could be of help and give him an honest opinion. Maddie could certainly be counted on to speak the truth without the slightest hint of tact.

'All right,' he said, straightening up. 'Let's go.'

He left the book for Rita on the table, said goodbye to Hannah, Eddie and Ezra Gunch, and climbed into his car, followed excitedly by Maddie. She was determined to make herself indispensable.

Once at the cottage, Harry lit the fire in his study and settled her onto the sofa with the manuscript of the book so far. She gulped at the weight of so many pages, but was encouraged to see that at least it was typed in double spacing. He put some Tchaikovsky on the gramophone, brought her a cup of tea and a biscuit, then left her to it, while he tapped away on his typewriter, disappearing further and further into the wintry world of war. Maddie noticed to her delight that the painting she had done of the bar-tailed godwit was framed and hanging on the wall above his desk.

She read the first few lines, took a bite of her biscuit then watched his back as he worked. She loved his tufty hair, his broad shoulders, the way his shirts always creased, however well they were ironed. He dwarfed the little desk and chair like a giant in a fairy tale, yet he was gentle and modest as if unaware of the power of his size. He didn't feel her stare for he continued to type, pausing every now and then to find the right word. During those moments he would lift his chin and search for inspiration out of the window. Then his fingers would type again, very fast and efficiently, before he lost his train of thought. But he never looked around. Maddie resigned herself to the fact that she wasn't going to get any attention however much she huffed and puffed behind him and began to read again. To her surprise by the third page she was scanning the lines with increasing speed and no longer taking a break to glance longingly over at him. He had an engaging, fluid way of telling a story. She felt she was really there in the small French town of Masmatre. She could smell the smoke in the café, hear the low hum of voices, taste the coffee and croissants. To her surprise she enjoyed it so much her tea grew cold in the mug and the rest of the biscuit remained untouched on the plate.

By lunchtime she had finished the first ten chapters and was reluctant to stop when Harry suggested they find something to eat. She stood up and stretched, leaving the manuscript on the sofa. She found cold meat and salad in the larder and a loaf of bread in the bread bin. She knew her way around his kitchen better than he did and laid the table with all that she could find. Then they sat down to eat.

'Lie if you don't like it,' he said with a shy smile, bracing himself for her commentary. He was used, but not immune, to Maddie's candour. Maddie was pleased her opinion mattered and chewed on a piece of bread to keep him in suspense. 'Please say you like it,' he begged finally. 'If you hate it, don't be too brutal, writers are very sensitive.' Maddie took a sip of water and sat back in her chair.

'I love it,' she replied truthfully. 'I really feel as if I'm there. I am Molly Cosgrove, the spy, the adventuress, the brave heroine of your story. She's daring yet sensitive, capricious yet vulnerable, beautiful but not in a conventional way. It would make a terrific film.' Harry seemed to swell with gratitude.

'You really do like it?' he asked, and finally Maddie felt important to him.

'I love the way you write. You don't go into too much detail. You keep the momentum of the story going. I'm dying to know what happens. I can't stand it, I've got pages and pages to go. I'm dreading the sad bits. Does she fall in love? Have I met him yet?' Harry grinned, a wide, infectious grin that consumed half his face.

'I'm not telling you,' he teased. Maddie giggled.

'Oh, please. Tell me she doesn't fall in love with Klaus the Nazi?'

Harry shook his head. 'I said, I won't tell you.'

'There's a dark chemistry already. He's handsome and cold, attractive but dangerous. Very dangerous and predatory. I hope she doesn't have an affair with him, she'll get hurt.' Then her eyes glittered. 'Oh no! She'll have an affair with him to glean information, won't she?' Harry raised an eyebrow. 'Tell me I'm right?'

She moved her face closer to his, but he simply smiled at her secretively. Then her impulses got the better of her. In her excitement she kissed him. The smile suddenly disappeared and a worried frown darkened his face. They stared at one another for a moment, Maddie in surprise and Harry in panic. Neither spoke. For once Maddie couldn't think of a clever thing to say. She waited for him to either kiss her back or tell her to leave. She suddenly wished she hadn't ruined the moment. He studied her face anxiously and she searched his eyes for an indication of his thoughts. She could hear their breathing and feel the heavy thud of her heart as if they were cymbals and drums in her ears.

'Maddie,' he began, but his voice was little more than a croak.

She was quick to take action. Instead of backing away she suddenly realised that the best form of defence was attack. She placed a finger over his lips and shook her head. Then slowly she removed it. His mouth remained shut but his eyes communicated his fears. Maddie leaned forward and pressed her lips once more on his. She opened them very slightly and traced her tongue over the inside of his mouth. Harry was unable to resist. He wound his hand around the back of her neck and drew her to him. Then he was kissing her passionately to the sound of Tchaikovsky's First Piano Concerto pounding loudly from the sitting room next door. She felt his rough cheek with trembling fingers. In that moment, when the lines of reality and fiction misted, she was Molly Cosgrove and he Klaus the Nazi. With one movement of his arm he swept the remains of the lunch to the other end of the table. A glass fell over and water spilt onto the floor but they didn't care, it simply enhanced the drama of their encounter. To Maddie's delight and amazement, she discovered that Harry was as impatient as she was. He didn't carry her up to the bedroom, as she had imagined, or make love to her on the sofa in front of the fire, but right there on the kitchen table. Under the influence of his sexual desire Harry Weaver became a different person. The lover so often found in fiction but rarely in reality. He was commanding, sensitive, generous and sensual. He made Hank Weston, Steve Eastwood and Bertie Babbindon look like amateurs. By comparison with Harry they were gauche and fumbling, their awkward attempts to excite her like the heavy-handed exploring of schoolboys. Harry had the slow, gentle touch of a man who knew exactly how to pleasure a woman and Maddie writhed and moaned beneath him like a brazen whore experiencing true orgasms for the first time after years of faking them.

When they lay together, bathed in each other's sweat and the juice of that forbidden fruit now picked and devoured, Maddie sighed with happiness, unaware that her lover's sighs were heavy with guilt and regret.

'Good morning, Miss Hogmier,' said Reverend Hammond as he popped into the village shop to post a parcel to his brother-in-law in Nottingham. 'Lovely morning, isn't it!' he exclaimed heartily.

'Quite beautiful. I hope Rita Fairweather doesn't walk out on the cliffs today.' She raised her thin eyebrows at him provocatively. Reverend Hammond nodded slowly.

'Quite so,' he replied cautiously as if he were afraid of being overheard.

'Fancy that! Wanting to kill oneself over a man!' Miss

Hogmier had never been loved or in love so the very idea was alien to her.

'Poor Rita. It's a harsh blow indeed to have one's dreams shattered so young.' He sighed heavily. 'I don't believe she really wanted to kill herself.' Miss Hogmier tuttutted and rolled her eyes at his naïvety.

'Of course she did. She was swaying over the edge, seconds from death. If it hadn't been for Harry Weaver she would have perished. Broken on the rocks. Imagine what a horrid sight that would have been.'

'She's a level-headed girl. I'm sure it was a terrible mistake.'

Reverend Hammond stepped back as the door opened with a tinkle. He frowned as there was no one there. Then his eyes fell to the ground where they caught sight of a large black cat slinking in like a silky breeze. He shuddered, remembering Mrs Megalith. Miss Hogmier's face contorted with fear.

'Don't breathe a word,' she hissed to the shaken Reverend. 'The Elvestree witch has spies all over the village and we're all under surveillance.' Elwyn Hammond left as fast as he could, forgetting altogether to post his parcel.

Rita awoke to the sound of her mother at her bedroom door. 'Darling, Max's here for you.' She blinked in the stream of sunlight that fell onto her bed through the gap in the curtains, momentarily uplifted by the enthusiasm of so bright a morning. Then she remembered George's letter and sank once more into depression.

'What does he want?' she groaned, rubbing her eyes that were still sore from crying.

'He's cycled all the way over. He says he wants to take you for a walk.'

Rita would have preferred to stay in bed. Sleep was the only way to forget. But she reluctantly dragged herself to her feet and into the bathroom. She didn't sense the contrived nature of Max's visit. Mrs Megalith had suggested he go. No one wanted her to walk out on the cliffs alone. Max had been only too happy to oblige and had bicycled over at once. Little did Mrs Megalith know that it served his own secret purpose to spend time with Rita. Besides, having lost his heart to her, he felt he was more qualified than anyone else to give her guidance.

Rita shrank back when she saw her bloated, yellowed complexion in the mirror. She looked grotesque. Splashing her face with water didn't do much to alleviate the problem, but at least it woke her up. She ran a brush through her knotted hair, wincing at the pain before giving up the struggle. She tied it back, unwittingly accentuating the unhappiness that drew in her cheeks and forced out her bones, then threw on some clothes, not really caring how she looked. What was the point now that George no longer wanted her?

When she saw Max waiting for her in the kitchen, ruddy-cheeked from the cold, bracing wind and smiling at her sympathetically, she felt her spirits stir a little. She let her mother bustle about, handing her a cup of tea and encouraging her to eat the porridge she had made especially for her. 'Put some honey on it dear, it's fresh from Elvestree and will do you good.' She watched her daughter with the scrutiny of an owl until she had taken her first, unenthusiastic mouthful.

'I thought you would like to walk up the beach on a day like this,' Max said. 'I spotted a couple of spoonbills in the estuary this morning,' he added, knowing this would cheer her up.

'Really?'

'Yes, they were sweeping up insects and small fish with their bills, making the odd grunting noise in appreciation. Primrose says they are rare in these parts.'

'But there's something rather magical about Elvestree,' said Hannah, watching her daughter take another spoonful of porridge and feeling heartened. 'It wouldn't surprise me if penguins started arriving all the way from the Galapagos.'

Rita and Max set out toward the cliffs. The resplendence of the morning was infectious and Rita found that, in spite of her unhappiness, the sunshine and blue skies soothed her hurt. She didn't fear the cliffs after the events of the day before. On the contrary, she was still drawn to them for they harboured the shadows of the past. They walked along the top and Max made sure that he walked on the outside. Rita found this amusing but pretended she hadn't noticed. She did, however, cast her eyes down to the rocks and beach below and imagine what her fate might have been had Harry Weaver not arrived in the nick of time to pull her back.

They walked down the grassy path to the beach and sat on the rocks in the shelter of the cliffs to watch the birds and listen to the soothing sound of the sea. Rita toyed with the little dove pendant that George had sent her the month before.

'Part of me wants to throw this into the sea,' she said sadly. 'But I just can't let it go yet.' Max pulled a shell off a rock and turned it over in his hands.

'It's hard to write someone out of your life when they've been such a big part of it.'

'George *was* my life,' she replied with emphasis. 'I can't quite believe it's happened. But the leaden feeling inside reminds me that I'm not imagining it.'

'It will get better.'

'I know.' She lifted her chin and let the icy wind caress her features. 'I feel as if he's died, but there's no funeral or body to mourn.' Max stared out to sea and smelt that familiar scent of his childhood reach him once again from the thawing corners of his heart.

'But George will come back one day. He is not dead. You

will have the opportunity to talk to him about it. One day when the wound is no longer raw.'

'I think I would have coped better if he had died in the war. Death isn't rejection.'

'It can be worse than rejection,' Max argued in a quiet voice. He threw the shell onto the sand and began to pick at another. 'They go without taking you with them.' Rita looked at him quizzically, then realised suddenly that he was no longer talking about her.

'But that gets better too, doesn't it?' she said in a soft voice. Max looked at her.

'Time makes everything better. That is one thing that experience has taught me. Some day you will have to take off that pendant. Keep it in a box, safely tucked away where it won't stare out at you all the time to remind you of what you have lost. Believe me, it works. Only when you have healed can you reminisce with nostalgia and without pain.'

'Megagran says that I have to talk about it,' she said, tucking the pendant back into her jersey.

'She's right. That makes you feel better too. But don't expect it to work overnight.'

'You rarely talk about your family.'

'You know Ruth and I had a little sister?'

'No, I didn't know.'

'Lydia. I don't remember her much. She was only a baby. I can still smell her, though. I can smell her bedroom. A soft, warm smell, like hot milk.'

'Did she . . . ?'

'Yes, she died too. In the camps.' He cast his eyes to the sand and focused on a small crustacean that was wriggling its way across a shallow pool of water. 'I'm lucky to have Ruth.'

'Do you talk about it with her?' Rita asked, without realising that the tragedy of Max's family was taking her out of herself.

'No. She's afraid to remember.' He lifted his eyes and looked at her. 'I talk to you.' Rita smiled.

'We can help each other,' she said, taking his hand. 'It can be our secret project.'

'I'd like to go back one day.'

'To Vienna?'

'Yes. To the theatre my father built. I dream about it sometimes. It seems so big in my dreams and yet, I know that my memory of it is distorted because I was just a small boy. It was beautiful, though. Full of golden lights and rich crimson velvet. Like the palace of a king. One day when I'm rich I'll buy it back.'

'Maybe you'll marry an actress like your mother and she'll sing in it.'

'Maybe,' he replied with a chuckle, but he was imagining taking Rita.

A flock of gulls flew overhead and Rita and Max shaded their eyes with their hands to watch them. Bathed in sunlight they swooped and glided, playing games with the wind that only they knew. Then they landed on the sand in a gaggle to search for food. The sight of those birds lifted their spirits, reassuring them both that while people change some things never do.

Chapter Twenty

Harry was mortified. He had taken advantage of a young girl without having thought through the consequences. It made no difference that she had the sexual experience of a much older woman, she was only nineteen and he was a middle-aged divorcé who should know better. Tormented by his own foolishness he withdrew like a tortoise into its shell, hoping that the problem would go away if he didn't confront it.

Maddie left his house delirious with happiness. Harry loved her. They'd marry and live happily ever after. He'd write his books, she'd edit them and raise their children and they'd make love in the afternoons in their cosy cottage in Bray Cove. But she was to be disappointed, for Harry didn't telephone her and when she telephoned him that evening he was distant and could barely manage more than a mumble.

'This afternoon was lovely,' she breathed down the line. Harry's gulp was audible. 'Why don't I come over tomorrow and make you lunch, then we can spend all afternoon together,' she whispered in case her parents happened to overhear her.

'Well, I really ought to get on with this book. I have a deadline, after all,' he muttered. Harry seemed to have developed a stammer. A sensitive woman would have understood the frantic back-pedalling and retreated with dignity, but Maddie didn't notice.

'I can help. You were grateful for my advice today. I'll cook you lunch while you write, then I'll read what you've written and tell you what I think.'

'That's really sweet of you . . .' he began.

'Good, I'll see you tomorrow. I can't wait, darling Harry.' When she hung up Harry was left bewildered. What was he going to do?

That night he lay uneasily in his bed. He had been weak and irresponsible and would have to pay the consequences tomorrow and tell Maddie that it had been a mistake. He muttered imaginary conversations into the darkness then, when those failed, tried to convince himself that his attraction to her had no substance, that it was no more than a sexual attraction he could easily live without. His thoughts drifted to his ex-wife and the error of judgement he had made there. He was no good with women. He didn't understand them. He couldn't risk failing again. Rolling over onto his side, he contemplated himself miserably. He was in his late thirties, divorced, balding, struggling to write a decent book, penniless and unlucky, what did he have to offer a young girl like Maddie? What on earth did she see in him? His attraction to her was obvious, but surely some sprite was playing a wicked trick with her eyes.

The following day Maddie walked over to Bray Cove in dazzling white sunshine. A light sprinkling of frost covered the ground and turned the world an icy blue. The beauty of the countryside was breathtaking and Maddie, who was usually far too self-obsessed to notice her surroundings, gazed about her in wonder. She pictured Harry's diffident grin, and smiled tenderly at the thought of his gentle face and kind, sensitive eyes. How surprised her family were going to be when they discovered that she had fallen in love with Harry Weaver of all people. He wasn't rich, he wasn't glamorous, he wasn't even handsome like George, but she loved him and after having made love with him she cherished him all the more. That was another Harry altogether; her own secret Harry.

When she arrived at Bray Cove she let herself in and bounded through the hall to the sitting room. Harry was grey-faced and anxious, stooped over his typewriter having written little more than a sentence that morning. Maddie smiled broadly and threw her arms around his neck, kissing his face with a loud smack.

'How's my darling lover today?' she said, pressing her lips to him again. She felt his unyielding body and drew away. 'What is it? What's the matter?'

Harry sighed heavily and raised his eyes to where she now stood before him. He hesitated and caught his breath as the luminous beauty of her face held him momentarily in a hypnotic trance. He inhaled the feminine scent of her body and felt the hair on the back of his neck bristle with nervousness. Silently scolding himself for his weakness, he tore his eyes away and resumed as planned.

'Maddie, what we did yesterday was wrong.' Maddie froze. She shook her head and frowned. Then she tried to smile but her lips only quivered for a moment before opening in panic. Harry continued. 'It was lovely . . . you were lovely,' he stammered. 'But it isn't right.'

'What isn't right?' Her voice was a high-pitched wail.

'You're young . . .'

'Young?' she repeated, extending her arms like the wings of a fearsome condor. 'Young? That's not what you thought yesterday when you made love to me on the kitchen table.'

'I shouldn't have.'

'A bit late for regrets, isn't it?'

'I don't regret, I mean, not like that. It was lovely . . . it's just that . . .'

'Was sex all you wanted? Now you've had me you don't want me any more?'

'No, it's not like that at all.'

Maddie placed her hands on her hips as her face began to match her hair. Harry only thought she looked more ravishing, which made his task almost impossible. He longed to kiss her again and taste the salt on her skin, but he knew he mustn't, though at this precise moment his arguments for restraint suddenly seemed negligible.

'I don't believe you, Harry!' she cried in fury. 'I thought you were different. I thought you were special but you're not. You're pathetic and weak and I deserve better!'

Before Harry could protest she marched out of his house and out of his life, leaving him more confused than ever.

As winter slowly thawed into spring, the ice on the birdbath in Hannah's garden thinned until it no longer needed breaking at dawn and Rita's crushed spirit slowly began to heal. Max put off his move to the city, his career could wait. Rita, he felt, couldn't. They walked out along the cliffs, up and down the beach, and picnicked on the sand reading poetry together, their laughter carried on the wind with the carefree chatter of gulls. Rita kept the little cave she had shared with George a secret. She couldn't bear to visit it. The memories within it still breathed with too much life. Max listened as she talked about George and sometimes, especially at sunset when he lost his reserve in the melting day, he would tell her about his childhood.

Rita resumed her sculpting lessons with Faye, and the family friendship that Faye had feared in danger of ruin was restored to something of its former strength. Trees had been right, but he didn't gloat or say 'I told you so' for he had moved on from what he believed to have been nothing more than a tiny pothole along the path of life. Only Humphrey still felt aggrieved but he kept his resentment to himself.

Maddie sulked. She put away her sketchpad and pencils

and no longer accompanied her mother to Bray Cove. When the swallows returned she cursed them. Why ever had she been interested in birds? To Hannah and Humphrey's dismay Bertie's car once more drew up outside their house and his arrogant, empty face was frequently seen pressed against the kitchen window, grinning inanely. Maddie let him kiss her in the lay-by outside Frognal Point, but her heart had frozen over.

Rita sensed her sister's unhappiness had much to do with Harry Weaver but she didn't dare mention his name. If Maddie's pride was hurt she would not want to talk about it. So she left her to smoulder about the house like an angry dragon without realising that, for the first time in their lives, they had something in common.

At the beginning of April Faye received another letter from George. This time she folded it away carefully and resigned herself with sadness to the fact that their much-treasured family friendship would now be over for sure. There was no avoiding a fall-out once this piece of news reached Hannah's kitchen.

George was getting married. His fiancée was called Susan and he had met her on the boat going out to Argentina. She was American and he was very much in love with her. Faye already despised Susan and immediately blamed her for ensnaring George so soon after he had left Rita. Only when she talked to Thadeus did she realise that she was wrong to cast blame.

'We all have the power of free will,' he said, sitting down beside her on the bench in his garden. The earth was now beginning to stir with life as the days lengthened and the weather warmed. Daffodils and snowdrops swung their pretty drooping heads and a pair of swallows danced in the air announcing their return and the long-awaited arrival of spring.

'How am I going to tell Rita that George fell in love

with this American woman no more than a few days after leaving her?'

'Why do you need to tell her the details?' he asked, taking her cold hand in his large warm one.

'Because I feel she has a right to know.'

Thadeus shrugged his big shoulders and growled. 'You don't have to lie, Faye, just tell her half the truth.'

'That George is marrying another woman? I'm so furious with him. It was bad enough breaking off his engagement. This news is going to destroy her.'

'Don't be angry with your son. He has the right to love whoever he chooses. He had not made his marriage vows to Rita. He was not committed to her in the eyes of God, only in the eyes of the Fairweathers. It is better to love honestly than to love like we do.' Faye watched the swallows disappear over the hedge, their song lost in the wind.

'At least he's marrying the right woman,' she said, squeezing Thadeus's hand. 'Or, at least, I hope he is.'

'People change. What he wanted as a boy is not necessarily what he wants as a man. Rita was right for him while he was young. Perhaps he simply grew out of her. Don't blame him for that. You wouldn't wish him to make a mistake, would you? Are you more concerned about your friendship with Hannah than your own son's happiness?'

'Of course not!' she replied quickly. Then she sighed heavily. 'I just want everyone to be happy.'

'Life is not like that. We're not meant to be happy all of the time. Life is full of problems and the sooner we realise that the better our chances of contentment. If your expectations are too high you will never be satisfied.'

'So what do I do?' she asked, resting her head on his shoulder.

'Go and see Hannah. Tell her that George has written to you saying he is to marry an American woman he met in

Argentina. That is all she needs to know. Then leave her alone to digest it. If she lets it come between you, so be it. There is nothing you can do. Go with the current because trying to swim against it will only wear you out.'

'Thank God I've got you!' she breathed. 'Why do we all make such a mess of love?'

'That I cannot answer,' he replied with a smile.

When Faye arrived at Hannah's house she leaned her bicycle up against the wall and walked through the hedge to the garden. She knew better than to knock on the door. On a day like this Hannah would be outside, looking after her birds and plants. As it was half term, Faye found Eddie playing with Ezra Gunch in the run that Harry had constructed for him on the lawn.

'Hi Faye,' Eddie cried with a giggle, for Ezra had just disappeared into a cardboard tube she had stolen from an unfinished toilet roll. 'I'm training him to be an acrobat,' she added when Faye came to see what she was laughing at.

'You're doing a terrific job of it,' she replied in a tight voice. She felt so nervous her whole body was shaking. 'Where's your mother?'

'In the vegetable garden planting sweet peas,' she replied, picking up the tube and pouring Ezra out onto the palm of her hand. 'Isn't he a dear little thing? We've become very close. He peed on Harvey's grave when I took him to visit it. I don't think he has much respect for the dead.'

Faye couldn't help but smile at the child's exuberance then, taking a very deep breath, she walked across the lawn to the old wooden door in the wall.

Hannah and Rita were working either side of the bamboo frame, chatting away happily while they planted the sweet peas. Hannah heard Faye approach and looked up.

'Faye,' she exclaimed. 'What a nice surprise.'

'Beautiful day, isn't it?' said Faye, putting off the dreadful moment for as long as possible.

'Finally. Winter did seem very long this year for some reason.'

Rita noticed the tension in Faye's face and stopped planting.

'I had a letter from George,' she said flatly, folding her arms in front of her. She looked at Rita and shook her head apologetically. Hannah paused her digging and her smile disappeared into a worried frown. 'He's getting married.'

Rita's cheeks flushed before blanching with shock. Hannah stared at her friend in disbelief. 'Getting married? Who to?'

'An American he's met out there.'

'What's her name?' Rita asked. Faye thought it an odd question.

'Susan.'

Rita began to cry. Hannah dropped her trowel and hurried around the frame to comfort her. Faye stood awkwardly watching them, not knowing what to do with her hands. She wanted to leave but feared she would appear rude.

'I'm so sorry,' she said. 'It's come as a total surprise. I never imagined he'd have met someone else. Agatha's farm is in the middle of nowhere.'

Hannah held her sobbing daughter against her breasts, mumbling endearments, as Faye looked on miserably. Eddie skipped through the door with Ezra Gunch perched on her shoulder. Her broad smile slid off her face when she saw her mother and Rita crouched down on the mud and she glowered accusingly at Faye.

'What's George done now?' she demanded and Faye was taken aback by the child's formidable tone of voice.

'He's getting married,' she replied. Eddie was horrified.

'How dare he!' she exclaimed, taking Ezra Gunch off her shoulder and sending him up her sleeve to safety. 'He was only in love with Rita five minutes ago. What a pig!'

'I think I had better go,' Faye stammered, backing away. 'I'm so sorry.' But neither Hannah nor Rita noticed her. Only Eddie glared at her as if she were guilty of betrayal too.

'I want to walk on the beach,' Rita said at last, extracting her face from her mother's spongy bosom. Hannah looked anxious.

'I'll go with you,' she suggested, standing up.

'No, I want to go alone,' Rita replied. Then she recognised the fear in her mother's eyes and added firmly, 'I won't throw myself off the cliff, I promise.' Hannah wasn't convinced.

'Oh, I really don't think you should be alone at a time like this,' she protested.

'I'll be fine. I'm angry. Angry people don't kill themselves.'

'You can take Ezra if you like. He won't talk to you,' Eddie suggested. Hannah placed a hand on Eddie's shoulder.

'Thank you, dear, but I think Ezra's happier with you.'

'I won't go up on the cliffs. I'll go straight to the beach.'

'All right,' her mother conceded grudgingly. 'But don't do anything stupid.'

Rita set off at a brisk walk. For the last few months she had nurtured a small flame of hope that George might return as planned after a year and want her back. It was a fragile flame and one which she knew she shouldn't fan with dreams and wishes. But while he was on his own there had always been that faint chance. Now he had fallen in love with someone else that flame had died, and her heart was plunged into darkness.

She hurried down the grassy path to the beach and then hovered momentarily, working up the courage to turn left to their secret cave. Slowly, she began to walk. With every step she remembered George. Now the footsteps in the sand were solitary ones. When she reached the mouth of the cave she stopped, unsure of whether to proceed, afraid of what she would encounter within.

Suppressing her anxiety, she stepped inside. When her eyes adjusted to the darkness she was surprised to see nothing but a gaping hollow of rock. There were no ghosts, no shadows, no demons dancing on the walls. Just her own memories locked safely inside her head. She walked up to the far end and sat down on the dry sand. She crossed her legs and listened to the hypnotic sound of waves breaking on the beach. Her fingers began to play with the dove pendant that hung between her breasts. She rubbed it with her thumb and forefinger for a while, deliberating whether she had the strength to take it off and lose it to the sea. There was no reason to wear it now. It only reminded her of George and the promises they had made to one other.

With a sigh she unclasped the pendant and let it drop into the palm of her hand. She looked at it through her tears. The lost letter had been an omen. She understood that now. Hadn't Thadeus said that a dove is symbolic of forgiveness as well as wedded bliss and love? She wondered whether George had known that when he had sent it to her. Well, she was unable to forgive him. He had betrayed her. Little by little she felt the burning sensation of hate seep into her heart like black tar. It was heavy and sticky and bitter and so dreadfully ugly that she was ashamed of herself. She strode out of the cave, down to where the sea crept up the sand, and flung the pendant into the waves. It made no sound or splash and was swallowed up by the greedy sea.

And what of the ring? The diamond solitaire that symbolised his promise to marry her. How often had she looked into its innocent sparkle and heard his words, '*Every time you look at it I want you to remember how much I love you.*' Now she took it off and slid it onto the third finger of her right hand. For some reason she was loath to let it go. Only when the last ray of hope had diminished would she send it, too, to the bottom of the sea.

As Rita walked through the village she decided to pay a visit to Thadeus. The last time she had seen him had been when she had lost George's letter to the sea. He had been a valuable source of wisdom then. She turned up the lane and hesitated outside the little gate that was partially obscured by the thick yew hedge. He would probably think her foolish crying once again over George. She should have visited him before to show him that she wasn't always broken-hearted. However, she dismissed her fears with the thought of his warm, cosy house and opened the gate.

She knocked on the door and waited. There was no reply. She knocked again and looked about her. She noticed a bicycle leaning against the wall in the sunshine. Deducing from the bicycle that he must be at home, she wandered round the house to the garden. It was such a beautiful day he was probably pottering about in his borders. As the started to make her way through the cluster of rhododendron bushes she saw him sitting on a bench with his arm around a petite woman with flowing white hair, whose head rested on his shoulder. As they were facing the other way she was unable to recognise the woman, but decided not to intrude on what was without doubt an intimate moment. She began to creep away. But curiosity pulled her back. She stole through the bushes far enough to get a better look. Horrified, she saw that the woman with long hair was none other than Faye. Clasping a hand over her mouth to smother a gasp, she scurried away as fast as possible, praying that they hadn't seen her.

When she was safely out in the lane she sank back into the hedge and covered her face with trembling hands. Her heart was thumping with fear and fury. She had never seen Faye with her hair down before. She looked like a young girl, a beautiful young girl. She immediately felt desperately sorry for Trees, toiling away on the farm while his wife led a secret romantic life with Thadeus Walizhewski. No wonder he kept one of her sculptures in his bedroom. One of her masterpieces. Did George know that his mother was an adulteress? Did betrayal run in the family? Run in his blood? A fine example she set, Rita thought bitterly. Faye of all people! She ran home, blinded by rage, and locked herself in her bedroom.

Rita realised she could never divulge what she had seen, not to anyone. But that day she lost all faith in love. She had always assumed that Trees and Faye had one of the happiest marriages in the world. She had based her own ideals of marriage on theirs and that of her parents. Now she not only felt betrayed by George but by his mother too, for shattering everything she believed in.

Mrs Megalith stood in the middle of her garden with Nestor, the ancient gardener, directing him with the aid of her walking stick. 'Over there are scarlet field poppies, purple verbena and violets,' she said, delighting in the thought of these opportunist seedlings. 'Lovely!' Nestor, half-bent with age and the force of Mrs Megalith's awesome personality, staggered over and pointed at the little sprouts that were already peeping out of the earth.

'It's difficult to imagine now, Mrs M, but when these little fellows flower it'll be a wonderland of vibrant colour.' He spoke slowly with a heavy Devonshire drawl so that even Mrs Megalith found him difficult to understand. 'A rainbow in your own garden!' he mused cheerfully. 'I did a fair bit of weeding in the autumn, you see, of campions especially. Created a bit of space for other fellows like poppies. I know how much you like poppies, Mrs M.'

'I do indeed, Nestor. Lovely!' She hobbled after him,

sniffing her approval at the immaculate state of the borders that promised to spill over with flowers in the summertime.

Mrs Megalith loved Elvestree. She had grown up in Frognal Point and the house had originally belonged to her grandfather. As much as people wanted to believe that the exotic birds and thriving animals, rare fruits and rich vegetables were due to her sorcery, she knew the truth: the magic had been there long before she was born and was as much part of the house as the very bricks it was made of. Nestor understood, for Nestor had worked for her parents as his father had before him. He didn't question the size of the potatoes or the abundance of beans, sprouts and cabbages. He didn't even raise an eyebrow when the garden threw up artichokes, rhubarb and aubergines out of season, and he was used to the grapevines and bananas in the greenhouses. While the rest of the country had to make do with plums and apples he could take home peaches and oranges to enjoy with his wife. When she praised the skill of the Elvestree witch, he simply shook his head for he knew better and remembered the strange lychees his father had brought home when he was just a boy.

Mrs Megalith was proud of the history of the place. The house dated back to the seventeenth century but the garden was far older. The walled vegetable garden was possibly as old as six hundred years. Legend had it that it was once attached to a monastery and that the monks fertilised the ground with nothing more than prayers. Mrs Megalith scoffed at that. She suspected they were more likely to be wizards in religious clothing and greedy wizards to boot.

She lifted her nose and sniffed the air. The sweet, fertile scent of spring had once more returned and nature quivered with life. She could smell the estuary too and hear the birds down on the sand, fighting over pieces of fish and small crustaceans.

Suddenly Nestor bent to the ground and waved aside

a clump of leaves. 'What have we here?' he exclaimed, straightening up to make way for Mrs Megalith.

'What is it, Nestor?' she asked, hobbling over to him.

'Looks like one of them cats has had a go at your swallow.' Mrs Megalith's face darkened in horror.

'A swallow? Is it alive?'

'I fear the poor little devil is, though it would be better off dead.'

'Let me see. Out of the way.' She pushed past him and peered down. 'Good gracious! Right, go and get Max.' Nestor hurried across the lawn, shouting for Max. Max emerged and recognised by the exaggerated movements of Mrs Megalith's arms that it was an emergency.

'I can't bend down to pick it up,' she said as he approached. 'But I want you to try and scoop the poor bird into your hands without frightening it. Imagine it's made of eggshell.' Max smiled indulgently and lifted the little bird with great care. When it lay still but trembling in his cupped hands she set off across the grass. 'Follow me. You too, Nestor. I need all the help I can get. We're going to nurse this little bird back to health if it's the last thing we do!' They followed her as she staggered towards the house. Ruth was in the kitchen devouring a Marmite sandwich when they entered in a flurry of excitement. 'Ruth, get me a cardboard box and fill it with hay. There's plenty in the barn.' Ruth frowned at her brother but was used to obeying orders and hurried off.

Mrs Megalith placed her glasses on the end of her nose and took the bird in her soft, doughy hands. 'Max, go and fetch my box of crystals. Nestor, I need a syringe from the medicine cupboard and a glass of water. I think it's only suffering a broken wing, but it obviously hasn't eaten or drunk for some time.' Nestor disappeared up the stairs to the cupboard on the landing where Mrs Megalith kept her medical supplies. Ruth returned with the shoe box that had contained the pair of sensible lace-ups Mrs Megalith had bought her for school. She had dutifully lined it with hay and punctured the lid in case she wanted to close it. Mrs Megalith placed the bird inside and, when Max returned with the box of crystals, she rummaged around until she found the ones she needed to aid the healing process. She fed it water with the syringe and bound the broken wing with a splint, securing it tightly to its body.

'Will he live?' Ruth asked, peering into the box.

'It's a she,' Mrs Megalith replied. 'And yes, she'll live. If I knew which cat had done it, I'd wring the little bugger's neck.'

Chapter Twenty-one

Reverend Hammond passed his eyes over his congregation. The pews were filled with the same faces in the same hats and coats, yet there was a subtle change that made today different from any other Sunday – and a great deal colder. Being a godly man he sensed it at once. It had nothing to do with the fresh sea breeze that swept in through the open windows or the fact that Miss Hogmier had fallen down the stairs and bruised her coccyx so that she now played the organ with such aggression as to suggest it was the organ, not the stairs, she blamed for her discomfort. He had heard from his wife who had heard from Miss Hogmier who had overheard Hannah talking to her sister in the bakery that George Bolton was engaged to be married to a woman called Cybil. It was a desperate situation and one which no doubt was being discussed in every shop and kitchen within a ten-mile radius.

To his dismay, he saw that the Fairweathers sat on the left side of the church while the Boltons sat on the right and neither family looked at the other. Instead of friendly waves and smiles a wall of resentment and guilt had risen up between them and, although they all knew it was there, no one dared acknowledge its presence. They kept their eyes fixed ahead or on their prayer books. Humphrey's face was grey and seemed to have collapsed like a soufflé while Hannah buried her chin into her neck, hiding her swollen features beneath her hat. Rita was tearful but pensive, seeking solace in the tranquillity of the church. She didn't have the courage to snatch a quick look at

Faye, *cheating* Faye, who no doubt sat with the innocence of one of those angels painted on the altarpiece. Eddie played with Ezra Gunch, having explained to her mother that he needed cheering up as much as everyone else for being a very small animal he sensed unhappiness but didn't understand it, and Maddie's cheeks were flushed with fury as she recalled over and over again her final conversation with Harry. Faye's hands toyed nervously with her engagement ring while Alice and Geoffrey looked very sombre indeed. Even their small children were unusually still and quiet in the pew. Trees was staunch in his belief that each man ploughs his own field in life and that one shouldn't get involved in the business of others, even one's children. He watched the Reverend, anticipating the service, viewing the whole melodrama as blown out of proportion by the women in both families. Surely Humphrey would rise above it as he did and consider the crisis nothing more than an unfortunate storm in a teacup.

Reverend Hammond met the challenge with zeal, considering it God's wish for him to unite these two families in obvious need of spiritual guidance. He quietly congratulated himself on ad-libbing a most inspiring sermon about forgiveness and love, without realising that Humphrey and Hannah were too hurt to forgive and Rita and Maddie were only too bitterly aware of the damage love could do. At the end of a service that left the rest of the congregation bewildered, Humphrey merely grunted at Trees before hurrying out into the sunshine, Hannah following hastily in his heavy footsteps. Trees was left dazed and bruised. He took Faye's arm and wandered slowly up the aisle blinking in the light of such a brutal awakening. Faye had been right all along. George's engagement had torn their families apart.

As Faye and Trees emerged, they found Rita standing by the door waiting for Eddie who had lost Ezra Gunch in the nave. When she saw them approach she backed away, pressing herself up against the wall hoping they would walk on without seeing her. But Faye had witnessed her sudden retreat. Sadly, she decided to persevere with a conversation in an attempt to make peace.

'Hello, Rita,' she said in a gentle voice. 'How are you?'

Rita's faced flushed and she looked anxiously over her shoulder for Eddie. 'I'm fine, thank you.'

Eddie was on her hands and knees trying to coax Ezra Gunch out from under the altarcloth where he had seized upon an old communion wafer.

'You haven't been for your sculpting lessons recently.'

'It's a bit difficult at the moment . . .'

'I understand. Of course I do. But you shouldn't let it go, you've got real talent.'

'I've been working late,' Rita explained lamely, then shuffled uncomfortably for it was common knowledge that the library always closed at six.

'Well, if you change your mind, I'd love to see you.' Faye touched her arm affectionately. But when Rita didn't respond she nodded at Trees and walked away, fighting her disappointment. Rita dropped her shoulders and took a deep breath. Finally Eddie appeared smiling, having forced the gerbil into a corner and lured him out with another piece of wafer.

'It's not as if I don't feed him enough, the greedy rat!' she complained as they walked down the path.

Faye was dismayed that Rita no longer wanted to sculpt with her and saddened that the bond that had held them all together for so many years had now been severed. It didn't occur to her that Rita's coldness might be due to having seen her in the garden with Thadeus, so confident was she that their secret was theirs alone.

'Well, you could have cut the atmosphere with a knife!' Miss Hogmier commented to Reverend Hammond once the congregation had departed. She hobbled up the aisle with the help of a stick, wincing every few paces so that her nostrils flared revealing thick black nasal hair like the brush of a chimney sweep.

'Oh dear,' Reverend Hammond sighed, watching Rita and Eddie walk down the road until they disappeared around the corner. 'I did my best to guide them in the way of Christ. I only hope the seed sown has fallen onto fertile ground.'

'A rift such as this will never heal,' Miss Hogmier stated spitefully. 'And young George is far away in Argentina, oblivious of it all.'

'I don't suppose he has the slightest idea of the suffering he has caused.'

'I don't imagine he cares. A selfish man, I've always thought.' Miss Hogmier sank carefully onto a pew, groaning as her bottom touched the wood.

'Dear Rita, it was only this time last year that they all welcomed George home with that party.'

'An extravagance for nothing,' she sniffed. 'Only ever thought of himself, that boy. Too handsome for his own good if you ask me.'

'She'll find someone else. She's young and pretty.'

'But the families will never recover. Better for the Boltons, I suppose. I wouldn't trust any descendants of the Elvestree witch, however pretty they were.' Miss Hogmier looked around suspiciously. 'No cats in the vicinity, I trust?' Reverend Hammond cast a quick glance at the altar, remembering with a grimace the time Mrs Megalith had brought her cats to sabotage his service.

'If there are, I shall throw them out,' he replied boldly.

'Surely not the way of Christ?' Miss Hogmier gasped in admiration.

'Christ threw out the moneylenders, did he not? Those cats

were emissaries from a pagan. If I see them again I shall do as Christ did and think nothing of it.'

'You brave man!' Miss Hogmier struggled to her feet. 'I suppose I will go home now and try to get on with things. No one to look after me. Of course, I don't complain. I shall simply suffer in silence, but what can one do? An old spinster like me? Society is not kind to old maids. Rita Fairweather had better find someone soon or she'll end up like me.'

'She would be lucky to, Miss Hogmier. You are a woman of faith,' said Reverend Hammond generously. Miss Hogmier clicked her tongue and took the compliment dispassionately, as if it were her due. Reverend Hammond watched her hobble out into the sunshine, wincing at the brightness like a vampire. He couldn't help thinking that she made Mrs Megalith look like the good fairy.

When Hannah returned home she changed out of her Sunday best and set about cooking lunch. She looked out of the window and sighed. She missed Faye. It wasn't her fault that George had met another woman in the Argentine, but she couldn't help but resent his whole family. She felt betrayed by Faye as much as by George and there was nothing she could do about it. Faye was obviously upset, but Hannah couldn't find it in her heart to forgive.

Rita sat on the window seat of her bedroom looking down at the pigeons on the lawn. Frognal Point had changed so much in the last few months and Rita hated change. She feared it. Her whole future, once so well thought-out, was now thrown into the air and she didn't know how it would arrange itself when the pieces finally settled. Even Maddie wasn't herself. She was moody and distant as if she feared intimacy would force her to divulge secrets she didn't wish to share.

Then one Saturday evening Maddie returned from a drive

with Bertie and marched straight into Rita's room, where Rita was busy composing poetry. When she saw her sister's ashen face in the doorway she put down her pen and stood up to embrace her. 'What is it, Maddie?' she asked after Maddie had finished sobbing onto her shirt. Maddie swept the clothes off the bed and sat down.

'I slept with Harry then he rejected me,' she stated, wiping her face with the back of her hand. Rita rummaged around on her dressing table for a hankerchief, and handed it to Maddie who dabbed at her cheeks with care so as not to ruin her make-up.

'Have you seen him since?' Rita sat down beside her.

Maddie sniffed and sighed melodramatically. 'No. And I don't want to,' she added hastily. 'I'm furious, that's all.'

'And hurt.'

'A little,' she conceded, dropping her shoulders. 'I think he's the first man I've ever been truly in love with.' Rita had never seen her sister so distraught.

'How did it happen?' she asked gently.

'I seduced him and it was wonderful.' For a moment the light in her eyes returned. 'Wonderful! He says I'm too young for him.'

'Too young? Is that all?' Rita was confused.

'He used my body and then discarded me.'

'I'm sure that's not true, Maddie! I denied George my body and he discarded me. Perhaps if I had slept with him he wouldn't have run off with another woman. I should have taken your advice.'

'You don't think he tired of me?'

'Of course not. Harry's not like that. He's sweet and kind, he's no cad. What else did he say?'

'I didn't hang around to listen.'

'You flounced out.' Rita knew her sister well. 'Then re-sumed your relationship with Bertie?'

'I was cross,' she said. 'I needed someone.'

After a moment's thought, Rita stood up and walked over to the window.

'Look at it from Harry's point of view. He's much older than you, divorced and poor. Perhaps he feels guilty that he took advantage of you when he has nothing to offer. I've seen the way he looks at you, Maddie. Maybe you should have been more persuasive. He's probably hurting just as much as you are.'

Maddie scoffed incredulously. 'I doubt it. He's buried his nose in his bloody book.'

'Go and talk to him. You have far more confidence than he has.'

'I'll think about it,' she replied, getting up. 'You know Rita, at times you can be very wise. It's a shame that wisdom's missing in your own love-life.'

Maddie considered her sister's advice. If Harry believed himself unworthy of her, then she would simply have to persuade him otherwise, and her greatest asset, she believed, was her sexuality.

Determined to win him back, she settled at her dressing table and carefully applied her make-up. She was beautiful with pale, translucent skin and wide-set, feline eyes that were the envy of all the girls she knew. He hadn't been hard to seduce a few months before; if she could just do it again she'd have a good chance of convincing him of her maturity. How foolish she had been to back down without a fight and how out of character. It had been the primitive reaction of a girl who had never known the sting of rejection. As she applied her rouge and lipstick she thought of war paint and the battle ahead.

In a thin summer dress she cycled over to Bray Cove. In spite of her confidence in her appeal she was nervous. She hadn't seen him for months. She didn't know what to expect.

She couldn't bear to be humiliated again. What if her plan failed and he rejected her? She winced at the thought, then banished it from her mind.

When she arrived at his cottage she left her bicycle on the gravel and crept around to his study window. As she anticipated he was bent over his typewriter, struggling to complete the book that he hoped would make his name as well as his fortune. Maddie's eyes stung as she watched him. He looked greyer, thinner and more dishevelled than ever. The room was a mess, with papers and books all over the floor and she could even see a thick layer of dust from where she was standing, exposed by the sunlight that managed to penetrate the dirty window. Then, as if subconsciously aware that he was being observed, Harry turned. Seeing Maddie's radiant face staring back at him he visibly jumped in surprise. His face creased into a frown and he called out her name. From where he was sitting she might well have been a trick of light for the sun shone brilliantly about her head. Flustered, he put up his hand to indicate that she stay right where she was and leapt to his feet, sending his chair crashing to the floor.

Maddie's heart hopped about like one of her grandmother's mysterious Indian jumping beans but his reaction had been encouraging. A few moments later he strode around the corner.

'Maddie?' he exclaimed. His appearance was hardly that of an adventurer who used women for his own sexual gratification. Maddie realised that she had clearly jumped to the wrong conclusion and set about putting it right immediately.

'Oh Harry, I love you,' she said, falling into his arms. 'I don't care that you're old and poor. To me you're rich in everything that matters.'

Harry was overwhelmed. He didn't know whether to be offended or flattered by her typically careless remark. He wrapped his arms around her and pressed his nose into her hair. She smelt warm and familiar. When she pulled away to look at him he was grinning down at her with boyish delight.

'I'm also divorced. I rarely go to church. I'm a misanthrope,' he began. Maddie noticed the colour return to his cheeks. 'I'm sure you have a few more disadvantages to add to the list!'

'If I did it wouldn't make the slightest difference. I love you just the way you are.'

'And I've been an oaf. I'm sorry I hurt you.'

She pressed her finger to his lips as she had done the first time she had kissed him but this time he took the lead and pressed his mouth to hers.

It was the middle of August when Max announced to Rita that he was leaving Frognal Point. The sun was intense, which was a relief after so much rain. Trees had had a hard time with the harvest, having to wait until the ground dried to cut the corn, which was still soaking wet and barely ripe, but the country-side had benefited enormously. The leaves sparkled on trees whose branches sagged under the weight of so many birds. Flowers turned their heads to the sun and shone resplendent at the height of their bloom, and the breeze was scented and fresh from having swept in from the coast. Max lay beside Rita on the lawn at Elvestree, watching the sick swallow – now well, but grounded – hop across the grass. Fortunately, the cats were asleep inside the house, but Max kept a keen eye out for any opportunists hopeful of an easy meal.

'When are you leaving?' Rita asked, surprised. She had taken Max for granted over the last few months. With Maddie spending so much time now at Bray Cove she had come to rely on him as her friend and confidant.

'On the first of September,' he replied, searching her face for signs of disappointment.

'Where will you stay?'

'With your great-aunt Hazel, Primrose's sister. She has a house close to Oxford Street which is very convenient as I'm going to work in Broadcasting House.'

'The BBC?' Her eyes widened with admiration. 'You kept that to yourself.' She pushed him playfully.

'I wasn't sure it had come off. I applied ages ago. They kept delaying it,' he lied. In fact, he had jeopardised his job there by stalling for Rita's sake. 'I would have told you if it had been a certainty. I didn't want to jinx it.'

'What are you going to do there?'

'Make the tea, probably,' he chuckled. 'I don't know. I'll do anything to get a foot on the ladder.'

'I'll miss you,' she said and pulled a pathetic smile. Max's heart fluttered as if it had wings and was about to fly away.

'I'll miss you too, but I'm not going for ever. I'll come down every now and then. You don't think I could be away from Elvestree for long, do you?'

'Megagran will miss you too. So will Ruth.'

'Ruth has grown so attached to Eddie, she'll be fine. In fact, she now wants a gerbil like Ezra Gunch but Primrose says the cats will have it in five minutes so she'll just have to content herself playing with Eddie's.'

'Will you telephone me once in a while?'

'I'll write too.'

'You're brave going to live in London.'

'The war's over, Rita, the only battle will be with the smog. I hear it's dreadful.'

'Pea soup!' she said with a laugh.

'So they say. I'm not looking forward to that. I'll get lost in a moment. I'm not good at finding my way around at the best of times.'

'Didn't Hazel's house get bombed?'

'Primrose says a doodlebug landed right on top of them. It was a miracle they survived.'

'It would take more than a doodlebug to finish off Megagran.' They both laughed.

'I'm really proud of you, Max. You're going to make something of your life. Your parents would be proud too.'

'Swallow's doing well, isn't she?' he said with a grin. Rita was surprised at the change of subject but replied, 'She might even fly one day.'

'If she has the will, she can do anything she wants to.' He looked at her with those intense eyes of his. Rita suddenly remembered Megagran's story of the two winged birds and felt herself blush.

'Thanks to you, I think she will fly again,' she said and turned onto her back so that the sun could warm her face.

With Maddie back at Bray Cove, Harry's creativity returned. He no longer stared miserably down at a blank sheet of paper but was inspired as he had never been before. Maddie took the new chapters into the garden to read in the sunshine, while Harry could barely type fast enough to put into words the sheer quantity of his thoughts. In the evenings, when the late summer shadows danced their way up the lawn to the tune of the breeze hissing through drying leaves, he would lead her up into his bedroom and make love to her until dusk. At the end of September Harry finished his book. To celebrate he took her to the theatre in town to see *The Importance of Being Earnest*, then to dinner in a quaint restaurant overlooking the sea.

'I think this book is going to be a bestseller,' he said. Maddie smiled indulgently. She was beginning to tire of his talking endlessly about his book, but each time she felt resentful she reminded herself of how lucky she was to have won him back. 'I couldn't have done it without you,' he continued. He looked at her radiant face, her thick and glossy hair, her sparkling blue eyes full of brightness and his heart stumbled at such unrestrained beauty.

'It's given me enormous pleasure, Harry,' she replied truthfully. 'We're a good team.'

'During the cold war,' he said, referring to the few months when they didn't see each other, 'my creativity dried up. I couldn't write a thing. Nothing worked. My prose was stodgy and awkward, my thoughts confused, my characters lacked life and became dead fish on the page. When you came back everything changed. You gave me inspiration and confidence, Maddie, and I owe you everything. Don't ever leave me again.'

'Don't ever tell me I'm too young for you then,' she replied with a grin.

'You're not too young, but you're too good to live like this.'

Maddie blanched. 'Like what?' she said, feeling a horrible sense of *déjà vu*.

'Making love to me then creeping home at dusk. It's not right.'

'But Harry . . .'

Harry smiled at her and took her hand in his large, rough one. 'It's time I made an honest woman out of you.'

Maddie's heart stalled and then started again. 'Are you asking me to marry you?' she asked hopefully.

'If you'll have me?'

'What? An impoverished old divorcé like you?' Her eyes suddenly brimmed with emotion. 'Of course I will, my darling Harry,' she laughed, wiping her cheek with her free hand. 'Whatever gave you the impression that I wouldn't?'

When Maddie and Harry announced their engagement Humphrey and Hannah were delighted, if a little surprised. But in the wake of Rita's crisis they welcomed the good news with warm embraces and a bottle of champagne from Mrs Megalith's bountiful cellar. They liked Harry enormously and were relieved that Maddie's ambitions were now reduced to a quiet life in Bray Cove. Eddie was excited to be a bridesmaid with Ruth and she planned to sew a little jacket for Ezra Gunch who would sit proudly on her shoulder throughout the service as she had trained him to do. Reverend Hammond clapped his hands at the thought of a wedding and began to prepare a lengthy address at once, kneeling quietly in the chancel in order to call upon the good Lord for divine inspiration. When Mrs Megalith offered Maddie her own wedding dress that she had worn at the same age Maddie screwed up her pretty nose and laughed out loud at the very idea of wearing one of Megagran's tents. But when she went with her mother and Rita to Elvestree to try it on she was pleasantly surprised.

'It's in my bedroom. Go upstairs with your mother. Rita and I will wait for you down here so you can make an entrance,' said Mrs Megalith, sitting on the sofa surrounded by a patchwork of cats. She held a glass of sherry and a faded red box. Rita perched on the fender in front of the dark chimney for the weather was warm enough not to have a fire. She watched her grandmother gloomily, wondering if she sensed her unhappiness, but Megagran was too preoccupied with Maddie's wedding to notice. Did it not occur to her that all this preparation and excitement should have been for her? If George hadn't gone off to Argentina she would have been trying on the dress today. After all, Megagran had offered it to her first, but she had obviously forgotten. They all had. She felt that familiar sense of hate writhe at the very bottom of her belly like a sticky black beast, then slowly rise up to her heart where it gnawed away at love, converting it into jealousy and resentment. But this time she wasn't at all ashamed of its ugly face. When Maddie appeared at the door, resplendent in ivory silk and lace, tailored as if it had been made especially for her, Rita surrendered entirely to the beast. She watched bitterly as Maddie walked up and down the room with a straight back and a long, elegant neck. Her fulsome body was restrained by a dress so exquisitely modest and feminine, she could almost have looked ethereal had she not smiled with such earthly pride. She knew it enhanced the smooth curves of her breasts and hips and the soft undulation of her belly. She was thrilled with the way she looked and waded through the cats to kiss her grandmother. 'I love it, Grandma. Thank you!' Mrs Megalith embraced her granddaughter.

'I'm very proud of you, Madeleine,' she said firmly. 'To be honest I always thought you were something of a drifter, but you'll make a fine wife and a mother a lot sooner than you imagine. You're a sensible girl, after all.' Maddie blinked down at her grandmother in surprise. She couldn't remember the last time she had praised her. She wondered whether she ever had. Rita had always earned her admiration and Eddie her amusement. But *she* only ever seemed to provoke disapproval and raised eyebrows. 'I think this will complete the look,' she added, handing her the little red box. Maddie opened it impatiently.

'Diamond and pearl earrings!' she exclaimed in delight. 'For me?'

'For you to keep. They belonged to my own grandmother and she gave them to me when I got engaged. I wore them on my wedding day with that dress. You will see they are a perfect match.' Mrs Megalith took them in her thick hands and clipped them onto Maddie's ears. Maddie jumped up to admire her reflection in the large gilded mirror that hung on the wall above the fireplace. Rita could only watch helplessly as if in a nightmare. This should all have been hers.

Then, just as she was beginning to wish she had followed that lone gull to heaven after all, Max telephoned her from London. She was so happy to hear his voice that her misery lifted and was replaced by a tender feeling of being loved.

'Are you all right?' he asked.

'I'm fine,' she replied, but her voice betrayed her sorrow.

'No you're not. I know what you're going through. This wedding should have been yours.'

'Oh, Max, you understand.'

'I care about you, Rita. I hate to think of you there without anyone to talk to. Is the whole village going mad over the wedding?'

'Yes.'

'It must be horrid for you.'

'It is. No one notices though. Not even Mummy. Suddenly, everyone's attention is on Maddie. Mummy's even invited Faye and Trees to the wedding. I think they're calling a truce. It'll never be the same, but at least they're talking again.'

'Does that bother you?'

'Yes, it does,' she replied, debating whether she should have admitted it.

'But Rita, Faye and Trees are guilty of nothing. You can't blame them for what George has done to you.' She said nothing. He endeavoured to fill the pause, for every minute cost money. 'I think it's terrible that the families should suffer because he let you down. They can all wring his neck when he comes back.'

'Max, if I tell you a secret, do you promise not to tell anyone?'

'I promise,' he replied, wondering what on earth could be so bad that her voice should lower in tone and turn so grave.

'I discovered Faye in the arms of Thadeus Walizhewski.'

'What? That old man in the village?'

'Yes.'

'Are you sure?'

'Certain. She had her hair down. She looked beautiful. Now I can't look her in the face without despising her. Do you think infidelity is in the blood?'

He chuckled. 'No, I don't.'

'Are you shocked?'

'Surprised but not shocked,' he said truthfully. 'It's none of my business and it shouldn't be any of yours, either. You can't let Faye's infidelity destroy your belief in love, Rita. Everyone's different.'

'I don't think I'll ever love again.' This time he hesitated and she filled the pause that followed. 'I don't trust it any more.'

'Someone will come along one day and love you so intensely you won't have any room for doubt,' he said after a while.

'Do you think so?'

'I know. Trust me.'

'When?' Max's heart at once ignited with a spark of hope.

'When you want him to,' he replied and shuddered at the realisation that he had just come very close to declaring himself. But Rita knew she would always love George and for as long as she did, there would be no room in her heart to love another.

Chapter Twenty-two

It was a perfect, sunny day for the wedding. An autumnal breeze swept gently across the countryside, but the sun was still hot as if reluctant to yield to the inevitable changing of the seasons. Agatha had enjoyed every moment of organising the event, ordering her army of staff around like a hearty general on parade. Rows of white chairs had been set out in front of the house forming pews, and a canopy of flowers had been erected under which George and Susan would exchange their vows. Father O'Bridie, an old Irish priest from Dublin who had been preaching in Buenos Aires for fifty-eight years, had agreed to perform the service of marriage even though neither the bride nor groom were Catholic. Fuelled by the promise of alcohol he would have agreed to marry anything so long as it professed belief in the one God. Agatha had arranged a morning wedding, in the hope that he wouldn't have time to get drunk. Dolores and Agustina had spent weeks planning desserts for the lunch, which was beginning to look more like a banquet, and the gauchos had slain three cows for the barbecue. Agatha had sent out invitations to all their friends, of which there were many, but she knew guests would bring their own friends and people she hadn't invited would turn up, such was the custom in the Argentine. Susan had given her a few names but George knew no one.

Agatha and Jose Antonio had been struck dumb when George and Susan had told them of their plans. Agatha hadn't expected him to return to England to marry Rita but she hadn't predicted he would fall in love with Susan. George was such a devilishly handsome young man and Susan was, well, so unfortunately disfigured. She would have understood him better had he lost his heart to a beautiful Argentine girl. Jose Antonio patted George so firmly on the back he nearly winded him. He now understood the young man's unwillingness to visit the whores of Jesús Maria and was relieved that his nephew was a normal red-blooded male. Susan was spirited and intelligent. She had an icy allure and was as mysterious to him now as she had been the day he had met her. He still didn't know the secret behind her scar and neither did his wife. He wasn't attracted by her blonde northern looks and slim, boyish figure, preferring more generous curves, but he understood the attraction of an older woman, and Susan was obviously as capable as Agatha, although she wisely left Agatha to organise the wedding. He had arranged to let them a pretty white house with stunning views of the plains and mountains which suited them both. George wanted to farm and Susan didn't want to live in the city. She had grown to love the languid life of the countryside and the gentle people who inhabited it.

Tonito and Pia adored her, and she loved them too and spent hours with them riding across the fields or at home inventing games for them and their small band of friends. They had asked her on her first day why one side of her face was 'broken' and she had replied with a smile that she had been clawed by a lion in Africa. Their eyes had widened and more questions had tumbled out as their curiosity increased with the thought of such delicious violence. Had he wanted to eat her? How had she got away? Had she been afraid? And she had answered each one with patience and humour, wishing that adults were as easy to deflect as children. Sometimes George would catch her watching them wistfully, a sad smile softening her face with tenderness and he would take her hand

and squeeze it. He didn't have to speak and she didn't have to explain for they understood each other perfectly. Her longing for her own children would stir inside her breast like a small, caged humming-bird, its wings tiny and quivering. She would place her hand there to calm it and will herself to be patient. Then she would look at George and hope would glimmer in her eyes that seemed so cold to everyone but him.

Now she sat in a simple ivory dress, while the hairdresser pinned her hair onto the top of her head, wondering whether she had been foolish to choose a dress rather than a suit that would have perhaps been more appropriate for a woman of her age. She felt a fraud playing the young bride. She believed herself tainted in some way, having been engaged and pregnant before, or too much of a woman for such a girlish wedding. The civil ceremony had been more comfortable. No confetti and a simple bouquet of flowers. They were already married by law, but George had insisted that they marry before God. To him that was almost more important. She heard voices downstairs and knew that Father O'Bridie had arrived.

'Praised be the Lord for bestowing on this young couple a morning of such splendour to bless their nuptials with sunshine!' he exclaimed in an exuberant Irish lilt. In spite of having lived in the Argentine for the best part of his adult life he spoke Spanish badly, preferring to speak English wherever possible. 'God's language is universal,' he was often heard explaining to people who asked him how come, after so many years, he hadn't managed to learn more than the odd phrase. 'Love is the same in all tongues,' he would say piously. But love didn't buy meat at the butchers or write his correspondence and there were many times he had to rely on a friend to translate for him. But today was different. He had been invited to conduct the service in English, as he did in the small Irish church of All Saints in Buenos Aires, and most of the congregation were well educated in English, if not English by birth. He would knock back a little tipple and give them an address they wouldn't forget. Like most good men of the clergy, he loved the sound of his own voice.

George mingled outside with the arriving guests. Dressed in a light summer suit he was relieved the breeze was cool and fresh for he was already hot with nerves. He knew very few people, but everyone made a great fuss of him for weddings tend to bring out the genial in most people. He hadn't thought of Rita in weeks, but now his attention turned to her. Frognal Point seemed so far away, so distant, no longer a real place at all. He was happy he wasn't marrying Susan there; he could imagine the fuss had he married Rita. The stifling attention, the overpowering excitement, the Reverend's pompous address and the simpering faces of the villagers who had all known him since he was a boy. He was glad he was in the middle of the Argentine, he was glad that none of his family had travelled out for the wedding, and he was glad that it was Susan who was preparing herself in the house to make her vows before God to love him until death parted them. He watched Aunt Agatha, resplendent in blue, meet and greet her friends and people she had never met before, and he was grateful to her for giving him a refuge from the war and from that small coastal village that had suffocated him so. If it hadn't been for her he might have lost his sanity staring out to sea, and perhaps he would never have seen Susan again. He would remember to thank her in his speech.

The guests took their seats and the small quartet Agatha had hired from Jesús Maria began to play. Father O'Bridie's ruddy face took on a grave expression of the utmost piety as he led George down the aisle to wait for his bride. Ernesto, one of the gauchos, stood as his best man in the front row, grinning at him crookedly as he approached. 'Good luck, gringo!' he hissed as George joined him. 'When I married Marta she was as thin as a pencil, how could I have predicted she'd grow into a cow?' He shrugged and turned to watch Father O'Bridie, who raised his eyes at the appearance of Susan, crossing the lawn, followed by Pia and Tonito.

George's heart stumbled when he saw her. She looked fragile next to the ursine Jose Antonio who had agreed to give her away, like an elegant arum lily beside a bulrush. She seemed to float towards him, the sunlight dancing off her simple dress and the flowers that were pinned into her hair fluttering in the breeze. She walked slowly, with her shoulders straight and her chin high, although her smile was shy and almost bashful. She held her bouquet tightly and looked directly ahead of her, while Jose Antonio grinned broadly at his friends as he passed them. The music rose in a melodramatic climax and George and Susan locked eyes in mutual understanding while they did all they could to contain their amusement. Hand in hand they stood together facing Father O'Bridie until the music finished. George could smell lily of the valley on her skin and that unique scent that was hers alone, and was reminded of the first time he had kissed her on the deck of the *Fortuna*.

The music stopped and the congregation fell silent. Father O'Bridie raised his bloodshot eyes and began to speak in a very slow brogue. Agatha sighed with relief that he hadn't had more than a shot of whiskey, although beneath his eyes the bags looked as heavy as wineskins. 'We are gathered here today, in the sight of God, to witness the marriage of this man and this woman. I stress the word witness, for that is what you good people are here for. Oh yes, you're here for the wine and the desserts and believe me there's a fair banquet out there for I've been into the kitchen and the work that's going on is quite spectacular!' He licked his lips. 'There's *dulce de leche* mousse and ice cream and meringues.' Susan squeezed George's hand again. They could both feel Agatha's fury rising behind them. 'But let's get back to the matter at hand. Yes, you are here to witness George and Susan make their vows, to love and honour each other until death does them part.' He opened the old, saggy, prayer book he carried in his unsteady hands and began to read. Agatha's relief was visible.

In spite of the melodramatic music, the kitsch nature of the garden 'church' with its floral canopy and white pews, and Father O'Bridie's questionable enthusiasm, George and Susan were moved by the service and made their vows solemnly. It didn't matter that they knew few people – for the witnesses were mostly strangers, for when they stood before God and promised to love one another for ever they were very much alone.

Agatha was reluctant to give Father O'Bridie anything more to drink, and could barely contain her annoyance: not only had he swayed from side to side as if on the deck of a galleon in a rough sea but his address had gone on and on without any recognisable point. She had softened, however, when she saw Susan and George's obvious happiness as they mingled with the guests and crouched down to praise Pia and Tonito who had both played their parts to perfection. She reminded herself that the day wasn't about Father O'Bridie; he had now served his purpose and could drink himself into a stupor if he so wished.

When she saw Dolores appear on the lawn with a tray of *empanadas* she forgot the inebriated priest, the bride and groom, even her own children, for the flimsy pink chiffon dress that Dolores had chosen looked like something one of the whores from Jesús Maria might wear to please a kinky client. It was completely transparent, crudely exposing her large white pants beneath. Agatha feared Dolores, too, had succumbed to the bottle.

'Dolores, where is your uniform?' she asked, recoiling at

the maid's extravagant make-up. Dolores smiled coyly and looked up from under congealed black eyelashes.

'I thought it would be nice to dress up for Señor George's wedding,' she replied with pride.

'Do you know that we can see your knickers?' Agatha retorted bluntly.

'Can you?' the old woman replied, a small smile tickling the corners of her pink mouth. Agatha was horrified that an employee could speak to her with such little respect.

'I think it's most inappropriate, Dolores. I would be very grateful if you could go and change into your uniform.' Before Dolores could reply Father O'Bridie staggered over, his lustful eyes doing their best to focus on the apparition before him. In his drunken state Dolores looked like a Botticelli Venus.

'Praise the Lord!' he exclaimed, reeling backwards then lunging forward, still on the deck of that imaginary galleon. Agatha had a brainwave.

'Dolores, Agustina and the girls can do lunch, would you do me the very great favour of looking after Father O'Bridie? I think the sun is too much for him. Take him into the floral spare room and give him lots of water. He must be dehydrated.' Dolores, recognising the lascivious glint in the old priest's eye, was only too happy to do as requested. She handed Agatha the tray of *empanadas* and took Father O'Bridie by the arm, leading him gently into the house. Agatha sighed. 'That kills two birds with one stone,' she said to herself. Then she picked up an *empanada* and took a bite, silently thanking God that the old woman was still able to cook.

Jose Antonio's laughter rose above the light chatter like a bellowing bull. He threw his head back and roared boisterously. Naturally, he was enjoying his own coarse jokes, but his charm was such that everyone laughed with him. The guests complimented the beauty of the bride, then asked each other in whispers how come she was so cruelly disfigured. When

Tonito or Pia overheard their conversations they trilled in loud voices the story Susan had told them about the lion in Africa. 'She was nearly eaten, you know! She said she wasn't frightened until afterwards because while she was in the lion's mouth she was too surprised to feel fear. If it hadn't been for a man with a gun she would have ended up as dinner.' The guests were so shocked by the story that they accepted it without question. Instead of regarding Susan with pity they looked on her with admiration. Her scar was heroic.

Suddenly the barking of Bertie and Wooster rang through the house. Agatha and Jose Antonio raised their eyes expectantly for the dogs rarely barked, except at the arrival of a very unwelcome visitor. George frowned and took Susan's hand while the rest of the guests continued to drink and eat *empanadas*, oblivious of the unexpected disturbance. Gonzalo, the gardener, hurried around the side of the house, hat in hand, bowing deferentially as he approached his mistress.

'Who is it, Gonzalo?' she asked, feeling the north wind rattle through her bones.

'Señora Velasco,' he replied, looking at her with fear. Agatha stiffened and turned to her husband who was wading through the crowd with a thunderous face.

'Your mother has turned up,' Agatha told him furiously. 'We haven't seen her in years and she goes and turns up uninvited on George's wedding day. It's unforgivable.' Gonzalo hovered anxiously, hoping to be released from any further task. He didn't like the idea of having to return to the prickly old woman in the car. Agatha, for once considerate of her employee, dismissed him with an uncharacteristic 'thank you' and stood her ground. 'I'm not dealing with her. She's your mother, after all.'

Jose Antonio didn't protest but took a deep breath, like a dragon working up a fierce fire, and marched purposefully around the house.

Señora Velasco sat in the back of the car fanning herself with an elaborately embroidered Spanish fan. She wore black, as she had done since the divorce from Jose Antonio's father, not because she mourned him, but to spite him: he had always hated women wearing black. She was very tall and bony with pigeon-grey hair, cut into a severe bob with a sharp fringe that rested just above reptilian eyes, and a large, hawkish nose. Her lips were thin and drawn into a tight grimace, scarlet lipstick bleeding into her skin, which was as white as death. She began to fan with more agitation and the chauffeur, a long-suffering man with the physique of a toad from spending most of his life in the front seat of a car, tapped his fingers on the steering wheel. 'Stop that tapping!' she snapped irritably. His fingers froze and didn't move again until Jose Antonio appeared at the window, Agatha in his wake.

'Mother, this is quite unexpected,' said Jose Antonio, barely able to restrain his fury.

'Oh, grow up! If I can't come and visit my own son for God's sake . . .'

'We're in the middle of a wedding,' he explained.

'Oh, good. Haven't you got rid of Agatha yet?' Agatha clenched her fists.

'If you're going to be rude I'll send you right back to Buenos Aires!'

'Have you lost your sense of humour, son? In spite of the hard life I have suffered I have managed to retain mine. It was a joke. Hello, Agatha, how nice to see you.' Agatha didn't smile. 'Who's getting married?'

'George Bolton, Agatha's nephew from England.'

'Well, don't just sit there, Blanco, I'm cooking in here.' The chauffeur struggled out of the car and came round to open the back door. Señora Velasco climbed out with some difficulty. Her bones were old and brittle and her muscles shrivelled. She ached all over.

'I've come to die,' she stated impassively, taking her walking stick from the melting Blanco.

'Oh good!' her son retorted. She smiled, and her lips disappeared completely, leaving only the red stains like rivers on a map.

'So you haven't lost your sense of humour, after all. But I don't joke. I have come to say goodbye.' Jose Antonio frowned at her and his eyes shifted, not knowing how to react. 'I won't be melodramatic about it, that is not my way.' Agatha rolled her eyes. 'I shall go quietly and you can bury me in the garden under that eucalyptus tree where I used to sit and cry when your father disappeared into Jesús Maria to lie with other women.'

'Will you come and enjoy Dolores's lunch before you pass away?' Agatha asked, knowing that the irritating old woman would now be with them for months.

'I never thought Dolores would outlive me,' she sighed.

'She hasn't yet,' Jose Antonio reminded her.

'But she will. At least I will enjoy her famous *empanadas* before I go.'

'There are plenty of those,' said Agatha, anxious to get back to her guests.

'I want to meet the bride and groom. They are just beginning their lives while I am ending mine. It seems significant somehow. Is the priest still here? Tell him not to go home. You might as well let the funeral run on while everyone is still in the mood for an event.'

They walked slowly around the house, Señora Velasco grimacing and groaning with each step, refusing to be helped when her son attempted to hold her arm with his large, calloused hands. 'You can hold me when I'm dead,' she barked. 'Until then I will walk unaided. I'm not crippled, you know.' The guests parted for her instantly for they could smell death on her breath. She staggered through without a smile for anyone. Finally Jose Antonio stopped in front of George and Susan who stood with Pia and Tonito. The children shrank back at the sight of the hideous old woman who resembled the witch in their fairy tales. Hidden behind the skirt of Susan's white dress they peered around fearfully. Señora Velasco raised her hooded eyes and settled them on George. 'What a fine-looking young man,' she said in perfect English. 'Who is the lucky bride?' She turned to Susan and her eyes flickered with surprise.

'Good God, girl. Whatever happened to your face?' she shrieked rudely. A gasp hissed through the crowd of guests. Susan straightened but retained her smile with icy calm. She could feel the children behind her bristling to tell the story for her.

'I was attacked by a lion in Africa,' she replied non-chalantly.

'A lion?'

'A very large lion. If it hadn't been for the guide who carried a gun, I would have been dinner.' Susan caught George's eye and she smiled triumphantly. Señora Velasco turned to her son.

'Take me to my room. I am weary after the drive. Bring me a plate of *empanadas*.' She took one last look at Susan before she stumbled away. 'Wear it as a badge of honour, my girl. A badge of honour!'

Another hurdle had been kicked down and how easy it had been. Suddenly Susan realised that her scar no longer hurt her so much. She watched the old woman retreat into the house and ran a hand over her wound. Señora Velasco was right, she would make a feature of it and wear it as a badge of honour. She bent down and embraced the children. They didn't realise she was silently thanking them for the lion story; if it hadn't been for their innocent questions she would never have thought of it.

Chapter Twenty-three

Much later, when the last of the guests had drifted away and the little nightlights that Agatha had lit around the garden twinkled through the darkness, George and Susan retired to bed. They were exhausted with so much happiness. Tomorrow they would leave for Mar del Plata where a friend of Jose Antonio was lending them his house, overlooking the sea. They would spend a few weeks alone together before returning to *Las Dos Vizcachas* and the rest of their lives.

Upstairs Jose Antonio knocked on the door of his mother's room. She made no answer, which was strange; he expected a bellowed command to leave her alone or to enter. The stale odour of death seeped out from under the door and clung to his nostrils. He grimaced at the smell of decay and the suspicion that his mother had, for once, been true to her word and passed away. When he entered, the little lamp on the bedside table illuminated her waxy features as she lay on her back with her mouth gaping in a silent scream. He approached the bed with reluctance. He felt nothing. No sadness, not even relief. He hadn't been fond of her, even as a child. Then he noticed the half-eaten *empanada* she still clutched in her hand and the foam that stuck to the corners of her mouth. She must have died from choking on one of Dolores's famous delicacies. He wondered whether she might have lived for years had it not been for her greed.

Agatha strode into the bedroom and covered the corpse with a sheet. She should have taped her mother-in-law's jaw together so that it didn't gape so grotesquely, but she couldn't bear to. It had been bad enough laying eyes on that dead flesh. She opened the window and lit a candle, less out of respect than to get rid of the stench. Then she left the room as quickly as possible in case Señora Velasco's ghost still remained there.

Jose Antonio and Agatha undressed and climbed into bed. Suddenly Agatha remembered Dolores and Father O'Bridie who hadn't been seen since she sent them inside at midday.

'Jose Antonio,' she whispered, as if death might hear her.

'What, Gorda? I'm trying to go to sleep,' he growled gently.

'I sent Father O'Bridie into the floral spare room with Dolores to sober up. I haven't seen them since. Have you?'

Jose Antonio chuckled throatily. 'No, I haven't.'

'What should I do?'

'Nothing. Leave them. When Father O'Bridie wakes up in the morning he'll get one hell of a shock if Dolores is still with him.'

'Perhaps she left him asleep and retired to her own quarters,' she said hopefully.

'Perhaps. Though it is strange that she didn't help the girls tidy up.'

'Oh God!' she groaned. 'You know, she's not of sound mind, Jose Antonio. Don't you think you should let her go?'

'Not while she makes such delicious *empanadas!*' he laughed.

'One of which killed your mother,' she reminded him in a serious voice.

'Exactly!' he replied and rolled over. 'The woman stays!'

The following morning George and Susan appeared flushed and smiling on the terrace under the vine. Agatha and Jose Antonio were already having breakfast with the children, who squealed in delight when they saw the bride and groom. Agatha, who firmly believed that their children should not be raised to fear death, had told them of their grandmother's passing and had been surprised when they had yelped with joy and relief and burst into commentary about how old and ugly she had been. George and Susan showed more respect, though neither could think of anything nice to say about her. 'She's here in this very house,' said Tonito, his eyes sparkling with excitement.

'Her body's upstairs,' added Pia through a mouthful of croissant. 'She's going to be buried in the garden so the worms can eat her all up!' Agatha was about to intercede when Father O'Bridie's pale face appeared at the door.

'Top of the mornin' to you,' said Tonito in a perfect Irish accent, then giggled. Father O'Bridie walked unsteadily, his eyes as shiny as two oysters in brine.

'What a beautiful day,' he said, taking a seat at the table. His voice wasn't quite as robust as it had been the day before.

'Are you all right, Father O'Bridie?' Agatha asked, searching his face for clues. 'You had a nasty turn yesterday. It must have been the heat.'

'Oh, yes. We Irish aren't too good in such strong sunlight,' he explained, pouring himself a cup of strong coffee. He shovelled three large spoonfuls of sugar into it and took a gulp, after which he seemed to calm down a little.

'I trust Dolores looked after you well?' Agatha persevered.

'Oh, she did. Thank you. She certainly did.'

'We haven't seen her all morning. Poor Agustina has had to make breakfast all on her own,' Agatha added, filling his cup. 'When you've had breakfast I have another job for you.' Father O'Bridie raised his eyes apprehensively.

'I'm afraid Jose Antonio's mother is dead upstairs. She died in the night, choking on an *empanada*.'

'An *empanada?*' he repeated, crossing himself.

'One of Dolores's famous *empanadas*.'

'We've called the doctor, but as it's Sunday he's enjoying his breakfast,' said Jose Antonio. 'I told him not to hurry, after all, she's not going anywhere, is she?'

'Her spirit is already with God,' said Father O'Bridie, thankful of the digression.

'If God can put up with her,' added Agatha drily.

'God is loving of all his creatures,' said Father O'Bridie piously. Agatha sniffed. 'How are Mr and Mrs George Bolton this good morning?' he said, turning to George and Susan who sat listening, amazed at the events that had taken place on their wedding day without their knowledge.

At that moment Dolores appeared on the terrace with a large oval plate of freshly baked pastries. She was once more dressed in black with her hair pulled back into its characteristic bun. She didn't smile and she didn't look at the priest. She said a tight good morning, put the plate in the centre of the table and straightened up self-importantly. The whole table gazed at her in astonishment.

'Are you all right?' Agatha asked. Dolores nodded.

'How many for lunch?' she asked, rubbing her hands together nervously.

'Señor and Señora George leave at eleven, so it will only be us and Father O'Bridie.' Father O'Bridie put down his coffee cup with a loud clank.

'I'll be leaving before lunch, I'm afraid. The work of the Lord cannot be delayed.' He smiled tightly.

'Of course,' said Agatha. 'I'll get Gonzalo to drive you to the station.'

Dolores then settled her eyes on the priest. For a moment there was an uncomfortable silence. The old maid sighed heavily, dropped her hands to her side and spoke in Spanish with a sudden burst of emotion.

'I'm a God-fearing woman, Padre O'Bridie.' The priest

seemed to understand and raised his right hand and made the sign of the cross.

'May God bless you, señora, and forgive you your trespasses as he forgives those who trespass against you.'

Dolores shook her head and frowned; she had failed to understand a single word. Agatha quietly translated for her. Dolores straightened up again and lifted her chin before snorting rudely and striding back into the house.

Jose Antonio chuckled and buttered a pastry. If Dolores had returned to her normal, irritable self, all was right with the world once again. Agatha disagreed; while Señora Velasco's decomposing body remained in her house all was *not* right with the world.

George and Susan left for Mar del Plata and Gonzalo drove Father O'Bridie to the station. Dolores scowled in the kitchen as she had done for the best part of forty years while Agustina laid the table for lunch. Jose Antonio organised his mother's burial because Agatha had refused to, retiring to her bedroom complaining of a headache. Pia and Tonito spied on their father, watching in fascination as the body was placed in a coffin and sealed. That evening, with little ceremony, a hole was dug in the ground beneath the eucalyptus tree where Señora Velasco had requested to be laid to rest, and the priest from Jesús Maria read the short service. Unlike Father O'Bridie he was a strict Catholic and took his duties very seriously indeed. Agatha, whose head still throbbed, was greatly encouraged by his humble piety and humility. She felt her faith return and stood with her head bowed during the prayers. When, after the service, Pia and Tonito tried to call the dogs, they would not obey, but pressed their tails down and thrust their ears back, trotting anxiously into the house. They had not liked Señora Velasco in life; even in death she unsettled them.

Susan and George were relieved to be left alone to enjoy

each other in peace and solitude. The house was a beautiful white bungalow overlooking the sea, with a little sandy path that led down to a deserted beach. Autumn had set in, drying the leaves on the trees and withering the flowers, and yet the place was rich in the song of birds and the chirping of crickets. A cold breeze swept off the sea and they had to light the fire at night, but that only served to increase the romance. Together with the smell of salt and wood smoke the distinctive scent of autumn made their hearts full of wistfulness. They walked up and down the beach as the setting sun simmered on the surface of the water, turning it pink, and recalled the time they had walked along the beach in Uruguay. Her rejection then had hurt him deeply. Now they had the rest of their lives to love each other.

One afternoon, while Susan lay reading on the terrace, George walked along the beach on his own. Memories of Frognal Point invaded his senses so that he could smell the ozone and hear the plaintive cry of gulls as they glided on the wind. He sat on the sand and rested his elbows on his knees, staring out across the ocean. It had been months since he had last given a thought to home. Happiness had shrouded the past in a fog so that he couldn't see it. Now, with the sound of the sea breaking on the beach and the sensation of sand in his toes, he remembered Rita.

He thought of Hannah and all those little birds she loved and nurtured in her garden. He remembered Megagran and her bags of crystals, and chuckled with affection. He thought of his mother, her love of art and music, and his father who said very little and cherished his walnut trees in the way that he should have cherished his wife. Geoffrey had returned from the war. Had war changed him too? Did he suffer from guilt? Did Alice understand Geoffrey like Susan understood him?

George no longer suffered nightmares but he often thought about his dead friends. He saw them in the strange formation of clouds or as misty reflections on the surface of a lake. Jamie Cordell, Rat Bridges, Lorrie Hampton – it was his duty to honour them by remembering them and his due to suffer the nagging in his conscience. What would they be doing now had they lived? Often he would daydream about his fights, the skirmishes up there in the sky, the danger, the adrenalin and the fear, the sense of purpose and camaraderie. Then he would sit back and look at the world around him, glad to be alive and on the ground.

He raised his eyes to see Susan walking up the beach towards him and waved at her. She wore a long cream cardigan, which she pulled tightly around her body against the cold wind, and her hair was loose and falling over her shoulders in waves. She sat down beside him. 'What are you thinking about?'

'Memories.'

'They've found you, have they?'

'I'm afraid so.'

'They were bound to. You can't hide from them for ever, you know.'

He kissed her temple. 'I'm glad I'm here with you. There's no place in the world I'd rather be.'

'I'm happy to hear it.'

'It's just the sound of waves lapping onto the beach and the stretch of ocean.'

'It reminds you of Frognal Point.'

'Yes.'

'You're not still worrying about Rita, are you?'

'Thinking about her, yes. But not worrying about her. I'm sure I did the right thing.'

'Good.'

'I feel nostalgic, though. Not so much the people but the place.'

'You'll have to take me there one day,' she said, nuzzling

against him. 'I'd like to meet your family and see the farm where you grew up. It sounds wonderfully quaint and English.'

He chuckled. 'Oh, I know you'd love it. Its landscape is a rolling patchwork of small green fields. Narrow, winding lanes lined with cow parsley and over-grown hedges. In the wood above Elvestree . . .'

'Where the witch lives,' she interrupted.

'Yes, where the witch lives, the blubells form an incredible carpet of blue, like a lake. The smell is intoxicating. The trees are full of birds because Hannah, Rita's mother, and her mother the witch, put out food for them all winter. Sometimes the wind is so strong you walk along the cliff top fearful that you might be blown off. Down below the sand is thick and grainy. We used to build sandcastles as children, it was like cement until the sea rushed in to wash it away. There are rock pools full of crabs and sea urchins, we used to collect the shells and show them off at school. The village itself is charming with a little shop, a school and an ancient church. You have to go into town to buy fresh meat and fish. Of course, as a child we took it all for granted, but after seeing a bit of the world I realise how lucky I was to grow up amidst such simplicity.'

'It sounds lovely, George,' said Susan truthfully. 'I look forward to seeing it.'

'We'll go one day. We'll take our children and I'll teach them to do all the things I did as a child.' Susan smiled with tenderness, imagining the children they might have. 'We'll picnic on cold beaches with sand in our sandwiches.'

'Is that why they're called sandwiches, do you think?' she said with a laugh.

'I don't know, but however hard you try it still gets in there somehow. Adds extra crunch.'

'In spite of your claustrophobia, George, you love Frognal Point.'

'I know. I just need to be away for a while. It will still be there when I want to go back, unchanged probably. I'll be ready for it then.'

At the end of the fortnight they returned to *Las Dos Vizcachas* and settled into the white house with the green-tiled roof and shady veranda. Susan set about planting flowers to creep up the walls and flutter about the windows while George returned to his work on the farm. Agatha lent her the services of the docile Gonzalo who knew all there was to know about nature, and Agustina's young cousin, Marcela, came to help clean the house. Jose Antonio was able to spare a couple of gauchos to paint the exterior and mend the leaking roof. Susan decorated the interior simply and tastefully, using craftsmen from Jesús Maria to furnish it, grateful for the generosity of the wedding guests who had all brought them presents, pretty crockery and fine bed linen. She was immensely happy with her new home. It was cool yet cosy, elegant but not extravagant, with the most magnificent views of the hazy blue sierras in the distance. Most importantly it was hers. A proper family home with enough rooms for children. She couldn't think of a better place to raise a family. The air was clean, the plains were safe, and the farm big enough for them to play in. There were ponies to ride, dogs to chase and prairie hares to watch leaping through the long grasses. It was a veritable paradise for a child. She hoped that it wouldn't be too long before they were blessed with a baby. Once again she felt the familiar quickening in her chest, that anxious humming-bird fluttering its small wings in an effort to break free.

Fifteen months rolled rapidly away. The winter was cold and bleak. Gales swept over the plains, flattening the long grasses and chasing the prairie hares into their warrens. Susan kept the fires lit, even in their bedroom, and wrapped herself in heavy coats and jumpers. Every month she hoped for signs of a pregnancy and every month she shed secret tears of disappointment. George made love to her often. She was irresistible to him and the flickering flames in the grate in their bedroom enhanced the romance of that small house in the middle of the plain. The winds roared, the windows rattled and George loved her in the tranquil warmth of their marital bed.

Sometimes during the day, when George was out, she would wander into the little bedrooms and imagine how she would decorate them for children. She envisaged the wooden cot, the mobile she would make of all the animals in the zoo, and the thick curtains to keep out the early morning light in the summertime. She yearned for a baby to love and nurture and her yearning began to choke her. Tonito and Pia, once so good for the terrible longing in her soul, now reminded her all the time of what she lacked. She watched them play and felt their warm bodies embrace her like little bears, and she had to make a monumental effort to hide the unhappiness that sometimes made it hard for her to breathe.

Then one night at the beginning of the summer, while she lay in George's arms listening to his stories of Frognal Point, she was struck with an idea. It was a devious one and probably unwise considering the circumstances, but Susan was desperate. 'Darling, tell me about the Elvestree witch.' George chuckled and Susan felt his laughter vibrate deep within his chest against her ear.

'The famous Mrs Megalith.'

'Does she really have magic powers?'

'I don't know. Strange things happen at Elvestree. I'd be a fool to dismiss her as a fraud.'

'What sort of things?' Susan felt the sweat gather around her nose, fearful that he might guess the reason for her curiosity.

'She's a healer.' He frowned in an effort to recall one or two of the many stories that circulated in the village. 'She's supposed to have cured Reverend Hammond's brother of stomach cancer with nothing more than a photograph. He lives in Bristol, you see, and was too ill to visit her. So she asked him for a photograph. I don't know whether it was just luck or coincidence but he's alive and kicking to this day, I believe. Reverend Hammond refused to accept that she had cured him but has been terrified of her ever since. I think she contradicts his views of Christianity although Christ himself was a healer, wasn't he?'

'A photograph?' Susan was eager not to go off the subject.

'That's all she required. She does that a lot. Rita said that she has a room full of photographs and candles for what she calls "absent healing". She picked up some strange habits in India. This bizarre ritual is probably one of them. She says that everyone has an energy field around them which is captured in a photograph. She can work with that. Rita told me of numerous successes. Her mother's back pain, too much crouching in the garden watching the birds, I suspect. My own mother once had a problem with her hand and my father is asthmatic. His asthma gets particularly bad during the harvest with all the dust. He sings her praises, but then she is the only person in the entire village to take an interest in his precious walnut trees.'

'I love the sound of your father. Are you close?' Now she endeavoured to divert attention from her curiosity by asking about other characters of Frognal Point.

'As close as one can be to a man who's in a world of his own. I only scrape at the surface. He says little but, judging by the lines on his face that resemble his own beloved walnuts, he thinks and feels a great deal. I love him deeply.' Susan listened with half an ear and George suspected nothing.

The following morning she wrote to Mrs Megalith enclosing the best photograph of herself that she could find, and an impassioned plea for help in starting a family.

Chapter Twenty-four

Mrs Megalith read Susan's letter with interest. The communication itself didn't surprise her. The content of it, however, did. Susan must be desperate to contact the grandmother of George's jilted fiancée. Naturally, Susan had requested that it remain a secret between them at which Mrs Megalith took mild offence for she respected the privacy of all her clients whether they asked for it or not. Alone in the room full of small candles, crystals and wind charms, Mrs Megalith sat in a leather armchair, closed her eyes and pressed her hands to the photograph. In her mind's eye she saw George's new wife as clearly as if she were standing in front of her. Unlike in the photograph, her long hair was loose and curling about her neck and shoulders; her eyes were cool and distant yet beneath them was a warm soul whose longing for a child was beginning to cripple her. Mrs Megalith felt her anguish and sensed the blockage of energy that such negativity caused. If Susan could only let go of those unhelpful emotions she would have no trouble conceiving.

The Elvestree witch saw the dreadful scar that marred a once celebrated beauty and, like a reel of film being played before her eyes, she watched the cause of it and the miscarriage that followed. Mrs Megalith was about to put down the photograph when she saw a vision of the future. George and Susan would return to live in Frognal Point driven by circumstances beyond their control.

She made a space for the photograph on the table beside the

window and placed a few carefully chosen crystal discs upon it: amethyst above the head, hematite between the feet and rose quartz on the area of the stomach. Then she lit a candle, closed her eyes again and called upon her spirit helpers. 'I dedicate this time to the healing of Susan Bolton. May she be cleared of all negative energy and conceive the baby she longs for,' she said in a clear, steady voice.

Then she sat back in her chair and reflected on the woman whom George had married. Their lives were very much intertwined with Rita's, although they didn't know it yet. They would never quite be free of each other. She remembered the little story she had told her granddaughter of the two winged birds. If Susan was a winged bird, with the terrible scar on her face that bore testament to an anguished past, then, with the conception of her child, she would learn to fly again.

And so it was. With the New Year came the good news of Susan's pregnancy. She had sent her letter to the Elvestree witch in absolute faith and her instincts had been right. Once or twice she had awoken in the middle of the night with a burning sensation in her belly, as if it were filled with hot treacle. It wasn't unpleasant, just extraordinary, and she had wondered whether it was the workings of Rita's gifted grandmother.

Susan kept her pregnancy quiet until she was absolutely sure. George had noticed that she wasn't quite herself but said nothing, pretending he hadn't noticed when she had hurried into the bathroom to throw up and seemed to go off her food. Finally, after a couple of months she greeted his return from work, her face aflame with excitement, with the news that they had been praying for.

'We're going to have a baby,' she declared joyfully, holding her arms out to him. George was ecstatic. Now hope shone in her eyes where before they had been dull with disappointment. He lifted her off the ground and began to dance her vigorously up and down the terrace. The hot evening sun continued to scorch the plains and they swept across the long shadows and slashes of gold into the happy ever after.

'I did notice you were a bit off colour,' he said finally, putting her down. They were both out of breath.

'I know, but I didn't want to jinx it by telling you too soon. I had to be sure.' She placed a hand on her belly and tears welled in her eyes. 'I'm so happy, George.' He gathered her into his arms and embraced her.

'Now you must take it easy,' he warned. 'No more scrubbing the floors on your hands and knees. We'll hire Marcela full time. I won't tolerate you overdoing it. You have a baby to think about now.'

'A baby!' she sighed contentedly. 'Just think, George, you're going to be a father.' Now it was his turn to flush. His face creased into soft lines. 'I'll decorate the baby's room nearer the time,' Susan continued. 'That nice man in Jesús Maria, the one who made our beds, can build a cot. Oh, I'm so excited, I don't know what to do with myself!'

'I know what you can do with yourself, rest!' he said firmly, leading her to the bench. She sat down and once again she felt the trembling wings of the small caged humming-bird in her breast.

'Pregnancy isn't an illness,' she said, but she knew he was right to treat her with care. Nothing in the world was as important as the baby growing inside her.

Charles Henry Bolton came into the world with the same enthusiasm with which he would bound through the rest of his life, on the 24th October 1949. He was a boisterous baby with his mother's ice-blue eyes and his father's lopsided grin. By the time he was one year old his thick blond hair had sprung into ringlets and if it hadn't been for his sturdy little figure he would have often been mistaken for a girl.

Susan had painted trains and aeroplanes all over his bedroom walls and made him the mobile of zoo animals that she had dreamed of long before he was conceived. She had recovered quickly from the trauma of giving birth, and settled happily into breast-feeding as if she had done it many times before. Charlie, as they nicknamed him, loved his mother with an intensity that melted the genetic frost in his eyes. As soon as he could, he put his little arms out to her and clung on like a milky white bear. He squealed when she left the room and crawled after her at such a speed that his father said he'd never have to bother learning to walk.

George was struck a surprising blow to the heart when his son was born. Speechless with awe, he looked upon the tiny creature who was a part of him and Susan and yet a stranger to them both whom they would have to get to know. The baby blinked up at him with his unfocused eyes and George knew that this being had simply passed through Susan from an unknown realm of heaven in order to live his life. He was unique, much of him unlike either of them. One day he would grow up and no longer need them. They would die and he would live on, perhaps fathering another generation, quite independent of them. Never before had George been so aware of the passing of time and the continuous river of life. In Charlie he sensed his own immortality. Even if he hadn't believed in life after death, he knew he would live on in his son. Then he thought of those friends who had lost their lives in the war and lamented that they hadn't lived long enough to experience such joy and wonder as this.

By the age of two, Charlie could ride a pony. Susan, pregnant with their second child, led him up and down the farm while he complained that he wanted to do it by himself. It wasn't long before the gauchos took turns taking him out across the plains on their own horses, one hand holding the reins, the other holding the small child tightly against their stomachs. This he adored and he yelped in delight, imploring them to go faster. The youngest of them, a dark-skinned youth with narrow, northern eyes that had earned him the name El Chino, would come for him in the evenings after his tea and canter with him slowly, scattering the hares and sending the birds into the air. Sometimes at night Jose Antonio would take him to the *puesto* to listen to the gauchos singing to the accompaniment of El Flaco's guitar. Jose Antonio, who wasn't allowed to sing at home, sang in his unsteady but enthusiastic voice, while Charlie danced around the fire like a Red Indian. George would watch his son with pride. He made him paper aeroplanes which they flew on the wind, and climbed the sinewy ombu tree. He taught him about the animals of the plains and those of the mountain ranges, and Susan bought him a box of paints so that he could draw them. Faye, delighted at the news of another grandchild, sent a parcel of storybooks and Trees planted a walnut tree in Charlie's honour, taking trouble to engrave a plaque with his name and the date of his birth so that when they visited he would know which one was his. But neither of them breathed a word to Hannah and Humphrey about their new grandchild; they had learned from past mistakes.

Neither Faye nor Trees suspected that anyone else in Frognal Point knew about George's son, especially not Mrs Megalith. Shortly after Charles was born Susan sent her a letter of thanks. Mrs Megalith was delighted to have been able to help. After all her years as a healer she still took immense pleasure when someone's pain was lifted. She could tell from Susan's photograph that she was now free of that dreadful longing. The bird had learned to fly higher and faster than ever before. She congratulated herself. If only Rita could do the same, but she still wallowed in self-pity as if she were determined not to move on. Mrs Megalith was growing tired of the girl moping around, retreating deeper and deeper into herself, as stubborn as the donkey Maddie and Harry had bought for their little boy. What man would want her like that? If there was one thing that Mrs Megalith despised it was inertia. Life was what one made of it, it was to be taken by the horns and wrestled with. 'God helps those who help themselves,' she mumbled to herself in exasperation, 'and so do I.'

It was not long after Ava Faye was born that a Texan friend of Jose Antonio, who lived in Buenos Aires, flew up to *Las Dos Vizcachas* in a small, private plane. To Charlie's great excitement the plane circled the farm while he waved along with his parents, Great Aunt Agatha and Great Uncle Jose Antonio and his cousins Pia and Tonito. Dolores crept out of the kitchen and stood like a little black *carancho* on the grass shielding her eyes from the sun. Gonzalo and Carlos, Agustina and Marcela rushed into the park to get a better look, ignoring the irritated shouts from Dolores complaining that they didn't have time to hang around gawping. They pretended they hadn't heard her, silently wishing that the groping priest hadn't caused her to relapse back into her black moods, as if she were determined to punish not only herself, but the rest of them as well, for allowing her virtue to be so wretchedly compromised.

The plane circled many times and Bobby Chadwin could be seen in miniature, waving through the small window. George hadn't been this close to a plane since he had left the RAF. He felt the palms of his hands grow sweaty and wasn't sure whether it was due to fear or excitement. Part of him yearned to take to the skies, to feel the slipstream through his hair again, to hear nothing but the roar of the wind, the vibration of the engine and his own silence. The other part of him remembered the battles, the black smoke of a plane spiralling uncontrollably into the sea, the smell of cordite, the rush of adrenalin and the sweat that stung in his eyes. He was reminded of the killing machine he had been reduced to in those moments when he had thought nothing of taking life. That part of him feared the skies for the man he had become still dwelt there, in the shadows between life and death, where dark clouds gathered to eclipse the sun. He didn't want to go back.

Bobby Chadwin landed and taxied up to the waiting crowd. He opened the door and climbed down triumphantly. 'What views!' he exclaimed. 'I took time to survey the farm. It's looking good, Jose Antonio.' Susan smiled as Bobby pronounced Jose as Josie with a strong Texan accent. Jose Antonio slapped him on the back and embraced him and she thought how much they resembled two rough bears, coarse and hairy yet charming and genial. Bobby kissed Agatha's hand and ruffled the children's hair. Then he saw little Charlie, as fair and pretty as one of Raphael's *putti*. 'Would you like to fly in my plane?' he asked. Pia and Tonito both cried that they would and clung onto his trousers while Charlie was too busy being thrown around to answer. Susan recoiled at the thought of her precious son in a small aeroplane and hoped the Texan would forget his offer.

They lunched on the veranda at Jose Antonio's house while Ava slept in a pram in the shade. After lunch Pia and Tonito pressed Bobby for a ride in his plane and Susan tried to distract Charlie with promises of *dulce de leche* pancakes for tea. Her efforts were to no avail for Charlie looked up to his cousins. Whatever they wanted to do, he followed blindly.

'Mama, I want to fly too,' he said. 'Papa, can I, please?' Susan looked at George and at once detected the fear behind his eyes, mistaking it for a reflection of her own.

'I really think he's too little,' she said, stroking his curly hair.

'Oh, go on, he'll love it,' Agatha encouraged. So charmed was she by the handsome Texan that she didn't sense Susan's reservations.

'Please, Mummy!' he begged. 'I'm nearly five.'

'I'm quite safe, I assure you,' said Bobby with a wink at Charlie.

'No one knows more about flying than George,' Agatha declared with pride. 'He was a fighter pilot in the war and thanks to his bravery we won.' George shuffled uncomfortably.

'Why don't you go too?' Jose Antonio suggested, wiping his face with a napkin where he had eaten his steak with too much enthusiasm. 'You can take all three children with you.' He chuckled and picked his teeth. 'Nothing would get me up there. I'm a man of the earth.'

'It would be a pleasure to show you around my lady,' said Bobby, referring to his plane. 'I'd be mighty honoured to pilot a man with your experience.' There was no way out. George had to fly or lose face.

They drank their coffee while the children played around the table, pestering Bobby every five minutes to take them for a ride in his plane. 'I want to go in your lady,' said Tonito to much laughter from the grown-ups. Finally the Texan drained his coffee cup and lifted Charlie onto his shoulders as he strode out into the park in the direction of the field where he had landed. Susan threaded her fingers through George's and whispered to him to look after himself and their son. 'I need you both,' she said nervously. George squeezed her hand to reassure her but inside his stomach had turned to liquid.

Bobby took time to show George around his plane, proudly showing off the latest gadgets. He patted it, the same way that George remembered patting his Spitfire. He felt a wave of nostalgia and had to steady himself with one hand on the wing. Bobby strapped the children tightly into the back seat then waved at George to climb into the front. George breathed heavily, nodded with confidence he didn't feel, and jumped into the cockpit. The sight of the dials, the stick and rudder bar reminded him of his first solo flight in a Tiger Moth. Most people had trouble landing the plane, but for George everything had gone wrong. He blinked away the memory but the nasty feeling in his stomach remained.

George felt naked without his oxygen mask, goggles and helmet, and light without the heavy parachute and Mae West life jacket. There he was in his shirt and slacks with nothing more than a pair of canvas shoes on his feet. The children were quiet in the back, their little faces peering excitedly out of the window. George quickly wiped away a trickle of sweat before Bobby noticed it. He passed a dry tongue over his lips and felt his throat constrict with panic. The aircraft shuddered a little then, as it picked up speed, it began to rattle like a toolbox. The smell of oil fumes reached his nostrils and his mouth suddenly began to salivate as the bile rose in his stomach. He tried to concentrate on his breathing so as not to embarrass himself by throwing up. Then, just when he was about to retch, the plane stopped rattling and soared smoothly into the air. The ground fell away and the sky filled the windows, much bluer than the sky above the coast of England, even on a midsummer's day. George gazed about him, at the miniature trees and dwellings and the vast, flat plain that erupted into the high sierras like a stormy sea on the horizon. He felt his anxiety slip away as once more he was close to heaven in a tranquil sky with only the low rumble of the engine and his own thumping heart to remind him of his mortality. There were no shadows, no death, and the man who had once lusted for blood had vanished.

Bobby looked across at him and smiled. 'Sure feels good, doesn't it?' he said into his speaker.

'Better than anything else in the world.'

PART II

Chapter Twenty-five

Frognal Point 1963

Faye sat listening to Thadeus play the violin. Outside, the afternoon sun was obscured behind black clouds that rolled angrily across the sky. The autumn wind clawed at the windowpanes as if struggling to get in to where the fire blazed in the grate, filling the small sitting room with warmth. She shivered, not from cold, but because she was afraid of returning home in such a storm.

She watched Thadeus, now seventy-eight years old, his long grey beard and deep-set eyes unchanged by the years, and knew that she loved him more than ever. They had grown together and fused like the branches of a tree, the past decade having only strengthened their affair and cloaked it in secrecy. He closed his eyes for he knew the music by heart and played it often. A sad tune that reminded him of his Polish past and all that he had loved and lost there at the outbreak of the war.

She, too, closed her eyes, felt the heat of the fire on her face and saw the shadows of dancing flames on the backs of her eyelids. The music made her melancholy. George had been away for so long and she doubted, in rare moments when self-delusion didn't convince her otherwise, that he would ever come home. She focused her thoughts on her son and the life he had chosen the other side of the world. She and Trees had travelled to see him twice, the last trip being over five

years before. They had met their two grandchildren, Charlie
and Ava, and spent three weeks staying with Agatha and Jose
Antonio. But the years had fallen away like leaves in autumn,
so many and so fast that now, at sixty-four years of age, Faye
worried that the last leaf might fall and she would never see
them again. And even if she did, her grandchildren would be
strangers.

Hannah had grown distant. Faye didn't see much of her
and Humphrey these days, except in church and sometimes
in the village shop. They never asked about George. Perhaps
if Rita had married they would have been able to put the past
behind them and forgive. But Rita was now thirty-six, still
single and leading an increasingly eccentric life in a rented
cottage the other side of Bray Cove. Like her mother, she
put out grain to attract the birds and spent hours taming
them. Faye had heard that she had cultivated a beautiful
wild garden, inviting all sorts of animals, from hedgehogs to
hares, to play among the foxgloves and lilac bushes. When
she wasn't in her garden or down on the beach she ran the
library in town where she had worked for over ten years. She
channelled all her energy into organising reader evenings with
authors with whom Max put her in touch and poetry classes
with a retired Oxford professor who had recently moved to
Frognal Point. She never dated and took little interest in her
appearance, her hair wild and unkempt and her clothes long
and flowing. In spite of her chaotic life style she retained a
natural beauty; her skin was pale and youthful and her eyes
an unusual shade of brown. She retained the naïvety of her
youth and seemed not to mature as others did. There was
something timeless about Rita. She had never resumed their
sculpting evenings, but Faye knew that she still sculpted for,
not only was there a rather dark and dramatic statue of a heron
in flight in the library, but the lady who ran the crafts shop in
town had told her that Rita came often to buy supplies.

Maddie remained friendly, and was lovelier than she had ever been. Happiness had given her eyes a healthy sparkle and motherhood had brushed her complexion with a gentle radiance. She had three children: Freddie, born in 1947; Daisy who came unexpectedly two years later; and Elsbeth, born some eighteen months after Daisy. Maddie told Faye that Rita loved her nephew and nieces as much as if they were her own. When she wasn't working or sculpting, she was at Bray Cove teaching them about birds, crustaceans and other sea creatures. They sailed out in a small boat and caught crabs, lobster and trout and lit fires on the sand at dusk, the wind carrying their voices as they sang songs to the hesitant strumming of Rita's second-hand guitar. Rita and Maddie made picnics as they had done as children and ate their sand-filled sandwiches on the beach watching the children make treasure trails as George had done. For Maddie life was an idyll. Harry had published his book to much acclaim and it was now translated into fifteen languages. He had made money, but they hadn't changed their lifestyle or bought a bigger house. They were happy as they were.

Eddie had surprised everyone by going to Bristol University where she had studied zoology. She had met her husband while working on an African game reserve a couple of years after graduating. Hannah now knew the pain of parting with a child as well as Faye did, but they never spoke of it. Eddie had made her life out there with the beasts of the jungle and it was doubtful that she would ever come back. Frognal Point couldn't boast lions and leopards and Eddie's interests had moved beyond bats. But Hannah was proud of her daughter and if she felt saddened by her absence she never let it show.

Faye opened her eyes as a sudden flash of lightning filled the room with a white phosphorescent light. She sat bolt upright as a crack of thunder ripped the sky apart and the clouds gave way to heavy rain. Thadeus stopped playing and put down his violin. They looked at each other in amazement at the unexpected viciousness of the storm. Another flash and Faye stood up.

'I had better get home,' she said anxiously. 'Trees will be wondering where I am.'

'You can't drive home in this storm. It's not safe.'

'Then I'll wait for it to pass. The thunder's so loud it must be right above us.'

'It won't be long. Let's watch it, shall we?' he suggested, walking over to the window. It was almost dark outside. Another blaze of lightning illuminated the garden for a moment with a shuddering flash of silver. Faye stood beside him and took his hand.

'It's beautiful, isn't it?' she said quietly. 'When I was a child, my father once told me that thunder was simply clouds knocking into each other. I believed it until not so long ago. It seemed so logical.'

Thadeus chuckled. 'Children accept what they are told, then adults forget to put them right. I laugh at some of the things I believed as a boy and continued to believe into manhood.'

'Adults try to make their children less fearful with stories.'

'Or more fearful in order to prevent them hurting themselves or going where they shouldn't.'

'I miss George,' she said suddenly.

Thadeus put his big arm around her and drew her against him. 'I know,' he replied and his voice was little more than a groan. He too knew what it was to miss one's children. 'Children belong to God and are put temporarily into our care. Still, it doesn't make it any easier, does it?'

'Love hurts so much,' she said, nuzzling her face into her chest. 'Loving you hurts, Thadeus.'

He cupped her face in his strong hands and stroked her

cheeks with his thumbs. 'But it is through suffering that we can experience joy, Faye,' he said with a smile and a tear trembled on his lashes like a ball of dew on the web of a spider.

When the storm had subsided a little, Faye drove home. She focused on the road but Thadeus was all she really saw. If only Trees would disappear, she thought disloyally, then she could spend the rest of her days with Thadeus. He needed her. Trees, on the other hand, needed no one but his walnuts.

When she arrived at Lower Farm the wind was still strong. Leaves were strewn all over the ground and were being blown up against the farm buildings like waves crashing against rocks. She ducked her head and ran inside, her shoes splashing through puddles that had collected on the pathway. Once inside, she shouted for Trees and, when there was no reply, she assumed he'd fallen asleep reading the papers by the fire in the little sitting room. She put the kettle on the Aga and took a couple of mugs down from the cupboard. The kitchen was silent, like a dark cavern. She made the tea and carried the mugs through the hall to the sitting room, only to find it empty.

'Trees!' she shouted into the hall, frowning in bewilderment. He couldn't possibly be out on a day like this, but there was no question about it, he was not in the house. She sat down in his armchair and drank her tea alone, wondering where he had gone and feeling a little afraid. Then she was struck by an idea. It was not unlikely that, even on an afternoon such as this, he was out with his walnut trees. 'Damn those bloody trees!' she swore, maddened that she had wasted time worrying when he was quite obviously nurturing his stupid trees. No doubt one of them had fallen over in the storm or been struck by lightning.

She decided to go and check. She put on her coat and strode across the grass to the copse where walnut trees of all sizes grew in more than an acre of lovingly cared for grounds. She shouted his name but there was no answer. Fear began to wind its fingers around her throat. Sensing something ominous, she walked faster. 'Trees!' she shouted again. Still no answer. Then she saw ahead a sight of terrible devastation. One of the thick branches of a mature tree had been struck by lightning and had fallen to the ground directly beside Mildred's grave. She swallowed hard and placed a trembling hand over her mouth. As she got closer she saw two booted feet, brown trousers and finally the inert body of her husband, his head beside Mildred's headstone. She ran to him and crouched down in an effort to resuscitate him. She pressed her ear to his heart, praying with all the force she could muster that she might hear a faint beat, but only the heavy silence of death filled his chest. He was gone. He must have fallen and hit his head on the gravestone. Cradling him in her arms she sobbed quietly and hoped it had been quick and that he had suffered no pain. She couldn't bear to imagine him calling out for help while she was in the arms of her lover.

News of Trees' sudden death spread around Frognal Point like sea mist in winter. No sooner had Faye watched his body depart in an ambulance than a car turned into the farm and drew up outside the house. It was Hannah. Faye was so distraught that Hannah forgot her resentment and embraced her old friend. 'I'm so sorry,' she said, her voice cracking with sincerity, for suddenly, in the face of death, she realised that their feud had been petty. The two women stood embracing in the gale and the drizzle, then walked inside where it was warm but silent and empty.

Faye slumped into a chair while Hannah put the kettle on the Aga, then leaned back against it. She folded her arms and her face crumpled with sympathy. 'I can't believe it, Faye. What was he doing out there on a day like this?'

Faye raised her bloodshot eyes and sighed. 'His blasted

trees.' She gave a bitter laugh. His obsession had finally killed him.

'He so loved his walnuts.' Hannah shook her head in disbelief. There was a long pause while she took a couple of cups down from the cupboard and two teaspoons out of the drawer.

Faye's lips had turned very pale and began to tremble. 'I wasn't even there,' she said in a whisper.

'Where were you?'

'I went into the village to see Thadeus.'

'That old Pole?' Hannah frowned. She had no idea that Faye even knew Thadeus.

Faye nodded. 'He commissioned a sculpture, a bear, and I had completed it. I took it over and stayed for hours. He's a fascinating man. If I had known . . .' She bent her head, guilty that lying came so easily. Hannah narrowed her eyes. She sensed there was more to Faye's story than she was letting on. 'He might have been calling for me,' Faye continued miserably. 'Perhaps he didn't die instantly. What if he had shouted for help? There I was enjoying a cosy tea with Thadeus.'

Hannah turned and poured boiling water into the teapot. 'Don't torment yourself, Faye,' she said soothingly. 'There was nothing you could have done. He's in a better place.' She filled the cups and went and sat opposite Faye at the kitchen table. It was then that she noticed Faye was wearing her hair down. Hannah couldn't recall the last time she had seen her friend with her hair loose.

'What are you going to do?' Hannah asked, taking a sip of tea. Faye stared into her cup.

'George will have to come home and run the farm. I can't do it on my own.'

Hannah stiffened. 'Do you think he'll come? Surely he's made a life for himself out there?'

'He'll come,' she said, smiling a little at the thought of being reunited with her son. 'He was only supposed to be away for a year to learn about farming, then he was planning on coming back here to work with his father. Things didn't turn out as any of us had hoped.' She raised her eyes and looked imploringly at Hannah. 'We didn't wish any of what has happened on either Rita or George. I wanted George to live here with us. He had been away at war for so long, it hurt me to watch him leave again. I love Rita like my own daughter and now I never see her. I only hear about her from Maddie.'

'It's all in the past,' said Hannah.

'I know it is. Eighteen years have passed since George came back from the war. We're old now. Who'd have ever thought it? I never imagined I'd live to the ripe old age of sixty-four. Trees was nearly seventy years old, that's ancient. It's the nineteen sixties, for God's sake!' She shrugged. 'It's right that George should come home and take over from Trees. He'll want to, I know. He loved his father. He'll be devastated.'

'Tell me,' Hannah ventured in a soft voice, her mind whirring with worry about how Rita would react to the news of George's homecoming. 'Does George have children?'

'Two, a boy and a girl.'

Hannah breathed sharply. 'How nice. Grandchildren are a blessing.'

'I only wish I could have watched them grow up. Now Trees will never know them.'

When Hannah left she felt downhearted. She was saddened by Trees' death and because she had allowed her friendship with Faye to unravel, but more acutely because George was coming home. She wondered how Rita would take the news. Why the girl hadn't married someone else, she couldn't understand. Things would be much less complicated if she had a family life of her own, rather than sharing Maddie's. She seemed happy enough, though. Kept herself busy. Max was a loyal friend. He was now an extremely successful producer in London. Her mother never stopped telling her how brilliant he was and how well-known he was becoming. He was spreading his tentacles into television, but Hannah couldn't see the advantages in that, she was more than satisfied with her wireless. More important than his career, to her, was the fact that he made Rita laugh in a way that no one else could, a deep, throaty laugh that made her eyes water and her cheeks flush. In those fleeting moments, Hannah saw Rita's potential, what she might have been had she made different choices. Max seemed to bring out the confident young woman whom George had sent into hiding. When he was around it was as if George had never existed. Of course, some day he would find a nice girl and marry and then he'd have no time for Rita. He was an attractive, successful man. If there had ever been a chance of a sexual attraction between them it would surely have happened by now.

When Mrs Megalith heard about Trees she sank into a chair and stared ahead of her as if in a trance. The cats gathered around her feet, sensing her unhappiness, and one brave tabby crept onto her knee and nuzzled his face against her arm; but she sat quite still as if she hadn't noticed him. She had been one of the few people in Trees' life to understand him. She had loved him too, as a dear friend. They had talked endlessly about his walnut trees and he had consulted her about how best to nurture them. No one knew of the crystals he had planted or of the saplings he had brought to her greenhouse for special care. With her, he had had the confidence to talk with eloquence about everything, even Faye. Although he had never openly said it, she knew he feared she had a lover. That fear had driven him further into his obsession with his walnut trees for they were constant and responsive and kept his mind from the hollow reality of his marriage. As Faye withdrew, he showered on them the love and attention he should have given to his wife and they grew better because of it. She would miss him terribly and so would his walnuts.

Hannah drove over to Bray Cove that evening to tell Maddie and Harry the sad news. She found them at home with their children and Rita, but they had already heard.

'I bumped into Reverend Hammond in town this evening and he told me,' said Maddie. 'Sad, isn't it? Still, he had a good innings. Wasn't he nearly seventy?'

'Seventy isn't old, Maddie, your father's not far off.'

'How has Faye taken it?' Harry asked. 'I had a lot of respect for Trees.'

Hannah breathed deeply and glanced at Rita. 'She's so sad,' she replied, knowing she would have to break the news about George's return.

'Didn't she find him under a tree?' Maddie asked. 'Ironic, isn't it?'

'She did, but she's dreadfully upset at not being there when it happened.'

'Where was she?' Rita asked, raising her chin.

'She had to deliver a sculpture to Thadeus Walizhewski. You know, the old Pole who lives up that little lane.'

'Really?' said Rita, her voice suddenly turning hostile. 'So, while Trees lay dying, his wife was with another man?'

Hannah straightened in amazement. 'Rita! I think what you are insinuating is an insult to Faye,' she retorted. Rita's cheeks blazed with fury. 'I have never seen her look so distressed,' Hannah continued. 'Her face was haggard and her eyes red from crying. She had sat with his body under the tree in the rain until the ambulance came. Alice said that the ambulancemen had to prise her away from him.'

'How gruesome!' Maddie gasped.

'You know, she was wearing her hair down. I don't think I've seen her with it like that in thirty years.'

Rita raised her eyes. 'I have,' she stated with studied nonchalance.

'Really?' said Hannah, raising her eyebrows.

'Yes. Thadeus was very kind to me after George left and I went to visit him one day, but he was sitting with Faye in his garden so I left without being seen. She had her hair down then, too.' No one spoke. Even Maddie remained silent as they all looked at each other in bewilderment. Not one of them would have suspected Faye of having an affair. Hannah took a deep breath and changed the subject to the one thing that would distract Rita from any more revelations.

'George is coming home to take over the farm,' she said, and watched as her daughter's mouth fell open in a silent scream.

Chapter Twenty-six

George was out on the plains when the boy arrived on horseback from the post office in Jesús Maria with the telegram. Susan signed for it with some foreboding. She knew instinctively that it didn't bring good news. The envelope felt heavy and formal, the kind of weight and formality that proclaimed the death of someone close. She longed to open it so that she could break the news to him gently and sensitively but she resisted, respecting his privacy.

The telegram sat menacingly on the table in the sitting room and each time she passed it she felt a strange sense of destiny, as if this small, ivory envelope contained news that would change the whole course of their future. In the afternoon Charlie and Ava returned from school with instructions for her to make them costumes for the school play. They dropped their satchels to the floor, hugged their mother, then ran outside in the direction of the *puesto* to where El Chino waited with a couple of glossy ponies to take them out across the plains, now flowering with the advent of spring. Susan watched them go and feared for them. If that telegram contained the bad news she suspected, their young lives would have to change, too.

Finally, George returned, dusty and weary from a hard day's work. Ava ran up to him and threw her arms around his waist but Susan held back and bit her lip, holding the telegram in her hand.

'What's that?' he asked, stroking Ava's eager face.

'It arrived this morning.'

'And you didn't open it?' George looked surprised.

'It's addressed to you,' she said, giving it to him. 'Charlie, Ava, go and tidy the playroom, it's time to change for supper.'

The children groaned for they couldn't understand why Marcela didn't tidy up after them like maids were supposed to. Once they had gone, George tore open the envelope. With desolation he read what was written there. Susan judged by the darkening of his features that it was bad news as she had feared.

'My father is dead,' he said, his chest growing tight with sorrow. Susan put her arms around him and felt his sadness penetrate her own heart. They would leave Argentina and build a new home in England. She had always accepted the idea of living in Frognal Point but now, faced with the reality, she was suddenly filled with dread. The children would see it as a great adventure. They would love the sea and the sand, the rock pools and caves, but she would be confronted with George's past as well as her own, and the demons she had left there.

George sat down and put his head in his hands. 'I never said goodbye,' he said in a hollow voice. 'I haven't seen him for five years. Now I'll never see him again.' He rubbed his face in disbelief, suddenly bereft. It was unimaginable. His father had always seemed as sturdy and enduring as a walnut tree. 'He wasn't even old. Mother must be devastated. We have to go back.'

Susan felt her stomach churn. 'Of course we'll go,' she said reassuringly, surprised how confident her voice sounded.

'You don't mind?'

She looked into his dejected eyes and felt her anxieties dissolve in the pity that his pain aroused. She kissed his temple. 'My darling, of course I don't mind. Home is where you are. We'll adapt. You'll show the children how to catch crabs and eat sandy sandwiches and we'll make a new life for ourselves. Life is an adventure and as long as we're all together we'll be happy.'

'You're an incredible woman, Susan. You have no idea how much I admire you.'

She ran a hand through his dusty hair. 'Oh, yes I do,' she replied.

The children were excited about going to England. George made it all sound so enchanting and Susan encouraged them with her own enthusiasm. Charlie could think of little else than the promise of hours and hours of flying in an aeroplane, but for Susan and George the journey ahead held nothing but dread. Jose Antonio and Agatha were saddened that they were leaving. In the last decade George had become a son to them and his children as cherished as grandchildren. The farm would be quieter and less bright without their laughter and vigour and the evenings long and empty. Agatha consoled herself that George had only intended staying a year and had lasted more than ten, but Jose Antonio couldn't understand why they couldn't just go for a while to console Faye and then come back. 'Their lives are here with us. They belong at *Las Dos Vizcachas* like we do,' he growled angrily. When Jose Antonio was hurt he lashed out in fury.

Not even Jose Antonio's rage, however, could persuade them to stay. Sorrowfully they packed up the house and the memories that would always remain tender and strong. Susan went for a last, solitary walk across the fields. She took a final look around at the place she had grown to love with such intensity. Now the outside world awaited her with challenges she'd thought she might never have to face. She hoped that Frognal Point would embrace her and forgive George for having left.

The night before their departure they dined with Jose Antonio and Agatha and then sat beneath the veranda on the swing chair as they had done over a decade before when Susan had just arrived. The air was sweet and balmy. They breathed in the smells of the countryside, the eucalyptus and jasmine, cut grass and honeysuckle, determined not to forget those things that they had taken for granted. Moths fluttered about the hurricane lamps and crickets cried out across the sleepy park.

'We've been very happy here, haven't we?' George mused wistfully. 'It's an idyll. I should be pleased to be going back to Frognal Point, but I'm not. My home is here.'

Susan took his hand and stroked his skin with her thumb. 'You'll probably find that nothing has changed there either.'

'Only Father's gone.' He dragged on his cigarette, contemplating Lower Farm without Trees. 'It just doesn't seem possible. He *was* home. It'll be halved now, diminished in every way. He was a quiet man but he filled that house with his presence. I'll always remember him in his boots and cap, striding around the farm with Mildred the sheepdog at his side. He loved the countryside, nature, trees and birds. He infected me with his passion. I grew up a countryman. He was wise too. He never said much. I think that frustrated Mother, she's a warm, lively woman. But she loved him. We all did.'

'He was a unique man. I'm so pleased I knew him. He was one of life's wonderful eccentrics.'

George smiled. 'He hated to spend money. Mother said that during the war he bartered with everyone. Eggs for clothes coupons, chickens for fish, pigs for fruit from Mrs Megalith's magical greenhouses. He dug up half a field for a vegetable garden. They wanted for nothing. While the rest of the country suffered terrible rations Pa produced his own bread and butter, milk and cheese, cream and eggs. I tell you, when I returned from France they looked better and healthier than I had ever seen them. He drove everywhere in that truck of his because petrol for farm vehicles wasn't rationed. He was a man of initiative and energy. He exasperated Mother with the buckets he put under leaks in the roof and the amateur way he mended everything himself. He was loath to pay for someone else to do it if he could do it on his own. Mother will cry over those buckets now, no doubt, because they'll remind her of him. She'll realise how much she loved all his funny quirks. She might even nurture his trees for him now that he's not around to do it.'

'If she doesn't, you will,' said Susan, leaning her head on his shoulder.

'I always knew in the back of my mind that I'd take over the farm when Father died, but I never thought it would be this soon. Part of me dreads going back, Susan. I'll be honest with you.'

'I know,' she replied softly, not wanting to enhance his fear with her own. 'But you're with me now. You have children, a family. Focus on all the things that you loved about the place. Like the sea and the beach, the farm where you grew up. You're going to be running it now. You couldn't really go on here, working for Jose Antonio, however much you enjoyed it. A man like you should be running his own business, calling the shots. It's the right time for you to leave, trust me.'

'Still, it will be hard parting, won't it?'

'We can always come back,' she said. But she knew that once they were gone, they would be gone for ever.

The following morning Dolores burnt the bread, overboiled Jose Antonio's eggs and spoiled the coffee. Pia and Tonito complained that the croissants tasted of charcoal and even Agatha had to agree that the milk was off. Then the disgruntled cook appeared on the terrace, wringing her hands and dabbing her tearstained face with the skirt of her apron.

'I cannot work today,' she declared melodramatically. 'I am not well.' And she left Augstina and Carlos to clear up what was without doubt the most unsatisfactory breakfast anyone had ever had at *Las Dos Vizcachas*. Agatha and Jose Antonio looked at each other in disbelief. Dolores had never shown the slightest affection for George, but it was obvious that his departure had upset her.

George, Susan and the children arrived at the house to say goodbye. They had little luggage, having sent most of their things ahead by boat. Agatha embraced them, drawing on her humour to see her through without tears. Pia cried uncontrollably, especially when she hugged Susan, whom she loved almost as much as her mother. Tonito's bottom lip quivered, but it didn't do for a young man to weep so he held his shoulders back and chin up as his father did. But Jose Antonio was devastated. He knew the seasons would come and go and that the cycle of life would continue to revolve as it always had done, but his world would never be the same once George and his family were no longer in it. He patted their backs too fiercely and made too many bad jokes and then, when their car had disappeared, leaving nothing but a cloud of dust and the silence of his anguish, he saddled his horse and rode out across the plains until nightfall.

It was well known that Mrs Megalith didn't like church – no one in Frognal Point could forget the occasion she had attended with all those cats – but for Trees' funeral she made an exception. She didn't arrive late and stagger self-importantly down the aisle. She was careful not to make too much noise with her walking stick and she wore black from top to toe for the first time in her life. Accompanied by Max, handsome in a hand-tailored suit from Savile Row, and Ruth, she sat behind Hannah, Humphrey and Rita without uttering a word. Only her moonstone pendant glinted in the light as if warming up for sorcery.

The church was filled with berries and fruit and branches of crisp autumn leaves. On the top of his coffin, long and thin as he had been, sat a small basket of walnuts from the first tree he had planted. Reverend Hammond stood in front of the altar, his bulbous eyes discreetly scanning the area for cats. He had noticed Mrs Megalith and had shuddered for, although she was unusually subdued, she looked even more like a witch, dressed in black, her moonstone pendant winking at him menacingly. But Mrs Megalith was in no mood for trouble. She had loved Trees and had come to say good-bye although, at her advanced age, she was sure it wouldn't be too long before she joined him.

Faye wished that George had got back in time for the funeral. She took her place at the front with Alice, Geoffrey and her grandchildren. She settled her eyes on the coffin and imagined Trees inside it, dressed in his brown trousers, blue shirt and cap. She had resisted placing his boots on his feet; somehow it didn't seem appropriate to meet the Lord in muddy boots. She had picked the walnuts herself from the Romanian walnut tree he had planted just after they had married. Now it was at least fifty feet tall with purple leaves, and had been his favourite. After his death she had been tempted to fell the lot of them, but there was no point holding a grudge against the tree that had killed him for, out of all the possible ways to go, he would have chosen that one himself.

She knelt on the hassock and buried her face in prayer. Contrary to Mrs Megalith's philosophy, Faye felt closer to God in His house. She had said countless prayers at home but she had more confidence He'd hear her in the quiet serenity of church. She thanked Him for Trees' life and for his love but she asked with more fervour that He forgive her for her adultery, crying tears that only Rita, Hannah and Maddie suspected were shed out of guilt.

Max could smell violets. No one but Rita smelled so sweet. He watched her from the pew behind, took in the small black hat and uncombed hair that tumbled down her back. She still wore George's engagement ring, but on the third finger of her right hand. He couldn't believe that a woman could hold onto the memory of a man for so long. She was as stubborn as she was misguided. He knew George was moving back to Lower Farm with his wife and children. Surely when she saw him she would realise that her pining was for nothing. She would have to let him go. Didn't she realise how much *he* loved her?

Max was not only producing radio shows but television programmes as well. He had an acute talent for predicting what would be successful and a sharp eye for judging people. He was rising faster than one of Hannah's walnut cakes and making more money than he could possibly spend. None of it, however, was for him. It was all for Ruth and Rita, the two most important women in his life. One day Rita would love him. One day he would take her to Vienna and show her the Imperial Theatre his father had built for his mother. They would go backstage and he would bring to life the stories he had told her down on the beach, of the one-legged whore who had seduced the Shah of Persia and the chorus girls who took turns to embrace him against their scantily clad breasts.

While Max ached with longing, Rita thought of George. She watched Faye and couldn't help but feel personally deceived by her adultery. Trees lay innocent and unaware in a wooden box while his wife shed crocodile tears like a dutiful widow. But her anger was overshadowed by apprehension, for George was on his way back from Argentina, with his wife and children, the family he should have had with her. She felt the hate simmering at the bottom of her heart and was ashamed that she could give in to such ill feeling in God's house, on the occasion of a funeral. She glanced down at the diamond solitaire ring that twinkled on her finger, oblivious of its own lack of purpose, and saw in its unfailing sparkle a small ray of hope. '*Every time you look at it I want you to remember how much I love you.*'

During the address Mrs Megalith closed her eyes and sensed the discreet presence of Trees. He was standing by the altar with his arms crossed, talking to his father. Mrs Megalith didn't blame him. Reverend Hammond was painfully self-regarding and sanctimonious. What amused her most, however, was the speed and eloquence with which Trees spoke. She couldn't hear what he was saying, she just knew he was chatting, and in her mind's eye she saw the animation in his expression. In life he had never been so articulate, not even when he talked about his walnut trees. *Making up for lost time, I suspect*, she said to herself, then wiped away a tear. When Max slipped his hand around hers she flinched, embarrassed to be caught in a moment of weakness, but she opened her eyes and gazed on him with tenderness and gratitude. He smiled back discreetly and felt, as he had done that first night when she had bent down and kissed him, the unconditional love of a mother.

Maddie had always been selfish. She watched the glassy-eyed congregation with detachment. She had been fond enough of Trees but he hadn't been a man to whom one could get close. Rita had more reason to be sad for she had worked with him and had almost become his daughter-in-law but, for Maddie, he had been something of an unremarkable presence. A man who had once been best friends with her father, until George had ruined it all. Not that she got involved in family feuds. She had her own family to think about now. As much as she had sympathised with her sister, seventeen years had gone by. Maddie had lost patience. If her sister wanted to wallow in self-pity so be it, but she wasn't going to let it dominate her life like it dominated her mother's. Men had come and gone, disappointed that their advances had been so swiftly rejected. Only Max had remained a loyal friend. He called Rita often, visited when he could and shared her past and, Maddie was sure, all her secrets too. Why she didn't marry him, Maddie couldn't understand. He was rich and successful and more handsome now than he had ever been. Time had beaten him about a little at the edges and rugged lines had appeared as if from nowhere, etched into his youthful skin by the hand of experience. His eyes seemed more intense, darker, less ingenuous, and his hair had begun to recede. If Rita didn't grab the opportunity he would fall in love and marry someone else. She wished she'd get rid of that dismal engagement ring George had given her. It was tragic to hold onto something that was so obviously over. She hoped that when George returned Rita would see the impossibility of her fantasies and throw that pathetically small diamond into the sea.

Faye sat sculpting in her studio to the sound of Thadeus' favourite *Alpine Symphony* and felt very alone. Without Trees the house echoed with an unbearable silence. Even when they hadn't been in the same room she had felt his presence. His company had been warm and thick like a blanket. Now he was gone she realised how much she had loved him. Not the passionate love she felt for Thadeus, but he had been kind and dependable. She wished she had tried a little harder to understand him. In the end, she had let him drift further and further into his trees; perhaps if she had made more of an effort he might not have drifted so far.

It would be harder to see Thadeus now. She was a widow, and mourning seemed a more essential duty after death than fidelity had been before. She couldn't risk being seen with another man while her own husband was still warm in his grave. She wished she could turn the clock back to the summer before George went to Argentina, when he was happy with Rita and when Trees and Mildred were as much part of Lower Farm as the walnut trees.

Chapter Twenty-seven

When Susan, George and the children arrived at the quaint Devon station they could see little more than thick, grey fog. Having left the Argentine in springtime they now arrived in England in the middle of autumn. A bitter wind swept in from the coast and only the most intrepid gulls ventured out to glide upon it. Charlie and Ava pulled their coats around them and looked on their new world with disappointment. Soggy leaves lay in drifts all over the train tracks and swirled around a lamppost whose light glowed feebly through the mist. They were tired from their journey and disenchanted by the cold reality of their situation. It was only four in the afternoon and yet it was already getting dark. The rain penetrated their bones and dampened any optimism.

Faye and Alice were there to meet them. George's heart stumbled when he saw how much his mother had aged. She looked smaller and more fragile, like a sapling suddenly exposed to the light when the tree that had protected her was gone. Her eyes brimmed with happiness as she embraced him and he was reminded of the day he had returned from the war. She smelt the same and the skin on her face was soft and familiar against his. They didn't need to speak. Leaving her son's embrace, Faye greeted Susan and the children warmly, marvelling at how much Charlie and Ava had grown up, then George introduced them to his sister. They all squeezed into the estate car that Trees had bought not long before he died and drove the short distance to Lower Farm.

'What a shame to arrive on a day like this. It's been foggy all week,' said Faye, sensing the children's gloom. 'You'll warm up once we get you home.'

'I wanted them to see the countryside from the train but all we could see was cloud,' said George, who sat in the front with his mother. He glanced back and smiled at Ava who sat on Susan's lap. Fortunately the child was small for her ten years otherwise they would never have all fitted into the back seat.

'They're just weary,' said Susan, kissing her daughter's head. 'It's been a long journey.'

'I think the novelty of the plane has worn off for Charlie,' George added, hoping to bring a grin to his son's face, but Charlie just stared in front of him with unfocused eyes. 'How are Johnnie and Jane?' he asked, changing the subject.

'Johnnie's at Exeter University and Jane's just finished school,' Alice replied. 'She's hoping to go to Bristol.'

'How time flies!' George marvelled, 'It seems like only yesterday they were children.'

'You've been away a long time, George,' his sister said, without resentment.

'I hope the place hasn't changed,' he said hopefully.

Faye smiled and shook her head, pleased that he cared so much. 'Lower Farm and Frognal Point are exactly as you left them,' she said. 'Perhaps a couple more houses here and there and a few new faces but all the things you loved as a child remain unchanged. We made sure of that, didn't we Alice?'

When they arrived at Lower Farm, Faye made them all tea with cake, sandwiches and biscuits, which they ate in front of the fire in the sitting room. George took one bite of the cake and remembered his wartime homecoming, eighteen years before. There was no way his mother had cooked this cake herself! The children devoured it, savouring the novelty, and began to talk to each other in quiet voices. Susan was immediately enchanted by the house. It was so English in a cosy, chaotic way. She noticed the stack of sheet music on top of the piano and the books scattered carelessly on tables and on the floor against the wall. Seeing Faye in her home enabled Susan to understand her more fully. Even she, who had never really known Trees, could hear the hollow echo his absence caused and, as much as Faye tried to dissemble, Susan could sense that she felt desperately incomplete without him.

However, once classical music resounded through the house and they were warm and their hunger satisfied, their spirits began to lift with the fog.

George asked about his father. Faye's face flooded with colour and she lowered her eyes. He wanted to know all the details. Faye's teacup began to tremble slightly as she relived the day of the storm and, when she confessed that she hadn't been with him when he died, she had to put it down, it was rattling so much in its saucer.

'Where were you?' George asked. His tone wasn't reproachful but Faye was immediately on the defensive.

'I was in the village, visiting a friend,' she replied cagily.

George wouldn't have been suspicious had it not been for the inner flame that burned through her cheeks. Suddenly he was reminded of an image, long forgotten, of his mother riding her bicycle out of the farm in the middle of the night. He had never asked her where she had gone and why now, after all this time, this image chose to surface, he didn't know.

'When I returned he was nowhere to be found,' she continued. 'I searched everywhere. I just knew that something was wrong. When I found him, he was already dead. He had been knocked down by a falling branch, bashing his head on Mildred's gravestone.'

'And the funeral?' George asked, devastated to have missed it.

'Just a simple service for friends and family,' his mother replied. Her face reverted to its natural pallor.

'Don't feel bad that you didn't make it, George,' said Alice kindly. 'He would have understood.'

'I know. I just wish I had said goodbye.' He sighed and smiled crookedly in resignation.

'We all do,' Faye added in a small voice.

'I'll visit the grave tomorrow morning.' He took Susan's hand in his, grateful for her presence. 'Hopefully the fog will have lifted and I can show you and the children Frognal Point.'

'We'd love that,' she replied, squeezing his hand reassuringly.

'I want to see some crabs,' interjected Ava, cheering up now that she had eaten.

'Even if the weather's bad we'll go and have a picnic lunch on the beach. I'll show you rock pools full of crabs and urchins and make you a treasure trail in the sand.' The children grinned excitedly, remembering all the stories their father had told them of his childhood.

'I've heard so much about sand-filled sandwiches, I'm really looking forward to trying one,' said Susan, happy that her children were no longer looking miserable.

'Oh, yes,' enthused Faye. 'They're part of Frognal Point. You can't have a picnic on the beach without them.'

After dinner, when the children had gone to bed, George and Susan sat outside on the terrace beneath a navy sky that glittered with stars. It was cold and they huddled together in thick coats, while George smoked as he had done as a young man, when he had struggled to come to terms with life after war. The flagstones were wet and slippery and strewn with dead leaves and small twigs. The low twit-twoo of an owl rang out from a treetop somewhere close, its haunting whistle rising above the wind. George was consumed with nostalgia.

The smell of rotting foliage and farm animals reminded him so much of his childhood. Even the sound of that old owl was the same as it had been when he was a boy. Home was unchanged, except for his father's absence. He looked out into the garden, as far as he could see, until the lights from the house faded and the fields beyond were shrouded in blackness, and wondered whether his father's spirit was among the trees he had so loved. Maybe he was there on the terrace, watching them with amusement now that he was so blissfully detached from the world. Maybe Mildred was with him. Maybe Mrs Megalith was wrong and there was no afterlife. He held Susan close and they sat in silence watching and listening, Susan to the place that would now be her home and George to the echoes and images of his past.

For George it was strange to be at Lower Farm without Trees. The house felt deserted as if its spirit had gone too, leaving only bricks and mortar. He lay in bed that night listening to the familiar creaking of floorboards, breathing in the smell of woodsmoke from the fire downstairs and remembering. If it wasn't for Susan and his children he could have been a boy again. But his body felt too big for the bed, like a man playing in a children's playhouse. He had moved on, made a life elsewhere and come back to find he had grown up and away. It was going to be hard adjusting. When he closed his eyes he saw the faces of his friends killed in the war, for his homecoming had reunited him with his past. The demons hadn't gone, they had just got lost on the Argentine plain.

The following morning dawned with splendour. Not a cloud marred the perfection of the sky and gulls flew once more, their cries of delight ringing out as they glided on the breeze. Susan looked out of the window and her heart inflated with joy. The garden glittered as if strewn with diamonds as the sun caught thousands of beads of dew on the grass and plants, illuminating them as if by enchantment. It wasn't long before Charlie and Ava bounded in. Ava squealed with excitement and jumped into bed to wake her father. She giggled as he rolled over and wrapped his arms around her, growling like a big bear. Charlie looked on in amusement, too grown up now to indulge in childish horseplay, although a part of him still longed to. Susan watched them in wonderment, reflecting on the amazing ability children had to adjust to new surroundings.

Faye hated sleeping alone. She had barely spent a night apart from Trees since they had married. Once or twice she had sneaked off to Thadeus, only when she had been desperate, but she had always awoken with her husband beside her. Now she awoke to a feeling of emptiness. She missed his warm presence in bed, the sound of running water in the bathroom as he brushed his teeth and shaved, the knowledge that she wasn't on her own. For a moment she suffered that cold ache in the pit of her stomach that she had had every morning since he had died, but then the events of the day before came flooding back replacing the ache with optimism. She opened the curtains and dressed quickly so that she could make breakfast for her son.

The noise in the kitchen as she walked down the corridor was heartening. It had been years since she had had people to look after. Since the children had grown up and left she had busied herself sculpting, a lonely hobby that required hours of solitude. Now she had a family to cook for and entertain. It would take time to warm to Susan; she was aloof and vigilant, which Faye felt had a lot to do with the scar she bore on her face, but the children were enchanting. She looked forward to watching them play in all George and Alice's old haunts like Johnnie and Jane had. They would love the farm and all the animals and she would teach them the piano and how to create with clay. Her evenings would no longer be solitary. Even if they moved into one of the farm cottages, which was the plan, she would be surrounded by her family, a dream she had given up long ago.

After breakfast George drove Susan and the children into Frognal Point. Charlie and Ava pressed their noses to the windows, noticing everything from the small, rolling fields to the quaint country cottages. At one point they had to wait behind a throng of Friesians meandering slowly down the lane on their way to the milking parlour. An old man walked behind them wielding a stick, which he brandished in the air like a weary warrior with a sword. He recognised George immediately and tapped his cap in respect. When George rolled down the window to engage in a brief conversation, the old man spoke with such a strong Devon accent, rolling his 'r's so tightly, that Susan couldn't understand a word.

The village was quiet. They passed the shop where Miss Hogmier brooded like an angry vulture awaiting more gossip to peck at and the White Hart pub where George had met up with his friends in the evenings for beer and darts. After the war there had been fewer of them, only a handful of survivors, all as jaded and cynical as he was, their youth gone and their prospects uncertain. He wondered what had happened to them in the years that he had been away. Had they married, had children and found their lives again? He could still envisage them leaning on the bar, staring into their beer hoping to find answers there. They drove past pretty cottages and a couple of large houses hidden up short driveways behind yew hedges and trees. At the other end of the village the church came into view. It was small and squat and very old. George remembered the services he had gone to on Sundays, dressed in his best clothes, the women in smart hats and gloves. It had always been as much of a social occasion as a religious one. He remembered how his mother used to stand for ages outside chatting to Hannah and their friends while he and Rita had played leapfrog over the gravestones, much to Reverend Hammond's disapproval. He recalled the time Mrs Megalith had made her surprise appearance and decided to tell the children the story. They were riveted by the tale of the Elvestree witch and enthralled by the thought of the magic cats appearing out of nowhere.

'Will we meet her?' Charlie asked, leaning forward between the front seats.

'Of course you will. She's legendary,' he replied. Susan smiled secretively; she had much to thank the witch for and looked forward to doing so in person.

'Does she really ride a broomstick?' Ava asked.

'I'm sure she does, but only at night,' her father replied.

Susan smacked his knee playfully. 'Oh, darling, you're wicked!' she scolded in amusement. 'What will they say when they meet her?'

George grinned. 'I'm longing to find out,' he replied mischievously and Susan shook her head as he launched into more outlandish stories.

George parked the car on the village green and led his wife and children across to the church. It was quiet in the graveyard, not a soul to be seen but presumably many that were beyond the awareness of human beings. Trees' grave was fresh and covered in flowers. George fell silent as he stood before the mound of earth. When his eyes settled on the grey headstone the reality of his father's death caused his whole body to tremble. He felt suddenly weak, as if the breath had been knocked out of him. There engraved in the stone was his name. 'Trees Bolton'. Not Edmund Anthony Bolton, his given name, but the name by which everyone knew him. Susan threaded her fingers through his, but said nothing. Charlie and Ava ran around the graveyard with as little reverence as a pair of excitable dogs.

'I can't believe Pa's in there,' George said, his forehead creasing into a troubled frown. 'I can't believe he's dead.'

'I know, my darling,' Susan replied. 'The gravestone really brings it all home, doesn't it?'

'That's what we're all reduced to in the end.'

'We all finish as dust, but you've still got many years of life ahead of you. Don't let this depress you.'

'I want to spend some time alone with Pa. Why don't you take Charlie and Ava to the shop and buy them some sweets?' he suggested.

She smiled at him sympathetically. 'Take as long as you like. We'll walk slowly, it's a beautiful day and I want to check out my new home town.'

When they reached the shop Charlie and Ava were thrilled to see a large, shaggy dog tied up to the letter box, so Susan left them stroking the animal and wandered into the shop. It was much larger than it seemed from the outside with a stand of magazines at the front opposite a window for the post office and the counter. Miss Hogmier stood in a starched pink apron with her arms crossed, guarding the shelves laden with tall jars of sweets. She scrutinised the stranger shamelessly. When her eyes settled on Susan's scarred face she recoiled in horror. Susan was aware of her reaction and greeted her coolly. Miss Hogmier tucked her chin into her scraggy neck and grunted. Not one for small talk, Susan wandered the aisles, taking time to look at all the goods, many of which were new to her.

Susan had noticed that she wasn't alone in the shop. A young woman with a basket walked discreetly up and down with her long, tangled hair doing its best to hide her face. Susan presumed the dog belonged to her. She heard the little bell tinkle as her children came in.

'Look at all those sweets!' Ava exclaimed, her mouth falling open in wonder.

'I'd like a bag of those big red things,' said Charlie, pointing past Miss Hogmier.

'Those are strawberry bonbons,' Miss Hogmier stated. She looked over at Susan and sniffed. The children must belong to her for they all spoke with strange accents. The mother was obviously American, but the children had accents that she couldn't place. 'Where are you from?' she asked.

'Argentina,' said Charlie importantly. 'But we're living here now.'

Miss Hogmier's eyes opened wide as if she'd been woken from a deep sleep. 'You must be George Bolton's children,' she said slowly, leaning on the counter to take a closer look. Charlie noticed her nasal hair, emerging like the legs of two large spiders and scrunched up his face in distaste. As Susan joined them and asked them to choose their sweets, the other customer came up behind her with her basket full of shopping. 'George Bolton's children!' Miss Hogmier exclaimed again in a loud voice. There was a sudden clatter as the young woman dropped her shopping basket, sending the contents rolling all over the floor.

'Oh, I am sorry,' Susan apologised, thinking it must have been her fault. The young woman mumbled something inaudible and dropped to her knees to retrieve the fallen items. Charlie and Ava crouched down to help while Susan looked on in bewilderment.

'At least nothing's broken,' said Charlie, picking up a can of beans.

'Thank you,' the young woman muttered, smiling nervously, but her eyes were wild and terrified.

'You go first,' said Susan kindly. 'My two haven't decided what to have.'

The young woman watched anxiously as Miss Hogmier

slowly added up all her shopping, placing each item in a brown paper bag. Finally she paid and hurried out, managing a timid 'thank you' from behind a curtain of hair.

'That was Rita Fairweather,' said Miss Hogmier, staring at Susan accusingly. Now Susan understood the young woman's nervousness. She pretended the name meant nothing to her and continued to help her children choose sweets.

'Make up your minds,' she encouraged, keen to leave the shop. 'Charlie, why don't you have a bag of strawberry bonbons and Ava a bag of liquorice?'

'She's never been the same since George Bolton left,' Miss Hogmier continued in a gloomy tone of voice. 'Has a dog now for company. Lives the other side of Bray Cove. Never has been like other girls of her age, but eccentricity is no crime, is it? Must be hard having a sister with three children and a happy marriage. Not that we ever thought Maddie would settle for a man like Harry Weaver. A glamorous, ambitious girl like her! But Rita, sweet, innocent Rita. Nearly killed herself when she heard he'd married. Poor girl. Tried to throw herself off the cliff. Never been the same since.'

'Right, one bag of strawberry bonbons and one bag of liquorice, please,' said Susan briskly, returning the shop-keeper's stare with her own unique brand of iciness.

Miss Hogmier flared her nostrils then reluctantly turned around and pulled the jars off the shelves, huffing to show that Susan was putting her to some inconvenience.

'Must have been hard for Rita to see you with your children,' Miss Hogmier continued relentlessly, holding her hand out for the money. 'Has she seen George yet?'

Susan pursed her lips, astounded by the woman's boldness. 'I really don't think that is any of your business,' she replied curtly, dropping the coins into her outstretched hand. She handed the bags of sweets to the children then ushered them hastily out of the shop.

Chapter Twenty-eight

Rita hurried up the lane as fast as her numbed legs could carry her, followed by Tarka, her shaggy golden retriever. Susan was beautiful. Even in that short moment of awkwardness Rita could feel the aura of serenity that surrounded her and see the cool sophistication of her dress and her speech. Susan made Rita feel clumsy, unkempt and inadequate. She had been too overwhelmed to notice the scar.

Struggling with her shopping bag, which seemed to get heavier with each step, she strode up the road, her breath short and the blood pounding against her temples. She had heard that George was coming home, but no one had known exactly when. It had been a shock to bump into his wife. His children were so grown up Rita felt like an old woman. If she had married George she would have enjoyed at least ten years of children by now. Instead, she could feel her womb withering away.

If Susan and the children were in the shop, Rita deduced that George couldn't be far away. The natural place for him to come would be the church, to pay his respects to his father. As she approached she sensed his presence before her eyes settled on the man who had dominated her sleeping and waking moments for most of her lifetime, and she stopped behind a slender tree on the green to watch him. His tall figure was stooped over his father's grave. Although he was much broader than Trees had been, his posture reminded her of his father. The way he inclined his head and dropped his shoulders. She felt her eyes sting and her throat grow tight with anguish. Tarka sensed her distress and whined softly.

At that moment George looked up and his eyes seemed to turn directly to where she stood, half-concealed. She saw him smile, a broad smile that transformed his face and he lifted his hand and waved. Suddenly the past seventeen years were swept away and he was reaching out to her as he had always done when they had been the very closest of friends. Rita's heart fluttered with the delicate quivering of tiny wings. Although her feet were firmly on the ground she felt weightless. She nearly waved back. She nearly cried out, but something made her turn around and catch her breath. Disappointment overwhelmed her as she saw Susan and the children walking up the lane, Rita shrank back and became a shadow that they couldn't see. She heard their cries as the children ran across the green and up the steps into the churchyard. Susan walked with composure but her expression was thoughtful. George pretended to stagger back as the little girl flung her arms around him and, when Susan joined him, he wound an arm around her waist and kissed her temple. The way he had kissed *hers* so many times.

Choked with misery she bent her shoulders and hurried up the lane to her mother's house, where she had left her car. She couldn't face lunch with her family now. The questions, the curiosity, the obvious pity. She needed to be alone. Throwing the shopping into the passenger seat she started the engine and reversed out of the driveway. She didn't notice the pigeons on the roof, basking beneath such a resplendent sky, nor did she take a moment to admire the garden that shimmered with golden shades of autumn. The world Rita looked out onto was murky and grey. George and Susan had eclipsed her sun.

Squinting through her tears Rita drove up the lanes to her small cottage overlooking the sea and, sobbing inconsolably, hurried onto the beach. She sat down, hugged her knees, and played with the ring on her finger remembering the promises they had made to each other in the cave the day George had left for the Argentine. 'Every time you look at it I want you to remember how much I love you,' he had said. Now he no longer did, but those words still echoed across the years, however faintly.

George left his father's grave and drove his family to the beach for a picnic lunch. His mother was right, Frognal Point hadn't changed at all. It still looked and smelt the same, and when he stood on the cliff he was suddenly consumed with nostalgia. The children ran down the path to the beach, followed by Susan with the rugs and George who carried the weight of so many recollections as well as the picnic basket filled with food and drink. Susan noticed he had grown subdued and left him on his own while she walked with the children along the beach. He spread out the rugs, placing rocks on the corners so that they didn't blow away, and poured himself a glass of wine. He sat down, sheltered from the wind, in the very spot where his family and the Fairweathers had always chosen to picnic and shivered as he began to remember. Memories found him now that he was back in the bay where he had played as a child and loved as a young man and he was at once besieged by mental pictures of Rita. He stared out to sea but his vision clouded and Rita's gentle face replaced the hypnotic swell of waves. Her sherry eyes and wild curls reminded him of the girl whose heart he had broken and he wondered whether she still lived in Frognal Point or whether she had moved away. Perhaps she now had a family of her own. He didn't have the courage to ask his mother.

When Susan and the children returned, George made a conscious effort to put away his wistful recollections and showed them the rock pools where crabs hid in the shadows and sea urchins sat menacingly, waving their spikes in the water. Charlie and Ava were enchanted and dipped their hands in to feel the seaweed and the small shrimps that swam there. Then he showed them how to build in the sand. They constructed a castle, and Susan and Ava decorated it with shells that they collected from the beach. George dug a moat and a tunnel that joined it to the sea so that after lunch, as the water crept up the beach, it served to protect the walls of the castle for a little while longer. Satisfied with sandwiches and chocolate the children fought against the elements to save their creation from ruin. They built dams and walls and tunnels to direct the water away from their castle, but as evening approached the sea overwhelmed it in spite of all their efforts and swallowed it greedily. 'We'll make another one tomorrow if you like.' George promised.

'Maybe Granny will come with us,' Susan suggested tactfully.

George took her hand. 'That's a good idea. We'll ask Alice too. I want to show them the farm in the morning, so we can come for an early tea. How does that sound?' The children ran off, leaping over the sand, sending the gulls squawking furiously into the air.

Susan began to pack up the picnic, wondering if she should have told George about Rita in the shop. Too late now. It would sound odd, as if she had deliberately hidden it from him.

'It's been a lovely day, darling,' she said, closing the basket and taking the rugs from her husband.

He smiled at her and nodded. 'I had forgotten how beautiful it is here,' he replied, turning to look out across the sea. 'It's an idyll for children.' He placed his hands on his hips and sighed. 'It was a paradise for us growing up here.'

'I can imagine.'

'It's strange for me to watch Charlie and Ava, so like Alice and me. We used to run up the beach like that and dip our fingers into rock pools.'

'Until something bites them,' said Susan with a chuckle.

'They'll settle in and Argentina will be a warm memory they'll always have to look back on. It'll be harder for us.'

Susan put her arms around him. 'But we'll settle in too. Goodness, I've moved so many times I can't count them. Once we move into the farm cottage and make a home for ourselves things will be easier. We won't feel so rootless.'

'Once I get to work,' George added, knowing the consolation of hard labour. 'It's what Father would have wanted. He'd like to think of us here, keeping an eye on Ma. He never considered leaving Frognal Point. As far as he was concerned everything he loved was right here and so it shall be for us.'

As they walked back up the beach George couldn't help but cast his eye over to where the little cave lay hidden behind rocks and long grasses. He wondered whether it was still the same inside and was suddenly gripped with an urge to go in and have a look. Perhaps in the damp darkness of their once secret place the memories would be tangible. He turned to Susan and almost suggested it. But something held him back. An intuitive sense that some things are better kept to oneself. Susan had given up her home to come and live in Frognal Point; the last thing he wanted to do was alienate her on the first day by showing her Rita's old haunts. It would keep. He would come one evening on his own, light a cigarette and wallow in the echoes of his past.

While George had been out, Faye had snatched the opportunity to go to visit Thadeus. She had taken the farm Landrover and parked at the top of the lane, walking the short distance to his house so as not to arouse suspicion. He had been standing by the door, as if he had waited there since Trees' death. He had embraced her without a word, then taken her inside to where it was warm in the glow of the fire. For the first time since her husband's death she had cried without shame or guilt, for in Thadeus' arms it was impossible to feel either. She no longer felt lonely and the dull ache in her head and in her heart eased with each gentle caress and each word of tenderness. His old eyes gazed upon her with understanding and she knew that in spite of her efforts to mourn as befitting a wife, she could never give up Thadeus. He was as much a part of her as the vital organs that kept her body alive.

The following day at church Faye sat with her chin up. She still wore black but her heart was blazing a shameless crimson and she smiled secretly for she could feel Thadeus' love consuming her spirit with fire. However, no one noticed Faye for they were all staring at George and the woman he had chosen instead of Rita. Their expressions were full of curiosity, which was natural enough, but as Faye put away her thoughts of Thadeus, she began to feel the resentment that vibrated in the air. She hoped that George hadn't noticed, but it was impossible not to, as people craned their necks for a better look. Faye turned her attention to Hannah and Humphrey and wondered whether their bitterness would resurface now that George was back. She noticed that Rita wasn't there. Hannah looked around anxiously as the place next to her remained obviously empty. Rita never missed church. Maddie and Harry sat with their three children who eyed Charlie and Ava curiously. When Charlie caught Daisy's eye she smiled at him broadly, which completely disarmed him, for fourteen-year-old Daisy, the image of her mother, was far too aware of her pretty features, long red hair and sparkling blue eyes. Charlie was aware of it too and buried his eyes in his prayer book, hoping that at the end of the service he wouldn't have to talk to her.

George was too busy scanning the pews for Rita to notice the stares and resentment. If she still lived in Frognal Point she would have definitely been at church, so he concluded with unexpected sadness that she must have moved away. He was surprised when Maddie smiled at him affectionately and felt himself smiling back in gratitude. Reverend Hammond was much aged and had developed a tendency to lose his train of thought and repeat himself. Miss Hogmier had reluctantly given up playing the organ because of her arthritis. Trees' funeral had been her swan song. She now sat in the front pew in a show of piety, standing up for the hymns and kneeling down for the prayers a moment before everyone else, as if keen to demonstrate how well she knew the service and how devout she was. She sang even more loudly than Hannah, who enjoyed singing with gusto, and her voice warbled so badly Charlie and Ava caught the giggles along with Freddie, Daisy and Elsbeth, joining them in a bond of mutual hilarity.

Susan was all too aware of the antipathy. She held her chin up and returned the stares with disdain, as one would regard a herd of curious oxen. She felt dreadfully out of practice having spent the last seventeen years on the plain where everyone knew her and no one made a fuss of her scar. She felt less confident, however, than she had been in the past because she wasn't sure whether people were scrutinising her because of her face or because she was the scarlet woman who had stolen their boy. Either way, their nosiness was rude and offensive. Satisfied that she had managed to stare them all down, one by one, she turned her eyes back to the hymn sheet.

At the end of the service, when George stepped into the aisle, Maddie pushed her way through the parting congregation to greet him. 'Welcome home!' she enthused, kissing him affectionately. 'I see our children have already made friends,' she added, patting the head of her youngest, Elsbeth, who was twelve. George turned to see Charlie and Ava hurrying up the aisle with a gaggle of other children. Elsbeth wriggled free and ran to join them. 'They'll all get along like a house on fire. How lovely that you've come home at last!' Susan felt a surge of relief at Maddie's unexpected geniality.

They proceeded slowly up the aisle and Susan noticed people moving away as if she had some disease they didn't want to catch. As her resentment mounted a tall woman with greying red hair tapped her on the shoulder.

'I hope you don't mind,' she said, her scarlet mouth curving into a pretty smile. 'My name is Antoinette. I'm . . . well . . . it's far too complicated to explain as I'm not related to George, but I jolly nearly was until you came along. I would like to welcome you most warmly to Frognal Point.' She extended a long, elegant hand, fixed Susan with feline eyes and lowered her voice confidentially. 'It's not the most sophisticated of places, which is why I have one foot in London, but it's very charming in a rural way. They'll embrace you once they get to know you, I'm sure. Rita's extremely popular here and everyone feels very badly that George left her for you. However, I don't care what everyone else thinks. Rita was far too immature for him.' Antoinette smiled graciously and added, 'If you feel lonely do come and see me, I live very close by and I can see you'll be needing a friend.' She handed Susan a white card with her name and address embossed in pale blue.

'Thank you, Antoinette,' Susan replied coolly, unimpressed by the older woman's saccharine charm.

Antoinette walked out into the sunshine, pleased that she had made friends with George's new wife – everyone was talking about her but so far, no one had managed to get to the bottom of her scarred face. *Poor creature*, she thought meanly, *beauty is such a valuable asset.*

George was still talking to Maddie and Harry when Susan joined him. At that moment he caught eyes with Hannah who was deliberating whether or not to greet him. On one hand she was fed up with Rita's foolishness, but on the other she was bound by a natural loyalty to her daughter. But now George was looking at her, his face cast in doubt, and she could see in his eyes the boy he once had been and she felt sorry for him: coming back to all those memories couldn't be easy.

'Hello, George,' she said. 'Welcome home.' She touched his arm. 'I'm sorry that your father has died. It must be a terrible loss for you.'

George was relieved that she seemed to hold no hard feelings. He longed to ask about Rita, but swallowed his words, frustrated that no one mentioned her. It was as if she no longer existed.

'I gather you're moving into the farm cottage,' Hannah continued, trying to act naturally.

'It will be strange living there, a few hundred yards from home. But we'll get used to it.'

'Your children look charming. I see they've made friends with my grandchildren.'

'How many grandchildren do you have?'

'Well, as well as these three, Eddie has two children. She lives in South Africa.'

'She always did love animals,' George commented with a grin.

'She moved on from bats the minute she saw a lion, I think.' They both chuckled, but George hovered expectantly for her next sentence. 'Rita has . . .' she began and George leaned forward with eagerness.

At that moment Susan said good-bye to Maddie and Harry and turned to join in her husband's conversation. As Hannah's voice trailed off George couldn't help but gasp with disappointment. He wished she had finished her sentence and satisfied his curiosity. *Has what?* he thought in desperation. *Died? Four children? Moved away? What?* He suppressed his frustration and put his arm around Susan's waist.

'Hannah, let me introduce you to my wife, Susan.' Hannah blanched and backed away.

'Welcome,' she said in a thin voice, then excused herself awkwardly. When she was gone Susan turned to George.

'That was Rita's mother, wasn't it?' she said. George nodded. 'I'm sorry that she still feels bitter. Darling, I have to confess something to you . . .' She was on the point of divulging how she had met Rita in the village shop when Miss Hogmier and Reverend Hammond bustled over to greet them like a couple of self-appointed village officials.

'We've already met,' said Miss Hogmier briskly and Susan felt her skin prickle with anger.

'Only in the shop,' said Susan, acknowledging the old woman with forced politeness.

'Well, you haven't met me,' interjected Reverend Hammond, extending his large, sweaty hand. Susan shook it reluctantly.

'What a charming service,' she said, desperate to distract Miss Hogmier from their previous meeting.

'Thank you, Susan. How very nice of you to say so. I've been a vicar for a good many years now so I've had some practice. But it's always nice to hear that one is doing a good job. I knew George as a little boy. How time flies. How long have I been a vicar, June?' he asked Miss Hogmier.

The old woman squinted and frowned. 'My mind's failing me,' she complained gruffly. 'Forty years, Elwyn? Not only am I losing the mobility in my fingers and the agility of my joints but I'm now losing my mind as well.'

'You've run the shop since I can remember,' said George, endeavouring to humour her.

'That I have,' she replied, lifting her chin and displaying three long black whiskers. 'There's not a customer I don't know by name. Frognal Point is full of good people. Most appreciate what I do for them.' She fixed Susan with a hard stare.

'Well, it's been very nice talking to you,' said George, stepping away. 'We really should be getting back for lunch.' But Miss Hogmier grabbed the sleeve of his jacket and leaned towards him. Susan held her breath.

'What of Rita?' she insisted. 'When she saw your wife she dropped all her shopping. Poor unhappy girl, what a state she was in. She lives alone, see. I know what it's like. No one to look after me either. Who'd have thought she'd end up on the shelf! Thought it was mine exclusively!'

George took Susan's hand. 'Oh it is, Miss Hogmier. Rita's far too generous-spirited to knock you off it.'

His smile was so charming that Miss Hogmier didn't know whether to be offended or flattered. She did, however, look disappointed and chewed on her dentures in dissatisfaction.

'Darling, I was going to tell you,' said Susan as they walked down the little path to the green where the children were playing with Freddie, Daisy and Elsbeth.

'It's of no consequence. Gossiping old vampire!' They both laughed. But George felt as if Miss Hogmier had just gutted him.

Chapter Twenty-nine

That night George crept out of bed, leaving Susan sleeping soundly, and tiptoed down the stairs, avoiding the squeaky floorboards. He took his father's old coat from its peg and put it on. It still smelt of Trees, that musty smell of dust and farmyard and his own unique scent. He grabbed his cigarettes and lighter from the kitchen table, then wandered out onto the terrace. To his surprise he saw the small figure of his mother sitting huddled in the dark on one of the damp garden chairs, her hands wrapped around a steaming cup of hot milk. Her fingers shone white in the phosphorescent light of the moon. When he appeared in the doorway she looked up, but she was not surprised to see him. How often they had met on that terrace in the middle of the night, unable to sleep, tormented by dreams.

'Are you all right?' she asked as he sat down on the chair beside her.

He leaned forward and sighed heavily. 'Tell me about Rita,' he asked, placing the cigarette between his lips and flicking his lighter.

'I thought it would make you feel guilty.'

'I appreciate that,' he replied. 'But I want to know. I still care about her, Ma.' He exhaled like a gentle dragon. He cared more than he dared admit to anyone.

'She has never got over you, George. I'm afraid that's the sad truth.' He stared out across the garden, which was strewn with leaves that caught the light and rustled in the breeze.

'Susan saw her in the village shop. She was so upset she dropped her shopping. So Miss Hogmier says.'

'Don't believe everything that old gossip tells you,' his mother said acerbically.

'But she does live alone?'

'Well, she has her dog.'

'Where?'

'The other side of Bray Cove. She works in the library.'

'Still?' George was shocked that Rita had allowed her life to stagnate.

'Yes, she runs it now. Actually, she doesn't mope around, George, she's very active organising events there. She's met some fascinating authors, all through Max who seems to know everyone. He's done so well for himself. To think he arrived in this country with nothing. He made it big in radio and then became a television producer. He's a very talented man and Frognal Point's finest export.'

George felt a prickle of jealousy. Little Max had grown up. 'Is he married?'

'No. Of course he's always in the papers with a pretty girl on his arm, but he's yet to settle down. These refugees are damaged souls, George,' she said thinking of Thadeus. 'They need a very special sort of woman. I hope he finds happiness, he deserves to. He does an enormous amount for others.'

George was anxious to steer the conversation back to Rita. 'Does she still sculpt?'

'Yes, she does. And she's rather good. I never thought she had that much talent, but unhappiness can do wonders for one's creativity.' Faye should know: her best works had been inspired by Thadeus or Trees – since his death.

'Why wasn't she at church? She never used to miss it.'

Faye took a sip of her milk. 'I suppose she doesn't want to see you,' she replied after a while.

'You really think so?' He stared at her with a wounded look in his eyes.

'Perhaps if you were on your own . . . but it's natural that she wouldn't want to see you and Susan together. Remember, she's hurt.'

'Still? After all these years?' He shook his head in disbelief. Never did he expect her to hold onto him for so long. He felt the incision made by Miss Hogmier slice even deeper, then a shameful satisfaction that in spite of the years that had passed, she still belonged to him.

Faye put a hand on his arm and flinched suddenly, for the familiar feel of Trees' sheepskin coat caused an unexpected pang of regret. 'Leave her,' she advised softly. 'It's better that way.'

'I have no choice,' he groaned. But he didn't mean it.

'Why are you out here?' he asked. 'Are you missing Pa?'

'You're wearing his coat,' she said, stroking it. 'I haven't thrown anything away. If there's anything you want you know you can choose.'

'It's too soon. It wouldn't feel right. Can I look after his walnuts though?'

'Of course you can. I'd like to but I don't know how.'

'He loved those trees.'

'It was one of his beloved trees that killed him. You know, I miss his company. You don't really appreciate someone until they're gone. Often we'd go for days without really speaking and yet he was a warm presence around the house. I never felt alone, just lonely. Does that make sense?'

'Not really,' he replied. She wanted to tell him about Thadeus, how he satisfied the part of her that Trees neglected.

'Sometimes I thought your father loved those silly trees more than he loved me. Can you imagine being jealous of a crop of walnut trees? It seems ludicrous now.'

'No it doesn't,' he said. Suddenly the image of her riding

her bicycle out of the farm in the middle of the night rose up again in his mind and he longed to ask her about it. But he held back, it didn't seem fair to intrude unless she volunteered.

'Towards the end we moved around the place like a couple of shadows, barely communicating at all. Now I wish I had made more of an effort to reach him.'

'No regrets, Ma. He knew you loved him.'

'I hope he did. If I had been there when he was struck perhaps I could have told him.'

'Where exactly were you?' He could feel the anxiety surround her like a thick miasma. She hesitated, scratched her neck and put down her cup on the garden table in front of her chair. The ground suddenly felt less solid beneath his feet.

'I had been making a sculpture for an old man in the village.' There was a long pause while George put all the pieces of this mysterious puzzle together.

'What is his name?'

Faye barely dared breathe. She knew he knew. 'Thadeus Walizhewski.'

He nodded in recognition of the name, although like most others in the village, he had never met him. 'And you're in love with him?'

Still his mother didn't move. 'Yes,' she replied in a whisper.

Now everything made sense. The solidity of his parents' marriage had been an illusion. As a child the fabric of his parents' marriage had never been questioned; now, as a man, he saw the holes in the weave only too well. But he didn't blame his mother for finding love elsewhere. Who was he to pass judgement? He was as flawed as she was. She had loved Trees *and* Thadeus. George was beginning to understand that it was possible to love two people at the same time for entirely different reasons and in completely different ways. He loved Susan and yet, now he was back in Frognal Point a part of his heart that had been asleep for a very long time was beginning to stir.

A couple of weeks went by. George took over the running of the farm, which kept him busy for so much had changed since the war. He strode around in a blue boiler suit, his hands and hair covered in dust, a far cry from riding out across the plains with the gauchos. He steered the Landrover around the farm tracks, surveying the fields with Cyril, reacquainting himself with the estate that was his inheritance. Nothing was too menial for him. He drove the tractor, swept floors, mended broken machinery, fed the animals and remembered how he had worked alongside his father as a young man. He wished he had been around when he had bought the new Massey Ferguson combine harvester. 'His pride and joy', Cyril told him, stroking the green metal flank as if it were an obedient animal. 'Chomps through the corn doing the work of a dozen men. There was always a smile on Mr Trees' face when he was at the wheel of this beauty!'

The children started at the same school as Maddie's children and didn't seem to miss the sunny plains of Córdoba. But Susan did. Barely a day went by when she didn't remember. She felt out of place in Frognal Point. The hostility she had felt at church had followed her back to Lower Farm and, however much Faye and Alice endeavoured to welcome her, she still felt as if she were watching them all through an impenetrable pane of glass. She wasn't suited to the damp, the coastal winds and sea. She hated sailing – the rocking of the boat made her nauseous – and she detested the cold. Picnics on the beach had lost their charm. Sand not only blew into the food but seemed to penetrate her clothes and chafe her skin. She missed Agatha and Jose Antonio whose warmth had enveloped her with the hot Argentine sun.

Finally their furniture arrived from Buenos Aires and they moved into the farm cottage. Perhaps, Susan thought, if I have my own nest to feather, I'll feel that I belong. So, with a heavy sense of *déjà vu* she scrubbed floors, painted walls and sewed curtains with Alice's sewing machine. She didn't have time to speculate about Rita. No one mentioned her name, out of tact, and Susan never saw her again in the village. She swept the shadows under pieces of furniture and the rugs that she laid out on the floor, transforming the cottage into a warm and elegant home.

One evening, when Susan took the children to meet Mrs Megalith, George stole the opportunity to walk the cliffs alone and smoke a cigarette in the cave that had become a symbol of everything he had once loved and let go. It was a magnificent evening. The sun was setting, dyeing the sky and fields below a rich, flamingo pink. The sea swelled like molten copper, the waves in the distance catching the light and glimmering like stars. With wistful nostalgia he walked towards the rocks where once he had carried Rita. They had been so full of joy and optimism then, blissfully unaware that their romance would die with the summer. That part of his life had been closed down. A chapter finished, collecting dust, forgotten. Perhaps one day he would teach his children about birds, perhaps Charlie would watch them and yearn to fly as he did. Or perhaps they would love different things, things they would make their own. He couldn't expect them to live his life.

He leapt across the sand that lay between the rocks and the opening of the cave, now flooded with a few inches of water. The sight of the opening had always held such excitement for him; now it seemed neglected, overgrown, sad. Inside it was dark and cold and empty. Once it had smelt of Rita even when he had come on his own. In those days he had felt her presence so strongly, as if her body warmth had vibrated off the very walls, as if the cave itself had breathed with life. Now it was distant and angry and he felt decidedly unwelcome. Whatever spirits had occupied the place had packed up and gone.

He wanted to go to see Rita. To talk about the past, say he was sorry, tell her that he had never meant to hurt her. He loved and respected Susan. She understood him and was his equal in every sense. But at the same time there was a longing for the boy he had once been and for Rita, who had been a part of that boy.

He swept his eyes over the walls, remembering intimate moments that he hadn't thought of in over fifteen years. He had deliberately shut them out. Now images fell about him, too many at once, and he blinked in an attempt to make sense of them. He remembered how she tasted when they kissed, the soft innocence of her skin when he ran his hands up her leg, and the sound of her laugh when she threw her neck back, exposing her pale throat for him to tease with his lips. He smelt the sweet scent of violets that she had made her own with the marshy fragrance of the sea, and his soul ached with a deep, insistent yearning.

Suddenly his attention was drawn to a shiny object, half-buried in sand, pushed up against the very back of the cave at high tide. He stood up and walked over, curious, brushed off the sand and picked it up. He recognised it at once. The little dove pendant he had bought Rita on board the *Fortuna*.

He walked slowly back up the beach, the pendant burning the pocket of his trousers. He touched it thoughtfully, reflecting on its significance. Why should he care? Why should the memory of Rita haunt him so? He had chosen to break off their engagement, to marry Susan, to start a new life the other side of the world. He had never regretted those decisions. But now he was back, he missed her.

Mrs Megalith had been surprised to receive a telephone call from Susan. She hadn't a good telephone manner, but she had a melodious voice and her accent gave her an air of sophistication that jarred with the simplicity of their small Devon village. Mrs Megalith was curious.

When they arrived Mrs Megalith was in a pair of boots and coat walking in the leaves in the garden. Susan had rung the bell several times then, when no one answered, she had walked around to the back of the house. To her surprise the garden was a large, exotic aviary. Birds in flight, their graceful wings catching the amber light as they seemed to dance on the last of the sunbeams, birds on the ground pecking at the leaves, hopping across the grass, chattering gaily to one another. The evening light slowly dimmed, setting the trees in a vibrant pink glow and turning the leaves a deep and extraordinary red. Even Charlie and Ava stood transfixed at the otherworldly sight.

'She really is a witch,' hissed Charlie to his sister.

'Shhh!' his mother chided, afraid that the old woman might hear and take offence. 'Papa was only joking,' she added hopefully. Charlie rolled his eyes.

When Mrs Megalith greeted them all three jumped like startled sheep.

'Ah, Susan. Isn't it a wonderful sight!' she exclaimed, hobbling towards them with the help of her walking stick. 'Love this time of day! So exhilarating watching the little feathered fellows settling down for the night.' They didn't appear to be doing much settling, Susan thought, but smiled and extended her hand.

'It's so nice to meet you at last,' she replied. 'These are my children, Charlie and Ava.'

'I do love it when things go according to plan,' said Mrs Megalith in a deep, fruity voice. She patted Charlie's head and Ava's eyes widened at the sight of the crystals that shone on her wrinkled old fingers. 'What a handsome fellow we made!' Susan laughed at Charlie's look of terror. He remained absolutely still until she removed her hand, then ran his fingers through his hair in case she had put something in it.

'You have a beautiful garden,' said Susan truthfully. 'What a stunning view of the estuary.'

'I'm very blessed and at my ripe old age one counts one's blessings and appreciates them. How are you settling in?' Mrs Megalith started hobbling towards the house. Ava and Charlie, so used to running wild, now walked slowly behind her like a pageboy and bridesmaid at a wedding. 'If it's any consolation, I'm an outsider myself and I've lived here all my life.'

'We're doing our best. The children have started school and have made friends, with your great-grandchildren in particular,' Susan replied. Mrs Megalith raised her eyebrows and wondered what Rita would think of that. 'It'll take time to adjust, especially for George. We were very happy in Argentina, but he belongs here, after all.'

'He was a very colourful young man as I recall,' said Mrs Megalith, opening the back door into the conservatory. Exotic plants hung from pots and a vine of grapes weaved up the walls and spread out like the roots of a tree on the ceiling. They followed her through the conservatory, down a corridor and into the drawing room where a large fire blazed beneath a mantelpiece of photographs.

Susan was at once drawn to the pictures. All framed or placed one on top of the other, they were mostly of her children, grandchildren and great-grandchildren. 'You have a big family,' she commented, eyeing a picture of Antoinette and realising at once what she had meant when she had said that she wasn't quite related to George but almost had been before Susan had married him.

'Like a rabbit's friends and relations, I can barely keep up with them. You haven't met Max, have you?' Mrs Megalith asked, her eyes suddenly turning a paler shade of blue. Susan shook her head. 'Now, he's exceptional. Not only handsome but gifted too. Terribly gifted.' Susan let the old woman ramble on while she seized upon a photograph of Rita. With her long, wild hair and soft golden eyes she looked carefree and happy. She wondered whether, if it hadn't been for George, *she* would have allowed herself to go to pieces over John Haddon?

'I don't suppose you've met my granddaughter?' Mrs Megalith asked, indicating with a wave of her hand that the children sit down. 'I can't cope with hoverers,' she said irritably, shaking her chins at them. 'They make me dizzy, so either settle or go and play with the cats in the hall, they don't get much ragging around from me, I can tell you.' Charlie and Ava left the room in silence.

'I met her briefly in the shop but we weren't introduced,' Susan replied carefully.

'Be thankful she didn't scratch your eyes out,' Mrs Megalith said with a snort.

Susan perched stiffly on the fireguard. 'I don't think our paths will cross again and why should they? I married the man she loved.'

'Dear girl, I think she believes she still loves him. However, if she took the time to see him she'd probably realise that she loves an entirely different man. People change and I'm sure George is no longer the George she grew up with. Reality is sometimes harsh, but Rita doesn't live there. Actually, she baffles me and I'm psychic.'

'You're right. George is a very different man now,' said Susan tightly.

'They were inseparable as children.' Mrs Megalith didn't realise that Susan would have preferred not to talk about Rita. 'But George was damaged by the war and dear Rita was simply another casualty. Hitler has an awful lot to answer for. Max is an entirely different story. His tragedy is the tragedy of

Europe. So many innocent lives. George believes he suffered, but he didn't lose his family in the concentration camps like Max did.'

'Everyone's suffering is relative, Mrs Megalith. George lost his friends and saw some terrible things. It's haunted him ever since.' Susan didn't like the old woman's insinuations.

'And he's fortunate to have found happiness with you.'

'I understand him.'

'Of course you do, my dear.' Mrs Megalith's fingers toyed with the moonstone about her neck. 'After all, he's not that complicated, is he?'

At that moment Charlie and Ava wandered into the room. They were both grinning and nudging each other. 'Are you a witch?' Charlie asked with a smirk.

Susan was horrified. 'Charlie, really!' she scolded in embarrassment.

Mrs Megalith looked at him steadily. 'Yes, I am,' she said with an entirely straight face. Ava shrank back.

'Do you cast spells?' he asked. Susan tried to intervene, but Mrs Megalith waved her hand at her. She hadn't had so much fun in years.

'I do.'

'What kind?'

Mrs Megalith leaned forward and whispered darkly. 'You remember all those birds in the garden?' Charlie nodded. 'They were once outspoken little boys like you.' Mrs Megalith turned to Susan with a grin. 'You can tell that husband of yours that if he spreads such nonsense he must take responsibility for it.'

Charlie insisted all the way home that he hadn't believed her. Ava teased him and called him gullible and various other names from school that Susan hadn't heard before, while she drove in silence, unable to take her mind off Rita. Her rosy face lingered in Susan's mind, reminding her that, as much as she tried to fit in to this coastal community, she could not. She had discovered another side to the man she thought she knew. The side that loved the same things that Rita loved. The side that belonged in Frognal Point. The side that she didn't fit into. Like an odd piece of a jigsaw puzzle, she was simply the wrong shape.

That night she was tidying up the bedroom. George was in the bath, singing the songs Jose Antonio had sung with the gauchos at *Las Dos Vizcachas*. When she folded his trousers she heard something rattle in his pocket and pulled out the pendant. She had never seen it before. To her fury her heart began to pound. She berated herself for feeling so insecure. If she had found it in the Argentine she would have thought nothing of it. Regaining her composure she strode into the bathroom. George's face was covered in shaving cream. He looked up at her expectantly. She held out the pendant and let it swing in front of his eyes. 'What is this?' she asked, trying to control the tremor in her voice.

'I found it in a cave on the beach,' he replied innocently.

'Really?'

'It was sticking out of the sand. I thought you might like it.'

She looked at it and lifted her chin. The suspicion still lingered. 'How sweet of you, darling. Some poor girl must have lost it.' She studied it more carefully. 'It's a dove, much more appropriate for a young girl, don't you think? A girl who loves birds.' She cast him a frosty glance. 'I'll give it to Ava.' She walked out and placed it on her dressing table, wondering if she had overreacted.

George dragged the razor down his face. Suddenly he flinched as the blade nicked the skin of his chin. He sat quite still and watched as the blood dropped into the bath water.

Chapter Thirty

The weeks went by and winter set in, bringing with it icy fog and sharp winds. Ava wore her pendant with pride after Susan bought her a smaller chain to hang it on. George admired it then never mentioned it again and Susan scolded herself for having jumped to the wrong conclusions. The children broke up for the holidays and spent much of their time with Maddie's children playing on the farm and building camps in the woods. Much to Susan's surprise she and Maddie became friends. Maddie didn't resent her like the rest of the community in spite of the fact that, out of everyone, she had the most cause. It seemed inconsequential to her that she should befriend the woman who stole the man her sister loved. They never discussed Rita. After a while Susan stopped thinking about her. She discovered that she and Maddie had a lot in common. As well as their children and Frognal Point, Maddie shared Susan's forthright nature and sophistication, though from where she had acquired it not even her mother knew. Neither enjoyed the seaside activities so beloved by Rita and George, preferring to sit over cups of tea talking in the cosy comfort of their sitting rooms. They laughed together and stood as allies sharing stories about the ghoulish Miss Hogmier and eccentric Mrs Megalith. They both found Reverend Hammond tiresome and exchanged looks during his sermons when his mind wandered and he began to repeat himself.

George, however, was unable to forget about Rita. He

noticed her absence every week in church and caught himself looking out for her when he walked on the cliffs or climbed the rocks with his children. In his mind she grew out of all proportion and Frognal Point became increasingly incomplete without her. He didn't notice the coolness that began to permeate his marriage. Susan withdrew more and more into the lives of her children while he scanned the beach for his past.

Then, the weekend before Christmas the two families were out on the cliffs when finally he saw her. It was a bitterly cold afternoon. The sun had melted the frost and was doing its best to creep under the trees to burn off the light covering of snow that had fallen during the night. He had run on ahead with Charlie, having made a kite that was proving hard to control as it danced and dived on the wind. Charlie was delighted and shouted back at his mother to make sure that she was watching. Susan broke off her conversation with Harry and Maddie to shout back every now and then but soon they were too far away, a pair of tiny figurines silhouetted against the sky.

Finally, as they approached the cove near the secret cave, George lost his grip of the string. He watched helplessly as the kite flew into the air in triumph, only to turn and dive suddenly over the edge to catch on the rocks directly below. Charlie followed his father to the verge where they both lay on their stomachs and peered over. George stretched as far as he could but the little kite remained just beyond his reach. 'I'm sorry, Charlie,' he said, shaking his head. 'We'd better wait until Harry gets here, perhaps he can help.' At that moment his eyes were distracted by a movement down on the beach. He caught his breath and blinked to focus. She was far away in the distance but he was in no doubt that it was Rita.

He stood up. 'Charlie, why don't you run back and tell them we've lost the kite,' he suggested. Charlie set off without hesitation, leaving George alone to watch his old love walk slowly in his direction, followed by a bouncing yellow dog. As she got bigger he could make out her long hair that blew about beneath a woolly hat pulled low over her forehead. She wore a beige coat and Wellington boots and had stuffed her hands into her pockets.

Battered about by the wind and the sudden cascade of memories, he stood high above their beach knowing that in a few moments she would raise her eyes and see him watching her. He wanted to run down the little path as he had done in his youth and talk to her but Susan and the others were now approaching, spurred on by an overexcited Charlie. He put his hands in his pockets and hunched his shoulders. Overwhelmed by sadness he gazed helplessly as Rita's features came into focus. Her face was impassive. Her nose was red and her skin as pale as the white throat of a tern. To George her tragedy endowed her with a beauty that in reality she did not possess and his heart lurched for what might have been. Inadvertently he romanticised her, casting her in a timeless spell that would have surely broken had he the chance to speak to her. But he did not and the spell remained complete.

Rita raised her eyes as he had expected and stopped walking. She stood quite still. Only her hair continued to dance about on the wind regardless of the sight that froze the blood in her veins. Silence seemed to descend upon the small cove where memories now merged into a surreal moment beyond the limits of time. The dog ran up and down the beach, barking at the waves that rolled onto the sand and the birds that scrounged for food. Then Rita raised her hand and her movement shattered the enchantment.

George turned to see Susan and the others now only a few feet away.

'Now where's that silly kite?' Susan asked. 'It doesn't

matter, darling. We can buy another one.' Then she looked over the edge. At first she saw the kite lying sheltered on the rocks, its tail twisting and curling like a long snake. Then her attention was drawn to the woman standing on the beach staring up at them. It seemed a long moment before she put her hand back in her pocket and continued to walk. She didn't look up again but kept her eyes fixed in front of her, determined not to give the American woman the satisfaction of seeing her pain. Susan recognised Rita immediately but pretended she hadn't noticed her. 'I think if you and Harry hold onto Charlie's ankles you might just reach it,' she suggested casually, but she felt as if she had been punched in the stomach.

The kite was retrieved and launched once again, but George didn't recover his light-hearted mood. He sank deep into his thoughts where even his wife was unable to reach him. Seeing his brooding face, she wished they had never come to Frognal Point. They had been so happy in the Argentine.

Rita's legs were shaking so much she was barely able to walk. He had seen her and he hadn't taken his eyes off her. During that long moment when their gazes had interlocked she could have sworn she saw, even from this distance, a glimmer of regret. She stepped along the sand aware that he was still there on the cliff top, his wife now at his side. She could feel his disappointment. Perhaps he had wanted to talk. Perhaps if he had been alone he would have run down the sandy path as he had done so often in the past and embraced her on the beach. Maybe he would have held her in his arms and told her how sorry he was, that he had made the wrong decision, that he had spent the last eighteen years regretting it. Rita played with the diamond solitaire ring. Somewhere in the most forgotten corner of his heart she was certain that he still loved her.

Now her spirits lifted and she felt a sudden urge to run up

the beach with her arms outspread. When she stole a glance back to where George had stood she saw that everyone had gone. Only wild grasses swayed against the sky, accentuating the void his absence made. Filled with the childish exuberance that had so dominated her youth she extended her arms and ran into the wind. She laughed as Tarka barked in excitement, wagging her tail and jumping across the sand with her. The birds scattered and flew into the air and Rita was sure that she could fly too, so light was her mood.

That evening Susan was subdued, wishing they could just pack up and return to Argentina. Tormented by her fears she opened the fridge to discover there was no milk left. George was in the sitting room reading the papers while Charlie and Ava played chess in front of the fire listening to their Jimmy Hendrix records. Knowing the village shop would be closed and that the milkman always arrived too late for George's breakfast, she decided to go over to Faye's and borrow a pint.

Across at the farmhouse, she followed the low sound of voices coming from the sitting room. She would have called out had she not heard Alice mention her name. She froze and held her breath as she realised they were talking about her.

'. . . Susan's perfectly pleasant, she's just rather cold,' Alice was saying.

'But she makes George happy and that's what's important,' said Faye. Pause.

'He doesn't look very happy,' came Alice's small voice. 'I think he would have been happier if he had married Rita. He grew up believing he could have everything he wanted. He's always been too ready to give up what's good for him in the hope that something better will come along.'

'Not now, darling. He's completely content with Susan. She's given him lovely children and stability. I agree she's not the warmest of people, but it must be hard for her here. She must find the English countryside dreadfully wet and cold.'

'She doesn't fit in. At first she made an effort to share all his interests, now she rarely accompanies him anywhere. I've bumped into him numerous times on the beach and she's nowhere in sight. I don't think she makes much of an effort any more.'

'That's no crime. I made no effort to love your father's silly trees and he didn't share my passion for sculpture.'

'That's different. I'm not talking about a hobby but a way of life. George *is* the sea, the beach, the cliffs, the birds. He loves people, she clearly doesn't. Have you noticed how she holds back after church as if no one's good enough for her? She reminds me of Antoinette . . .'

Susan couldn't bear it a moment longer. With tears stinging in her eyes she crept back down the corridor and out into the wind once again. The cold dampened the flames in her cheeks and quietened her thumping heart. So that's what they all thought of her. That he would have been better off had he married Rita. She felt the resentment rise in her chest. Is that what George thought too?

She wouldn't take it any more. She was fed up of stepping aside and pretending nothing was wrong. When she got home George was in the kitchen helping himself to a biscuit. He saw her ashen face and closed the tin. 'What's happened?' he asked, immediately thinking of his mother.

'We need to talk,' she stated firmly. He followed her upstairs, wondering what on earth had inspired her wrath. Once in the bedroom he closed the door behind him so the children wouldn't hear.

'What's wrong?'

She turned and folded her arms in front of her chest. Two small red stars appeared on her white cheeks where they smarted angrily. 'I've just overheard your mother talking to Alice.'

'What about?'

'Me.'

'What did they say?'

'That you would have been better off had you married Rita.'

George dropped his shoulders and chuckled. 'And you believe them?'

'I saw the way you looked at her today. I'm not blind, George.'

'She lives here, Susan. I'm bound to see her.'

'It's not that you saw her, it's the way you looked at her. Do you still love her?'

'Of course I don't. I love you,' he said, as if he thought the whole conversation ridiculous.

'Even though I don't fit in?'

'You do fit in.'

'Not according to your mother.'

'It's according to me that matters.'

'God, George,' she raged. 'I'm now haunted by *your* demons!'

He strode over and drew her into his arms where she yielded without resistance. 'We've only just arrived. It was never going to be easy, you knew that. It's not easy for me either. I'm tormented by memories of the war, not Rita.'

'We were so happy in Argentina,' she said, wrapping her arms around his waist. 'I wish we could go back.'

'Give it time, Susan. It'll get better, I promise.'

The following morning George felt the need to be alone among his father's beloved walnuts. Perhaps amidst those trees he would feel him close. If Mrs Megalith was to be believed, he was there, separated only by the intangible wall of vibrations that made it impossible to see him. In his mind's eye he pictured his tall weathered frame, complete with the tweed cap and heavy boots he had always worn, standing beside the friends he had lost in the war: Jamie Cordell, Rat Bridges, Lorrie Hampton. He put his hands in his pockets and hunched his shoulders against the bracing wind that swept in from the sea. Then the sight of a small grey plaque at the foot of a young tree diverted his attention and he bent his head to get a better look. *Charles Henry Bolton, 24th October 1949.* His father had never told him he had planted a tree for his grandson. He crouched down to run his fingers over the words and his eyes misted with sorrow. He missed him. He missed the boy he had once been, and then his thoughts turned to Rita. He missed her too.

Max looked forward to returning to Frognal Point for Christmas. Christmas at Elvestree was always memorable, although it wasn't their event to celebrate. Mrs Megalith had respected Max and Ruth's Jewish roots and had read up on the festivals that had punctuated their childhood in Austria. According to what she had learned she had decorated their playhouse out of fruit for Sukkot, lit candles on a Friday night, and hidden their presents at Hanukkah, displaying the eight-candled Menorah in the window according to the Law. She had never taken them to church and had on occasions made a synagogue out of her drawing room. The first time Max and Ruth attended synagogue in England was long after the war, when she had made a point of taking them, as teenagers, to London to stay with her sister. She had sat through an entire Saturday morning service in Bevis Marks without understanding a word of Hebrew so that Max and Ruth could stay faithful to the religion of their parents. That was the first time Ruth had cried for her home. Hearing in the language and ritual of synagogue such distinctive echoes of her childhood she had sobbed all the way back to Devon in the train. Max had wanted to cry too, but he knew he had to be strong for his sister. He had clenched his fists and blinked away tears, for the associations were almost too much to bear. When he got home he had filled the hollowness in his spirit with his mother's little book of poetry. Reading the verses she had once read to him, he had given in to memories usually too painful to remember.

Sorrowfully, he had recalled the last supper she had prepared for them before their long journey to England on the Kindertransport train. His father had sat solemnly, his thick whiskers twitching, the distinctive smell of tobacco surrounding him in a familiar cloud. Talk of war had dominated their small house, but that night they had tried to talk about other things. No one could have predicted the horror that was to come or the lucky escape that was to be his and Ruth's destiny. Lydia slept unaware of her fate in her cot upstairs. Their little suitcases were packed and placed by the door, full of warm clothes and hope. Max had noticed his mother's white hands trembling as she served him from a large pot of steaming soup and he had felt a solid ball of anguish forming in his throat. Had she known that she would never see them again? That she wouldn't live to watch them grow up? The pain must have been unbearable. She had tried to hide her anguish behind a tight smile, but she was unable to control the trembling in those slender white hands. Max's heart had filled with fear and the dreadful sensation of suddenly being cut loose from the strings that supported him.

The following morning he had sat on the train with Ruth, staring out at the bleak wintry landscape, remembering with all his might the colour and majesty of the Imperial Theatre. Those crimson velvet chairs, blazing golden lights and the smell of paint and perfume. The sound of raised voices, the scraping of furniture, the screeching of actresses in fur and lace. He imagined he was hiding in his father's box watching rehearsals, crouched low so no one could see him, enveloped in the warm fog of familiarity.

Christmas had always been a pleasure. It didn't remind Max and Ruth of the family they had lost in the war or of the childhood that had been so abruptly snatched from them. Christmas was shiny and novel and full of new memories. Most notably for Max, however, Christmas meant time with Rita, more eagerly anticipated than any present could ever be. This yeat it would be even more special because he was going to ask her to marry him.

He was certain that he could make her happy, especially now that he had made a name for himself and enough money to satisfy even the most materialistic of women. Rita wasn't materialistic, she had simple tastes. He would buy them a house by the sea as close to Frognal Point as possible and give her children of her own. There she could watch the birds and run up and down the beach. He'd take her to Vienna and show her the theatre his father built, the one he hoped to buy. They'd hold hands on the opening night and stand above the crowd watching them filing in as his father had done on his opening night when his mother had performed there for the first time.

He knew Rita cared for him. He sensed it in the pauses between sentences when their laughter trailed off and they looked at one other with tenderness. He wasn't sure that she lovd him in the same way that he loved her. That was too much to hope for. But there was more to marriage than the passionate excitement of lovers. It was about stability, family and affection. The last few times he had been to Frognal Point she had seemed so much happier and hadn't mentioned George in their conversations. They had chatted over glasses of wine and walked on the estuary by moonlight. With the exuberance of children they had run up the sand, laughing into the wind, teasing each other. He had never told her he loved her, he hadn't dared. But time was running on and they were getting older. He couldn't wait any longer.

Max drove down to Devon in his new MG. It felt good to be at the wheel of a shiny sports car, humming down the country lanes on his way to starting the rest of his life with the woman he loved. Although it was bitterly cold he drove with the hood down, wrapped in a woolly hat, scarf, heavy coat and sheepskin gloves. He liked the feel of the wind on his face, biting into his skin with tiny, sharp teeth, and looked about him through old-fashioned driving goggles with the appreciation of a man who's spent too much time in the city. The sky was pale but resplendent, the sun doing its best to thaw the frosted fields below. Max's heart soared in his chest and he sang loudly and energetically to the radio that he played at full volume. As he drove up the drive to Elvestree he turned off the music and inhaled the sweet scents of home. He could already smell the wood burning in the fireplaces and taste the champagne from Denzil's bountiful wine cellar. He pressed his foot on the accelerator and grinned at the thought of Mrs Megalith who no doubt would be dressed in velvet drapes and silk scarves and glittering with crystals. The world had moved on, but Elvestree was unaffected by fashion and the influence of time.

He parked the car on the gravel and bounded in through the front door decorated with a wreath made of holly and red berries. Stumbling over the cats, he made his way into the drawing room where the smell of the fire and the sound of music lured him enticingly. When Mrs Megalith saw him she rose from her card table to embrace him. 'My dear Max!' she exclaimed happily. 'You must have either driven like the wind or risen at dawn.'

'Both!' he replied, wrapping his arms around her large body. She smelt of mothballs and cinnamon, a scent that made him as nostalgic as the smell of the woodsmoke. She stepped away and eyed him up and down, sniffing her approval. *What a fine young man he has grown into,* she mused proudly. 'Where's Ruth?' he asked, helping himself to a glass of wine.

'In the kitchen preparing lunch. She's been very morose recently. I think she's working too hard. She's very pale,' Mrs Megalith replied, sinking into an armchair and balancing her reading glasses on the bridge of her nose. Ruth still lived at Elvestree, earning money cooking for local families. 'You wouldn't believe the stories she has to tell,' Mrs Megalith continued, picking up the newspaper. 'Some of the families she works for are so eccentric!'

Max raised his eyebrows and grinned to himself for no one was more eccentric than Mrs Megalith. She hadn't seemed to age in all the years that he had known her. She still suffered from the effects of the doodlebug that had fallen on her sister's house during the war and had walked with a stick for as long as he could remember, which made her appear older and more vulnerable than she really was, but her debility was deceptive. Perhaps her hair was whiter but it was still thick and glossy and her skin was as plump and dewy as that of a much younger woman. Like the rest of the house and gardens she had been touched by that inexplicable magic and would probably outlive them all.

'Bring me a sherry,' she said and looked at him over her glasses with a knowing glint in her moonstone eyes. There was little that escaped her notice. 'Why are you looking like the cat that's got the cream?'

Max longed to tell her that he was going to propose to Rita. He was barely able to contain his nervousness, but he didn't want to spoil it for her. If she didn't know already then he had a rare opportunity to surprise her. 'I'm just happy to be home,' he said. Mrs Megalith snorted through her nose and raised her eyebrows suspiciously.

'You've always been a dark horse,' she said, taking the glass of sherry from him. He sat down opposite her and leaned back and stretched. 'It's high time you found a girl to spend all that money on.'

Max chuckled. 'They don't grow on trees, you know,' he replied.

'Sometimes all a person has to do is look under his nose.' Max narrowed his eyes and wondered whether she already sensed his intentions. Had Rita spoken to her? Did Primrose know something of her feelings?

He decided to double bluff. 'How's Rita?'

Now Mrs Megalith put down her sherry glass and took off her glasses. 'Thanks to you Max, she's very content.'

'How do you mean?' He barely dared breathe.

'She's happy. You've enabled her to make something interesting out of that dreadfully tedious job in the library. You've encouraged her to read books and meet fascinating people. She's busy and her life has purpose. I think she's seen George and Susan and realised that she's got her own life to lead. That silly pining is done with, I hope. She's looking marvellous and has a spring in her step. About time too!'

Max took a sip of wine and tried to steady his twitching nerves. He was greatly encouraged by Primrose's words. It was only natural that their friendship should flower into something deeper.

'I'll go and see her this evening,' he said, draining his glass.

'She's spending Christmas at Bray Cove so she can enjoy the children.' Mrs Megalith noticed his disappointment and added, 'Why don't you wait until tomorrow? They're all coming for Christmas lunch. Ruth's chosen the fattest turkey especially.'

'I suppose she'll be having a quiet Christmas Eve with Maddie and Harry,' he said flatly.

'I lit the Menorah with Ruth, you know. Old habits die

hard,' she said with a chortle. 'Do you remember how I used to tell you the story about the wicked King Antiochus who tried to stop the Jews from worshipping God in their own way?'

'Yes, and we used to make stars out of foil and hang them from the kitchen ceiling.'

'You used to love hunting for your presents. One day you'll do all that for your children so they know where they come from.'

Max brightened up at that thought. He imagined a house like Elvestree, a roaring fire in the grate and Rita surrounded by their children. He had waited years for her. What was another day? He would propose to her tomorrow.

That night Ruth and Max went for a walk around the garden. They wandered across the lawn where the moon shone so brightly in a crisp, starry sky that the estuary glittered below like a diamond-studded gown draped over a sandy bed. Max smoked, wishing that he were there with Rita, for the night was as romantic as he had ever seen it. Ruth confided in him about the young student doctor with whom she had fallen in love, but Max felt unable to share his own secret with her. He had kept his feelings to himself for so long he was reluctant to open up now until he had something definite to divulge.

'Do you know, if she had lived, Lydia would be twenty-six and a half now,' said Ruth suddenly. Max stopped walking and stared at her. It was the first time they had ever talked about her. Even on the train after the service at Bevis Marks she hadn't mentioned their baby sister. 'I wish I remembered her,' she said. 'I wish I could remember what she looked like.'

'I don't remember either.'

'I sometimes feel so afraid, Max, because I can't see Mother and Father. I can't visualise their faces. I try, but it's a mist. Then I have to look at that photograph. That old, fading photograph. It's all I have left. Even memory fades.'

Max put his arm around her and kissed her temple. She

had been withdrawn all day, but neither Mrs Megalith nor he had taken much notice. She had always had a quiet nature, a reserved figure who said little and kept her thoughts to herself.

'Why now, Ruth?' he asked.

She turned to him with eyes that sparkled in the moonlight. For a moment she hesitated as if having second thoughts, but then she blinked away a tear and her lips quivered. 'Because I'm expecting a baby and I wish Mother were here.' Max drew her into his arms and hugged her.

'You're pregnant?' he asked in amazement.

'Yes, and I feel so alone.'

'God, Ruth, you're not alone. I'm here.'

'I know but . . .'

'Is the father standing by you?' he asked. 'If he's not I'll . . .'

'Yes. Oh, Max, we love each other,' she interrupted hastily, sensing his anger and feeling heartened by it.

'Will he marry you?'

'He wants to, but he doesn't have any money. He hasn't qualified yet. He lives with his parents.' She sniffed and lifted her chin.

Max was horrified at his neglect. He had been so pre-occupied with Rita he hadn't noticed his sister's predicament. He was ashamed of his own selfishness and determined to put it right. 'Why didn't you tell me before?'

'I'm telling you now.'

'You're the only family I have, Ruth. You know I'll take care of you.' She smiled at him gratefully and wiped her eyes. 'You'll never want for anything, I promise you.'

'You're so good to me, Max.'

'You're family. What belongs to me belongs to you.' He curled a stray piece of hair around her ear. 'Is he a good man?' he asked.

'The very best.'

'Then marry him and pretend you've inherited money from Primrose or something. Don't tell him I'm financing you, it might hurt his pride.'

Ruth wound her arms around him. 'Thank you, Max,' she whispered into his neck, unable to believe that all her problems had been solved in a single conversation.

'I only ask one thing,' he said in a steely voice. 'Never hesitate to come to me again, do you understand? Father would turn in his grave if he knew that you hadn't asked for my help when you needed it.'

'I promise,' she replied happily.

This would be the best Christmas ever. They walked with their arms around each other towards the house and Ruth told him all about Samuel Kahan, how they had met when she cooked for his parents one weekend the previous spring. The wife of a handsome Jewish doctor, their parents would have been so proud.

As they passed the drawing room window they both stopped suddenly at the astonishing sight within. Mrs Megalith was holding an animated conversation all on her very own. She was laughing, gesticulating, frowning her disapproval and flirting as if talking to someone she greatly admired. 'My darling Denzil, there are plenty of bottles left in your cellar,' she said with a coy smile. 'Remember that 1928 Krug? Ah, what an occasion that was.' Then she leaned back in the armchair and laughed a deep-throated laugh in response to something Denzil must have said. She tilted her head to one side and sighed wistfully, without taking her eyes off what must have been the spirit of her dead husband. Ruth looked at Max and giggled.

'Come on,' he said leading her away. 'I think we should creep in through the back door, don't you?'

Chapter Thirty-one

The following morning Max awoke with an intense feeling of optimism and excitement. By the time the sun set Rita might have agreed to marry him. He didn't allow his nervousness to ruin so perfect a dawn, or consider that she might refuse him. He bathed and dressed and joined Mrs Megalith and Ruth in the kitchen for breakfast, which Ruth was cooking on the Aga, her cheeks flushed with happiness. Her cheerfulness was infectious and soon the three of them were laughing and joking over poached eggs, toast and tomatoes. Only Max knew why Ruth ate enough for the entire household and why she quietly kept raiding a plate of olives.

When Max saw Rita he was struck immediately by the change in her countenance. She looked as radiant as when he had first fallen in love with her. Her cheeks were as rosy as Elvestree plums, her eyes as gold and shimmering as Mrs Megalith's sherry. She smiled at him – a wide, carefree smile – and he felt his stomach lurch as it did when he drove his car too fast over the bridge just outside Frognal Point. She embraced him affectionately and he breathed in the familiar scent of violets that always clung to her skin.

'You look so well,' he said, looking her over appraisingly.

'Thank you.'

'Will you come for a walk with me after lunch? I want to catch up with you properly. I feel I haven't spoken to you in ages.'

'Of course. Just like old times,' she said brightly. 'We can take Tarka. I had to leave her in the car because she hates Megagran's cats.'

'I should imagine the feeling's mutual.'

'You look well too, Max,' she remarked, noticing how his eyes shone a bright cornflower blue.

'I have so much to tell you, Rita. I wish we were alone,' he said, looking at her steadily.

'Later,' she whispered, crinkling up her nose. 'I have lots to tell you too.' And they smiled at each other as old friends do.

Maddie and Harry helped themselves to drinks while Freddie, Daisy and Elsbeth ran over to the tree which stood in the corner of the room decorated with old-fashioned glass balls, red and gold ribbon, and velvet figurines that were much older than Mrs Megalith herself. Beneath the tree were strewn piles of brightly wrapped presents which each family had brought. The children immediately began to hunt around for their gifts until Rita told them to wait patiently until their great-grandmother decided to hand them out. Aunt Antoinette and David arrived with Harrods bags full of extravagant parcels which had all been wrapped in the same red paper by the shop assistant. William followed with his snooty, glamorous wife and young children, and Emily with her dull solicitor husband and screaming baby. Antoinette told her daughter to take the baby upstairs. In her opinion small children should be rarely seen and never heard. David was pleased to find Humphrey with Hannah in the hall, draping their coats on top of the cats on the sofa. He took his friend into the small sitting room, away from the chaos of the drawing room, to discuss Macmillan's government over a large cigar and a glass of Bell's whisky.

Hannah kissed her grandchildren, handing Elsbeth a bunch of feathers she had gathered from the garden to add to the child's growing collection. Like her parents Elsbeth adored birds and knew all the regional ones by name. Hannah suddenly thought of Eddie far away in Africa and her heart was pinched with sorrow. She would have loved her to be there, celebrating Christmas with the family. Of all her daughters Eddie had been the most special to her and now she was gone. If only she had managed to work that broomstick then she could have flown back just for the day. She sat next to her sister on the fender but didn't voice her regret to Antoinette. Instead Hannah listened to her sister praising her daughter-in-law who she obviously regarded as a pretty reflection of herself. 'William has always had good taste in women,' she declared with misguided pride. 'I set him a rather high standard. I thought he'd never be satisfied, but in Caroline he's found not only good looks and class but intelligence too. I've always said a woman ensnares a man with her beauty but keeps him with her mind. She's a very bright girl.' *She's also glum and unpleasant,* Hannah thought to herself. She had never seen a more dissatisfied face in all her life. On reflection Antoinette never really smiled either; she just pinched her lips together, screwed up her face as if she was in pain, and simpered in an artificial way. She noticed that her sister's hair was bigger and redder than was natural and her lips a harsh scarlet that did not become her face. She was too old to wear such vibrant colours.

Mrs Megalith sat regally in her armchair surveying the room with disdain. The children were too noisy and spoilt. Antoinette smoked far too much and looked utterly ridiculous modelling herself on the fashion magazines she so slavishly followed. Hannah was covered in feathers from the new dovecote Humphrey had installed for her to compensate for Eddie's absence, and William and his monosyllabic wife made no effort to join in but stood against the wall drinking all her champagne and looking down at everyone from the dizzy heights of their egos. Maddie hung onto every word her ludicrous aunt said while Harry watched her with eyes that dripped with love, quite absurd still to be so infatuated with one's wife at his age. Rita was full of joy, which was a blessing, but no doubt Antoinette would burst her bubble by the end of the day and send her into a rapid decline. Ruth worked away in the kitchen listening to the wireless; Mrs Megalith gave her little thought. At least she could trust that the food would be good. At her age, food was one of life's greatest pleasures.

However, her face softened when her old eyes settled on Max. She watched him with ill-concealed adoration. She turned to Emily who had put the baby to bed upstairs but was too anxious to concentrate on anything other than the faint sound of his crying, and said, 'Now there's a fine example of a man with the best of everything. Why didn't you marry someone like Max?'

Emily still took offence in spite of having grown up with her grandmother's often tactless comments. 'Because there's only one Max, Grandma, and he wouldn't have me,' she replied.

'He's very gifted. Very gifted indeed. Always has been. I recognised his talents when he was a little boy and nurtured them. If you don't water a plant it doesn't grow. Look what a fine young man he has grown into. Nurture is everything, Emily. Don't forget that with . . . what's his name?'

'Guy,' Emily retorted unhappily.

'Silly name, Guy!' Mrs Megalith exclaimed, smacking her lips together. 'You know it's not too late to change it. Why not call him Denzil after your grandfather? A fine man was your grandfather. He'd be very fortunate to wear his name. With any luck it might endow the child with a bit of character!' Emily didn't have the confidence to hold her own with her grandmother and fled the room with the excuse of checking on her son. Mrs Megalith barely noticed she had gone for her attention was firmly fixed on Max. When Rita asked if they could start the present giving, Mrs Megalith withdrew her attention and snorted in disapproval. 'In my day we only had one present each and that was considered a luxury. Nowadays Christmas is all about gifts. A perfect consumer *fest*! You hand them out, Rita, or get the children to do it, teach them a bit about giving. If I hear anyone whining because they haven't received the present they requested I'll burn the lot of them!'

Mrs Megalith caught Max's eye and winked. With a smile he got up and went to sit next to her on the sofa. He poured her another sherry and whispered into her ear, 'Are you bearing up?'

She chuckled and placed her plump hand on his knee. 'You're the only person here who spares a thought for me,' she said.

'I know you secretly hate Christmas.'

'Wasn't Hanukkah always lots of fun? Just us.' She sighed wistfully.

'Christmas is a national day of compulsion, that's why you hate it.'

She looked at him and narrowed her eyes. 'You're so right, Max. I've always loathed following the pack, just like you.'

'But it gives your family an enormous amount of pleasure,' he said, watching the children handing around the presents, their little faces alight with excitement.

'Today's young are spoiled. They didn't live through the war. I have lived through two.'

'You can't expect them to appreciate what we went through, how can they? We can only try to teach them that family, love, loyalty and respect are far more valuable than possessions.'

Mrs Megalith gazed at him steadily. 'You do know that you're more valuable to me than anyone else in the world?' she said suddenly. 'When I die I'm leaving everything to you.'

'Don't talk of dying, Primrose. You'll outlive us all,' he said, turning serious.

'No I won't. You love Elvestree. You understand it. You're the son I never had. I want you to know that. I don't want to go without having told you.'

'Just don't go yet,' he said, trying to lighten their mood. 'You have to marry me off first.'

Mrs Megalith laughed. 'That's my boy!' she exclaimed. 'But mind she's good enough for you or you'll have me to contend with.'

After the presents had all been opened and the champagne bottles drained, Ruth announced that lunch was ready. She opened the door to the dining room and smiled proudly as her decorations were met with gasps of admiration, even from Mrs Megalith who hobbled in first, assisted by Max, the only person she allowed to hold her elbow as she walked. The tables were decorated with Christmas crackers, chocolates in bright wrapping, and holly. She had lit candles and dimmed the lights so that the room glowed with a festive golden radiance. The smell of turkey wafted in from the kitchen as she disappeared with Maddie and Rita to bring in the dishes. Humphrey poured the wine and Mrs Megalith was relieved that Ruth had written place cards seating her between Max and David. The children looked out of the window to see to their delight that it had suddenly clouded over and begun to snow. Everyone sat down, filled with the joy of being all together on such a splendid day. Even Mrs Megalith appreciated the wonder of snow and when she took her first mouthful of turkey her spirits lifted and she raised her glass to Ruth, to family and to the future. Then she added as she did every year, aware that Max and Ruth were guests at their Christmas table. 'I would like once again to welcome our two Jewish friends to our festival. Let us not forget that there is only one God and in His eyes we are all the same. To Max and Ruth and to those who are with them in spirit.'

After lunch Rita and Max sneaked away to walk together

down on the estuary. Wrapped in coats, hats and the glow of their own exuberance, they wandered down the garden and onto the sand that stretched for miles across the mouth of the sea. Tarka was thrilled to be let out of the car and bounded down the slope, her tail almost lifting her off the ground like the propeller of a helicopter. They discussed lunch and laughed as they recalled various conversations, especially Aunt Antoinette's whose lying had taken on a new dimension.

'It's a disease,' said Max.

'I know, it's terrible. I don't know how Uncle David puts up with it!'

'He's never there. If you noticed he's been hiding in the sitting room with your father all day. I don't think he even likes her.'

'Some people stay together simply out of habit or because it's easier than separating. Can you imagine the flak if he said he was going to leave her?'

'It's not worth his while, is it?' They began to walk up the beach. The snow was now falling heavily, like the dove's feathers stuck to Hannah's clothes. Rita threw back her head and tried to catch them in her mouth.

'Haven't you had enough to eat!' he teased.

'The more you eat the more you want,' she said, running up the sand, followed by Tarka barking at her heels. 'Isn't this marvellous! I love snow!'

He ran behind her and grabbed her hand. Suddenly overcome with emotion, he pulled her around to face him. 'And I love you!'

Rita stared at him, her eyes wide and glassy in the cold.

'I love you,' he repeated.

'Oh, Max!' she sighed, her face darkening with anxiety.

'Don't say anything. Hear me out.' He took both her hands in his. They were warm but rough from working with clay.

Her breath floated up on the icy air like smoke as the snow fell around them and the cloud closed in. The estuary was shrouded in a heavy silence. 'I have loved you from the first moment I saw you, Rita. I love everything about you. I know you hoped to marry George and that your dreams were shattered when he left for Argentina. But I know I can make you happy. If you agree to marry me you'll make me happier than I ever dreamed possible.'

Rita watched him nervously. She bit her lip while she hastily worked out what she was going to reply. She had known he loved her as a friend but it had never occurred to her that he felt something more profound. Now her heart buckled because she knew that she could only disappoint him and possibly lose him for ever. 'Oh, Max. That's the nicest thing anyone has ever said to me,' she replied, her voice cracking.

'It's all true. I can't tell you how good it feels to tell you. I've kept my feelings secret for years.'

'I can't marry you,' she said simply.

'But why?' Max felt his stomach plummet.

'Because my heart will always belong to George.'

Max felt years of hope unravel before him. 'Oh, come on, Rita,' he exclaimed in exasperation. 'He's married to Susan. He has a family of his own. You can't hold onto a memory. A memory won't make you happy, give you a family to love and a life to live.'

She dropped her hands and put them in her pockets. 'I saw him last week.'

'And?'

'He was up on the cliff and I was walking up the beach with Tarka. He was alone for a few moments. We just stared at each other.'

'Just stared at each other.' Max wondered what was so special about that.

'When I stopped and returned his stare he didn't look away.

He stared right back at me. I know he regrets losing me. I could feel it.' She pressed her fist against her heart.

'Oh, for goodness' sake, Rita. You're imagining it.'

'I wasn't. I've known George all my life. I know what he's thinking.'

'Well, why didn't he walk down and tell you instead of just staring at you?'

'Because Susan was with him.'

'That's hardly the behaviour of a man who feels he's married the wrong woman!' Max was intensely irritated by her stubborn refusal to see the truth.

'I know how hurt you are. I love you as friend. A dear, dear friend. But how can I marry you when I love another?'

'But he doesn't love you, Rita. Why can't you get that into your head?' He knocked his own head with his fist to emphasise the point.

Rita began to get flustered. 'Look, Max, whom I love is my choice.'

'But the years will roll by and you'll be old and childless and bitter. I can't watch you waste yourself. We're given one life. One life!' He thought of Lydia, denied that precious gift and here was Rita thoughtlessly throwing it away. She didn't understand what it was she was discarding. He felt his throat tighten with fury and resentment. 'What do you hope for, Rita?' He was aware that he was now shouting. 'That George will leave Susan and marry you? You don't believe in divorce any more than I do. Even if he did love you how could he look at himself in the mirror and respect himself if he were to leave his wife and children? Do you want him to? Is that what you want? To destroy all those lives?'

There was silence as Rita digested his words. They stared at each other, chewing on their anger, fighting their disappointment. Rita knew that their friendship would never be the same again after this, but at that moment she was too affronted to care.

'I'm sorry,' she said huffily. 'I know you don't understand. No one does. I love George and always will. I'll die loving him.'

Her words struck Max at the very centre of his being. 'No, I don't understand,' he groaned. 'One day, Rita, you'll wake up and realise that you made a grave mistake today and I'll be gone. I have offered you a real chance at happiness but you have chosen to remain in your dark world of make-believe. If that is where you want to stay I cannot help you. But I can no longer be your friend. I must learn to live without you.'

With that, he walked back towards the house, disappearing into the fog that had now swept in from the sea. Rita watched him go. A part of her wanted to run after him. He was the only real friend she had. But the stubborn, angry part of her, the part that clung to George like bindweed, held her back. She stared down at the little solitaire diamond that twinkled on her finger and wondered whether she had made the right decision.

Max couldn't remember the last time he had cried. There had been many times when he had wanted to. But he had always braced himself, strained his throat against tears until it ached with the effort, bit his lip until it bled. He had always had to be strong for Ruth. But this wasn't about Ruth, his parents or his little sister who perished in the camps. Now he sobbed for Rita, and for himself. He bowed his head and cried into the collar of his coat, relieved that the fog was so thick that no one could see him. He climbed back up to the garden and walked straight past the children without saying a word. They barely noticed him, continuing to build their snowman as the fog crept up the lawn to engulf them too.

It didn't take Max long to pack his bag. He wrote Mrs Megalith a note explaining the reason for his hasty departure. Then he climbed into his car and drove back to London.

Chapter Thirty-two

When Mrs Megalith read Max's note her forehead darkened into a frown and she shook her head in bewilderment. 'This isn't right,' she muttered, taking off her spectacles and staring out at the white fog and snow that fell silently outside her window. She read the note again then pursed her lips with impatience. 'Silly girl!' she sighed, unable to understand her granddaughter. She stood up, grabbed her walking stick and paced the room slowly and unsteadily. Max and Rita were a natural partnership. They always had been. How Rita could prefer to love a man she could never have rather than marry Max was beyond Mrs Megalith's comprehension. What frustrated her more than anything was that she was unable to help him. She wanted to shake some sense into her granddaughter but knew she must not intervene. Destiny had other plans and she knew better than to meddle.

When Rita returned to the house she realised from the expression on her grandmother's face that she knew what had happened. It didn't surprise her that Max had fled back to London, though it saddened her. Unable to meet the disapproval, incomprehension and pity in Megagran's eyes, she went about the drawing room tidying up all the wrapping paper and hiding her misery behind a bustle of efficiency. She was relieved when Maddie and Harry decided to leave after tea. The children were weary and the snow was now falling heavily, which would make the roads dangerous.

Max returned to the New Year and to a bleak future. He

buried himself in his work, leaving home early and staying in the office until late. He missed Rita dreadfully but felt angry towards her. He had many friends and a busy social life: dinners, cocktail parties, theatre, opera and ballet. The invitations weighed heavily on his mantelpiece and yet he had never felt lonelier in his entire life. Friends introduced him to beautiful women. Girls even approached him on their own initiative. He could have had any he wanted, but only Rita would do. 'I have everything and nothing,' he would say when his friends commented admiringly on his success and his wealth: none of them understood what he meant.

The moment he returned to London he had set about transferring money into his sister's account, lavishing his wealth on her because now she was all he had. He bought her a pretty manor house in Frognal Point, with a large garden complete with an old barn and duck pond, where she moved with Samuel Kahan after marrying him in the Register Office in Exeter. Mrs Megalith threw a small party for them, but didn't invite Rita. Max was happy for his sister. He knew his parents would be proud of them both. But he felt bitter envy. Ruth had everything he wanted for himself.

Ruth kept in close touch by telephone. Although she knew about Rita's rejection, she didn't dare mention it, for her brother shied away from discussing his personal life. So she supported him as best she could by being a constant presence in his life. Mrs Megalith was saddened that he didn't come down to Elvestree as often as he used to. She understood that it was painful for him to be so close to Rita, but she missed him. Angry with Rita for having hurt Max, she sought her company as little as possible. When she did see her, she was impatient and brusque, leaving Rita feeling more isolated and misunderstood than ever.

Rita missed Max more than she had anticipated. An empty, Max-shaped space echoed in her heart and no one else could fill it. She retreated again into her sculpting. Once she had moulded clay in order to maintain her links with Faye and indirectly, with George, but now she sculpted to ease the pain of losing her friend. She didn't notice that as spring brushed off the winter pallor and painted the countryside once again with colour, the shadow of Max's absence began slowly to eclipse George.

Reverend Hammond was aware that Rita no longer attended church. He knew it was because of George and Susan, which he considered a weak excuse for not worshipping as one ought. As God's mouthpiece he felt it his duty to teach her about forgiveness and to guide her back into the light. After the Christmas service when her non-attendance had been shamefully noticeable he resolved to pay her a visit. Miss Hogmier wasted no time in filling him in with the details of the latest developments. 'That Jew-boy asked her to marry him,' she said with a snort when he went into the village shop to buy tea-bags for his wife.

'Max?' Reverend Hammond exclaimed in surprise.

Miss Hogmier folded her arms in front of her and nodded. 'And she refused him.'

'Was that not a foolish move?'

'I would say so. A girl like Rita should be grateful for small mercies. She's not getting any younger and a Jew-boy is better than none.'

'Perhaps a quiet word from me might change her mind. I would hate to see her growing old alone. Not that there's any stigma attached to that,' he added hastily when he noticed Miss Hogmier's nasal hair begin to twitch.

'I don't think even God can change that girl's stubborn mind,' she said huffily.

'She's one of God's lost sheep, Miss Hogmier. It is my job to lead her home.'

'Do what you will, Reverend Hammond, but don't say I didn't warn you. She has quite a tongue on her at times, like her grandmother.' She shifted her eyes about the shop for cats, then added in a low voice, 'About time the old witch met her Maker and took all her little spies with her.'

Reverend Hammond waited for a suitable moment to approach Rita. His opportunity came in the summer, after Ruth Kahan was delivered of a rosy little girl whom she named Mitzi, after her mother. To his dismay he heard from Miss Hogmier, who made it her business to know everyone else's, that Rita had left her job at the library to become a full-time sculptress.

'She's cavorting with a group of scruffy-looking rich kids who have set up camp down on the beach for the summer,' Miss Hogmier informed him, pursing her lips in disapproval. 'They're leading her astray. It's because of them that she feels she no longer has to work for a living, as if the good Lord will rain down manna from the heavens. They sit around camp fires, singing and playing guitars. I don't know who she thinks she is these days with those strange dresses and beads. I imagine her mother despairs of her with her uncombed hair. It's practically reached her waist. In my day women took more pride in their appearance. Look at me, it might be the nineteen sixties but I still sleep with my hair in rollers and wouldn't be seen dead in the street without a little makeup. I'd scare off my customers if I didn't make an effort to look my best.'

Reverend Hammond drove up the coast, beyond Bray Cove, to where Rita lived in her little cottage overlooking the sea, with the intention of persuading her to open her heart once again to God. On the passenger seat sat an old Bible with faded gold edging and a frayed ribbon marking the place from which he was going to read to her.

It was a warm summer's day. Gulls flew overhead, the tips of their wings catching the sunlight as they dived and glided over the cliffs. He felt God's presence in the beauty of the morning and knew that He was with him on this very important mission. Of all his jobs as vicar of the parish this was one of his favourites. Yes, he enjoyed weddings, and funerals were an important part of the cycle of religious life, but individual meetings with members of his flock gave him the most satisfaction.

As he drove into the driveway he was impressed by the pretty home Rita had made for herself. Clematis climbed up the front of the house, tangled with white roses and honeysuckle, and large pots of lavender were placed outside the front door. He breathed in deeply, savouring the sweet smells of summer, and knocked on the door. Rita didn't hear him for she was in the garden, weeding the flowerbeds. Reverend Hammond waited a while, with his Bible clamped under his arm, then wandered round the side of the house. When she saw him she stood up in surprise and frowned at him beneath her sunhat. Reverend Hammond had never visited her in all the time she had lived there. Someone must have died.

'Ah, Rita, how nice to see you,' he said, walking across the grass.

'Is everything all right?' she asked.

'Yes, yes, everything is just dandy.' He swept his eyes over the garden. 'What a charming place this is.'

'Thank you. I'm very attached to it.'

'Lots of birds I see,' he stated, noticing the birdbath and feeding trays.

'I don't attract as many as Elvestree, but the odd nightingale sings in the hedge and of course there are always swallows.'

'How very nice.'

She looked at him quizzically, wishing he would get on with his business for she wanted to get back to her weeding.

'I have come to talk to you,' he said in a pompous tone, expecting her to be grateful. 'I hear you're now a full-time sculptress?'

'Yes.' Surely he hadn't come to talk about sculpture!

'No longer working in the library then?'

'No.'

'Right. Well, I suppose you know what you're doing?'

'I think I do,' she replied coolly. 'Is that what you want to talk to me about?'

'Why don't we sit down?' he suggested.

She led him to the small terrace where there was a teak bench and table, and watched him settle comfortably. She dropped her shoulders in resignation. 'Can I get you something to drink?' she asked, realising that he was intending to stay some time.

'A glass of water would be most welcome. It's a very hot day, don't you think?'

When she returned with a jug and two glasses he was reading the Bible with his thick round spectacles perched on the bridge of his nose. 'I gain great strength from God's word,' he said, looking up at her gravely.

'It's your job to,' she replied with a grin. There was something comic about the old Reverend beating about every available bush to avoid getting to the point of his visit.

'You don't have to have my vast knowledge of the Bible to derive courage from it. I have noticed, Rita, that you no longer attend church. Do you want to talk about it?'

'Not really.'

He took a gulp of his water and silently asked the Lord for assistance. This was one very stubborn sheep. 'You used never to miss a Sunday. The place seems empty without you.'

'I very much doubt that,' she said crisply.

'God used to reside in your heart, Rita.' Now he peered at her over the top of his glasses like a schoolmaster.

'Oh, but He still does, Reverend. My grandmother says that God is everywhere and that one doesn't have to go to church to talk to Him.'

He stiffened at the mention of Mrs Megalith. 'She's right,

of course,' he said hastily. 'God is indeed everywhere. I feel, however, that it is not due to a lapse in your faith that you are avoiding worship but due to the presence of George Bolton and his wife Susan.'

Now it was Rita's turn to look uncomfortable. She closed her eyes in exasperation and shook her head. 'I suppose you heard that from good Miss Hogmier?' she asked, her voice steely.

'No, no, of course not,' he lied, silently asking forgiveness at the same time.

'Well she's right. I don't go because I don't want to see George with Susan. That's very petty of me, I know. But I'm not holy like you, Reverend Hammond. I am a frail sinner.'

'God teaches forgiveness,' he ventured bravely.

'I'm not ready for that yet.'

'Rome wasn't built in a day.'

'It will take me a lifetime, Reverend.'

'But you have to start sometime.'

'When I'm ready.'

Reverend Hammond scratched his head. 'Then let me leave you with this Bible. I was going to read you a passage or two today, but I've suddenly remembered another appointment.'

'Are you sure? It's a lovely old one.' She took it and stroked the leather cover that was rough and worn with use.

'Perfectly sure. You need it more than I. A man in my position has many Bibles. Return it one day when you no longer have need of it.'

Rita sighed, feeling that she had perhaps been a little harsh. He wasn't, after all, a bad man. 'That's very kind of you,' she said truthfully. She thought a moment then added in a firm voice, 'I shall come to church from time to time.'

The Reverend's face lit up and he quietly thanked the good Lord for His guidance. Rita watched him go, then took the

Bible inside, put it on the sitting room table, and forgot all about it.

The following Sunday she kept her word and went to church. Knowing that George would be there, she spent a long time in front of the mirror, combing her hair, trying to remember how Maddie had suggested she wear a little foundation and rouge, choosing which summer dress to put on.

By the time she parked on the green her nerves were in tatters. She sat for a while watching people go in, frightened that she would find herself face to face with George and not know what to say. Finally she saw her parents with Maddie and the children and she quickly got out of the car to meet them. Their surprise was obvious. Humphrey patted her back a little too hard and Hannah persuaded her to join them for lunch, tempting her with treacle sponge and a possible sighting of a spotted flycatcher. Maddie had left Harry at home; he was now working on another book, which kept him deep in his office or in his thoughts. Daisy was looking out for Charlie, who had become her closest friend, Freddie was sulking because he didn't like sitting through Reverend Hammond's boring sermons, and Elsbeth had made a flamboyant hat out of some of the feathers she had collected. Rita was happy to be among them and felt stronger as they all walked in together.

'About time you wore a little make-up,' said Maddie approvingly once they had sat down. 'It suits you. You don't look so pale and sad.'

'I never look pale and sad,' retorted Rita in offence.

'Yes you do. All that pining for George is nonsense.' Rita felt irritated and opened her hymn book. 'You should have married Max.'

'How do you know about that?' Rita asked in surprise for she hadn't told anyone of his proposal.

'Megagran told Mummy.'

'Typical!'

'Well, you're a fool,' she hissed.

'Will you mind your own business!'

Maddie suddenly grabbed her arm. 'Look, there's George and Susan. You know Daisy has a crush on Charlie. History repeating itself somewhat!' Rita turned around to see them walk up the aisle, flustered because they were late. Reverend Hammond was already tapping his foot on the floor with impatience.

Susan saw Maddie and smiled before she noticed Rita sitting quietly beside her. To Susan's surprise Rita's face had acquired a subtle beauty, quite different from the ashen young woman she had seen in the village shop the previous winter and from the plump child who had grinned out from Mrs Megalith's mantelpiece of photographs. Her skin glowed with a delicate translucence and her hair was thick and shiny, cascading down her back in curls. Her cheekbones were accentuated by the weight that she had lost but her loveliness had more to do with her poise than with individual features. Susan's eyes darted quickly to her husband but he was searching for a place to sit and hadn't seen her.

Rita felt as if the eyes of the entire congregation were upon her, eager to see her reaction. She remained very still as the sweat gathered behind her knees and under her arms. Reverend Hammond waited for George and his family to settle down before he began the service. As they were sitting a few rows in front of her on the other side of the aisle Rita was able to watch him without fear of him noticing.

George was now forty-two. He still had a thick head of curly hair but it was greying at the temples and receding a little at the front. His shoulders were broader and he had certainly filled out around the waist. No longer the lean hero of the Battle of Britain, he was still handsome and charismatic and Rita believed she still loved him. Rita transferred her gaze to Susan. The tidy blonde hair pulled back into a shiny chignon at the nape of her long white neck reminded her of Faye, and the neat pearl necklace, elegant dress and understated hat betrayed a sophistication that she could never acquire. She now noticed the scar but time had done much to heal the wound that had once sliced through Susan's face so cruelly, making it fainter and less harsh. Rita thought it detracted nothing from her beauty and couldn't help but envy her, for she had everything that Rita wanted. It was like watching someone else living her life for her. Someone lovelier, more urbane, making a much better job of it than she could ever have done. She didn't feel Susan's discomfort or sense the hostility that surrounded her, preventing her from becoming a real member of the community. She wouldn't have guessed it was out of loyalty to her, because she was one of them and Susan was a usurper. Only when she went up for communion did George see her and his look of surprise made her falter as she walked back down the aisle.

George's face drained of colour and turned as sallow as wax. Time had done nothing to diminish her loveliness, in fact, it had enhanced it. She wasn't the tragic creature his mother had described, but the confident girl he had dreamed of, running up the sand with her arms outstretched, chasing the birds into the air on the tail of the wind. He could only watch helplessly as she floated towards him, a few feet away but so out of reach as he stood in the queue for communion with Susan and the children right behind him. Rita steadied herself and drew her shoulders back. She felt as if she were walking in slow motion for the moment seemed unnaturally extended. As she moved closer she saw something in his countenance that unsettled her. Something alien. Something unfamiliar. Hastily she searched beneath the surface for the insouciant young man she loved but couldn't find him. He was no longer there.

She settled back into her seat beside Maddie, who took her hand and held it for support without realising that she no longer needed it. When George walked back down the aisle he cast a fleeting glance in her direction then swiftly withdrew his eyes and turned into his pew. His face was grim. Susan followed him but she didn't look at Maddie. Determined not to let Rita cause her any more anxiety she tried not to dwell on the intense manner in which she had gazed upon her husband. She had no reason to feel insecure. George had made his choice a long time ago and they were very happy together. If Rita made him feel uncomfortable it was simply that seeing her so obviously alone must make him feel guilty indeed.

At the end of the service the congregation spilled out into the aisle and George was unable to reach Rita. He longed to talk to her. Perhaps that would do something to settle his rattled spirit. He saw the top of her head as she made her way out of the church with Maddie and struggled to move past the gossiping villagers. Susan watched him closely. She knew what was on his mind and she tried to convince herself that it would be a good thing if they spoke. Perhaps it would exorcise the ghost once and for all. She noticed that Charlie had already squeezed past his father and was talking to Daisy outside in the sunshine with her mother and grandparents while Ava had found Elsbeth doing pirouettes on a gravestone.

Frustrated that he couldn't move any faster, George was tempted to throw people out of his way with brute force. Finally the slow-moving herd fanned out into the churchyard and he squinted in the bright sunshine. He scanned the faces for Rita's. Susan saw her husband scour the yard and the disappointment that caused his face to sag. Then the rumble of an engine caught his attention and he cast his eyes across the green to where Rita was starting her car. Susan walked up behind him but she didn't slip her hand into his as she once would have done. They both watched the car pull out. They both saw Rita turn and look at them. Her eyes settled on George for what seemed an interminable moment. Then she drove away.

Chapter Thirty-three

Rita sat on the beach with Pepper, one of the young bohemians who had been camped up on the bank in their orange Volkswagen all summer. It was early September. The amber glow of sunset seemed all the more wistful through the wafting cannabis smoke. The low strumming of a guitar resounded across the bay, carried on a gentle breeze that brought with it the cool undertones of autumn. Pepper's friends were at the other end of the beach, building the fire and setting up for the night. Rita had grown tremendously fond of them all, especially Pepper, whose positive, untroubled nature reminded her of herself as a young girl, before George had returned from the war.

But right now her thoughts weren't for George but for Max whom she missed as much as if she had lost a vital part of her body. What bothered her most was that their friendship had ended so viciously. They had shouted at each other, said things they regretted and they were both too proud to extend the olive branch. Rita longed for him to telephone her and apologise. She had played the conversation over and over again in her mind, imagining what she would say. However, she hadn't yet the courage to acknowledge her deepest feelings.

'You're thinking of Max, aren't you?' said Pepper in her aristocratic voice. Christened Petruska she had been born in the highlands to an eccentric Scottish earl who left his staid English wife for a famous Russian dancer he had met in

Moscow between the wars. Pepper was the product of that union. She had more money than she could spend and parents who were a great deal more interested in each other than in her. 'Why don't you just telephone him and apologise?' she asked, running a hand through her long red hair.

'He should apologise to me,' Rita replied indignantly. She patted Tarka who lay sleeping by her side and dragged on her joint. 'After all, he walked off and left me.'

'One of you has to do it or you'll end up a lonely old maid.'

'I'm not lonely, I have all of you.'

'We'll be leaving soon.'

'Leaving?'

'Well, you didn't expect us to hang around here indefinitely, did you?'

Rita was shocked. 'I thought you liked it here.'

'In the summer when the weather's good. It's getting colder now. I thought I might go to art school. I like painting. Mother wanted me to be a dancer like her, but my feet are too big. She would have preferred me to be pretty and petite like her. Sadly, I take after Papa. Maybe I'll go to Florence.'

'I'll miss you,' said Rita truthfully. Pepper had become a good friend. Someone she could confide in who was nothing to do with Frognal Point.

'Come to Florence. You can learn to sculpt with the masters, surrounded by the best works of art in the world.' It amused Rita that Pepper thought everyone had as much money as she did. In fact Rita was having trouble paying her bills now that she had given up working in the library.

'I couldn't leave Tarka.'

'Bring her with you. Florence is the city of love. You'll forget all about George and Max with all those delicious Italian men.'

'That's my problem, Pepper, I don't want to forget. I like

it here, surrounded by my memories and my family. If only Max hadn't gone and ruined it all by proposing.'

'He'll have got over you by now. You know what men are like. Fickle. Archie gets through women like an anteater on an ant hill.' She giggled at the thought of her friend who drove into town every evening in search of fresh blood. 'He's got to go back to Oxford. Term starts in October. I don't want a boyfriend or a husband. They just complicate your life.'

'Love complicates everything. To think that all the time I thought we were best friends, he was in love with me,' she said. 'I had never looked on him in that way. Now I've broken his heart.'

'And George's,' Pepper added.

Rita sighed. 'I have loved George all my life. Or have I?'

'What do you mean?' Pepper scrunched the butt of her joint into the sand.

Rita narrowed her eyes as the blinding sun slowly began to sink into the sea. 'Maybe Max was right about George.'

'What did he say?'

Rita frowned. 'That for all these years, I've been in love with someone who no longer exists.'

Autumn swept in with gales and storms and Rita's small band of drifters packed up and left, returning to their privileged lives. The winter months were dark and cold. Rita thought about Max often, picking up the telephone before losing courage and replacing the receiver. She didn't see George again for Susan had convinced him to attend church in the neighbouring parish and, little by little, he ceased to occupy her thoughts as he had done before. Once or twice she visited their secret cave to feel the warmth of his presence there, as if he too had sought the comfort of memories in that special place only moments before. Now the bittersweet taste of those memories was distant and intangible for she had learned that she could never bring them back, or the George with whom she had grown up: Max had been right.

Christmas was damp in every sense. Max didn't come home so Mrs Megalith was more cantankerous than ever, vociferously blaming Rita for his non-attendance. How could Rita explain that she missed him as much as her grandmother did? Elvestree wasn't the same without him. It was far less magical and that year it didn't even snow.

Rita settled into sculpting, a solitary occupation that cut her off even more from life outside. At first Mrs Megalith helped out by ordering the odd piece and Hannah had made endless requests for birds, but the reality was that she could barely scrape by.

By the spring Mrs Megalith had lost patience with her granddaughter's foolishness and had withdrawn her patronage. Hannah had far too many sculptures of birds and nowhere to put them and the odd commission that had come from the library dwindled. Charming as her objects were, they didn't have much appeal for those who didn't know her. She was beginning to feel a dark sense of hopelessness. She had been imprudent to give up her job in the library, but since her fight with Max she had lost the confidence to continue her author events. Max had been the mastermind behind them and it was he who had put her in touch with all the authors. When she had approached publishers independently no one had been interested in her small library and some of them had been extremely rude. The change of occupation had been good, but it didn't bring in much money. Rita wondered whether Max missed her as much as she missed him, or whether he had cut her out of his life and moved on. Occasionally she read about him in the national press or heard about him from Ruth, who had taken to visiting with Mitzi.

Ruth's happiness was obvious. Her daughter was a constant source of delight to her, and her husband quite clearly loved her. They both exuded joy and serenity and Rita couldn't help but feel envious.

Max coped with his unhappiness very differently. He lost himself in the scented flesh of beautiful women. He took them home to his town house in Cheyne Walk, made love to them, looked for the unique and special in every one, but awoke in the morning repulsed and disillusioned because each was the same as the last: lovely to look at but hollow inside. There was nothing singular for him to fall in love with. He thought of Rita and despaired that he would never find someone with whom to share his life. He longed for children. He thought of Lydia who didn't even have the chance to live more than a couple of years. She had been less than mortal, a grain of dust in the wind that never found a place to settle, but he was determined to settle and sow and continue the cycle of life. In that way he would ensure his immortality and that of his entire family.

Secretly he fed upon the dream of buying back the Imperial Theatre, as if in some way he might recapture the world that was lost to him as a small boy. He fantasised about sitting in his father's private box with Rita while an actress of unparalleled loveliness retraced his mother's footsteps on the stage below. It was childish. Castles built in the air by the part of him that had never grown up. But he didn't travel to Vienna. He feared he wouldn't recognise it.

When Max met Delfine Bonville he saw a gentle character he thought he could grow fond of. She was an elegant French girl in her early twenties whose parents had settled in London just after the war. She worked at the French Embassy as a secretary, carrying home a bag of scrunched-up paper every day because she was embarrassed to fill the bin with all the typing errors she made. She was impressionable and naïve but charming. He liked the way she looked, with her dark chestnut eyes and short brown hair cut into a chic bob, because she didn't remind him of Rita. Petite and feminine she was like a little magpie, seizing with unrestrained fascination upon anything that shone. There was no doubt that she was awed by Max's celebrity and wealth but he was the first man she had taken to her bed who knew how to pleasure a woman. Most of the English lovers she had had considered sex a competition, like a game of tennis, the first to orgasm being the winner. Max was different, he was sensual and earthy and the longer he could make their lovemaking last the better. He would feast on her for hours and her Continental enthusiasm for sex made them both laugh.

He bought her jewellery, which she would take out every evening before she went to bed and play with like a child with a doll. She'd try on the rings and necklaces, striking different poses in the mirror, slipping in and out of the pretty dresses he bought her. Max found this childlike delight enchanting and took pleasure from her happiness. He spoiled her. Took her away for romantic weekends to Paris, Venice, even Morocco, and bought her everything she admired. He overwhelmed her with material things because he couldn't give her his love. Rita had always held his heart and always would. How he wished she had treated it with more care.

When Rita finally swallowed her pride and prepared to make the first move, her intentions were dashed when Mrs Megalith announced in her tactless way that Max had fallen in love. 'She's French,' she said admiringly. 'Very pretty and charming and Max says he's never been happier.' Rita was stunned by her own reaction. She was devastated. Max was now lost to her for ever because of her fruitless obsession with George.

Months slipped away and Rita only noticed the passing of time because of the changing seasons. She grew increasingly desperate. She couldn't face going back to the library. She couldn't bear to admit that she had failed. Besides, working at home now suited her. She could sculpt all day in her dressing gown if she so wished and she was grateful for the privacy of her house where no one could see her miserable decline. Then, one winter day, when she was at her lowest ebb, a stranger came calling.

Rita was in her kitchen spooning condensed milk out of a tin to make fudge for Maddie's children when there was a knock at the door. Tarka sprang up and barked excitedly. Rita was immediately irritated for she hadn't bothered to get dressed and was still in her dressing gown and slippers with her hair in tangles. She hoped it was someone she knew well enough not to mind. When she opened the door to find an elderly man standing bent in the doorway her face flushed crimson with shame. 'I'm so sorry to call unannounced,' he said in a deep, fruity voice. Rita pulled her dressing gown tightly around her and swept her hair off her shoulder with her hand.

'Not at all. What can I do for you?' she asked, noticing at once his smart suit, navy blue cashmere coat and felt hat.

'You are the talented sculptress from the library, are you not?' he asked with a small smile. Rita immediately straightened up and took more interest. 'My name is Benjamin Bradley,' he said, extending his hand.

'Rita Fairweather,' she replied, shaking it. 'Why don't you come in?' She closed the door behind him and led him into the kitchen. Tarka followed him curiously, wagging her tail. 'Can I get you something to drink?' She wished she had taken the time to tidy up, the room was as messy as the beach at low tide.

'A cup of tea would be very nice,' he replied, clearing a space for his briefcase on the table. Rita put on the kettle and tried to find a clean teacup and spoon.

'Please, do sit down. I'm afraid it's a little chaotic around here.'

'You're an artist. It's called creativity.'

'You're far too kind. I'm not even dressed.'

'That's the luxury of working at home. What are you cooking? It smells delicious.'

'Fudge for my nieces and nephew. It's always a favourite.'

'No children of your own?'

'I'm not married.'

'Not for want of offers, I'm sure.' He smiled at her warmly and Rita felt herself blushing again. He took off his coat and hat and sat down.

'Would you excuse me while I dress?' she said, leaving the kettle to boil on the stove. She returend a few moments later in a pair of trousers and sweater with her hair drawn into a ponytail. She noticed that Tarka was sitting down at Mr Bradley's feet, rubbing her face on his trousers.

'You've made a friend, I see,' she said with a smile. 'Tarka doesn't take to just anyone.'

'I'm flattered,' he replied, stroking her gentle yellow face.

Rita poured him a cup of tea and decanted the milk into a jug in an effort to appear more civilised. She sat down at the kitchen table and raised her eyebrows expectantly. 'You've seen my work?' she asked hopefully. He nodded, stirring sugar into his tea.

'Indeed I have and I'm very impressed. The heron in the library is a very good piece. A very good piece indeed.'

'Really?' she exclaimed incredulously, scrunching up her nose.

'I think you have great talent and potential.'

'It's a hobby really. I don't make much money out of it.'

'I think you should.' He took a sip of his tea. His white fluffy eyebrows met in the middle as he frowned with pleasure. 'Ah, this is just what the doctor ordered. How very nice.'

'I don't sculpt for money but because I love it,' she said, trying not to think of the bills that were piling up on her desk.

'Well, I've come to make you an offer. You see, Miss Fairweather, I own a small gift shop in London. I'm always on the lookout for fresh new talent. I want to commission you to produce a certain number of sculptures a year, if that sounds agreeable to you.'

Rita looked at him askance. 'This all seems too good to be true.'

'If it's too much, I understand,' he began.

'No, no. It's not too much. A commission like that would be a wonderful opportunity. How many pieces would you want?'

'Let's say we start off with five or six, see how they sell and then take it from there? I have a painter who produces about thirty to forty works a year. He sells very well. Very well indeed.'

Rita bit her bottom lip. 'How much would you pay me?' she asked, trying to sound as if she had some business experience.

'I'll pay a hundred pounds a piece initially then, depending on how they sell, I'll consider raising it.'

'A hundred pounds a piece?'

'Is that not enough?' he asked, suddenly embarrassed.

'That's more than enough.'

Mr Bradley smiled again. 'London prices are different from those in the countryside. People in London have more money and are willing to spend more. Your work is of the highest quality. If we price things too low customers will think they're not buying the best.'

Rita couldn't believe her luck. She gave Mr Bradley a few pieces that he admired in her studio and promised to send more within a month. He opened his heavy black briefcase and pulled out £300 in crisp twenty-pound notes. Rita had never seen so much money all in one go and held the bundle with reverence. That afternoon she went for a long walk up the beach, excited that she now had a purpose, something to wake up for, a goal. When she returned home she telephoned Maddie and told her the good news. Maddie was impressed. 'Better than rotting away in that dreary old library,' she said. 'Sculpting is much sexier. Now all you need is a lover and you'll be entirely satisfied.'

Rita ignored this and asked herself over for tea. 'I've made some fudge for the children,' she explained.

'Good,' Maddie replied, with a little smile. 'They've invited some friends over from school so they can all enjoy it. I've only got Marmite sandwiches and trifle.'

Rita hid the money beneath a loose floorboard in her bedroom then drove into town to buy more supplies. The woman in the craft shop was very surprised to see her looking so happy. 'I'm selling my work in a gift shop in London,' Rita told her with pride. 'They want up to forty pieces a year!'

'That'll keep you busy,' said the salesgirl, impressed. She couldn't wait to tell Faye Bolton of Rita's change of fortune.

In the afternoon Rita walked Tarka to Bray Cove. She took the path that wound its way along the coast, taking pleasure from the little bays and choppy sea. The air smelt of salt and ozone and the grey clouds were swept across the sky by a strong, icy wind. Rita walked with a spring in her step. Finally a ray of light had penetrated her dark soul.

When she arrived at her sister's house, the children were all outside in the garden, playing 'kick the can' with an empty baked bean tin. Elsbeth waved at her from 'prison' as Freddie stalked the lawn hunting for the others. She wore a tall witch's hat that she had made at school and an old black cape from the dressing-up box in the playroom. Maddie was in the kitchen, reading a magazine at the table with a cup of coffee and a biscuit.

'Doesn't Elsbeth remind you of Eddie?' Rita said, as she hung up her coat and wriggled her feet out of her boots.

'That's Eddie's cape she's wearing. She always wanted to be a witch,' Maddie replied with a chuckle.

'I thought I recognised it. Strange how history repeats itself, isn't it?'

Maddie nodded and raised her eyebrows. 'It certainly is. You should see Daisy and Charlie Bolton, they're just like you and George were. Can't separate them for anything in the world.'

Rita suddenly looked apprehensive. 'Is Charlie here?'

'Yes,' said Maddie, getting up to start preparing their tea. She noticed her sister's sudden wilting, and huffed impatiently. 'For goodness' sake, Rita, don't let Charlie rattle you. He doesn't look a bit like George. He's his mother's son entirely.'

'I'm not rattled,' said Rita, putting the kettle on the stove and taking a cup from the cupboard.

'Congratulations on your commissions. Just shows, I know nothing about art.'

'What do you mean?'

'I thought that heron was dreadful!'

'Did you?'

'I like the ones you do of children. They're charming in a rough kind of way. As I said, it just shows that I know nothing about art.'

'Well, Benjamin Bradley thinks he can sell up to forty a year,' said Rita, trying not to feel hurt.

'Good luck to him. He must know his market and if he doesn't, it doesn't matter. As long as he keeps paying you.' Rita changed the subject and asked her about the book Harry was working on. 'It's about unrequited love,' Maddie replied. 'You've been a perfect example, Rita. We should pay you a commission. Lucky you're going to be so rich now, you won't need one!'

Before Rita could retaliate, the back door opened and the

children hurried in from the cold, scrambling out of their coats and hats and leaving them in a heap on the floor. Elsbeth rushed over to Rita and hugged her. 'I'm a witch,' she said. 'Shame I'm not a real one or I'd turn Freddie into a toad. I've spent all afternoon in prison.'

'You shouldn't hide in such dumb places, then!' he retorted, striding past her to take his place at the table. 'Any chocolate cake, Mum?'

'Rita's made you some fudge,' she replied, placing the trifle in the middle of the table.

'Goodie!' he exclaimed eagerly. 'You can come again, Aunt Rita! Hey, Charlie, come and sit over here, I'm about to tuck into the trifle.' Charlie sauntered over and climbed onto the bench against the wall. Rita had seen him already in the village shop and once in church, but now she could get a better look. Maddie was right about his resemblance to his mother, but only marginally. The crooked way he smiled was very much his father's.

'Daisy, grab the cream for me, will you?' said Freddie, spooning a huge dollop of trifle onto his plate.

'What did your last slave die of?' she replied coolly, taking the place next to Charlie. 'Go and get it yourself.'

'Elsbeth!' he ordered.

His little sister sighed and opened the fridge. She pulled out the carton of cream, found half a gherkin in the vegetable drawer and dropped it in. With a completely straight face she handed it over and sat down next to Ava, who was chewing quietly on a piece of fudge at the head of the table. Daisy narrowed her eyes. She could always tell when her sister was up to something. Elsbeth pulled an innocent expression and took a sip of her milk, leaving a thick white line on her upper lip. Freddie didn't even say thank you and was talking so much to Charlie that he didn't notice the piece of gherkin fall into his trifle. Daisy did and she stifled a giggle. She nudged Charlie under the table with her leg. He turned to her and frowned. She indicated her brother's plate with her eyes. It wasn't long before Freddie had taken a large mouthful. When he bit on the gherkin he let out a loud yelp, spitting all the fruit, sponge and cream onto the immaculate table cloth. Maddie just rolled her eyes and shook her head.

'If Frognal Point doesn't send me mad, my children will,' she said with a wry smile.

Rita watched Ava. She was quiet and shy, with sensitive grey eyes like her father and long white hair like her mother. Rita wondered what *her* children might have looked like had *she* married George. While she was dreaming she noticed a pendant hanging around the child's neck. When she looked closer she saw, to her amazement, that it looked like the very same dove that she had thrown into the sea. Unable to contain her curiosity she approached the table.

'What a lovely pendant you have, Ava. Where did you get it from?'

Ava touched the little dove with thin white fingers. 'Mama gave it to me,' she replied. 'Papa found it in a cave on the beach.'

Rita felt as if she had been winded by an unexpected punch to the stomach. 'It's lovely,' she said in a thin voice.

'Thank you. Luckily for me, Mama said that she didn't want it.'

Rita felt the anger rise in her chest as she thought how close Susan had come to wearing it. She wondered why George hadn't kept it for himself. It seemed so careless to have given it away. Once it had been very special to both of them. She tried to ask Ava a few more questions about her parents but the child answered in monosyllables, so Rita had to give up and retreat to the other side of the kitchen where Maddie was flicking through her magazine again. She suddenly felt uncomfortable, as if she didn't belong there. A small, sticky hand slipped into hers. She looked down to see Elsbeth the witch gazing up at her fondly.

'Aunt Rita, will you play with me?' she asked.

Rita's heart softened. 'I'd love to. Why don't we go outside and sit on the rocks in the dark? I'll tell you about witches. Real witches like your great-grandmother,' she said, leading the child to the door.

Maddie didn't even look up from her magazine and the other children were too busy feasting on fudge and trifle to notice that Aunt Rita was about to weave her much-loved stories under the bright crescent moon.

Having given up on Rita and determined not to live on the residue of broken dreams, Max asked Delfine to marry him. She was too young and blinded by the brilliance of her jewellery to notice that he didn't love her. She accepted his proposal and moved into his house.

'Everything that I own will be yours,' he told her. 'But there is one room in the house that belongs only to me. It is my private room and I always keep it locked. I don't want to share that room with anyone, and I trust you to respect that and not to try to go in there. Every other room in the house is yours.'

Delfine reassured him that she would never betray him. She was too happy to care about a secret room locked with a mystery key. She was going to be Mrs Max de Guinzberg and that was all that mattered.

When Rita heard the news from her grandmother, she was broken-hearted. He hadn't even bothered to tell her himself. She obviously meant nothing to him any more. She felt betrayed. She walked along the cliff top with Tarka, recalling the time she had nearly thrown herself over the edge for George. It seemed like an age ago, another era, when she had been a very different girl. Suddenly she realised that everyone else's life was continually moving, like a river, on and on and on. Her life, however, was a stagnant pond where nothing could grow. She was tired of it.

Chapter Thirty-four

It had been almost three years since Trees' death, and Faye had had enough of mourning. Secret visits to Thadeus's house were simply no longer enough. George was busy with the farm and his children, Alice had her own life. What of her? She sculpted in her studio and enjoyed her grandchildren, but she felt incomplete now she had no one to look after. She longed to take care of Thadeus. He was old and needed her. She wanted to cook for him, wash and iron his clothes, keep him company during the long winter evenings by the fire in his sitting room, discussing books they had read and music they loved. She dreamed of playing the piano, accompanying him as he played the violin, sharing those melancholy moments when his memories turned his heart to liquid. She loved him. It wasn't enough to see him only occasionally.

Faye was now in her late sixties and no longer cared what other people thought of her. Hannah could disapprove, Miss Hogmier could gossip to Reverend Hammond and his wife if it gave her pleasure, the church could vibrate with the shattering news of her love affair, it no longer mattered. *Freedom is when you no longer care what people think of you,* she thought to herself as she packed her bags, *I'm going to live for me.* That evening when George popped in for tea after a busy day on the farm, Faye's bags were piled up in the hall.

'Where are you going?' he asked her as she took his crumpets out of the Aga.

'I'm going to live with Thadeus Walizhewski,' she stated casually.

George sat down and rubbed his chin. 'What about the house?' he asked, for he couldn't think what else to say.

'It's yours, darling. Trees left everything to you.'

'Why doesn't Thadeus come and live here?'

Faye put the crumpets on the table and pulled out a chair. 'Because this was your father's house. I have too many memories of him ever to be happy here with another man.'

'Have you told Alice?'

'No. Only you.'

'Everyone will ask questions. You're ready for that, are you?' He thought of Susan and the hostility she still faced for being an outsider. He didn't wish the same fate for his mother.

'As ready as I'll ever be. I loved your father and I mourned for him as a widow should. But it's been three years now. Three Christmases without him. I don't want to waste more time. Life is short and I don't have years ahead of me. I want to spend the rest of my life with the man who loves me. I can't live without love, George.'

'No one should live without love,' he agreed solemnly, thinking of Rita.

'You know, Max asked her to marry him,' she said, reading his thoughts.

'Max asked Rita to marry him?' His possessiveness stunned him. 'She didn't say 'yes', did she?' He hastily corrected himself. 'I mean, I'd never put those two together.'

'She refused him,' his mother replied, watching the jealousy tinge his cheeks red. George bit the skin around his thumbnail, ashamed of his profound sense of relief.

'Have you seen her, George?'

'Only from a distance.' He lowered his eyes and buttered a crumpet.

'I see.' She watched him eat for a moment in silence then she added, 'Funny how one can live only a few miles away from someone and never see them.'

As much as George had tried to put Rita behind him he was unable to stifle the yearning that was slowly choking him. As long as he lived in Frognal Point, amidst all the memories of their growing up together, he would never be free of her. Her ghostly figure would continue to haunt him on the rocks, in the cave and on the beach. He would look out for her on the cliff tops, afraid yet longing for her at the same time. She was as much part of the place as the birds that flew there – and so was he. He couldn't bear it any more. Dizzy with excitement he didn't consider his wife; all he could think of was Rita. He had to talk to her.

With his heart in his mouth he drove up the coast. The roads were strewn with autumn leaves that danced about in his wake, the sunlight catching their golden edges and causing them to sparkle. He rolled down the window and enjoyed the cold wind on his face. He was nervous. His stomach was tight. He felt as if he were in the cockpit of his Spitfire, looking out for German bombers. The prospect of seeing Rita again was almost as frightening. When he arrived at her cottage he sat in the car a little way from the entrance, wondering what he was going to say, anticipating her reaction.

He bit the skin around his thumbnail, which was now raw and bleeding. His hands were rough from farming. Not the hands of the pilot he had once been. He caught himself in the mirror and noticed suddenly the lines around his eyes, the broader face, the tougher, redder skin, the thinning hair. He wasn't the man Rita had fallen in love with all those years ago and she probably wouldn't be the girl, either. He braced himself and climbed out of the car, leaving it parked in the lane. He felt as guilty as if he had already been unfaithful.

He walked up the short driveway, beneath tall chestnut trees that shed their conkers onto the ground to rot with the leaves and fallen twigs, and approached the cottage. He was aware, as he stood in the doorway, that the next few moments could either stamp a seal on the past or rip it open again, leaving him more disoriented than before. It was a gamble. He hoped to find a paper tiger in Rita. Taking a deep breath and pulling back his shoulders he rang the bell. There was no sound from within, only the desperate beating of his own heart. He rang it again. Remembering she had a dog, he listened for a bark or the patter of paws. Nothing. Nothing at all. His nervousness turned to frustration. She wasn't here. He doubted he'd have the courage to come again, and fought his disappointment. After hovering a while in the doorway he reluctantly decided to leave.

He was about to walk out of the driveway when curiosity motivated him to turn back and take a quick look around her property. What sort of woman was she now? After all, a place reflects the person who lives in it, he thought, as he walked back towards the little gate in the hedge that led into the garden. He was surprised at the size of the garden; it was much bigger than he had expected because the cottage was small. The lawn sloped down to the beach and the sea swelled below the wheeling gulls. He put his hands in his pockets and swept his eyes across the bay where the waves gently rose and fell in the soft autumn light. Following his instincts he wandered down the well-trodden path to the beach. The sand was damp for the tide was slowly edging its way out, leaving small crabs and crustaceans exposed to the birds. A salty breeze ran through his hair like the familiar caress of a lover's hand and his head felt light with nostalgia. He thought of Rita. He thought of Jamie Cordell, Rat Bridges and Lorrie Hampton, and their faces merged with hers as pictures arose in his mind from the misty corners of his past. To the hypnotic music of the surf he spread out his arms like a mighty eagle and ran up the beach. The farther he ran the higher his spirits soared until he laughed out loud at the absurdity of it. But suddenly, in that brief moment of ecstasy, he rediscovered the boy who had grown up in Frognal Point. He found him deep inside himself, in his carefree, laughing spirit, and he searched the cove for the girl who had lived there with him.

He strode back up the path into the garden. He could smell Rita in the flowers that grew there and in the grass that now glistened with dew. He would wait for her to return and then he would tell her that he still loved her and that he should never have let her go.

To the left there was an old, crumbling wall. The rickety gate was open. He sauntered over, taking pleasure from this wild house that seemed to reflect Rita's nature to perfection, and peered through it. There, lying on the grass beside a sleeping dog, was Rita. She was some distance away and could not see him, for she was partially obscured behind the netting that had protected the raspberry bushes from birds in the summer. Her hands were outstretched and she was taming titmice with pieces of walnut. She lay quite still as the dainty little birds hopped about her hands, debating whether or not to trust her. The dog looked old, her face grey around the mouth and eyes, and did not sense his presence at the gate. George shrank back in horror, suddenly afraid that she might see him.

He breathed as quietly as he could, regained his composure, then peered around the wall like a spy. Rita looked beautiful in the burnt light, her face pale and serious with concentration. She was exactly as he remembered her. She didn't look a day older. Her hair was still long and unkempt, her body fulsome, her clothes carelessly chosen. Even when she had tried to dress well she had looked scruffy. He tilted his head to one side, forgot his nerves and enjoyed the tranquil scene as his spirit remembered and filled his heart with love.

A light breeze rustled through the desiccated raspberry bushes, sweeping away her hair and exposing the side of her face. The face he had so often brushed with kisses and stroked with tender fingers. Where he had tasted the salt of the sea and the bitterness of her tears. How many times had he held that body in his arms? He could feel her now as if it had been only yesterday. The warmth of her flesh, the solid confidence of her affection, the unbound enthusiasm of her youth. He had thrown it all away. It was then that he noticed a small twinkle of light as she altered the angle of her hand. He recognised the little solitaire ring immediately and felt a flutter of pride tickle his stomach. She had kept the ring he gave her. Suddenly the promises they had made to each other the day of his parting came back in words that echoed across the years in ghostly whispers. *'Every time you look at it I want you to remember how much I love you.'*

'And I want you to remember, every time you look up at that moon, that I love you too.'

Now the titmice began to eat from her fingers. He shrank back against the wall as if he had been scalded. He had made vows before God to love Susan for ever. If he gave into his desire now he would surely lose everything. His heartbeat accelerated and thumped against his ribcage. Choked with regret, his head buzzing with confusion, he staggered across the lawn, desperate to get away before she noticed him. He couldn't possibly see her now; he didn't trust himself. How was it possible to love two women? The thought of losing Susan filled him with complete desolation. The thought of coming face to face with Rita filled him with terror.

He hurried to the road and climbed into his car. As he turned on the ignition he saw in the rear mirror the yellow retriever running out of the driveway. He sped away without another backward glance.

Rita called for Tarka. 'You silly dog!' she exclaimed as she came trotting back into the garden. 'What did you see out there?' She patted the furry coat and shook her head. 'You're getting on, old girl. Chasing ghosts!'

She was pleased the titmice were now eating from her hands. She had learned how to tame them from her mother. Maddie used to paint such pretty birds, she thought to herself, such a shame that she had retreated once again into magazines and movies. As she wandered into the house she had no idea that George had only been a few yards away, watching her, or how close she had been to realising years of futile dreams.

As George drove back to Lower Farm he realised that he could never see Rita again. As his mother had said, it is possible to live close to someone and never see them. Perhaps he would live out the rest of his days in Frognal Point and never come across her. For Susan's sake and for the sake of their marriage, Rita must simply cease to be a reality.

Susan prepared supper. She was now getting used to living at Lower Farm. Faye had taken all her books and manuscripts, odd photograph frames and trinkets, but it was still full of their family things. Susan planned to redecorate. Faye's taste was eccentric at best, shocking at worst. A blind person could have chosen better. She was grateful for the excuse for she wanted to make it into *their* home. At the moment she still felt like a guest, embarrassed to move anything for fear of offending her mother-in-law. George loved it just the way it was, for it reminded him of his childhood, but he understood her need to feel that she belonged. She looked at her watch and wondered when he'd be finishing for the day.

She was distracted by the sound of a car. She looked anxiously out of the window to see George pull up and turn off the ignition. As he climbed out she noticed that he looked different. His cheeks were flushed and his hair ruffled. He seemed younger, like the boy she had met on the deck of the *Fortuna* all those years ago. She wondered where he had been. And with whom.

He walked through the door to see her standing in the kitchen, leaning against the sideboard. In that moment, she appeared older. Her face was gaunt and lines had formed around the corners of her mouth, dragging it down. How strange that he hadn't noticed before. They stared at one another warily. Neither spoke. The aroma of her cooking filled the room. Susan had never been a very good cook. In Argentina they had had the fortune to have Marcela. In Argentina they had had the fortune to be happy.

Susan studied her husband's face with cold, unfriendly eyes. 'Are you having an affair, George?'

Her question was as unexpected as it was aggressive. George was stunned. His eyes widened and their boyish expression disappeared to allow the man to reassert himself.

'No,' he replied firmly.

'Where have you been?'

'On the beach.'

'Alone?'

'You don't ever want to come with me.'

'Because you never ask me.' She felt her chest tighten with anguish as she realised that he had drifted away from her, and that she had allowed him to.

'Then I'm asking you now,' he smiled at her hopefully and the skin creased around his eyes. 'Will you come down and watch the sunset with me?'

She fought hard against tears. She had always detested self-pity and weakness, in herself as much as in others. She turned to take the supper out of the oven, lest it burn while they were away, and said, 'I'd like that.'

After that, they never spoke of Rita again. Her ghost slowly faded from their marriage, relegated to the cave, the beach and the windy cliff tops where it remained as whispers in the rise and fall of the tides. George felt her presence there when he took solitary walks but he did not let it interfere with his life and certainly did not allow his occasional yearning to show. He had made his decision.

'Do you suppose, Reverend, that Faye was seeing Thadeus Walizhewski during her marriage to Trees?' asked Miss Hogmier, leaning eagerly across the counter so that the poor Reverend could smell the stale odour that surrounded her. She spoke in a loud hiss even though the shop was empty.

'That is not for us to judge, Miss Hogmier,' replied the Reverend reproachfully. 'Her husband is with God now. It is right that she should love again.'

Miss Hogmier's eyes narrowed and she grinned as far as her bitter little mouth allowed. 'I've heard, although I won't mention any names, that she was with him the night Trees died.'

'Yes, she was delivering a sculpture.'

'So she says.' She stood up and crossed her arms. 'If you ask me, and I'm not one to gossip, live and let live is my motto, she's been itching to move in with Thadeus ever since she buried her husband. She thinks no one will be any the wiser. But she doesn't fool me.'

'She keeps herself to herself,' said the Reverend, tapping his goods with his fingers, hoping she'd notice and start adding up the shopping.

She nodded slowly. 'Dark horse more like,' she retorted with a sniff. 'What are the young supposed to think? It's our job to set a good example. Not surprising that George married an American, his mother's run off with a Pole!'

'We are all God's children,' said the Reverend irritably. He was beginning to lose patience with the woman. 'Have you put all this on my account?'

'In a hurry are you? Well, no one has time to talk to an

old spinster like me these days. Rushing around, too busy to stop for a nice chat. Not that I'm complaining. I'm a humble woman. Live your life with humility, as my mother used to say to me. I don't expect much. Just a little kindness. People can be so unpleasant these days, can't they?' She opened the red account book with arthritic fingers and wrote in small, squiggly writing.

Reverend Hammond was left uneasy. If Faye had indeed committed adultery it was a grave and dreadful sin. He decided to pay her a visit. The way to heaven was through repentance. It was his duty to see that she got there.

Chapter Thirty-five

Two years went by and Max was still finding an excuse to avoid setting a date for the wedding. At first Delfine didn't complain. She brandished a large engagement ring with three dazzling diamonds and set about redecorating the house at great expense. She made no attempt to open the door to her husband's secret room. She was too busy shopping, lunching with friends, joining the committees of high-profile charities and accompanying him on business trips when the destinations were glamorous enough. She relished being the future Mrs Max de Guinzberg and posed shamelessly for photographers at parties and was only too happy to give quotes to the press. Max derived pleasure from her enjoyment and lavished her with more gifts. He laughed when Mrs Megalith dismissed her as little more than an ornamental poodle, but he grew intensely serious when she spoke about Rita.

'Her work is selling very well in London,' she informed him on the telephone. 'It's given her a sense of independence and achievement. Why don't you get rid of that simpering fool and propose to Rita again?'

'She doesn't want me, Primrose. She said so herself, she'll love George until she dies.'

Mrs Megalith clicked her tongue loudly. 'Women are often conquered with persistence, dear boy. What are you doing with that ghastly poodle?'

'I'm very fond of Delfine. She makes me happy,' he said lightly.

'She's a spoilt child. Wait until she's a spoilt woman and then she won't make you so happy.'

'Don't be so cynical. She's charming, everyone loves her.'

'Except you,' she stated flatly.

'How's Ruth?' he asked, changing the subject. Didn't she realise how much it hurt to talk about Rita?

'Her pregnancy is beginning to show now. She wears it well.'

'That's good!' he exclaimed, dwelling for a moment on his own deep-rooted yearning to create new life for the sake of his family who had lost theirs. He never confided in Delfine the haunting dreams he had about the baby sister who had never lived to grow up. Only Rita knew the remote corners of his heart and the shadows that dwelt there.

'Thanks to you she's happy and living well. You're a very generous boy.'

Max chuckled. 'Money means little to me, Primrose, you know that. I'm in a position to help. I do what I can.'

Mrs Megalith knew he would have liked to do the same for Rita. 'If Rita married you, she wouldn't have to work so hard,' she said, continuing her thoughts out loud.

'That was her choice, not mine.'

'Fools, the both of you. Really, you do make life very hard for yourselves. Still, thank God for Mr Bradley. Long may he live!'

When Max put down the telephone he felt depressed. It was usually such a pleasure talking to Primrose. He knew that she was wrong about Rita. As long as George was alive she would never have room in her heart to love *him*. Besides, he didn't want the role of understudy to George Bolton. When his secretary tried to put through a call he snapped at her for no reason. He'd bring her a bunch of flowers at lunch time to apologise.

To Max's intense irritation Mrs Megalith seemed to be

right as usual. As Delfine grew up she became less charming. All the things that Max had liked about her were discarded like clothes she'd grown out of. Little by little she failed to be impressed by his gifts, the hotels they stayed in weren't luxurious enough, the parties she went to bored her, and the charities that had launched her into society were time-consuming and dull. Having been like an adoring puppy, happy with the odd pat or smile, Delfine became demanding of his attention and bitter when she didn't get it, pressing him all the time to confirm a date for the wedding.

Delfine realised that there was an invisible presence that stood between her and her fiancé. She refused to go and stay at Elvestree because, not only did she get the impression that Mrs Megalith didn't like her, but she sensed there, more intensely than ever, that invisible but inescapable presence. Max never told her he loved her. He told her he was fond of her, that he adored her, that she made him happy, but he never used the word 'love'. She hadn't noticed at first. His gifts had been so generous. She had never expected a man like Max to want her. She was flattered by the simplest of smiles, the smallest of gestures. Now they had been living together for over two years, she had grown accustomed to his wealth and his celebrity. She wanted the man, but she couldn't have him. Someone stood in her way and she was sure that the secret was hidden behind the locked door to the only room in the house that didn't belong to her.

Then one bleak winter day Ruth telephoned Max, her voice heavy with sorrow, 'Primrose is dying and she wants to see you.' Max left a message for Delfine with the housekeeper and drove as fast as he could to Devon. When he arrived at Elvestree the house looked naked and cold as if some of the magic were also dying. Choked with misery, he hurried inside to find his sister waiting for him in the hall. 'Thank God you've come. She's barely holding on,' Ruth groaned, sinking into his arms. He kissed her affectionately, then bounded up the stairs two at a time. He walked to the end of the corridor where the door to her room was open and expectant. Ruth followed, biting her fingernails and fighting her tears. To Max's horror the room was filled with cats. They lay on every surface, watching the bed with eyes wide and knowing. Mrs Megalith was sitting up, propped against large white pillows. Her face was as grey as the sky outside and her eyes glistened with rare emotion.

'Come to me, Max,' she said, putting out a feeble arm. She wore a purple dressing gown but her hands were free of rings. Only the moonstone hung against her bosom as it had always done. 'Ruth, I want to speak to you too,' she added weakly. Max sat on the edge of the bed and sandwiched her hand between his. Ruth went around to the other side and had to push off a couple of cats in order to make a space for herself. 'My time is up. Denzil and Trees are waiting for me in the world of spirit with a bottle of the best Dom Perignon, bless them. I bet it tastes even better in spirit.' She managed a chuckle but then coughed and wheezed with difficulty. 'You are my children,' she continued seriously. 'I love you both more than I love either of my own daughters and I'm not a bit ashamed of it! When you two little refugees arrived in my house, forlorn and fearful, I think I loved you instantly. My Max,' she said with a long sigh, removing her hand from his and running her fingers down his face. 'You're a good boy. Don't give up on Rita, she needs you. Foolish girl, she has a funny way of showing it, though, doesn't she?'

'I'll look after her, I promise,' he replied, turning to kiss her hand.

'I know you will. That is why I've left the house to you. Time will reveal that I'm not as batty as you all think. I have a reason for every one of my actions.'

She turned to Ruth. 'Max will make sure that you have

everything you need. You're a good little mother, Ruth. That baby will be big and bonny and blessed with great charm. I leave to you this little fellow,' she said, touching her moonstone pendant. 'Barely taken it off in all the years I've had it. God knows what you're going to do with all these cats! Will you make sure that Eddie and Elsbeth share my box of goodies?' By that she meant her tarot cards, crystals and other mystical objects. 'I've written it all down in that letter over there on my bedside table.'

She turned to Max again and her voice became brisk and businesslike. 'Now, I don't want a funeral. God forbid the pompous old Reverend having the last word! I want to be cremated and scattered in the garden. This body has served me well. I want it treated with respect. No tears and all that mawkishness. I shan't be gone, just out of sight, though Eddie and Elsbeth will see me, they have inherited my gift. Damn lucky Antoinette didn't, wouldn't be so much fun haunting her if she knew the truth about spirits.' She suddenly raised her eyes and shook her head impatiently. 'Not yet, Denzil, I've got one more thing to say.' She took both their hands in hers and said with deliberation. 'All was not lost . . .'

But before she could finish her sentence her spirit was dragged from its body. She fought it, determined to have her say, but death could not wait. She managed to utter one final sentence. 'A stranger will come to you for help . . .' Then she departed with her habitual snort of irritation.

'She's gone,' said Ruth, leaning over to close her eyes.

'What do you think she meant?' Max asked, pressing his lips against her hand.

'I don't know.' Ruth wiped her tears on her sleeve. 'The world suddenly feels very empty, doesn't it?'

Max nodded gravely. 'I can't believe she was human after all.'

'What are we going to do with all these cats?'

Max scratched his head. 'That's not a priority. First, we must tell Hannah and Antoinette, Maddie . . .'

'And Rita?'

'And Rita.'

Ruth looked at him with sympathy. His face suddenly looked so desolate. 'Go and see her, Max. So much water has gone under the bridge since that Christmas. Life is too short.'

When Max parked the car outside Rita's cottage he was heartened to see smoke rising from the chimney, signalling that she was at home. He looked about at the frozen trees, gnarled and twisted by the wind, then at the white sun that shone weakly down from a pale, watery sky. He felt a gentle thawing in his heart, inspired by memories of the countless times he had drawn up outside her front door. He imagined the warmth of her kitchen, the smell of coffee, the familiar chaos, and he smiled inside. Outside, however, his mouth twitched nervously.

He climbed out and slammed the door. He heard Tarka barking in the hall, then footsteps as Rita came to open the front door. When she saw his grim face she blushed in surprise, not knowing how to react. She had been so furious that he hadn't spoken to her since that day on the estuary, not even to tell her of his engagement, but his sad eyes and hunched shoulders caused her heart to stumble and she shook her head in resignation.

'I've missed you,' he ventured, putting his hands in the pockets of his coat. He lowered his eyes in shame. 'I'm sorry. I've been a rotten friend.'

'I've missed you too,' she replied softly. 'Although you made me angrier than I've ever been in my entire life.'

They stared at each other for a long moment. The muscle in his jaw began to throb, anticipating her fury, but her mouth extended into a shy grin and she began to laugh. Max's relief was overwhelming.

'We've been friends for too long to let a proposal of marriage come between us,' he said, walking up to her and drawing her into his arms. She still smelt of violets.

'What fools we've been!' she sighed, winding her arms around him and resting her head on his shoulder. She savoured the feel of his embrace, like the familiar sense of home, and wished she could remain there a little longer. 'I'm glad you've come back.' She withdrew and studied his face, bleak in spite of his smile. She frowned. 'What is it, Max?' She stood aside as he walked past her into the hall where Tarka sniffed his trousers excitedly.

'I'm afraid I've come with some very sad news,' he said. 'Your grandmother died this morning.'

There was a long pause while she digested his words. Her sadness was tempered by gratitude, for it was obvious that her death had inspired their reconciliation.

'I was very fond of the old witch. She was good to me,' she said. 'Let's go and put the kettle on.'

He followed her into the kitchen, where they had so often sat and shared secrets. It smelt so much the same – of fudge, baking bread and coffee – that Max felt the years melting away like the frosted trees outside in the sunshine. He took off his coat and sat in his usual place at the kitchen table just like old times. For a while neither spoke. He watched her as she boiled the kettle, took the mugs down from the cupboard and searched around for clean teaspoons. She hadn't changed in all the years that he had known her, rather like her grandmother. Her skin was still as pale and speckled as the egg of a thrush, her hair was still wild and knotted; only her eyes had lost their innocence and were now cast in shadow. She might as well be a child of the sea, he thought wistfully, and he was suddenly gripped with longing to hold her.

She turned and caught him gazing at her. She smiled shyly

and brought over the tea. 'Were you with her when she died?' she asked, pulling out a chair and sitting down.

'Yes, Ruth and I,' he replied. The desolation he suffered at the loss of her grandmother seemed to pull down his whole face. Rita was filled with compassion and extended her hand to touch his.

'I'm so sorry, Max. I know she was a mother to you.'

'She was old. She'd had a good life. But I'll miss her.' His eyes shone as he smelt the familiar scent of mothballs and cinnamon as if she were in the room with them. 'She was the only link Ruth and I had with the past. Now she's gone, I feel as if a little of me has gone with her. But I mustn't keep looking back. Yesterday is only memories, after all. Today is real and each moment is precious. It was just so unexpected. I never thought she'd die.'

'Her life is to be celebrated, not mourned.'

'You're right. She wouldn't want us all to mope around feeling sorry for ourselves.'

'I can't imagine she went quietly?'

'She said Denzil was there waiting for her but she was determined to have her say before she went. I think he had to drag her off.'

'That sounds like Megagran.' She laughed affectionately. 'I hope she forgave me before she left. We didn't really get on in the last few years.'

'She told me you're selling your work in London now,' he said, changing the subject.

'Yes, this wonderful old man called Mr Bradley buys about thirty sculptures a year to sell in his shop. I can barely keep up with his orders. I can't imagine who buys them.'

'You're very talented. Don't put yourself down.'

'At least it pays the bills. I never thought I'd make it. Thought I'd have to go back to the library.'

'I'd hate to think of you still toiling away in that stuffy old place. I'm glad you're creating. It's good for the soul.' He cocked his head and swept his eyes over her face with an intensity that made her stomach swim. 'You look well. You look happy.'

'I am well and I am happy,' she said with emphasis. 'Now you're here.' It was his turn to blush. 'I was lonely without you. The old cliché is true: you don't appreciate people until they're gone.'

'I won't leave you again, I promise.'

'What are you going to do now? I'm pleased that Megagran has left Elvestree to you. You love it more than anyone else. I love it too, but now we're friends again I can come and visit as often as I like.'

'I don't know. I have to sort things out with Delfine. She hates it here.' The name Delfine grated and Rita felt herself bristle like an animal suffering a threat to her territory. She had completely forgotten about his fiancée. She withdrew her hand. 'One thing is for certain, I'll spend far more time down here. Elvestree is a house that needs to be lived in. Who's going to feed all those cats for a start?'

Rita recovered her composure, grateful that Delfine would never belong in her grandmother's house, and screwed up her nose. 'Let's pretend Megagran left them all to Antoinette!' she said with a mischievous smile.

When Max returned to Elvestree all the cats had gone. Ruth had been busy telephoning and organising the cremation. Mrs Megalith's body had been taken away and the house suddenly felt empty as if its spirit had gone too. Ruth was as bewildered as Max. 'Where could they all have gone?' she exclaimed, raising her hands to the sky.

Not far away in the rectory the telephone rang. Reverend Hammond picked it up to hear Miss Hogmier's screeching voice. 'Calm down, Miss Hogmier, I can't understand a word you're saying.'

'They're everywhere! Everywhere! Making a mess of my shop!' she wailed.

'Who are? Shall I call the police?' he replied in alarm.

'Cats. The witch's cats.'

'Mrs Megalith's cats? Are you sure?'

'You have to come down with a shotgun. They're destroying my business as well as my sanity. I, who have no husband to protect me. I'm alone in the world. No one cares for an old spinster like me.' Her voice resonated with a heavy vibrato.

'I'll be over at once, after I've called the RSPCA.'

'Don't be a bloody fool, Elwyn, shoot the buggers!'

But when he looked out of his own window, he was shocked to see at least twenty cats playing among the borders of his own garden and rolling around on the grass. He rubbed his chin thoughtfully. Mrs Megalith must have finally passed away.

Delfine was not happy that Max had gone to Devon without her. Although she hated the place she didn't trust him there on his own. She paced the drawing room deliberating what to do. She thought of the invisible presence and the locked door and knew that all the answers lay behind it. Resentful that he didn't trust her with his innermost secrets, she set about searching for the key. She would take a quick look and he would be none the wiser. As she was rummaging through the drawers in his study the doorbell rang. The housekeeper had left for the day due to a bad cold so she had to answer it herself. She huffed with frustration and strode across the hall, her high heels clicking briskly on the marble chessboard floor.

'Yes?' she enquired impatiently when she saw an old man in a three-piece suit standing on the steps in the cold. He was tall even with his shoulders bent. In his hands he held a large package.

'My name is Benjamin Bradley. Are you the lady of the house?'

'Yes. Is that for me?' she enquired crisply.

'It's for Mr de Guinzberg.'

'What is it?'

Mr Bradley masked his hesitation behind a kindly smile. 'Is Mr de Guinzberg at home?'

'No.' Her voice betrayed her annoyance.

'Then I'll come back another time.'

Delfine narrowed her eyes suspiciously. 'There's no need, I'll make sure he gets it,' she said, taking the package from him.

Mr Bradley frowned, but there was nothing he could do. He watched helplessly as she closed the door in his face, then turned and walked down the steps to the pavement. He knew he had made an error. He usually gave his packages to the housekeeper. He hoped Mr de Guinzberg wouldn't chastise him for it. He paid him well and he certainly needed the money. Who else would employ a retired butler of his age?

Delfine tore open the package to find a sculpture of a sleeping child. It was rough but charming. She ran her hands over the gentle curve of its body as it slept like a cat, with its little fingers holding a cloth of some sort. Her fury dissolved into compassion. There was something about the piece that made her eyes fill with tears; it was so innocent, so vulnerable and so beyond her reach. She suddenly felt guilty. Perhaps Max had bought it for her as a surprise. Hastily she did her best to wrap it up again.

She placed it on the table in the hall and resumed her search for the key. When she couldn't find it she decided to try her hand at picking the lock. She used various implements without success. Her curiosity mounted with her frustration. She'd get into that room if it was the last thing she did. Finally, to her delight, the lock turned. She stood up and hesitated, her hand on the knob, ready to turn it. Suddenly, now that she was able to get in, she wondered what horror lay inside. What if he was a murderer and stored the bodies of his victims there? What if he found out? Would he kill her too? Shaking but determined, she opened it a crack and peered inside. The room was darkened by shutters. She felt for the light switch and turned it on. What she saw within made her jaw fall open in a silent gasp. Shelf upon shelf of sculptures. They ranged from rather crude to quite impressive and they were all obviously by the same sculptor who had fashioned the sleeping child.

The room was dusty and neglected, but Delfine could smell the scent of love as a sommelier identifies the very best of wines. She swept her eyes over each piece. There were many birds. Birds in flight, with their wings outstretched, birds on the ground, pecking at sand. She was astute enough to work out at they were all coastal scenes, for there were seagulls and fish and children with small nets. She suspected the sculptor came from Devon. She recognised the female touch and she knew, beyond any shadow of doubt, that the sculptress was the invisible presence in their life, the presence that was constantly between them. Why he collected her sculptures, she didn't know. The room behind the locked door answered many questions yet raised many new ones.

When Max returned a few days later he found the package in the hall and the door to his secret room locked as before, but Delfine was sitting on the stairs waiting for him. He could tell by the look on her face that she was weary with anger. His eyes darted to the package where he noticed the evidence of her tampering.

'You've been into my room, haven't you?' he said quietly, putting down his bag and taking off his coat.

'Who is she?' she demanded, standing up. 'Don't lie to me Max. The woman who sculpts those dreadful pieces is the woman who you love. You always have. Why are you with me if you don't love me? They're not even very good, you know. In fact, they're appalling!' She stood up and slapped him hard across the face. He recoiled, but when he looked back at her, his eyes misted with sorrow. 'I despise you for taking advantage of me,' she continued, her voice rising into a scream. 'Who is she? I demand to know. It is my right to know.' When she was angry her French accent was exaggerated. Max sighed in resignation and pulled a key ring out of his breast pocket. He walked down the hall and opened the door to his secret room. She followed him inside.

'I'm not going to lie to you, Delfine,' he said quietly, switching on the light. 'She is called Rita and I grew up with her in Frognal Point. She is the granddaughter of Mrs Megalith, the woman who adopted me when I fled Austria at the beginning of the war. I love her. I always have, but she doesn't love me.'

'So you buy all her sculptures. That's pathetic!' she snapped scornfully.

'I buy her sculptures because she was in financial trouble. I knew she wouldn't accept my money so I sent a man down to pose as the proprietor of a gift shop interested in her work. It is my way of supporting her.'

'You expect me to believe you?'

'I have no reason to lie.'

'How long have you been buying these pitiful things?'

'About three years, I think. I've lost count. It doesn't matter. I will buy them all until I have no more room to store them.'

'I've suspected you loved another woman for ages. Tell me, why are you with me?'

'Because I'm fond of you. You make me laugh. I enjoy you. Weren't we happy in the beginning?'

'It is all ruined now. You never loved me. If we were happy

at the beginning I wouldn't remember now because you've tainted my memory.' She began to cry. 'I'm leaving.'

'Delfine!'

'No, you listen to me for a change. I want a man who loves me. I've never been second best to anybody and I'm not going to start now.'

Max watched her pack up her belongings and climb into a taxi. His overwhelming emotion was one of relief.

So Max returned to Elvestree. He moved into Mrs Megalith's magical house, wondering whether it would ever be the same now that she was gone. He knew a happy relationship and the laughter of children would put back the magic, but he was denied both, in spite of all his efforts. He thought of Lydia and sobbed into his pillow that first night, when darkness hid his despair from all but the ghosts who inhabited the place. He wished he could remember her face, but he had barely any memory of her at all. He wanted to telephone Rita but it was the middle of the night. But then, as he felt the hollowness in his spirit engulf him completely, he experienced a strong feeling of warmth and love like that first night all those years ago. Then he felt someone pull up the blanket and kiss him tenderly on the forehead. He dared not open his eyes in case he woke up from what must surely be a dream, but he was certain he wasn't asleep. Then he breathed in the familiar scent of mothballs and cinnamon and knew that he wasn't alone.

Chapter Thirty-six

In the months that followed, Max controlled his business from Elvestree, making occasional visits to London for meetings. He also pursued his other cultural interests, inviting foreign politicans, famous writers, artists and composers from all over the world to Mrs Megalith's once magical home. He sponsored exhibitions, bought a publishing house which he renamed Guinzberg & Megalith, and continued to work tirelessly for the charity he had set up in support of Jewish causes. He kept himself busy in order not to focus on his sterile private life. However, there was one ambition which smouldered continuously in his restless soul: to buy back the Imperial Theatre in Vienna, if only to smell again the musty, perfumed scents of his childhood and listen to the echo of voices reverberate across the years to fill the gaping hole that decades of silence had carved upon his soul.

Without Primrose's indomitable presence Elvestree wasn't the same. Not only had the cats gone but so had the magic. The exotic fruit withered and died, the vegetables ceased to grow in such large proportions, spring blossomed unexceptionally, as it did everywhere else. Strange birds no longer diverted off course to summer in the gardens. Only the swallows still nested in the far corner of the drawing room as they had always done. Max changed nothing in the house. He gave Primrose's box of crystals and other mystical things to Elsbeth and Hannah to share with Eddie, as promised, but he moved nothing. Still, the feeling of the place had altered.

'How can one woman make such an imprint on a house?' he said to Rita one day in mid-summer. 'Elvestree is still lovely, but it's no longer special in that magical way. Nothing tastes as good as it did when Primrose was alive. Nothing grows like it did. Even the birds are the same as anywhere else. Typical Devonshire birds.'

'That's nothing to complain about. Most people would be enchanted with a beautiful place like Elvestree,' she said, sipping elderflower cordial that didn't have quite the same flavour as when Mrs Megalith had made it. She looked around at the manicured borders and clipped lawns and beyond to the estuary, which would always remind her of their argument that day in the snow, and marvelled at the memories she had built there.

'I know they would, but we know what it was like before,' he argued.

'Megagran was a witch, Max, you're not,' she laughed, shaking her head.

'Can a house really reflect the personality of the person who lives in it?' he asked, perplexed.

'I'm sure it can. You'll make your imprint on it the same as she did in time. It'll be just as special, only a different type of special.'

Max longed to ask Rita about George, but he knew he could not. It was a sensitive subject. He was certain that she still loved him and that the chances of her affection diminishing were slim. Their friendship was the same as before except she no longer shared that part of her life with him. It was a question that never came up although it was at the very forefront of both their minds. Rita seemed contented with her life, but Max had physical needs that had to be met. He knew he couldn't have the woman he wanted so he took lovers whenever he spent time in London. These were meaningless encounters but they served their purpose and saved his sanity.

He tried to come to terms with his platonic relationship with Rita, but his yearning for a family often drove him to despair. He wanted to ask her again to marry him, to persuade her that they could be happy. He was even prepared to accept that she didn't love him. She could continue to love George if she so wished, if only she'd settle for a marriage based on affection, friendship and trust. They could raise a family at Elvestree, after all; she loved it as much as he did. It was where she belonged. However, he didn't dare risk asking her again; he had made that mistake once before. As long as she wore George's ring she belonged to him.

Then one Sunday evening in mid-winter, as he sat in his study watching the snow falling outside his window, brooding on that fateful Christmas day he had fought with Rita on the estuary, there was a loud knocking on the door. He put down his brandy and padded through the hall where the fire blazed in the grate like it had always done in Primrose's day, though the smoke didn't smell quite as fragrant. He opened the door to see a bedraggled young girl standing in the snow, holding a small baby.

'Come in, for God's sake, you'll catch your death of cold,' he said briskly, taking her sodden arm. She stood in the hall, gazing around her with large, fearful eyes. The pallor of her face was accentuated by her white-blonde hair and purple lips. She must have been no more than sixteen years old, barely adult enough to have an infant. The baby slept against her, wrapped in her coat. 'Are you in trouble?' he asked, assuming her car must have broken down or lost her way in the snow.

'Yes,' she said and sniffed. 'Are you Max de Guinzberg?'

'Yes, I am. Look, I don't want to interfere, but you're very wet. Why don't you take off that coat and I'll lend you a dressing gown?'

'Thank you,' she replied and he detected a strong German accent. Curious, he left her by the fire and hurried upstairs to bring down a towel and gown. When he returned she had slipped out of her coat and was standing warming herself in front of the flames. Without a word she handed him her baby while she dried her hair with the towel and put on the dressing gown, which was delightfully warm from hanging against the hot pipes in the airing cupboard.

Max gazed down at the sleeping baby and felt something insistent pull at his heart. In his mind's eye he saw the face of his baby sister. He remembered as a little boy holding Lydia in his arms as he held the infant now, staring into her features in wonder. He blinked away the image, but he recalled the prettiness of her face and the sense that she belonged to him. 'What is her name?' he asked.

'Mitzi,' replied the young girl. Max stared at her in amazement. 'Mitzi was the name of my grandmother. Your mother, Mr de Guinzberg.'

'Who are you?' he asked slowly, his eyes misting with the trigger of a distant memory.

'My name is Rebecca. My mother was Lydia, your sister.'

Max sat down on the old leather armchair beside the fire. *So this is what Primrose was trying to tell me*, he thought to himself. *'All was not lost.'* 'But my sister died in the camps with my parents,' he said, bewildered, handing back her child.

'No, she didn't.' Rebecca shook her head. 'When your parents sent you and Ruth to England a generous neighbour offered to look after Lydia until the trouble passed. The Germans came for your parents and took them away, but Lydia was safe. Lydia, my mother, grew up with these good people. At the end of the war they adopted her and in a bid to protect her they never told her about the family she had lost. She believed she was Lydia Steiner right up until she died a few years ago of a tumour.'

'She never knew?' Max was devastated that all the time he

and Ruth had assumed their sister was dead, she had in fact been alive and living in Austria.

'They felt very guilty about it and told her of her true identity just before she died. They gave her a box of photographs and sentimental things her mother had left her.'

'Do you have that box?'

'Yes, I do.'

'Where?' he asked, looking at the sodden coat she had draped over the hall table.

She lowered her eyes. 'I left my bags outside.'

'In the snow?'

'I wasn't sure you would want to see me.'

Max strode outside and retrieved the brown leather suitcase, wiping the snow off with his hand. 'How did you get here?' he asked. There was no sign of a car.

'I took the train and a taxi.'

'You're a brave girl,' he said kindly.

'I'm desperate,' she replied. 'You're the only family I have.'

'Where is your husband?'

'I don't have a husband.' She blushed.

'I see.'

'My boyfriend left me when I got pregnant.' Max thought of Ruth and how close she had come to ending up in the same predicament as Rebecca. They had even both named their daughters Mitzi.

'Have you come all the way from Austria?'

'Yes.'

'Let me see the box,' he said, wanting to be certain that she was the person she claimed to be.

She bent down to open the case. She had packed everything with great care. The few items of clothing were neatly folded. She lifted them up and pulled out a weathered cardboard box. Placing it on the table she lifted the lid. To Max's amazement it was full of photographs of him and Ruth as children, of Lydia as a baby and later of her growing up. He slowly studied each one, dizzy with nostalgia and wonder.

'This is my mother just after she had me,' she said, pointing to the black and white photograph of a pretty young woman holding a small baby who strongly resembled Mitzi. 'I miss her so much.'

'What happened to your father?' he asked.

'My mother didn't have a happy marriage. Life was hard. My father left her for another woman, who he married after she died. They were never divorced. I have no relationship with him.'

'Are you an only child?'

'Yes. I would never have bothered you, Mr de Guinzberg, if I hadn't been desperate. I didn't know where to turn. I have no money and a small baby . . .' Her voice trailed off and she began to cry.

'Rebecca,' he said in a gentle voice, standing up and putting an arm around her. 'You don't know how happy I am that you have found me. Fate has led you to me. You are my sister's child. You are all I have left of her.'

'I have never been curious to find you,' she began, but he interrupted.

'It's okay, you don't have to explain. You're a child yourself. You're too young to bring up a baby on your own. You're home now. You and Mitzi. You're safe and I'm going to look after you, I promise.' He put the lid on the box. 'Come into the kitchen and let's get you something to eat. You must be hungry, and how about Mitzi?'

'I'm still feeding her myself, Mr de Guinzberg,' she said, following him.

'Call me Max,' he said. 'I'm your uncle, after all.' With that Rebecca began to cry again, which woke Mitzi.

Max cooked her a Spanish omelette while she fed her baby

discreetly beneath the dressing gown. She told him about her mother but he wanted to know more, right down to the smell of her skin. 'She always smelt of roses, you know, the old-fashioned kind. As a child I used to play with her hair. Tie it up, plait it, wash it. She had lovely thick hair. Like yours. I have my father's hair. He is blonde too, but his hair isn't thick.'

'Mine is not as thick as it was, but that is age,' he said, turning to look at her.

She was a beautiful girl, now that she was no longer crying. Her eyes were the same colour as his, sodalite blue, the very bluest of blues, and her smile was wide and charming like her grandmother Mitzi's, who had been celebrated for her loveliness.

Rebecca ate her omelette hungrily while Max went through her box with growing curiosity. There was a gold Star of David pendant and a diamond butterfly brooch that had belonged to his mother and a notebook of his father's with prayers written out in his wiry handwriting, an old black Bible and a gold signet ring. He was amused to find an old theatre programme with his mother's name emblazoned on the front. They had obviously scrounged around for keepsakes to leave in case they never returned. Max felt his throat constrict with emotion as he handled each item with reverence. Rebecca was too young to understand the significance of these things.

Once he had settled her into the bedroom that he and Ruth had slept in on their first night now over thirty years ago, he telephoned Ruth. She was as surprised as he had been. 'Are you certain she is not a fraud?' she asked.

'Absolutely, she even looks like us.'

'How could Lydia have had a child of sixteen now?'

'Work it out. She would have been eighteen.'

'That's incredible.'

'I know. It's amazing. Rebecca barely looks old enough to have a child, but she's made it all the way here from Austria on her own. She's no fool and she's efficient and capable, her suitcase was immaculately packed. She's not a child. You have to come over tomorrow, as early as you can. The photographs are a miracle.'

'I can't believe that Lydia lived,' she said quietly. 'All this time we thought she was dead.'

'I wish we had known her. The least I can do is look after her child,' he said in a low voice.

'You're a very good man, Max.'

'No, Ruth. Rebecca and Mitzi are a blessing.'

It was true. Max suddenly felt complete. The hollowness of spirit had been filled. He had a purpose far greater than any business could inspire.

The following morning when Max pulled open the curtains he saw to his amazement a pair of snow geese standing in the middle of the lawn. He blinked, then blinked again. They were still there, the sunlight catching their shiny white plumage as they looked down their short bills at the snowy garden. 'I thought they lived in Canada,' he muttered to himself, recalling the famous story of *The Snow Goose* by Paul Gallico. He shook his head and hastily dressed, smiling as he remembered the details of the evening before. How suddenly his life had changed. In a single moment. No day had ever looked more lovely.

As he walked down the stairs to the hall, the scent of wood from the dying embers in the grate was as it had been when Primrose had been alive. The house even felt the same again. With a light step he wandered into the kitchen. Mrs Gunter, the cook, would be arriving later to prepare lunch and dinner; until then he had the kitchen to himself and set about making coffee, tea, fruit juice, poached eggs, toast and porridge for

Rebecca, not knowing what she would like best and wanting to please her.

When she came down she looked entirely different. She had washed her hair, applied some makeup, dressed in a pair of jeans and a pale blue sweater. She looked older than her years and her smile betrayed her contentment. In her arms she held Mitzi, who was awake and blinking around with curiosity.

'Is all this for me?' she asked, when she saw the breakfast laid out on the table.

'I didn't know what you'd want,' he replied with a shrug.

'Thank you. I don't know where to begin.' Her laugh was soft and woody.

'Why don't you give Mitzi to me? She won't mind, will she?' he suggested enthusiastically. 'Then you can eat.'

'Are you sure?'

'Of course I'm sure. She's my great-niece.'

'You're not a typical man, are you?'

'I don't have children of my own,' he replied, smiling sadly. He took the baby from her. She lay in his arms, trying to pat his chin with her small, podgy hand.

'Max, when you said last night that I had come home, did you mean it?' she gazed at him apprehensively.

'I meant every word. You're family. You belong here.'

'I don't know how to thank you.'

'You don't have to, Rebecca. You see, I have grown up believing my sister to be dead. That thought has haunted me for years. If you hadn't turned up last night, I would never have known the truth. I would have died an unhappy man. Now I will die happy knowing that she had you and little Mitzi here. She had a future after all and it is my future too.' He looked at her puzzled face. 'Do you understand?'

'I think so,' she replied slowly.

'It doesn't matter. Eat your breakfast because my sister Ruth is coming over to meet you this morning, then

I think we should go shopping. Poor Mitzi doesn't even have a cot!'

When Ruth arrived she embraced her brother and then spontaneously wrapped her arms around Rebecca. She gazed at her niece with glassy eyes not knowing what to say. In her features she recognised her mother and Max, even herself. She no longer needed explanations. She knew that Rebecca was family. She sensed it in her heart for she had shed light into the dark corner that had contained the same shadows as Max's. Finally, she was able to speak about the past. The three of them walked around the garden in the snow, sharing stories, igniting memories, asking questions that only Rebecca could answer. They took turns carrying Mitzi, showing their niece her new home, staring into the face of the future, the horrors of the past lost in her innocence. They drank coffee and cried over the photographs. Rebecca remembered her mother, and Ruth and Max were at last able to remember theirs.

When Rita arrived for lunch she noticed at once something magical had taken place. 'Do you know the house feels different?' she said to Max. 'It smells different.'

'Yes, I smell it too,' he agreed with a smile.

'Smoky, woody, cosy, like it used to.'

'Did you see the snow geese?'

'There are snow geese?' she exclaimed excitedly.

'Two of them. I opened my curtains this morning and there they were.'

'You know they come from Canada. They migrate to Mexico.'

'Well, they're right here at Elvestree.'

'That's miraculous,' she gasped.

'Not nearly as miraculous as Rebecca.'

'That is true.' She touched his arm fondly and said a little sadly, 'I'm so happy for you, Max.'

*   *   *

Rita wished she could turn her life around, too. She was now in her forties and the hope of having children had gone. George was no more than a memory, a transparent puff of smoke with no substance. She toyed with her ring absentmindedly and wondered what her future held, now that Max had a family. Once he had loved her. The irony was that now she loved him. It hadn't come in a flash of lightning but grown slowly upon her so that she had barely been aware of the changing nature of her heart. For a long time she hadn't dared acknowledge it. But now Max's life was taking a different course she realised that he was leaving her behind and she minded.

As Rebecca and Mitzi settled into Elvestree the magic returned with the spring. The blossom was far more spectacular than anywhere else, the rare vegetables and fruit grew in abundance, baffling the gardeners, and birds from all over the world settled to build their nests in the leafy trees that had observed this mysterious corner of England for centuries. Wagtails and puffins, waxbills, even an albatross was seen on the estuary. The house once more resonated with laughter as Rebecca and Ruth watched their children play on the lawn. Rebecca made friends easily and Max enjoyed the sounds of clattering in the kitchen as she invited other young mothers for tea with their toddlers. They grew as close as a father and daughter could ever be. Rita watched them with mounting envy. Although she too had grown to love Rebecca and Mitzi she was saddened that his attention was now diverted. He no longer gazed upon her with longing. She remembered the snowy day on the estuary and wondered whether he had forgotten how to love her.

Then in the midst of all this joy, George suffered a stroke. Hannah heard it from Faye and told Rita, who was devastated. She longed to go and visit him, but she knew she wouldn't be welcome. Certainly in his fragile state it would be unwise. She badgered her mother for more news, any news at all, but it wasn't good.

The years had caught up with him. The trauma of the war perhaps, or the pressure of living. Or maybe the strain of loving, for George had loved intensely and he had loved too much.

Chapter Thirty-seven

Susan sat on the beach and cried. She rarely cried. At least no one could see her there in the dusk, watching her happiness disappear into the mists on the horizon where the sea flowed into eternity, the gateway of death. She stared into it as if George had already gone. He had been so physical and vital, like a solid oak tree. He had been her strength and her support. Now he could barely speak or move, like a decrepit old man. He was only forty-seven.

It had all happened without any warning. George had been on the farm, working as usual, when a pain in the head had seized him like a hand of iron squeezing his brain. One of the farm boys had run to the farmhouse for help. Susan had been in the garden with Charlie, now a strapping twenty-year-old, in love with Daisy Weaver. They had called an ambulance and he had been taken to Exeter hospital. Like his father, Charlie had been dependable and level-headed, but Susan had been too worried to indulge in feelings of pride. Now George was in the Yew Tree Nursing Home down the coast, being cared for by professionals who knew how to nurse him better than she did. She could barely look at him in that state because she knew how wretched he must feel, like a bear without claws or a lion without teeth. A part of George had died and a part of her had gone with it.

She let the sound of lapping waves soothe her tormented spirit; like music it had its own rhythm. She allowed her mind the freedom to wander down the alleyways of her past and remembered their meeting on the deck of the *Fortuna* when she had coldly rebuffed him, then later on the beach in Uruguay when her body had stirred with something uncontrollable and infinitely more primitive than friendship. She smiled at her foolishness, how she had mistrusted him, not knowing that he would be the best thing that would ever walk into her life. How canny she had been to get invited up to Córdoba and what joy they had built there. Her mind focused on the first time he had kissed her scarred face and tears began to tumble for he might never kiss her there again. He had taught her how to love herself and to be loved in return. He had galloped through her soul like a knight on a white horse and slain all her demons.

And what of his demon? Had he managed to slay his own or had he allowed it to get the better of him? To curl up at the very bottom of his soul in the form of a snake, waiting its moment to uncoil and strike him down? The past had tortured him. Memories of the war and of Rita. Perhaps he still loved her and it was that suppressed, unrequited love that had choked his heart. It didn't really matter now. Their love had endured even though Frognal Point and its ghosts had robbed it of its intensity.

She remained on the beach until darkness wrapped cool arms around her, until the stars studded the sky and twinkled down reassuringly. The sea swelled and crashed against the rocks and a whisper of wind swept across her face. She felt part of nature, like a shell on the beach or a crab sitting watchfully in the sand, and suddenly she sensed the presence of God, telling her in those windy whispers that everything in life has a purpose, that nothing is left to chance, like the rise and fall of the tides. This was George's destiny. His stroke was meant to happen. She now felt relief because she accepted that fighting it wasn't going to make any difference. It was all out of her control. She would simply have to surrender herself to this higher power and pray. So she prayed hard that He would be merciful because she didn't know how to live without George. She had forgotten how to be on her own and she had grown dependent on his love.

On that dark beach she realised, for the first time, that she now truly belonged in Frognal Point. To her surprise, after an unsettled life, she had managed to build a home there out of memories and affection, a home that would last. She would never belong in quite the same way that George belonged – his footprints were embedded in the sand while hers were fresh – but they felt right there, beside his. She watched her son and Daisy, and hoped that one day they might marry and show their children the tidal pools and sea birds as George and Maddie had shown them. She took pleasure in Ava's friendship with Elsbeth and knew that it was one that would sustain her throughout her life. In spite of her fears her children were as much part of the place as their father and this small, coastal village had affixed upon her soul.

When she returned home Charlie and Ava were in the kitchen waiting for her. Ava had cooked dinner while Charlie had spent an hour on the telephone to Daisy. They saw their mother's tearstained face and barely recognised her. She had slowly wilted over the last few weeks. Each visit to their father seemed to squeeze another ounce from her, but they didn't understand her love for they were too young and their love was too green. Charlie planned to marry Daisy. He had been able to forget his devastation and sense of helplessness in the white plains of her flesh down in the secret cave that they had discovered by chance, hidden among long grasses and by the rise of the tide. Ava knew because Elsbeth spied on them occasionally and told her when they took the little boat out together to fish and share secrets.

Susan was grateful for the support of her children. Ava did the shopping and made sure there was always food on the table. Charlie drove her to the nursing home so she didn't have to go alone, and sat outside on the terrace smoking while she spent time alone with his father, reminiscing, sharing news of the children or simply reading to him. He liked short stories best of all. Oscar Wilde and Maupassant in particular. He would gaze upon her with sad eyes and she would strain all the muscles in her face in order to appear cheerful when her heart just wanted to fold up and go to sleep.

Now Charlie and Ava watched her come inside. Her cheeks were red from the wind and her hair, that she now wore shoulder length, was unkempt.

'Can I get you a glass of wine, Mama?' Charlie asked.

'That would be nice, thank you,' she replied, wandering into the room. 'Something smells good,' she added, turning to her daughter.

'Roast chicken and roasted vegetables. I've done potatoes too for Charlie. He needs his strength if he's going to keep up all this exercise.' She grinned mischievously, trying to lighten the atmosphere by making a joke about her brother's lovemaking in the cave.

Susan frowned but she was too drained to ask questions. Charlie and Ava were constantly teasing each other and most of the time she ignored it. Charlie handed her a glass of chilled Chardonnay and she sank into a chair. In spite of their company she felt alone. Their futures were spilling over with the possibility of love and fulfilment whereas hers was slowly dying in the Yew Tree Nursing Home. She knew she would never love again.

As they ate dinner, Charlie declared that he wanted to marry Daisy, but didn't feel he could ask her until their father's health improved.

'Don't be silly,' said Susan. 'It would cheer him up. He needs good news at the moment.'

Charlie's eyes shone with excitement and Susan realised

that, as much as they grieved for their father, they both had their own lives to think about. She envied their youth. If only she could start all over again with George. Would she do anything different? Would she stay at *Las Dos Vizcachas*? She observed her children's happiness and knew in her heart that their decision to come to Frognal Point had been the right one, however hard it had been for her.

The following day dawned bright and warm. The August sun blazed down with more enthusiasm than it had during the entire summer. Charlie and Ava accompanied their mother to the nursing home. They both wanted to see their father, Charlie to tell him of his intentions with Daisy, and Ava because she hadn't been for a few days. They drove in silence, watching the light catch the waves and glitter as they meandered down the coast. George was outside on the terrace, which looked over a sheltered bay of smooth sand and dark blue sea. He was in his wheelchair with a blanket over his knees, a pad and pen ready, his only means of communication. When he saw his family he managed a crooked smile, more crooked now due to the stroke. He blinked at them and Susan was sure his eyes shone with unusual cheerfulness. Her spirits lifted with hope. Perhaps this was the turning point. A new mental attitude that could kick-start his recovery. She kissed him affectionately on his cheek and took his hand in hers. Inside his useless body his heart swelled with love.

Susan noticed the change in him. She didn't know the cause of it, but suddenly George seemed to have accepted his condition and his enthusiasm for life radiated from him like a warm aura of light.

'I'm going to ask Daisy to marry me,' said Charlie, anxious to tell his father his news. *How little children notice*, thought Susan to herself. George's transformation seemed to her as obvious as if he had suddenly begun to speak, yet Charlie was only interested in talking about himself. George blinked at his son in encouragement and scribbled in his wobbly hand-writing 'Hope she says "yes".' Charlie chuckled, sure that she would. George hadn't failed to notice the parallel, but there was no war to distort Charlie's values and scramble his mind. George had a strange sense that Charlie and Daisy would live the life that had been meant for him and Rita, that they would achieve the happiness that had eluded them. 'I want to marry in the church in Frognal Point,' he continued.

'Thank goodness Reverend Hammond is no longer preaching there,' Susan said, lowering her voice for he had also taken up residence in the nursing home. 'He was a rather arrogant man, I always thought. The young vicar is extremely nice.' George pulled a loose smile and nodded slowly in agreement.

'You can be bridesmaid,' said Charlie to his sister with a smirk.

'Not if you paid me!' replied Ava with a giggle.

'I'll pay you to keep quiet,' he hissed at her.

Ava smiled and whispered in her father's ear. 'They've found a cave on the beach.' She looked at him and raised her eyebrows suggestively.

'Shut up, Ava!'

'Papa's amused, silly!' she chided, pulling a face. For an instant George's eyes misted over. So they had found their secret place and indented the sand with their own special brand of love. He felt wistful, as if the tide had crept up and washed his and Rita's footprints away. And they had believed them indelible. Soon there would be no trace of them left at all, just new prints and new memories all belonging to other people; that is the immutable fact of life.

Soon Charlie and Ava went for a walk up the beach, leaving their mother alone with their father. She sat beside him, watching their children wander off and squeezed his hand.

'You seem better today, George.' She sighed. 'I know it must be frustrating not being able to talk, but you will in time because your spirit is so strong, you'll overcome this. I know you will.' She turned and looked into his eyes, now shadowed and forlorn. Her heart buckled at his helplessness. 'We love you so much,' she said, appalled that her voice had been reduced to a mere whisper. He blinked back at her and a single tear caught in his long eyelashes. With a tender hand she gently wiped it away. Bending forwards she kissed him. He gazed into her face for a long while, then scribbled on his pad, 'I don't deserve you.'

'But you do,' she protested, pressing her cheek to his. 'You deserve all the love I have to give.'

George stared out across the wide expanse of ocean. The sky was bluer than he had ever seen it and the sea glittered and sparkled. He felt drawn to it, as if a strong force were pulling at him, beckoning him towards it, to bathe his broken body in the healing waters. He wanted to leap out of his wheelchair and run down the path to the beach, but he was paralysed and imprisoned within the bondage of useless flesh and bones. Then he saw a figure running with her arms outstretched, her tangled seaweed hair flying out behind her, her laughter like the chuckle of gulls as she let the wind carry her up the sand. She wore a thin summer dress and cardigan and her freckled face was alive with exhilaration. He tried to cry out. 'Rita! Rita!' but his voice was lost deep in his chest, where his heart now began to burst with longing. He managed to lift a hand. Perhaps she would see that small gesture and know that he was calling to her. Then she turned and began waving at him, encouraging him to follow. Didn't she know that he couldn't? Her hands moved in slow motion, her smile large and inviting. He tried to shake his head, to tell her that he was a cripple. That he couldn't move, however much he wanted to. But then his will grew greater than the physical resistance of his flesh. He floated out of his wheelchair, leaving his decrepit body limp and crumpled behind him. He felt a surge of relief as he drifted up across the lawn, over the beach where Rita was waving at him joyously and out across the sea. He felt the easy movement of his limbs as if they were made of sunbeams. His spirit was filled with bliss as he passed wheeling gulls towards a greater light. Then he saw them, their faces bright with youth and contentment. Jamie Cordell, Rat Bridges, Lorrie Hampton and his father, Trees and many more, in the distance, welcoming him home.

Rita had never read Reverend Hammond's bible. It had sat on the side table, ignored, for years. Until now. She picked it up and ran her fingers over the leather cover. He had only been trying to help. They all had, but she hadn't understood then. She had been too afraid to move on in case of more disappointment. The disappointment of the past was familiar – she had grown accustomed to living there – but now Rebecca had rewritten Max's past, everything had changed. She wanted to be part of that change.

She got into her car and drove over to Elvestree. Max was in his study working. When she stood in the doorway, smiling and radiant, he cocked his head to one side and frowned at her.

'Will you join me for lunch?' she asked.

'What's up?' He was baffled by the sudden change in her expression. She looked younger somehow, as if she had shed an old skin like a snake. He felt his stomach turn over. After all these years she still had the power to turn his insides to jelly.

'I need to talk to you.'

'Where do you want to go?'

'I want to go and give this bible back to Reverend Hammond. He's in the Yew Tree Nursing Home. It's not far. We can find a pub and eat outside. I haven't done that in years.'

Max was too curious not to accept her offer. 'I'll just go and tell Rebecca.'

With Max at the wheel they drove down the coast. 'So why are you giving it back now?' he asked.

'He lent it to me a long time ago. It's a rather beautiful old book. I thought it would be right to give it back.'

'Why did he give it to you in the first place?'

'He thought I was one of God's lost sheep because I stopped going to church.'

'Did it work?'

'You mean, did I start going to church again? Yes, I did. But I never read it.'

'I'm surprised he didn't come and try to convert me and Ruth.'

'No, you were far too lost for him. He didn't like to fail. Only liked semi-lost sheep like me, then he could feel he'd done God's work when we returned to the flock. He didn't try to convert Megagran either. Knew it was a losing battle.'

'He had some sense then.' Max smiled as he looked out at the road in front of him. He began to feel nervous too, as if they were both teenagers again. He gripped the steering wheel and concentrated on driving.

They drove through the smart white gates of the nursing home and up the driveway lined with shady yew trees. A magnificent Victorian building loomed up ahead, once the private mansion of a millionaire. Max accompanied her into the hall where the receptionist sat behind a dark wooden desk. He could see the sea through the open french doors in the sitting room and told Rita that he would wait for her out there on the terrace.

'I won't be long,' she said, then turned to the young girl in a nurse's uniform.

'I've come to see Reverend Hammond. My name is Rita Fairweather.'

The nurse nodded and smiled toothily. 'Of course, first floor, room fourteen. If you turn right here and walk up the corridor, the staircase is straight ahead.'

The corridor smelt of polish. The original wooden floor shone brilliantly and the walls were hung with brightly coloured paintings of landscapes and boats on the sea. The staircase squeaked as she walked up it, reminding her of Lower Farm, except here it was wider and grander with a vast window letting in an abundance of light. When she got to his room she discovered to her disappointment that he wasn't there. She waited a while then decided to write him a note instead, leaving it on the bed with the Bible where he was sure to find it.

'I'm sorry to have missed you, Reverend Hammond,' she wrote. 'As you said, Rome wasn't built in a day. I'm now ready to lay the first stone. My thanks, Rita.' She looked down at the small solitaire ring that seemed to shine with less brilliance and wondered why she had continued to wear it so long after it had lost its significance. There was only one thing left to be done.

With a light step she began to walk back down the corridor, too preoccupied to see the solemn young woman walking towards her carrying a cardboard box. She bumped straight into her, sending the box crashing to the floor. The younger woman fell to her knees. 'I'm so sorry,' Rita cried in horror. 'I was miles away.' Then she recognised Ava. Ava blinked up at her, knew she had seen her before but couldn't place her. 'I'm Rita Fairweather, you must be Ava Bolton. What are you doing here?'

'My father died yesterday. I'm clearing out his room.'

'George died?' Rita repeated incredulously, slowly shaking her head. 'But he was so young.'

'Another stroke.'

There was a lengthy pause as Rita digested the news. *George is dead? George is gone?* 'I'm so sorry,' she gasped, bending down to help pick up his things.

'Thank you,' Ava replied. 'It was very sudden, but he's in a better place. I really believe that.'

'So do I,' said Rita, gathering up his books and a pen. To her surprise, although she felt sad, she also felt oddly detached, and realised that the George she had once loved had died years before and that she had already mourned him.

At that moment she noticed the little faded Polyphoto she had given him, carefully protected within a transparent envelope. She sat down and studied it wistfully for a moment, amazed that it was there.

'Who is this?' she asked.

'I don't know. Someone special, I expect,' Ava replied, putting the lid back on the box. 'I found it in his breast pocket. He must have always kept it there.'

Rita smiled and handed it back. Ava nodded and thanked her again, and Rita watched her walk down the stairs, her heels clicking on the polished wooden floor. So he had never stopped loving her after all. As he had promised, he had carried her photograph until his death. But it no longer mattered. It would have meant everything a decade ago but she was no longer that girl, she had finally outgrown her. She toyed with her ring a moment then strode purposefully down the stairs.

She found Max outside smoking on the terrace. Without a word she took his hand and led him down the path to the beach. He followed, wondering why her face was flushed and her eyes shone with a light he had never seen before. With her shoes almost in the waves, she turned and looked at him steadily, then pulled off the ring. 'I should have done this years ago,' she said and threw it into the sea. They both watched in silence as it fell with a small plop into the water, then disappeared for ever. Max didn't know what to say. He felt the habitual churning in his stomach, but dared not hope too much. 'You once asked me to marry you,' she began and then her voice trailed off. Perhaps she had missed the moment. Perhaps he no longer wanted her. She wasn't young and pretty like she had been then and, besides, he had Rebecca and Mitzi now. But Max needed no further encouragement. He took her face in his hands and kissed her as he had longed to for almost thirty years. She closed her eyes to withhold the tears and wrapped her arms around him, kissing him back.

Finally he pulled away and traced her cheek with his fingers. There was so much he wanted to tell her but he couldn't find the words with which to unburden his heart. He simply gazed down at her lovingly. She pressed her lips to his hand.

'I want to grow old with you, Max. I want to walk down on the estuary, in the fog and the snow and tell you how much I love you as I should have done that Christmas when I almost lost you for ever. I want to share everything with you, your future, your past.' Her eyes began to glisten. 'Take me to Vienna, Max. Show me the Imperial Theatre where your mother performed for your father. Perhaps one day soon it will be yours and all the memories that lie within it.'

Max looked at her for a long moment, awaiting those familiar scents of his childhood to reach him once again from the far corners of his heart, but they did not come.

'No,' he said at last and his gaze was so intense that she almost had to look away. 'The Vienna of my childhood is gone. They destroyed that long ago. Even my ghosts don't walk those streets anymore.' Then he slipped one arm around her waist and took her hand in his. To the formal steps of a waltz he thought he'd forgotten, he held her. 'Let's go home Rita. We'll build Vienna together.'

*Now read on for a glimpse of
Santa's new epic romance,*

LAST VOYAGE
OF THE VALENTINA

Chapter One

London 1971

'She's enjoying the attentions of that young man again,' said Viv, standing on the deck of her houseboat. Although it was a balmy spring evening, she pulled her tasselled shawl about her shoulders and took a long drag of her cigarette.

'Not spying again, darling!' said Fitz with a wry smile.

'One can't help noticing the comings and goings of that girl's lovers.' She narrowed her hooded eyes and inhaled through dilated nostrils.

'Anyone would think you were jealous,' he commented, grimacing as he took a sip of cheap French wine. In all the years he had been Viv's friend and agent she had never once bought a bottle of decent wine.

'I'm a writer. It's my business to be curious about people. Alba's a very selfish creature, but one can't help being drawn to her. The ubiquitous moth to the flame – in my case not a moth at all, but a rather beautifully dressed butterfly.' She wandered across the deck and draped herself over a chair, spreading her blue and pink kaftan like silken wings. 'Still, I enjoy her life. I'll put it in a book one day, when we're no longer friends. I think Alba's like that. She enjoys people then moves on. But when the dramas of her life no longer entertain me and I'm bored of the Thames too, when old bones ache from the damp and the creaking and bumping keep me up at night,

I shall buy a small chateau in France and retire to obscurity. Fame having become a bore too.' She sucked in her cheeks and grinned at Fitz. But Fitz was no longer listening, although it was his job to.

'Do you think they pay for it?' he said, putting a hand on the railing and looking down into the muddy water of the Thames. Beside him, Sprout, his old springer spaniel, lay sleeping on a blanket.

'Nonsense!' she retorted. 'Her father owns the boat. She's not having to fork out twelve pounds a week in rent, I assure you.'

'Then she's simply sexually liberated.'

'Just like everyone else of her generation. Following the herd. It bores me. I was before my time, Fitzroy. I took lovers and smoked cannabis long before the Albas of this world knew of the existence of either. Now I prefer bog standard Silva-Thins and celibacy. I'm fifty, too old to be a slave to fashion. It's all so frivolous and childish really. Better to set my mind on higher things. You may be a good ten years younger than me, Fitzroy, but I can tell the world of fashion bores you too.'

'I don't think Alba would bore me.'

'But you, my dear, would bore her. She'd have you for dinner then spit you out like a chicken bone. You're too sweet, darling. I'd hate to see your lovely brown eyes seeping with sorrow. Your face is made for laughter. Besides, you're too good for her. You know she's half Italian.'

'Ah, that explains the dark hair and honey skin.' Viv looked at him askance and her thin lips extended into an even thinner smile. 'But those very pale eyes, strange . . .' He sighed, no longer noticing the taste of cheap wine.

'Her mother was Italian. She died when Alba was born. In a car crash, I think. Has a horrid stepmother and a bore for a father. Navy, you know. Still there, the old fossil. Has had the same desk job since the war, I suspect. Commutes every day from Hampshire on the train, very dreary. Captain Thomas Arbuckle, and he's definitely a Thomas and not a Tommy. Not like you who are more of a Fitz than a Fitzroy, though I do love the name Fitzroy and shall continue to use it regardless. No wonder Alba rebelled.'

'Well at least he's a rich bore.' Fitz ran his eyes over the shiny wooden houseboat that gently rocked with the motion of the tide. Or with Alba's lovemaking. The thought of the latter made his stomach cramp with jealousy.

'Money doesn't bring happiness. You should know that, Fitzroy.'

'Does she live alone?'

'She used to live with one of her half sisters, but it didn't work out. I can't imagine the girl's easy to live with, God bless her. Don't even think about it, Fitzroy. She's bad news. Ah, about time too! You're late!' she exclaimed as her nephew Wilfrid hurried down the pontoon towards them with his girlfriend Georgia in tow, full of apologies. Viv could be quite fearsome when they showed up late for bridge.

The Valentina was a houseboat unlike any other on Cheyne Walk. The curve of the prow was pretty, upturned, coy as if she were trying to contain a knowing smile. The house itself was painted blue and white with round windows and a balcony where pots spilled over with flowers in springtime and leaks let in the rain during the winter months. Like a face that betrays the life it has lived, so the eccentric dip in the line of the roof and the charming slope of the bow, like a rather imperious nose, revealed that she had perhaps had many lives. The overriding characteristic of The Valentina was her mystery. But the secrets of her past she was unwilling to share. Like a grand dame who would never be seen without her makeup The Valentina would not reveal what lay beneath her paint.

Her mistress, however, loved her not for her unusual features, or her charm or indeed her uniqueness; they meant very little to her. No, Alba Arbuckle loved her boat for a very different reason.

'God, Alba, you're beautiful!' Rupert sighed, burying his face in her softly perfumed neck. 'You taste of sugared almonds.' Alba giggled, thinking him absurd, but unable to resist the sensation of his bristles that scratched and tickled and his hand that had already found its way past her blue suede Clog boots and up her Mary Quant skirt. She wriggled with pleasure and lifted her chin.

'Don't talk, you fool. Kiss me.' This he did, determined to please her. He was heartened that she had suddenly come alive in his arms after a sulky supper in Chelsea. He pressed his lips to hers, relieved that as long as he occupied her tongue she couldn't verbally abuse him. Alba had a way of saying the most hurtful things through the sweetest, most beguiling, smile. And yet, those pale grey eyes of hers, like a moor on a misty winter morning, aroused a pity that was disarming. Drew a man in. Made him yearn to protect her. To love her was easy, to keep her, unlikely. But along with the other hopefuls who walked the well trodden deck of The Valentina, Rupert couldn't help but try.

Alba opened her eyes as he unbuttoned her blouse and took a breast in his mouth. She looked up through the skylight to wispy pink clouds and the first twinkle of a star. Overwhelmed by the unexpected beauty of the dying day, she momentarily let down her guard and her spirit was filled with a terrible sadness. It flooded her being and brought tears to those pale grey eyes, tears that stung and reminded her of the loneliness of her childhood. Appalled by such weakness she wound her legs around her lover and rolled over so that she sat on top, kissing and biting and clawing him like a wild cat. Rupert was stunned but more excited than ever. He eagerly ran his hands up her naked thighs to discover she wore no pants. Her buttocks lay smooth and exposed for him to caress with impatient fingers. Then he was inside her and she was riding him furiously, as if aware only of the pleasure and not of the man who was giving it.

Soon Rupert's thoughts were also lost in the fevered excitement of their lovemaking. He closed his eyes and surrendered to the animal inside who sought nothing but sexual gratification. They writhed and rolled until they exploded onto the floor with a thud, gasping, laughing and wiping the sweat from their brows. She looked at him with shining eyes and said with a throaty chuckle, 'What did you expect? The Virgin Mary?'

'That was wonderful. You're an angel,' he sighed, kissing her forehead. She raised her eyebrows and laughed at him.

'Now that is absurd, Rupert. God would throw me out of Heaven for misbehaving.'

'Then that is not the Heaven for me.'

Suddenly her attention was diverted by a brown scroll of paper that had been dislodged behind the wooden slats under the bed. She couldn't reach from where she was lying, so she pushed Rupert away and crawled around to the other side, stretching her arm beneath the bed.

'What is it?' he asked, blinking at her through a post coital daze.

'I don't know,' she replied slowly, pulling it out and withdrawing. As she stood up she grabbed her cigarette packet and lighter from the bedside table and threw them at him. 'Light me one, will you?' Then she sat on the edge of the bed to take a closer look at what appeared to be a drawing. Rupert didn't smoke. In fact, he loathed cigarettes, but not wanting to appear gauche he did as she asked and handed it over, throwing himself onto the bed beside her and running an appreciative hand down her back. She stiffened. Without looking at him she asked him to leave. 'I've enjoyed you, Rupert. But now I want to be alone.'

'What's wrong?' he asked, astounded that she could suddenly turn so cold.

'I said I want to be alone.' For a moment he remained, unsure how to react. No woman had ever treated him like this. He felt humiliated. When he saw that she wasn't going to change her mind, he reluctantly began to dress, clutching onto the intimacy they had shared only moments before, now all but gone. He was aware that he sounded desperate.

'Will I see you again?'

She shook her head, irritated. 'Just go!'

He did up his shoe laces. She still hadn't looked at him. Her attention was entirely captivated by the scroll. It was as if he had already gone.

'Well, I'll let myself out then,' he mumbled.

'Oh dear! Someone doesn't look very happy,' commented Fitz as Rupert walked slowly up the pontoon towards Chelsea Embankment before disappearing beneath the streetlamps. His comment suspended their bridge game for a moment. Sprout cocked his ears and raised his drooping eyes for a second before closing them again with a sigh.

'Well, she does get through them, darling,' said Viv, curling a stray wisp of blonde hair behind her ear. 'She's like a black widow.'

'I thought they ate their mates,' said Wilfrid. Fitz contemplated that delicious thought before placing a card on the table with a snap.

'Who are we talking about?' asked Georgia, crinkling her nose at Wilfrid.

'Viv's neighbour,' he replied.

'She's a tart,' added Viv caustically, winning the trick and swiping it over to her side of the table.

'I thought you were friends?'

'We are, Fitzroy. But that doesn't mean I'm blind to her faults. After all, we all have them, don't we?' She grinned and flicked ash into a fluorescent green dish.

'Not you, Viv. You're perfect.'

'Thank you, Fitzroy,' she replied, then turned to Georgia and added with a wink, 'I pay him to say that.'

Fitz glanced out of the little round window. The deck of The Valentina was still and quiet. He imagined Alba lying naked on her bed, flushed and smiling, with curves and mounds in all the right places and was momentarily distracted from the game.

'Wake up, Fitz!' said Wilfrid, snapping his fingers in front of his face. 'What planet are you on?'

Viv placed her cards on the table and sat back. She took a drag of her cigarette and exhaled with a loud puff. Gazing upon him with eyes made heavy with drink and the excesses of life she said,

'Oh, the same sad planet as so many other foolish men!'

Alba stared at the portrait, sketched in pastels, with a rush of emotion. It was as if she were looking into a mirror, but one that increased the loveliness of her image. The face was oval, like her own, with fine cheekbones and a strong, determined jaw, but the eyes weren't hers at all. They were almond shaped, mossy brown in colour, a mixture of laughter and a deep, unfathomable sadness. They held her attention, stared right back at her and through her and when she moved, they followed her. She gazed into them for a long while, absorbed in hopes and dreams that never bore fruit. They contained a certain wistfulness and yet, although the mouth only hinted at a smile, the whole face seemed to open up with happiness like a sunflower. Alba's stomach twisted with longing. For the first time in living memory she was staring into the face of her mother. At the bottom of the picture, written in Latin were the words: *Valentina 1943, dum spiro, ti amo*. It was signed Thomas Arbuckle with a small I/III in ink, presumably added later. Alba re-read those words a dozen times until they blurred with her tears. '*While I breathe, I love you*'.

Alba had learnt Italian as a child. In an unusual moment of charity her stepmother had suggested she take lessons in order to maintain some contact with her Mediterranean roots, roots that in every other way the woman had tried to ignore. After all, Valentina had been the love of her father's life. Her stepmother was all too aware of the shadow that woman cast over her marriage. She was unable to erase so powerful a memory; all she could do was attempt to smother it. And it seemed beyond her father's ability to oppose her. Or perhaps he went along with her for an easy life. They simply never talked about her mother. They had never travelled to Italy. She knew none of her mother's relatives, and her father avoided her questions so she had long since given up asking. As a child she had shrunk into an isolated world of patchwork facts that she had managed to glean and sew together through devious means. Alba would retreat into that world and derive comfort from the invented images of her beautiful mother on the shores of the sleepy Italian town where she had met and fallen in love with her father during the war.

Thomas Arbuckle had been handsome then; Alba had seen photographs. In his naval uniform he had cut quite a dash. Sandy hair and pale eyes and a cheeky, confident grin that the Buffalo (as Alba nicknamed her stepmother) had managed, with the sheer weight of her forceful personality, to reduce to a disgruntled scowl. Jealous of the houseboat he had bought and named after her mother, the Buffalo had never set foot on its deck, referring to it as 'that boat' and not as 'The Valentina' that conjured up memories of cypress trees and crickets, olive groves and lemons and a love so great that no amount of stamping and snorting could denigrate it.

Alba had never felt she truly belonged in her father's house. Her half-siblings were physical reflections of their parents but she was dark and alien, like her mother. Her half-siblings rode horses, picked blackberries and played bridge, while she dreamed of the Mediterranean and olive groves. In despair, she had moved into the houseboat that carried her mother's sacred name and there she felt her ethereal presence, heard her voice in the rise and fall of the tides, a mere whisper away.

Alba lay on the bed, beneath the skylight where the stars now glimmered in their hundreds and the moon had risen to replace the sun. Rupert might just as well have never been there. She was alone with her mother, her soft voice speaking through the portrait, caressing her daughter with those soft, sorrowful eyes. Surely now Thomas would have to tell her about Valentina. This picture must melt the layers of ice that had built up over the years.

Alba did not waste any time. She placed the scroll carefully into her bag and hurried out of the boat. A couple of squirrels played tag on the roof, and she shooed them irritably away before setting off up the gangplank. At that moment Fitz, having lost at bridge, was leaving Viv's houseboat, light-headed with wine and startled by the coincidence that should set his path and Alba's in tandem. He didn't notice that she had been crying and she didn't notice Sprout. 'Good evening,' he said jovially, trying to ignite a conversation as they walked up the gangway towards the embankment. Alba did not reply. 'I'm Fitzroy Davenport, a friend of your neighbour, Viv.'

'Oh,' she replied in a flat tone. She crossed her arms and dug her chin into her chest.

'Can I give you a lift somewhere? My car's parked around the corner.'

'So is mine.'

'Ah.' Fitz was desperate for her to notice him. He watched her long legs strutting out in front of her, clad in blue suede boots and a very short mini skirt, and felt the anxiety tighten about his throat. Her loveliness debilitated him completely. 'I've just lost at bridge,' he persevered frantically. 'Do you play?'

'Not if I can help it,' she replied.

'Very wise. Dull game.' He chuckled awkwardly.

'Like the players themselves,' she retorted, then gave a small smile before climbing into a two-seater MGB and roaring off down the road. Fitz was left alone under the streetlamp, scratching his head in bewilderment, unsure whether to be offended or amused, his loins aching with longing.

Alone in the car where no one could see her Alba sobbed. She could fool everyone else with her bravado, but there was no point trying to fool herself. The sense of loss that had overwhelmed her earlier now resurfaced and this time with greater intensity. Her imaginary world of cypress trees and olive groves was no longer sufficient. It was a lonely place to live. She had a right to know about her mother, and now she had the picture, her father would have to talk about her. How it had got there, she didn't know. Why and when he had hidden it was a mystery. Perhaps the Buffalo didn't know about its existence. Maybe he had put it there so she wouldn't find it. But now Alba would tell her. She changed gear and turned into the Talgarth Road.

★   ★   ★

It was late. They wouldn't be expecting her. It would take her a good hour and a half to get to Hampshire in spite of the clear roads. Not a cat on them. She turned on the radio to hear Cliff Richard singing *'Those miss-you nights are the longest,'* and her tears cascaded all the more. Out of the darkness and into her headlights her mother's face loomed. With long dark hair and soft, moss coloured eyes she gazed upon her daughter with love and understanding, and her love was big enough to heal the entire world. She would have smelt of lemons and she would have rested her lips on her daughter's face and held them there. Alba had longed for her mother all her life. Without even a photograph she had hungered for stories. Simple things: what had she worn? How had she done her hair? Had she sung to her when she slept? Had she chosen her name? Tears blurred her vision and she swerved. With a sharp intake of breath, she steadied the car and wiped her face with her hand.

It was easy to see why the Buffalo hated Valentina. Margo Arbuckle wasn't beautiful like Valentina had been. She was a big woman with sturdy legs better suited to Wellington boots than stilettos, a large bottom that moulded itself well into the saddle and freckly English skin that was bare of make-up and scrubbed with Imperial Leather soap. Her style of dress was conventional: tweed skirts and billowing blouses from Country Casuals. Her bosom was overlarge and she had lost what waist she had once had. Alba wondered what her father had seen in her. Perhaps the pain of losing Valentina had driven him to chose a wife who was the complete opposite of her. Why he had married again, Alba couldn't imagine. Wouldn't it have been better to live with Valentina's memory than compromise in such a pitiful way?

As for the children they had had together, well, they had

wasted no time in that department. Alba had been born in 1945, the year her mother died, and Caroline only three years later, in 1948. It was shameful. Her father had barely had time to mourn. He had barely had time to get to know his firstborn child, the one he should have loved more than anyone else in the world for being the living part of the woman he had lost. After Caroline came Henry and then Miranda – with each child Alba was pushed a little further into her world of pine and olive groves. Her father didn't seem to notice that she cried out for him. He was too busy making another family. But it wasn't her family. *God*, she thought unhappily, *does he ever sit down and think about what he's done to me?* Well, now she had the portrait she was determined to tell him.

She knew they dreaded her visits. She couldn't resist kicking up and being difficult. Goading the Buffalo was the only amusement she got at home and it was fun to watch everyone tiptoe carefully around her as if they were afraid of stepping on drawing pins. Well, she'd give them one hell of a shock tonight.

She turned off the A30 and headed down narrow winding lanes. Her headlights illuminated the hedgerows bursting forth with cow parsley and the odd hare that darted hastily back into the bushes. She rolled down the window and sniffed the air like a dog, taking pleasure from the sweet scents of spring that swept in with the rattling sound of the motor. She imagined her father smoking his after dinner cigar and swirling brandy around in one of those large, swollen bellied glasses he was so fond of. Margo would be rabbiting on about Caroline's thrilling new job in a Mayfair art gallery and Henry's latest news from Sandhurst. Miranda was still at boarding school; little to report there except top grades and fawning teachers. How dull and conventional, Alba thought. Their lives would all run predictably, along tracks laid down at birth like perfect little trains. 'The runaway train came down the track and she blew, she blew . . .' sang Alba, her misery lifting as she contemplated her unconventional, independent existence that ran along a track entirely of her own making.

Finally she turned into the driveway that swept up for about a quarter of a mile beneath tall, slender lime trees. She could just make out a couple of horses in the field to her right, their eyes shining like silver as they caught the lights of her car. Hideous beasts, she thought sourly. Amazing they weren't all buckling at the knees considering the weight of the Buffalo. She wondered whether the woman rode her father like she rode her horses. She couldn't help but giggle at the thought, then swiftly dismissed it. Surely they were too old for that sort of thing!

The wheels of the car scrunched up the gravel in front of the house. The lights blazed invitingly but Alba knew they didn't blaze for her. How Margo must resent her. It would be easier to wipe away Valentina's memory if she weren't around as a constant reminder. She parked her car beneath the imposing walls of the house that had once been her home. With its tall chimneys and old, weathered brick and flint it had withstood gales and storms for well over three hundred years. Her great-great grandfather had apparently won it at the gambling table, though not before he had lost his wife as a consequence of his addiction. She had swiftly become mistress to some Duke who had just as big as an addiction but a much deeper pocket with which to indulge it. Alba rather liked the idea of the mistress; her stepmother had forever tainted her concept of marriage.

She sat in the car, watching as three small dogs scurried out of the darkness to sniff the wheels and wag their small, stumpy tails. When her stepmother's face appeared around the door she had no option but to climb out and greet her. Margo looked pleased though the strain showed around the eyes where her smile didn't quite reach. 'Alba, what a lovely surprise! You should have telephoned,' she said, holding the door so that the orange light flooded the steps leading up to the porch. Alba went through the ritual of kissing her on autopilot. She smelt of talcum powder and Yardley's Lily of the Valley and around her neck hung a fat golden locket. As she shouted to her husband, Alba noticed the locket bounce on the shelf of her bosom and blinked away the image of Margo riding her husband like a horse.

Alba walked into the hall with its wooden-panelled walls hanging with austere looking portraits of deceased relatives. At once she smelt the sweet scent of her father's cigar and her courage flagged. Thomas emerged from the drawing room in a green smoking jacket and slippers. His hair, although thinning, was still flaxen and brushed back off his forehead, accentuating pale eyes that appraised her steadily. For a fleeting moment Alba was able to see beyond the heavy build and extended belly, past the ruddy skin and disgruntled twist of his mouth to the handsome young man he had been in the war. When he had fallen in love with her mother.

'Ah, Alba, my dear. To what do we owe this pleasure?' He kissed her temple, as he always did, and his voice was thick and grainy like the gravel outside. Jovial, inscrutable; the young man had gone.

'I was just passing,' she lied.

'Good,' he replied. 'Come on in for a nightcap and tell us what you've been up to.'